USA TODAY bestselling author **Natalie Anderson** writes emotional contemporary romance full of sparkling banter, sizzling heat and uplifting endings—perfect for readers who love to escape with empowered heroines and arrogant alphas who are too sexy for their own good. When not writing, you'll find her wrangling her four children, three cats, two goldfish and one dog…and snuggled in a heap on the sofa with her husband at the end of the day. Follow her at natalie-anderson.com.

Marcella Bell lives in the mostly sunny wilds of Southern Oregon with her husband, children, father, and three mismatched mutts. The dry hot summers and four distinct annual seasons of the region are a far cry from the weird rainy streets of Portland, Oregon, where she grew up, but she wouldn't trade her quirky mountain valley home for anywhere else on the earth. As a late bloomer and a yogini, Marcella is drawn to romance that showcases love's incredible power to transform.

THE QUEEN'S
IMPOSSIBLE BOSS

NATALIE ANDERSON

STOLEN TO WEAR
HIS CROWN

MARCELLA BELL

MILLS & BOON

First Published in Great Britain 2020
by Mills & Boon, an imprint of HarperCollins*Publishers*
1 London Bridge Street, London, SE1 9GF

The Queen's Impossible Boss © 2020 Natalie Anderson

Stolen to Wear His Crown © 2020 Marcella Bell

ISBN: 978-0-263-27844-6

MIX
Paper from
responsible sources
FSC™ C007454

This book is produced from independently certified FSC™ paper
to ensure responsible forest management.
For more information visit www.harpercollins.co.uk/green.

Printed and bound in Spain
by CPI, Barcelona

THE QUEEN'S
IMPOSSIBLE BOSS

NATALIE ANDERSON

For my Bubble.
Thank you for being so supportive and patient
while I wrote this when we were all holed up together—
the apple sponges were amazing!!!

CHAPTER ONE

'GIVEN YOU'VE NOT BOTHERED to reply to any earlier messages, don't bother coming back at all.'

Jade Monroyale shivered as that stern dismissal echoed in her head, but for once in her life she was going to disobey a direct order. She strode along the Manhattan pavement in her travel-stale clothes, masking her nerves as she wheeled the one small suitcase she'd been able to bring with her. The number of people heading to work was amazing, given it was still very early and so cold her fingers and toes were numb. She'd have loved a hot shower, but, having heard that message only an hour ago, she'd known she had no time to waste. She had to get to the office and fix things.

'Don't bother.'

His low tone had been underlined by an edge of danger. Authoritative and uncompromising, his anger had been barely leashed. Jade knew that kind of man well—impatient, dismissive, arrogant. But there'd been another frisson in his voice—a passion that had alarmed her more than the accusation had.

Navigating the subway had been something else. She'd run her sister's MetroCard the wrong way a few times before figuring it out. Swiping cards through machines ought to be something anyone could do but, as Queen of a prosperous, albeit small, European country, Jade Monroyale had never carried either cash or cards before. Her father had deemed it unnecessary given destiny dictated her future. She was 'different', she had a 'rare duty'…and he'd ensured she never forgot it. But now she felt a very different duty. Her twin needed her help.

'Juno? This is Alvaro Byrne.'

He'd introduced himself brusquely as he'd left the last of the many messages on Juno's phone. A couple of workmates and her immediate manager had left several, but Alvaro Byrne—the CEO himself—had left just that last one.

Juno, Jade's younger sister by a mere two minutes, had lived here in New York for more than a decade, the identical twins separated by much more than their parents' traumatic divorce. But for the first time Jade was in a position to be able to help Juno. She was not having her sister's job lost because of a lapse in communication. Her twin hadn't been able to respond to those calls because she'd been travelling. She hadn't even *heard* them. Jade was so glad Juno didn't understand the degree to which her job was in peril. And if Jade could finesse it, she need never know. All Jade had to do was pull off this impersonation to perfection...

Yes, their twin switch was *crazy*—especially considering they'd not been together for years and knew so little of each other's daily lives—but it was worth the risk. Juno desperately needed time in Monrova. While Jade?

Finally, for just a few weeks, she'd be free.

Until last night, Jade had barely left her home. As she was the only heir her father had acknowledged in recent years, there could be no risk of them both being in an accident. So they'd never travelled together. Jade had been strictly limited in where she could go, what she could do. Her entire life had been spent preparing for the role she was destined to fulfil. She'd studied several languages, history, geography, absorbed political and diplomatic theory, mastered manners and etiquette and, most of all, emotional control. She'd learned never to let fear or hurt or anger show—for, according to her father, a monarch must remain impassive in public. That was absolute.

Pretty ironic given that, behind that pretty palace facade, her parents' separation had been so acrimonious and bitter that they'd forced Jade and Juno apart when they were only eight. Jade, as firstborn, had remained with her father to be groomed as future Queen, while Juno had been sent to the United States with her mother. It was a decision Jade still struggled to forgive, even all these years later. She'd been forbidden to see her mother again. And their authoritarian father had disapproved of their mother's more permissive parenting style and the defiance that an independent Juno wasn't afraid to display when she was allowed to visit for holidays that were too brief. Finally, in the summer in which they'd turned sixteen, Juno had stormed from their father's autocratic displeasure in Monrova, never to return.

'I expect my employees to be team players and to value their colleagues.'

Alvaro Byrne's stinging rebuke had stopped Jade in her tracks. Juno had suffered enough thanks to one unforgiving man, Jade wasn't letting it happen again. Especially not for something so minor. *No one* was as loyal as Juno, and this jerk hadn't even given her the chance to explain.

In the past Jade's only act of defiance had been to stay in touch with Juno after that last fight, despite her father's ever-looming disapproval. A month before they'd turned eighteen their mother had passed, leaving Juno alone and isolated miles away. Jade had been prevented from going to the funeral and unable to offer any real comfort and Juno had made it clear she had no desire to return to Monrova. Jade had learned to bypass the Internet security wall that had previously stopped her from seeing her sister's social media postings and they'd video conferenced when they could. Juno had regaled her with tales of her life as the media-dubbed 'Rebel Princess' in New York…

But Juno still hadn't come back when their father had

died just a year ago. And while her choice had saddened Jade, she'd understood that some things were so painful they were impossible to overcome…or at least, took a long, long time. So Juno's surprise visit to Monrova at the weekend had been the best thing ever. And her suggestion of a three-week twin-switch?

Yes, it absolutely was crazy. But Juno needed time in her own country—she needed time to understand the heritage and the life that had been denied her.

And yes, there was a selfish element to Jade's ready agreement. For Jade to have just a little time to herself and live like a 'normal' person with relative anonymity? To experience a few of those freedoms that only a city like New York could offer? To have time to herself before fulfilling her late father's last wish? And Christmas—an actual special, even if alone, Christmas. She'd barely been able to admit it even to herself, but the chance to experience life a little more 'normal' had been irresistible.

'How could you just ignore their calls?'

There was that emotive edge in Alvaro Byrne's tone that had scalded Jade. It seemed her 'little more normal' now included dealing with Juno's irate boss at work. She was determined to defuse this situation. Duty—responsibility—was everything and right now she was responsible for Juno's reputation.

Jade had her own challenging choice ahead. She would do anything for her country—even marry the man her father had decided would be the best match for her politically. Since his death, her advisors had unanimously insisted that the marriage was still the best course of action for both Monrova and for Queen Jade herself. If it *was*, then of course she would do it. But Juno had been horrified that Jade was even considering marriage to King Leonardo of Severene—the neighbouring nation—and she'd wanted to give Jade space to consider everything. Juno had handed over her phone, passport, passwords…and Jade had been swept along by her twin's insistence and enthusiastic assurance that they could pull this off.

Because she'd not just wanted it, she'd needed it too.

But Juno had said there was no need for Jade to go into her work as she could work from home in this last week before the office closed early for the Christmas break, lessening the chances of someone suspecting their switch. Only when Jade had landed at the airport in New York and turned on Juno's phone, it had pinged incessantly, signalling an insane amount of messages and voicemails. And this last—from the CEO himself—was the one that spurred Jade's action now.

This is Alvaro Byrne.'

He was CEO of a conglomerate that had started with an eclectic suite of popular apps and mushroomed since to include both property and financial investments. Juno had been recruited to work in the social media marketing arm for the suite of apps, including that original fitness tracking one—Byrne IT. Juno had mentioned a minor issue at work in passing, but when Jade had looked online after hearing those messages, she saw the fuss was more major than Juno had realised and it was only escalating.

On her journey in from the airport, Jade had searched online for any information she could find about the office and her co-workers but there'd been little about the structure. So she'd listened again to the catalogue of increasingly concerned voice messages and memorised the names of the callers—grateful for the disciplined memory techniques drilled into her from a young age. Then she'd coiled her hair into a bun to hide the fact that hers was longer and straighter than Juno's and hoped that her plain black trousers and white shirt were suitably 'Juno office wear'. She figured her black coat covered much anyway, and if she could somehow fix this quickly, she could be out of there before the others arrived for the day.

Finally, at Byrne HQ, in Tribeca, she stared through the gleaming glass to the brightly lit, funky atrium of the re-purposed brick-fronted industrial building. She shuffled through Juno's battered wallet to find the office security card. To her relief the door lock clicked when she swiped it through the security pad. So Juno hadn't been banned from the building, despite the unreasonable rancour in that man's tone.

She quickly read the signs and ventured deeper into the quiet building. She shivered again, nerves biting. But she had no choice but to ignore their agreement for her to stay away from Juno's work. She had to fix it so every-thing would be well when Juno returned. She knew this job mattered to her sister—she'd shut down the social media sites she'd been running for years because she'd wanted to pull back from that public 'Rebel Princess' persona. She'd wanted a normal marketing job for a company and to get some anonymity back. So, more than anything, Jade wanted to help her sister keep it.

Those two minutes that separated them as 'heir' and 'spare' were merely fate, but Jade hated that Juno had ef-fectively been ejected from the kingdom. She knew her fa-ther's hard-line stance stemmed from a deep, devastated hurt, but that didn't make it okay. And Jade had been too scared to challenge her father on it. Too scared that if she too hurt him, or let him down in some way as her mother had, then she too would be rejected. She'd tried for years to be the perfect princess daughter. Now she had the chance to be a decent sister.

She took the elevator to the sixth floor, grateful for the clear signs. There was a large open-plan area with several desks in groups, separated by a couple of sofas, and a num-ber of glass-walled offices ran along the side. How was she meant to know which was Juno's desk? She paused, taking in the personal items on each one in the hope she might find a clue. Then she spotted an enormous hot pink coffee mug with *Princess* emblazoned on the side. Jade smiled the second she saw it, her amusement bubbling up. That 'own it' attitude was pure Juno. She wheeled her cabin bag up to the desk, shrugged out of her coat, hung it on the back of the swivel chair and eyed up the computer. All she needed to do now was get online, get a few messages and emails sent and she'd be out of here.

'What do you think you're doing?'

Jade wasn't listening to that icy but irate phone message now, but there was no mistaking that voice. She instantly swung round, drawing in a breath to reply—but then she choked.

'Oh.' She gulped, staggered by the sight before her.

First impression? Skin. Second impression? Muscles. Third? Fury—in the heated tension in his tight stance. All of it up close and personal and towering over her.

Jade suddenly felt as if she were being incinerated from the inside out. Awareness—purely, *mortifyingly*, sexual—swamped her, frying her brain. He was huge. Like really, *really* tall and muscular in a way she wasn't used to.

Of course, she wasn't used to it.

The man was gleaming and hot—literally. She could almost see the steam rising from his body. Why—*why*—was his chest bare? Finally—far too late—she dragged her gaze up from his abs and pecs, past his wide shoulders to the tanned column of his neck, his sharp-edged jaw, grim-set mouth and then there, to the blazing anger in his amber eyes.

'Juno, right?' he said tightly. 'You need to leave.'

This wasn't the setting for so much skin. That was why she was reacting so primally, right? Frankly she wasn't used to seeing half-naked men, *ever*. No matter that it was an office situation, not in *any* situation was she used to this.

'You're…' she trailed off, forced to swallow in an attempt to ease her dry throat.

'Still wondering why you're here,' he snapped.

Couldn't the same be said for him? It was ridiculously early and what was he doing here *barely dressed*? Black sports shorts and trainers were all he had on.

Alvaro Byrne.

Tall, dark and wild. Even his hair was a little long and now he swept it out of his eyes with an impatient hand. The already tense muscles in his chest rippled.

'Why are you here?' he demanded. 'Didn't you get my message?'

'I—'

'Don't need to be here. Leave. Now.'

Seriously? He wasn't even going to listen to her? Wasn't going to take a breath? 'No. I'm here to—'

'Why aren't you moving?'

'Why aren't *you* listening?'

He folded his arms in front of her. The stance just made his biceps pop more.

Jade, who'd held her nerve for so many years, in so many public situations in Monrova, was completely distracted. For the first time ever, her brain slipped into mush territory and her tongue slipped away from her.

'You…' It wasn't good enough. She needed to do better for Juno. She drew a deep breath and began again. 'You need to give me a chance.'

'You've had plenty of chances. But you haven't answered any calls or messages for forty-eight hours. And now you walk in here looking…'

Jade tensed warily. Looking what? Had he guessed already?

'Like butter wouldn't melt,' he finished with a growl.

She was buffeted by a wave of relief that she might pull this off. He hadn't instantly recognised that she wasn't Juno. She struggled to stare calmly back at him. Never had it been so hard to stand still and stay cool.

'Forty-eight hours, Juno,' he repeated. 'Why didn't you return any calls?'

It was always best to answer with honesty, right? Or at least with as much honesty as she was able at this point in time. 'I was out of range.'

'Really? That's what you're going with?' He couldn't look more disbelieving. 'Maybe you should have stayed out of range.'

'I'm here now.'

'Why?'

'Why do you think?'

'What do you think you can possibly do to make this better?'

She had no idea. Never had she been challenged with such hostility or fury and she was lost for words.

His eyebrows lifted. 'Way too little, way too late.'

Jade was tired from the flight. Stressed from maintaining a stupid lie for such a short time already. This had been such a bad idea. The little 'snafu' that Juno had mentioned had apparently morphed into something bigger. But this—creature—couldn't be that unreasonable. And she needed to re-engage her brain. 'I couldn't...'

'I'm going to shower and dress,' he interrupted, apparently bored already. 'You'll be gone when I return.'

He'd turned his back on her and was walking away before she could blink.

Jade gaped as she watched him stride through the office. He thought he could just fire her? Be that dismissive? He hadn't even given her a chance to properly explain, let alone offer a solution. Never had she met someone so unreasonable.

She'd bitten off more than she could chew. She'd been impetuous and foolish and she had no way of pulling this off. But this was for Juno and she had to succeed at saving her sister's job. She was *not* giving up.

Alvaro strode through the office to the bathroom and flicked the shower to cold, desperate to regain control over the appallingly base reaction of his body. That woman had walked in here at stupidly early o'clock—wheeling a case, for some strange reason—and frankly almost looking furtive. He'd finished his workout only five minutes earlier and followed her progress from his office. He'd seen her smile as she'd made her way to her desk. A smile of pure joy. Why was she so amused by this situation?

And worse was that *he'd* been flooded with a heat that was outrageous in its intensity. Anger, right?

Not entirely.

But that visceral betrayal of his body had only exacerbated his anger. He refused to be physically attracted to Juno Monroyale. Hell, he barely knew her. His marketing manager had pitched hiring her to him only a few weeks ago, but he'd been overseas setting up a major deal and hadn't spent much time in the office since her arrival.

Unfortunately, it turned out that the princess was stunning. Her eyes a gorgeous, bewitching green. Her brunette hair was swept up in a high bun that emphasised cheekbones and plump lips and her pretty little chin tempted him to tilt it upwards so she could take his kiss.

It was appalling. He'd not been paralysed by lust like this in quite a while. Not as instantly or as intensely or as inappropriately. She was an employee. Worse, she was an employee who'd screwed up. *Royally.*

So the sooner she was out of here, the better.

He glared at the shower wall as if his eyes were lasers

and could burn right through the tile and wood to where that woman was wheeling her damn case out of here.

She'd *better* be walking out of here—in those thin-soled stupid shoes with their little high heels that were useless for the snow-threatened streets of New York. It said it all, right? Ill-equipped for real life? She was a literal princess who didn't own up to her mistakes. She'd apparently abandoned her colleagues—did she just assume that someone else would clear up the mess?

He knew too well how that worked. He knew people with such privilege who'd refused to carry the burdens of their own responsibility—their own *mistakes*. His own 'family' were the perfect example of that—while he'd been the 'mistake'.

So he had little time to sympathise with Her Royal Highness. And he had little time to get this sorted. But he would, because *he'd* built this entire company—with determined, round-the-clock effort. Its increasing success had meant he'd had to assemble teams around him, but at heart he preferred independence and self-reliance. He'd never liked asking anyone to help him. Never expected anyone would—not unless there was something in it for themselves. Something like a fat pay cheque.

This princess had no idea what building this success had taken. Whether her cluelessness was based in pure entitled privilege, or mere carelessness, it didn't matter. Whichever it was, he didn't want her around.

To be honest, it wasn't the actual social media post he was bothered about. While that app was his oldest and he had a soft spot for it, it wasn't his core business now. But it was the *trust* that had been damaged. And he was in the middle of a delicate acquisition and the last thing he needed was for his prospective target to be frightened off.

He exited the shower and dressed, yanking a shirt from the hanger and swiftly buttoning it. Then he strode back out to the office to check that she'd obeyed his order and had gone.

She hadn't.

He paused a few paces away from where she sat at her desk, focusing hard on the computer screen before her. 'Why are you still here?'

She didn't stop typing. 'Because I'm sorting out this issue.'

'The only issue here is that you haven't left yet,' he scoffed.

'Then call your security, I'm not leaving.' She spun her seat round a few inches and glared up at him.

Oh, really? Adrenalin rippled within him at her audible defiance. 'I don't need security to help haul your ass out of this building. I can scoop you up with one hand.' In fact, both of his hands were itching right now.

'Try it and see how far you get,' she snapped back.

Jade never snapped. Ever. And to her absolute amazement, she just had. Their gazes clashed. Never had she felt as small as she did sitting on this chair, nor had she felt such appalling anticipation.

'Not going to give you the thrill,' he muttered through clenched teeth.

'Not going to move,' she replied.

She'd laid the challenge with loathing, but a second later a wave of longing swept over her. She *wanted* to feel his hands grab her waist and haul her to her feet and press her against his hard body. She wanted it so intensely, with such ferocity that for a second, as she stared into his eyes, she actually believed that *he* wanted it too. That he envisioned exactly that—the two of them pressed tightly together.

Her heart thudded as they silently squared off. Impossibly, he was more dangerous now in that sharp white shirt and the black trousers. She could sense the heat and strength of the muscles she knew full well were primed beneath that expensive fabric. But she refused to flinch, or shrink back…right now she refused to even breathe.

He still just stared at her. But where his stance was furious, his eyes were nothing but warm—a honeyed amber iris and melting, deep pupils that widened the more she watched—daring her nearer, willing her to dive in and drown.

'Let me have a go at fixing this,' she eventually croaked.

'And make it worse?'

'Why not trust me to do the job I was hired to do?'

'You've already shown you're incapable of doing that. You chose to walk out.'

'So a person can't make a single mistake? You can't give someone a second chance? This wasn't a capital offence, Alvaro. This wasn't even *illegal*.'

It had been the tiniest mistake and he was totally overreacting.

'It was a data breach.'

'Actually, it wasn't,' she said firmly. 'It clearly states in the terms and conditions of the app that Byrne IT has the right to use that data in any publicity.'

His gaze narrowed on her.

Yes, she'd spent the time waiting for the train reading up all she could. And she was good at reading long, boring documents and legalese.

'While it wasn't ideal and while it certainly might not have been best policy,' she continued, 'it *wasn't* illegal. And you can change the policy to better reflect what your consumers are now saying they want.'

'You're not going to admit to doing anything wrong?'

'Actually, the contrary.' She straightened on her chair—pointless as it was because he was still so much taller than her. 'I take full responsibility. It was *my* mistake and I'll apologise for it.'

Juno had posted the wrong graphic on one of their social media channels. Version one instead of version two. Version one included user names whereas version two had been made anonymous. It had been such a simple mistake but some of those users had noticed and didn't like their usernames being displayed. The lack of initial response had led to that small flame of discontent flaring to a dumpster blaze and an online debate about privacy rights.

'Fine. You've apologised. Now you can leave.'

'Not leaving.' She spun back to the screen.

'What are you doing?'

She didn't glance away from the computer. 'I said I'd apologise.'

'You just did.'

'Not only to you.'

He paused. 'You're emailing the team before you leave?'

'I already have. Because I'm sorry for going AWOL at the weekend, but I'm back. And now I'm replying to the complainants.'

'What?'

'*Everyone* makes mistakes,' she said heatedly. 'And most people deserve a second chance, right?' she said. 'Most *normal* people are willing to give that.' She sent him a look.

He folded his arms across his very muscular chest. 'You think a little apology is going to make this all go away?'

'An acknowledgement can mean a lot.' She nodded.

'As can getting something for free,' he added cynically.

'Then I'll give them a month free on their subscription. You can take it directly from my salary.' She swallowed. She could cover that cost for Juno once she was back in Monrova. And it would be worth it just to prove herself in front of the furious one here.

'You're willing to the pay the price all by yourself?' he asked.

She glanced back and looked directly into those heart-stopping eyes. 'I'm willing to do whatever it takes.'

'I didn't think royals were known for admission of any kind of guilt,' he commented acidly.

Oh, so he had a thing against all royals? Not just Juno in particular? 'Did you think we're all spoilt and entitled?'

'I think...' He paused, his words coming soft but dangerous nonetheless. 'I think you need to prove yourself, Princess.'

She looked at him a moment longer and then lifted her chin. 'Fine,' she breathed, bluffing as best she could. 'No problem.'

CHAPTER TWO

No problem?

The annoying thing was, that appeared to be the case. Three hours into it, Alvaro studied the princess from the relative privacy of his office. She looked pale and thinner—at least he thought she did. Truthfully, he'd not spent much time considering her as he'd been away working on a deal. But Juno was right, this wasn't a 'data breach' and they hadn't actually contravened their own privacy policy, and perhaps her suggestion they amend their terms was worth considering.

So now he watched her messages appear online with interest. She was responding to every comment already made, signing each one 'PJ'.

I'm sorry for the error. It was entirely my mistake. This was your story to share.

To his amazement, the diffusion of emotion was happening before his eyes. Comments kept appearing—more, then more replies to her responses. Now people were telling her not to worry about it? People were feeling sorry that she'd made a mistake? How had she got them onside so quickly?

Everyone makes mistakes, but mine impacted directly on you. I can only apologise and thank you for accepting my apology.

She'd written to one formerly cross customer and now they were asking her which was her favourite workout and chatting like old friends?

He looked up to observe her again. She was almost smil-

ing as she typed—a whisper of a sweet smile. He'd had his
doubts about hiring her, cynically thinking that his marketing manager just wanted to sprinkle some quasi-celeb-
rity glitter about the place. And that Juno was cynical too,
only doing this for profit. Prior to this she'd been an 'influ-
encer' or something—he'd assumed that meant she merely
peddled whatever product people would give her just to
make a buck.

But maybe he'd been wrong about that, because she
was genuinely engaged and actually enjoying this interaction. She worked quickly, using two computers to check on
different social media channels, answering comments as
quickly as she could. But the comments were snowballing
now. One made him flinch. It was personally abusive. *Vile.*

Instinctively he stood, but before he could move she'd
posted a polite, finite response. And now others had boosted
her response and, in only moments, the abusive comment
was buried in an avalanche of support for the princess.

So why had she skipped out for the weekend, then? Why
hadn't she replied to any of those messages from her workmates? No one had heard from her. No one had been able to
reach her. Sophy, her direct manager, had been stressed—
now Alvaro buzzed for them both.

'Sophy, can you help Juno moderate those comments?'
he said shortly when they appeared in his doorway. 'She
shouldn't have to see some of those...'

'I can handle them,' Juno replied before Sophy had the
chance. 'They're only words and this shouldn't impact on
anyone else's workload any more than it already has.'

Alvaro stared, his breath stolen by her restrained dignity—so different from the flare he'd seen from her this
morning. 'Are you sure?'

She nodded.

Through the afternoon he drank another two coffees
and kept an eye on Juno. She didn't move from her chair

for hours. Surely, she needed food or a bathroom break? She'd didn't stop to chat to colleagues much either. On the socials, there were more comments than ever. But not angry ones. Somehow, she'd got people sharing stories about when they'd screwed up. The community was more active than it had been in ages.

'We've had a bump in sign-ups today.' Sophy reappeared in his doorway, looking smug. 'Across all the apps. They love her response and her apologies. She's given us a masterclass in social media management,' Sophy added. 'Talk about the power of authenticity. And somehow she's done it in a way that hasn't made her a martyr.'

Alvaro didn't respond. He was facing the discomforting fact that he wasn't going to be able to fire her now. It ought to be good to have someone with such expert social media skills on his team. So why did he feel thwarted? And what was with this prickling sense of danger?

He clamped down on the obvious reason. He refused to acknowledge the heat that had hit the second he'd clashed with her at five o'clock this morning.

'They want to talk to her.' Sophy turned and watched Juno from his office. 'They like being able to talk to a real princess.'

He stiffened, bothered by that being the reason for her success. Were they *using* her because of who she was? He didn't feel comfortable that he was benefitting in some way because of the name she had and the family she'd been born into. That he was taking advantage of something that was beyond her control…

And yet it wasn't beyond her control. *She* was the one out there commenting, choosing how to respond, choosing to take the time. She could have chosen not to come back at all. She could have left when he'd told her to first thing this morning. But she hadn't.

Then again, perhaps that was because she *needed* this

job, needed to utilise whatever skills or assets or abilities she had—ones she was born with every bit as much as the ones she'd developed. Just because she was a princess, didn't mean she had everything.

He knew what it was like having to do whatever it took to survive—sucking up crap jobs or working all hours. His foster carer, Ellen, had done that, taught him through her example that work ethic was everything. The one thing you could control.

So all he could do was respect and appreciate Juno's effort and dignity. Yet he remained uncomfortable. He hadn't felt this wary in years—not since that dreadful day when he was nine years old and had been dragged to face his biological 'family' only to be rejected all over again. And then abandoned. Again.

'We need to clarify those terms and conditions,' he said to Sophy irritably. 'Get legal on it for me.'

'Sure thing.' But Sophy didn't leave. 'One of the online news bulletins has requested to interview you and Juno—she'd be good—'

'Juno's busy,' he said decisively. 'I'll handle it.'

He wasn't using her more today. Furthermore, he needed to get his inappropriate attraction under control. What was with *that* landing on him today? Why when he'd barely noticed her before now?

Maybe he was coming down with some kind of fever because within one second of seeing her this morning, he'd been burning up and hadn't cooled since.

She was still responding to that online chaos. Incredibly focused and calm. Too calm. Had he imagined that fiery argument from her this morning? Irritated, he stood to escape the office for a breather.

'You sound different today, Juno,' one assistant mused.

'I was with some people from Monrova over the weekend,' Juno answered. But as Alvaro passed her she saw him and a slow flush clouded across her pale cheeks. 'My accent always becomes stronger then...'

He tore his gaze from hers and strode out of the office. He barely managed to maintain his smile through the interview as her words from this morning rang in his ears.

'Everyone makes mistakes and most people deserve a second chance, right?'

Exhausted and stiff, Jade tilted her head to stretch out the tension in her neck and shoulders.

Why are you still here?'

Surely, he didn't mean that? Her heart thudded as she spun once more to face the penetrating amber eyes of Alvaro Byrne. She'd been waiting for hours for him to return from that wretched online interview she'd watched, fiddling with the computer system and avoiding talking too much to Juno's colleagues before they finished for the day and left her alone.

'I'm glad you agree everyone makes mistakes,' she said quietly. 'And that everyone deserves a second chance.'

'You saw the interview?' His lips twisted. 'You argued compellingly—are you not pleased I took your thoughts on board?'

Jade was too tired to be left in any doubt. 'Does everyone include me?'

His gaze softened. 'I'm not afraid to admit when I'm wrong either, Juno. I appreciate everything you've done today.'

But she shrank, because him calling her 'Juno' made her feel guiltier than ever.

His jaw tightened. 'Look, you weren't to know, but I've been away working on a sensitive deal,' he said. 'I didn't react well this morning and I apologise for that.'

Oh. His quiet apology almost broke her last defences.

'I know it looked like I'd just walked out...' She drew

breath, determined to be as honest as possible while still protecting Juno. 'There was something I had to attend to at the weekend. I'm sorry I wasn't in touch sooner.'

He gazed at her, too still, too intent, for her comfort.

'Sophy said that before this happened you'd planned to take leave from work this week?'

She nodded warily.

'Would you mind coming into the office instead? I'd appreciate your input on a couple of project streams and I think the team could benefit from your expertise. Unless you have plans you can't change?'

'Um—I…' This nightmare was going from bad to worse, yet she couldn't seem to say 'no' to him. 'Of course, I can come in.'

Ordinarily she could maintain a calm facade better than anyone. Ordinarily she would never say 'um'…but at this moment in front of Alvaro Byrne, she was a breath away from falling apart.

'That's great. Thank you.' Though he didn't look all that thrilled. 'But for now, it's late and you've had a long day. How are you getting home?'

Jade had no idea how to answer him. She didn't even know where home was. She had gone into this without properly thinking it through. Too late she'd realised the utter stupidity of her decision to come into the office this morning. Because while she'd secured Juno's job today, she was probably going to lose it for her tomorrow. She couldn't possibly keep this up. And she certainly couldn't cope with the hot bomb that was Alvaro Byrne.

'You shouldn't go on public transport this time of night.' He frowned.

'I can manage,' she lied.

'Just humour me,' he growled. 'You've gone above and beyond and been here hours. The least I can do is ensure you get home safely. I'll call a car.'

'I don't need—'

His gaze narrowed again. 'Company expense, Juno.'

She *really* didn't like him calling her by that name. But she couldn't tell him not to.

The easiest thing to do right now ought to be to say yes, to stop arguing with him. Except oddly it was the hardest task she'd faced all day. Drawing on that mantle of polite courtesy that had been drilled into her from birth was almost impossible.

'Thank you,' she finally said. 'That would be wonderful.'

'Wonderful?' He stared at her for a long moment.

Jade had the sudden suspicion she'd inadvertently jumped from the frying pan to the fire.

'Oh, sure,' he muttered softly but so dryly she nearly shivered. 'Let's call it wonderful.'

CHAPTER THREE

JADE SHRUGGED ON her jacket, extended the handle of her cabin bag and followed Alvaro to the elevator.

'You really were out of range?' He glanced at her bag as he pushed the buttons.

'I really was.' To her relief, he didn't ask for any more detail.

She was hugely relieved at the prospect of a car taking her straight home too. All she had to do then was unlock Juno's apartment. She was so tired she might fall into bed fully dressed.

She exited the lift ahead of him, increasingly desperate to escape his company. He was too tall, too intense, too magnetic and she was too aware of his every movement.

A sleek black sports car was parked right outside the building. The kind of low-slung roadster, capable of lethal speed, that her father and her protection officers would never let her near. To her horror, Alvaro walked around to the driver's door and got in. When she didn't move, the passenger window glided down.

'Come on.'

'I thought you said you called a car,' she said stupidly.

'I did. My car. The building valet brought it to the front for me.'

She'd thought he'd meant a taxi.

'You're driving me home?' Her audible breathlessness made her wince. If only she could instantly shrivel to ant size. The thought of having to spend more time with him ought to be terrifying, but her suddenly sprinting pulse was actually due to *excitement*. So awkward. And that restless ache inside was so wrong. She stared at the car and then back at him and tried not to melt in the warm amber of his eyes.

There was a long pause.

'You know you're not at risk from me,' he finally muttered. 'I'm not in the habit of harassing my employees.'

And now she was beyond mortified. 'I didn't think that you were.'

'So take this as all that it is, an apology and a small service to show my appreciation for your extra effort today. But if you would prefer I get a driver—'

'No, please don't,' she said hurriedly. 'I was just surprised. You've had a long day too.' She climbed into the car and fastened the belt and resolutely stared ahead.

'If you say the address the navigation will pick it up,' he said blandly.

Relieved, Jade parroted the address she'd memorised and sat back as the automated instruction began. The car silently glided along and she realised it had an electric engine. As she relaxed into the comfortable seat, tiredness swept over her. She could hardly keep her eyes open, only then—

'Is that your stomach rumbling?' Alvaro laughingly glanced at her as the mortifying gurgle continued.

The tension broke and she giggled too.

'You haven't eaten all day,' he said reprovingly. 'You barely left your desk.'

He'd noticed that? And now he intercepted the amazed look she shot him and countered it with a smile.

'Of course not, you might've locked me out if I left the building,' she answered. 'And you were in your office all day too.' She struggled not to react too obviously to his distracting charm—how could he have gone from infuriating to fascinating like this?

'You were watching me?' His eyebrow quirked.

'I was prudently keeping an eye on a *threat*, yes.'

'A threat?' he teased with mock outrage. 'Little old me?'

Oh, the man totally knew the impact he had on people—most especially women.

'You were all for throwing me out of the building,' she said. 'And I need my job.'

'You've saved your job.' His expression turned serious again. 'But I had my lunch delivered, whereas *you* need food *now*.'

'And I'll get it. *Shortly*.' Though she had no idea if Juno had any in her apartment. Or whether there was a store nearby. Not that she had any cash to buy anything with.

'Push that button.'

'Pardon?'

Alvaro leaned across, reaching past her to touch a discreet button. The glove compartment slid open with controlled smoothness and a light automatically illuminated the interior.

'Oh. Wow.' She stared at the incredibly ordered contents in the surprisingly large space.

'Help yourself,' he invited.

'You get hungry?'

'What kind of a question is that to ask a man my height?'

She resisted the urge to feast her eyes on his physique yet again. She was already far too aware of his height and muscularity and doubtless he did need a tonne of food to keep his…*energy* up. And she needed an immediate distraction from her shockingly inappropriate thoughts.

'What's this one?' She pulled out one bright rectangular package.

'Protein bar. They're pretty much all protein bars.'

'Do you carry them on you too?'

'Sure. I go too long without fuel, I get ugly.'

Laughter bubbled out of her before she could stop it. The concepts of 'Alvaro' and 'ugly' were absolute opposites of the reality spectrum. 'So, an endless supply of protein bars?'

'And fruit bars, sometimes chocolate bars…' He shrugged.

'This isn't just a bar at the bottom of your bag.' She gazed at the compartment again. There had to be at least twenty different bars in there. 'This is like survivalist mode.'

'Like I'm prepped for the zombie apocalypse?' He reached past her again and picked one with a scarlet and black wrapper, expertly tearing it and taking a bite while still driving.

'You ever gone hungry for days on end?' he asked after a moment.

'No.' She'd never gone without. Her meals had always been perfectly nutritionally balanced affairs, carefully prepared by the palace chefs. They still were. And she still put up with the annoying monthly medical checks with the palace physician—as she had all her life—because her advisors expected it. It was, now she thought about it, ridiculously over the top.

'It's not a nice feeling,' he said.

She gazed at him, but he didn't add anything more, he was too busy chewing. Deliberately avoiding answering her unspoken questions, she realised. A horrible sensation washed through her. Alvaro knew that feeling of hunger *well*. And she'd just been mentally moaning about her privileged palace food.

'Go on, try it,' he encouraged after a while, nodding to the bar she still held. 'Don't be polite, I know you're starving.'

For diversion from those horrible thoughts as much as anything, she unwrapped it and took a bite.

'Well?' he asked, that laugh back in his voice.

'It's actually…not bad.' She nodded.

'I know.' He laughed. 'Take another for later.'

'I can't do that.'

'Why not? As you can see, I have plenty.'

'Do you get through them or do they get old and go to waste?'

'None go to waste.'

She heard that hint of history again in the serious edge of his answer.

'I give them away if they start to get too old. I don't throw food out.' Alvaro shook his head, regretting the small truths escaping him the way air escaped through the smallest tear in a once-tight seal.

He never discussed personal things, never answered to anyone, never hinted at what had once been… His past was irrelevant; his reasons for his action remained his own.

Yet here he was, telling her little truths that added up to a horror story. She wouldn't know that though. She'd think he was just a perpetually hungry man mountain.

He tried to clear his head, but the scent of vanilla permeated the air. It wasn't from the stupid snacks, it was her. He'd noticed it before and now, in the close confines of the car, it tantalised—making his mouth water and his body tense. He liked vanilla, a lot.

She'd fallen silent again, apparently focused on the road he was taking. Ironically *her* reticence bothered him more than the lapse of his own. She'd smiled at him before with that same open smile he'd seen first thing this morning when, oblivious to his presence, she'd got to her desk. When she'd turned it on him, it had almost caused him to veer off the road. But now she'd stilled, masking those turbulent emotions. He itched to brush the veil from her eyes so that mobility of expression was revealed. Because it was there. She was more sensitive, more volatile than he'd expected and yet, most of the time, so *controlled*.

He couldn't shake the suspicion she was somehow vulnerable—which was stupid when she could clearly take care of herself. She didn't need him getting all unnecessarily gallant… But he couldn't stop his acute awareness of her, while a million and more questions mushroomed in his mind. Because while he couldn't put his finger on it, something was off. Maybe the feeling was merely a residual hangover from that social media mess.

He should've cut himself free of that old app a while ago, but it had been his first success and he'd been loath to lose anything from his arsenal of enterprise. Back when Plan A—to be a professional sportsman—had been destroyed when the ligaments in his knee had been torn, that little idea he'd had, when he'd been captain of the school basketball, football and volleyball teams all at once, had come into its own. He'd been desperate not just to survive, but to succeed at getting out of the poverty hell he'd been in for ever. To escape that insecurity and lift his elderly foster carer, Ellen, with him. And he had. All on his own—with the determined independence he still treasured.

'This is where you live?' he asked.

It was his navigation system, not Juno, who confirmed it. And his discomfort grew. The run-down building on the edge of Queens looked as if it needed a better landlord. It was hardly a palace for a princess. Alvaro pulled over in front of it, his muscles clenching as he glanced around the darkened neighbourhood.

'Thank you for the lift. I so appreciate it,' she said with slightly haughty dismissiveness.

But he was already out of the car. It was too late and the corners too dark for him to leave her yet. He used to meet Ellen and they'd walk home together from night shifts. He'd never leave anyone to walk streets like this alone. He picked up Juno's case, followed her up the stairs and waited while she fished in her purse for the key.

'What's wrong?' he asked eventually.

'Nothing.'

The raw edge in her answer set his nerves on edge. Something was wrong. He leaned past and saw her struggling with the door. 'Can I help?'

'I just…' She looked mortified. 'It sticks sometimes.'

So, the last thing she wanted right now was to accept more help from him? Frankly, that put him out. 'Let me have a go.'

Silently she held out the key.

'You don't have any security guard or anything?' He glanced down the side alleyway, loathing the still shadows and the thought of her arriving here alone night after night.

'No,' she murmured.

'But you're a bona fide princess.'

'Not really.' She sounded choked. 'They changed the line of succession after my mother and I left.'

'And cast you out into the world, alone and defenceless?' he muttered as he forced the key to turn in the half-rusted lock. He didn't know too much about the situation in her home country, but it didn't sound right.

She stiffened beside him and he heard her sharply inhale.

'I can take care of myself,' she said valiantly.

Jade cringed as she stepped over the threshold. It was *such* a lie. How could she claim that when she didn't even know which of these doors off the vestibule led to Juno's apartment?

Panic rose. She couldn't pull this off. She didn't have any cash, didn't know where to get food or how to even order a damn pizza. Now she had to go into the office for another few days and pretend she was the capable, smart and savvy Juno. It was mortifying.

She'd never made a meal in her life. Everything had been brought to her. She was the *definition* of spoilt—to be so incompetent in all basic life skills? She'd been supposed to come here and eat pizza and doughnuts without being judged, to walk around sightseeing, blending in like any other tourist, childishly soaking up the Christmas lights and candy… It was supposed to be her secret escape, a few days of anonymous freedom. Only now?

Alvaro's mouth compressed as he gazed down at her as she stood frozen in the open doorway.

'It's not right to deny someone their birthright. To take away their identity and place in the world,' he said roughly.

Once again, his tone held an emotional, personal edge she didn't understand and hadn't expected. What did he know of identity and loss? Obviously something, because he was right.

'I know,' she said huskily.

She burned with guilt at lying to him, yet his empathy drew her to him at the same time. She had the most appalling urge to lean close—not for the safety or the security a big strong man like him could offer. But for quite the opposite—something far more tempting, far more dangerous.

She didn't, of course. She stiffened and forced herself to step further into the relative safety of the building. She was *not* screwing this up for Juno. But she wished her twin had told her how ridiculously attractive Alvaro was, because her inability to cope with the reality of him was something terrible. If only she'd known.

'Goodnight, Juno.'

For once in her life Jade couldn't execute a polite reply. She simply nodded and closed the door, before leaning against it to stop herself opening it again and saying something stupid.

Why now? Why *him*?

She'd met several attractive men: advisors, guests, even King Leonardo of Severene—who her father and his advisors suggested would be a suitable husband...

But she'd never felt her pulse skip and sprint the way it did around Alvaro. She'd never felt restless or had an ache burning deep and low in those secret parts that had stayed resolutely silent before.

How was she to survive the next few days with Alvaro Byrne as her boss?

It was impossible.

CHAPTER FOUR

'So, Juno—'

'Please,' Jade interrupted Grace, another of the social media assistants. 'Please call me PJ.'

'PJ?' Alvaro, sitting just along from her, frowned.

'Yes.' She forced a smile and grabbed assertiveness with both hands. 'For—'

'Pineapple Juice?' Grace joked.

'Plain Jane?' Jade giggled back.

'Poor Joke?' Alvaro added blandly.

Jade shot him a look. 'Yes, it's a new thing, but it's good to refresh, right?'

'Refresh?' Alvaro echoed.

'Like we need to do with some of your social media channels,' she said with more bravery than she felt. As a comeback it was weak, but it was the best she could muster in front of everyone.

It was her own fault that he was watching her with that wary, almost disapproving eye. She'd been late, thanks to figuring out the damn subway system again, which would've been fine except he was waiting by her desk to ask her to join in this never-ending meeting with so many other people.

'You did an amazing job turning this issue around for us yesterday,' Sophy, the marketing manager, filled the sharp little silence. 'It's the honesty and authenticity that people have responded to.'

Jade wasn't either honest or authentic. She was sitting here lying to them all right this second. And she couldn't bear to look at the tall man sitting to her left, yet she couldn't seem to stop herself. Her pulse still wouldn't settle but worse was the heightened state of awareness, the heat, the craving she felt for his attention.

'Are you all okay to work through lunch?' Alvaro asked. 'I've ordered catering.'

A noisy cheer echoed around the meeting room. Jade's stomach cheered too. Turned out Juno didn't keep her fridge well stocked and Jade hadn't had time to stop to get anything on the way to work this morning. So yes, she was starving again.

'Lunch is important, after all. To keep us going.' Alvaro's gaze landed on Jade again. 'And it's our last week before our Christmas break, right?'

Try as hard as she could, she couldn't tear her gaze from that knowing glint in his—as if he'd somehow twigged she'd gone without again and he'd deliberately ordered in.

'And the sooner we refine these plans, the sooner we can break up early,' he added.

While the rest of the staff looked delighted, Jade wished she could melt and slide into a gooey mess under the meeting table. She *never* tripped over her words. She never felt *nerves* like this. But she was far too conscious of him.

'Can you work up a proposal, PJ?' Sophy asked. 'It doesn't have to be fully costed or detailed. I'd just like the concept to mull over during the Christmas break.'

'Of course.' Jade scrambled to catch up on what it was they'd been saying and on what topic it was she was supposed to propose…and she'd get to researching 'how to write a proposal' the second she was back at her desk.

'Wow, did you get hair extensions?' Grace paused beside her when they finally stood to leave the meeting room, almost three hours later.

'Pardon?' Jade lifted her hand to her head and realised some of her hair had fallen from the topknot she'd tied it in early this morning, and it was now hanging in a long streak over her shoulder. 'Oh, yes, I did.'

'It looks amazing. I love the length and the colour.'

'Thank you.'

But yet again her errant, apparently uncontrollable gaze glided across the room to collide with Alvaro Byrne's once more. He impacted every sense—her vision and hearing were so attuned to him, but most of all he struck a need for touch within her. It was appallingly inappropriate. Even after the meeting—after he was locked away in his own office—he still oozed animal magnetism, dominating every damn one of her thoughts. It was as if she'd walked into a cloud of heated, sensual fog. She couldn't see beyond him, couldn't think of anything else. It was *mortifying*—mostly because it seemed so beyond her control.

There were plenty of other men in the office and there were those personal trainer guys who worked at the gym downstairs who walked around with equally ripped muscles on show all the time… But none of them had the effect on her that Alvaro Byrne did, even now when he was covered up in his perfectly tailored suit.

The worst thing, though, was that she was sure *he* was aware of her response to him. There was an arrogant tilt to his lips and an astute glint in his heavy gaze, as if he could see through her superficial layer to that guilt just beneath. He watched her as if he knew, or at least suspected, something was wrong.

And he was right, of course.

She didn't want to wreck Juno's reputation, but she didn't think she could sustain this lie. She'd gone too public and what had been a minor error was now getting more attention than before. That online bulletin had asked again to interview *her*—it was ridiculous—and more people were trying to follow her online. Thank goodness Juno had shut down her social media platforms because, as it was, some of her old pictures had been recirculating. If anyone looked too closely and spotted any differences between them and the 'Juno' in the office now? It was a nightmare waiting to come to life.

But it was that internal battle that was the most hideous. She'd prided herself on her ability to contain her emotions, to be the calm, polite princess who could control her own thoughts and get the job done. But all that control had slid the second she'd encountered Alvaro Byrne.

And now she'd got to know a little of him? He wasn't the autocratic bully who didn't bother to listen…in reality he did hear, he did see. He even apologised.

Which meant he was impossible to stay mad with, impossible to say no to, impossible to ignore. But he was her boss. So she had to. Because he was so, *so* out of bounds.

Something still didn't add up. And that fact that he was still obsessing over her *days* later? Alvaro couldn't wait for tomorrow—Friday, finally. The office was officially closing for Christmas and it would give him a few days alone to sort out his head—and other parts. Because he did *not* screw around with employees. Ever. It wasn't as if he hadn't had the chance. He'd had to be very distanced from one former recruit who'd made a pass at him, but he didn't like it messy in the workplace.

Outside the company? For a while seduction had been a sport like any other, and Alvaro always played to win. But he'd matured since the days when he'd taken what had been offered just because he could. And he'd swiftly learned it was simpler to stay single. With his workload he couldn't meet the commitment or expectations of a long-term relationship. Nowadays he enjoyed an occasional brief affair with a woman willing to enjoy the lifestyle—and lack of strings—he offered. A woman unencumbered by unrealistic dreams of happy-ever-after, or drama.

But this woman? An employee. A princess—even if cast off from her kingdom… There was so much drama. So much that was forbidden.

Yet he couldn't tear his attention from her. Couldn't stop

the urges whispering within—they'd been his constant, irritating companions every minute since he'd sparred with her first thing last Monday morning. Every day since had only added to the weight of temptation. And his curiosity—sexual and otherwise—had equally magnified as the days had passed.

Why had a supposedly streetwise 'rebel' struggled to unlock her own front door? Why had she fleetingly looked panicked when she had been late the other day? And he couldn't be sure, but he suspected that for some reason she wasn't eating much. He'd seen her pour herself too many coffees from the office filter, adding doses of sugar and cream as if to magically bulk it into a meal… He was probably projecting his own old feelings and fear of hunger on that one, but he'd ordered lunch into the meeting on Tuesday just in case. He'd done the same again every day since, calling it his new Christmas tradition. As if he knew anything about those. But he couldn't stand to think of someone starving. Sometimes she seemed miles away—Sophy had had to call her name twice the other day. And her immediate apology, the polite smile she offered? The stillness in the way she sat? Her quietness in the office? She was a contradiction. Because he knew that, beneath that supposedly serene exterior, she was stifling a snappy fighter. He wanted *that* Juno to emerge again. Instead, she'd buried herself in that stupid proposal Sophy had requested.

He'd had to resist, employing every ounce of self-control not to try and provoke the feisty determination he'd discovered lay beneath that poised facade. She was *too* perfectly contained. Where was the wild 'Rebel Princess' her old social media posts showed her to be? Where was the flash of spirit she'd shown him on Monday morning?

While she looked the same, she didn't *seem* the same.

But *he* didn't need to be wasting his time contemplating her. It was the slide into the holiday season, right? Maybe he'd fixated on her as a distraction from all the happy family, festive tinsel stuff filling the city. Speaking of which, he clicked into his email system to check that his orders to Ellen had been delivered. His foster carer had always worked Christmas, as had he as soon as he was able. He still did. Satisfied when he saw the receipts were signed off, he pushed back from his desk and stood. Thankfully it was Thursday night and he'd made it. He'd not gone near her, not noticed those slim-fitting black trousers and pristine white shirt. He'd ignored the fact that his fingers itched to skim over her lines and that he ached to discover what softness and curves lay beneath...

His staff were going out tonight, celebrating the holiday starting tomorrow. He'd never been more glad that he'd agreed to close the office a few days ahead of Christmas. He told his assistant to pass on his good wishes. They were used to him not stopping in to socialise.

He took the stairs down to the gym, once more trying to work out the never-ending frustration, knowing that when he got back, she would be gone and out of reach. The relief would be immense. Avoidance was his only remaining strategy.

But when he returned to the office in gym shorts and tee, a full fifty minutes later, she was still sitting at her desk, still in that same self-contained pose, still silently focused on her screen. The only other person on the floor.

'*What* are you doing?' he demanded, his patience blown.

'Oh!' She spun on her chair and drew in a shocked breath. Her jade eyes widened.

Déjà-vu. Suddenly he was hotter than he'd been mid-workout. Because once again she was staring at him as if she'd never seen a man before. Honestly, it took everything not to flex. But every muscle was already tense—they'd been on high alert for days.

'I thought you worked out this morning,' she blurted, then blushed.

Alvaro smiled faintly. She taken note of his routine? Good, because he'd been barely able to tear his attention from her for days now.

'I did,' he said. 'I work out twice a day. It's how I manage stress.'

It was a discipline too. The habit branded within him from his youth. He'd learned that if he wanted to succeed at something, he had to work harder, longer, heavier, than any competitor. Only this time his competitor was his own lust. So in fact he'd gone for another session in the middle of the day today, desperate to burn some of the energy coiling tighter and tighter within him.

'I'm sorry you're stressed.' She bit her lip. 'I don't think I've helped you there.'

That was incredibly true, but not in the way she meant.

'It's habit as well.' He shrugged, trying to rein himself in and at least act casual. 'Twice a day, every day. I like it.'

Another blush swept across her cheeks. He stared. Was she interested in what he *liked*? In what made him feel *good*? Because really, the best thing of all was the most instinctive, the most animal of urges…was she thinking about sex? Because he not so suddenly was. Damn, if he didn't have the overriding instinct that the chemistry between them would be instantly combustible.

'Why are you still here?' He growled, irritated with his one-track mind. 'The others have gone for Christmas drinks.'

'I know.' Her expression pinched. 'But I wanted to finish up that report before leaving.'

'There's always tomorrow morning.'

'I don't want to leave it until the last minute. I want to be sure it's done and done well.'

Seriously perfect, wasn't she? His skin seemed to have

shrunk too small for his muscles. Why didn't the 'Rebel Princess' want to party? He'd overheard one of the guys ask her out yesterday and she'd made some weak excuse about getting home to her cat. But there'd been a large 'no pets' sign at the entrance of her apartment building the other day and definitely no felines yowling around. She'd been lying.

'You're not going to join them?' Her glance was wary as he silently stared at her.

'I'm the boss. They'll have more fun if I'm not casting a shadow over proceedings.'

Jade stood, her nerves too strained for her to remain still. He was no shadow. He was a light that commanded all attention, who made her incredibly aware of every movement, every breath. She needed to *leave*.

She couldn't believe she'd come across him in his wretched workout gear all over again. This time he hadn't stripped, he still had a tee shirt on. But the arms on show? The skin? All those muscles? It was impossible not to stare even as she burned to a crisp, her brain overcooked and immediately unproductive. She'd been struggling all week— hyper-aware, absurdly impressed. And it was evident his staff were completely loyal—no wonder they'd all phoned Juno so desperately when that little post had gone awry. They would do anything for him and no wonder—with his patience in meetings, his insights, and those incredible catered lunches?

Yes. She had to get out of there. *Now.* Before she did something mortifying. Because now he was nearer, now there was an element in those amber eyes that expressed… *care*.

'Are you okay?' His voice was low and husky and soothing. 'Juno?'

She closed her eyes. She hated hearing her sister's name on his lips. She hated that she'd lied to anyone, but most of all him. And she hated how much his opinion of her mattered to her.

'I'm not used to...' *Having a stunning man stand so close.* She opened her eyes and sighed. 'I'm just a bit tired.'

'You've had a tough week.' He was looking at her as if he were trying to solve a puzzle. 'What do you do to unwind? If it's not heading out for a drink and it's not burning off stress in a gym...'

She froze. The only other thing she could think of was the one thing she'd *never* done with anyone. Why was that utterly inappropriate suggestion leaping into her mind now and flashing like an unavoidable neon sign?

'What are you going to do?' A frown intensified the amber depth of his warm eyes. 'You're obviously strung out.'

She'd thought she'd done a good job of holding herself together, and he was telling her everyone could see right through her?

'You're pale. When did you last eat?'

'Actually, I had a protein bar for afternoon tea.' And that was after a huge sandwich from that lunch he'd had delivered.

His mouth quirked but he shook his head slightly. 'Not enough.'

'A protein bar lasts a long time.'

'Rot.'

'Maybe my engine doesn't need the same amount of fuel as yours.'

His gaze drilled into hers. 'All engines need good fuel and good, regular service.'

She suppressed a shiver. She was misinterpreting what he was saying, reading something inappropriate into every word.

She tried to laugh. 'You take this interest in all your staff?'

She felt his tension immediately treble.

'You've had a difficult few days,' he clipped. 'Dealing with that stuff online can become overwhelming, even when mistakes haven't been made. I want to make sure you're okay.'

'I'm okay.' She forced a smile. 'Thank you.'

'Are you sure?'

This didn't feel like a normal conversation between boss and employee, or colleagues, or even friends. This was heavier. Her heart thudded, bolting her in place right there before him. He didn't move either. The world telescoped. They were inches apart and no one else was there and there was no threat of interruption...and the longing sweeping through her was crazy. Any rational capacity lapsed, leaving only the ache of temptation. Her limbs trembled as yearning flooded. It was almost a dream when he slowly lifted his hand and lifted a lock of her hair, then ran it through his fingers. She held her breath, not wanting to move, not wanting this mirage to end.

'It's so long,' he muttered. 'I can't believe it isn't real.'

She sucked in a breath as hurt whistled through her. He'd heard her lie and lie and lie and every one burned. She *never* should have thought this switch was a good idea. Yet, if she hadn't, she never would have met Alvaro. She would never have had this moment. Suddenly the urge to lean into his light touch was unstoppable. 'I...'

He blinked and jerked his hand away in a negating gesture and she knew he was about to step back. But she didn't want anything to spoil this one, precious moment. She couldn't.

'It is real,' she blurted, so lost in staring up at him that she lost control of her tongue, telling him things she shouldn't. But she'd never been drawn to anyone the way she was to him. She needed him to *see* her—truly.

'What?' He stood like a hot granite statue.

'My hair,' she muttered helplessly, so stupidly. 'It's real. It's mine.'

His eyebrows pleated. 'But—'

'I'm not Juno.'

His mouth opened.

'I'm…' She paused to swallow, horrified yet unable to halt her confession. She didn't even want to. She wanted—needed—him to know the truth. 'I'm not Juno Monroyale.'

'What?' While his eyes widened, their focus was laser-like.

'I'm her sister.'

For an endless moment neither moved. But beyond his unnatural stillness she knew he was processing and she could feel his reaction rising. A howling heat emanated from his tense body, while loss welled in hers. She'd broken his trust, so now she braced for his fury.

But what emerged was almost a whisper. 'You're not Juno.' He stared so hard he paralysed her. 'If you're not Juno…'

She was Jade. She was the Queen of Monrova.

Confessions were supposed to relieve, instead desolation slid deep, painfully making hidden cuts, as she watched him make the connection.

'Then that means…' He trailed off again, his focus still intent upon her. But as he blinked, the reaction behind his frozen countenance flared and she saw a blaze of emotion heating his whisky-amber eyes.

'If you're not Juno,' he said harshly, 'then I'm not your boss.'

He suddenly stepped forward and that desolation was swept away by a tsunami of something so much hotter. So much more that she couldn't think to answer.

'I'm not your boss,' he repeated angrily, almost to himself.

And she realised that he'd just let something within himself go.

His hand hit her waist in a firm, heavy hold that made her heart thud. She couldn't tear her gaze from his— couldn't move, or speak. Her lips parted, yet she still couldn't breathe as an enormous wave of want tumbled over her again, drenching her with a desire so powerful it knocked over any hesitation, any caution, any reality. All she could hear was her heated blood beating, all she wanted was the touch she'd craved for days.

Just a taste.

She still couldn't speak as he pulled her so close her breasts were pressed against the sizzling strength of his chest, nor could she speak as he slid his other hand to cup the nape of her neck. And she still couldn't say a thing as she leaned against his hold, arching her neck to maintain that impossibly intense contact with his gaze. And then, beneath that penetrating stare, she realised she didn't need to speak. Nor did he. They both knew the answer was obvious and undeniable. In reality, there wasn't even a question.

His head lowered and her breath released on a gasp just as his mouth slammed on hers, his strength making her knees buckle. His hold instantly tightened, and he hauled her fully against him. The impact of collision—chest to breast, hip to hip—destroyed her. His heat, his arousal, made hers burn hotter. She was literally caught up in his passion and his vitality and she could do nothing but be carried along the road he'd chosen. The sensuality poured from him, filling and stirring her, until she had no choice but to release her own, kissing him back as best she could beneath his onslaught, clutching his shoulders, not just to touch, but to hold—to *keep*. Because she needed more of this. Of *him*. She needed so much more. She burst with the need to race with him, to beat him, to hit some near-but-far dizzying destination. Oh, she was suddenly so, so desperate.

Somehow he spun them both and moved her back until

the wall was behind her. It was literally the hard place supporting her while he—like a rock in front—crushed closer, caressing her, kissing her sensitive lips with unrestrained passion. And it was so good because he was so big, so powerful and every muscle, every movement was utterly focused on her. Initially she'd been stunned, rendered immobile, but with each sweep of his plundering tongue her response rose, drawn out of her like a release of a power she'd not known she had. And then she didn't just open for him, she met him with a seeking, demanding slice of her own force. Every particle within her tensed and tingled, filled with energy that couldn't be contained.

These weren't soft, gentle, teasing kisses. These devoured. Fast and long and hot as pent-up passion exploded. It was an almost animalistic seeking to sate long aching hunger. He kissed her as if he'd been thinking of nothing else for eons and she kissed him back just like that because for her it was true. She tightened her arms around his neck, threading her fingers through his unruly thick hair and holding him to her. His fingers slid beneath her shirt, caressing her waist, lifting higher to smooth her ribcage, and she leaned into the sweep of his palm, all her skin ablaze, aching for such touch from him over every inch—inside and out. Exhilaration soared. Her toes curled and she pressed her hips forward, grinding them back against his to feel the shockingly huge reality of his arousal. Heated pleasure stormed, setting off a volley of vibrations within. Lust coiled higher still, the yearning inside widened. His hand at her breast. The scrape of his thumb across her nipple. The ache to be naked. All consumed her.

'Alvaro...'

He smothered hot, wide kisses across her face and down her neck and his hips pressed against hers again and again, mimicking the ultimate act of passion and possession. Never had she felt such excitement, such abandonment.

Never had she wanted anything as much. Never had anything so instinctive overtaken her so completely. She cried out as he savagely sucked, then nipped, her sensitive skin.

'J—' He broke off the guttural mutter and abruptly flung back from her, leaving her slumped back against the wall.

Shocked and suddenly cold, she put her hands palm down for balance, absorbing certainty from the solid wall as she watched him transform before her in the blink of an eye—from passionate lover to furious stranger.

His hair stood in tufts from where she'd tugged at him like some untamed creature. His chest rapidly rose and fell and there was a wild look in his eyes. But his glare solidified and scoured her insides. 'If you're not Juno, then you're...'

Her lips felt puffy and oversensitive and she couldn't bear to press them together. She licked them but it didn't soothe their hungry ache. And she had to answer him. 'Jade.'

His hands curled in fists and he jammed them onto his hips, his chest rising and falling as if he'd just run a life-or-death sprint. 'Juno's identical twin sister.'

'Yes,' she confessed. But his angry reaction horrified her. 'I'm sorry you thought I was her.' Oh, God, she realised the worst and whispered, 'You wanted to kiss her.'

'What? *No!*' His frown deepened. 'I've never wanted to kiss Juno. Never wanted to order her into my office and slam the door behind her so I could grab her and strip her—' He broke off and cursed—a full sentence of self-berating filth.

She stared at him as something feral inside roared with primal pleasure. Every millimetre of her skin tightened again with awareness and want.

'I've never wanted to do that with *any* of my employees,' he said more calmly a few moments later. 'I've never been unable to control my reaction to anyone before.'

'But your reaction to me?' Her mouth dried because she was stupidly nervous. As if she were facing all the exams of her life in the one moment. Pass or fail were the only options. Win or lose. Have or have not. She wanted to win. She wanted to have.

Just this one moment.

But she could see him calculating and she could feel him cooling…so quickly. His emotional withdrawal wasn't just visible, wasn't just audible, it was palpable. And she felt it as the devastating loss it was. She wanted his heat, his body, his intimacy. For once in her life, she wanted to obliterate her isolation.

'If you're Jade,' he said quietly, 'you're the Queen.'

Her heart dropped to the floor, but she tried to pull herself together, to answer with her old, customary politeness. 'That's correct.'

The change in the atmosphere was as strong as if a foehn wind had lifted and turned all the fallen leaves over, presenting the whole world in a different colour.

But it wasn't the whole world. It was only her. *She* was being seen in a new light. No longer an employee. No longer a woman.

She was merely—*only*—a monarch.

CHAPTER FIVE

'YOU SWITCHED PLACES,' Alvaro said with cold clarity. 'At the weekend.'

'Yes,' Jade admitted miserably, mortified by her unthinkable, inappropriate actions. All of them. 'I'm…'

Unable to think.

Why had she said anything at all? Why had she betrayed Juno so swiftly? She'd only been here a few days and she'd let desire overrule everything. She'd *never* let personal wishes get in the way of professional duty before. And her duty right now was to Juno. She'd let her sister down badly. But she'd not been able to resist him any longer, and certainly not been able to lie to him any longer.

'What are you playing at?' He watched her from those few paces back. *'Why?'*

'Juno needed time in Monrova.' But without further explanation her reason sounded weak. Yet those reasons were private to Juno.

His fists tightened. 'You lied. Not just to me, but to everyone.'

'To protect my sister, yes. I'm sorry. It wasn't just for fun. It *mattered* more than that.'

'Not just for your sister. You wouldn't take such a big risk if there wasn't something in it for you too. Something that *matters*.' He echoed her emphasis, but his had an edge. 'So what is it?'

'It's just a few weeks,' she muttered, glad of the steadying wall supporting her back. 'But it's the only chance I was ever going to get to be…a normal person.'

'Normal?'

'As normal as either Juno and I can get.' And yes, she knew she sounded like the ultimate spoilt princess right now.

But he nodded, as if understanding. 'A few weeks—in a lifetime?'

'Yes.'

'Yet you're spending them working round the clock on some stupid job for me?'

'For my *sister*. I don't want her to lose this—'

'She won't.'

'Thank you.' She couldn't bear to look at him.

'Does she know what's happened here at work?'

'We've not been in touch since we switched. We thought it was safer not to.'

'Safer?' He sounded astounded. 'It's a shocking risk you've taken. I *knew* something was off.' He expelled a harsh breath. 'Why have you told me now?'

'Why do you think?' she mumbled. 'I...was drawn to you.'

Such an understatement. The real risk was what she'd just done and the terrible thing was she wanted more. The sheer rush still rampaging through her.

'Nothing more can happen between us, Jade. You're a *queen*.'

His immediate rejection hurt. 'Am I suddenly inhuman?'

'Aren't you supposed to be engaged to another man?' he threw back at her. 'Don't you have to marry some prince?'

Shocked, she stared at him. Had he heard the rumours about King Leonardo of Severene? It was what her father had wanted and the plan had still been progressing. She'd been supposed to give King Leonardo an indication of her willingness at the Winter Ball. Instead she'd run away— seizing on Juno's mad switch suggestion to stop herself having to make that decision just yet. She'd literally run away from it.

Ironically now Jade seized that exact prospect as a way of putting a barrier between her newfound recklessness and her duty. Because of her own weakness, she needed to put Alvaro at a distance. *Now.*

Yet she couldn't lie to him completely. 'Nothing has been settled.'

His eyebrows shot up. 'But it's under consideration?'

'Several options are…' She fudged, but he silently waited her out. 'It's more like a…political contract. An alliance to benefit both our countries.'

'You'd really marry for duty?'

'If that's what's required,' she said determinedly. 'It wouldn't be the first time it's happened in history.'

He stepped closer and her wretched body hummed with temptation anew.

'What's in the fine print?' His voice was both harsh and husky, that thread of anger strengthened. 'Would you produce heirs?'

'Of course,' she said stiffly. 'For the succession. We would have a shared heir between Severene and Monrova.'

'And unite the two into one country? So this is an acquisition? Who'll have the greater power—Monrova or Severene?'

Jade straightened. She would never cede power over Monrova to another nation. Not even a friendly neighbour like Severene. It would be an *alliance.* But Alvaro's distaste grew more evident with every sarcastically enunciated question.

'Does this prince of yours expect you to be a virgin queen?' he asked. 'Is that part of your promise too?'

'I imagine he'd think my virginity is a hindrance, actually,' Jade retorted, stung by Alvaro's judgment. 'He probably wouldn't be at all pleased.'

'You…*what*?' Alvaro's eyes widened. 'He *what*?'

She realised he'd not expected her to answer that virginity question—let alone honestly.

'Well, it is inconvenient,' she said, explaining it with

bald businesslike briskness to cover her embarrassment. 'But neither of us would consider sex as anything other than a biological transaction. Fortunately, there are other ways for me to become pregnant.'

'*What?*' He actually gasped. 'Are you talking about artificial insemination?'

She shrugged. 'It might be a preferable option for us both.'

His jaw slack, he slowly shook his head. 'You're a virgin. An actual, real-life twenty-something virgin.'

'I'm sure I'm not the only one in existence,' she retorted testily. 'But I've been very sheltered all my life.' All but imprisoned, to be more accurate. 'There really hasn't been the opportunity.'

He stared at her, then glanced away, visibly processing it all. A few moments passed and she felt relieved that the subject was closed. But then he faced her again—muscles flexing as he moved, the faint sheen of sweat making his bronzed skin glow.

'Have you ever kissed anyone else?' It was a whisper.

One she couldn't answer.

'Jade?' Alarm flashed across his face, but he stepped closer again.

She was indescribably pleased by that small shrinking of that gap between them, but there was no hiding the obvious truth.

'Never?' He lifted his hand and brushed her lip with his fingertip. 'I'm sorry. Did I hurt you?'

'No,' she breathed. And she didn't want him to be sorry.

'It was a little more than a kiss.' His frown hadn't fully eased, but there was the smallest quirk of his lips as he softly questioned her. 'What did you think?'

That blush burned again. 'You know already...'

He waited but she couldn't say more.

'Are you always this careful with your words? This...

reticent?' That quirk became a complete smile. 'Not officially a risk taker, Queen Jade?' He leaned closer. 'Yet I think you're *exactly* that.' He brushed her lower lip with that lightest of fingertips again. 'Is that the real reason you switched with Juno? So you could have a couple of weeks to sow all the wild oats you can?'

That smile, that touch, provoked her. 'Would it be so awful if it was?' she challenged, even though it had been nothing of the sort. 'Why shouldn't I? King Leonardo has certainly enjoyed life to the full. There shouldn't be a reason why I can't do the same.'

Alvaro's frown instantly returned. 'Are you really considering marriage to him?'

She paused.

'You don't see something wrong with fooling around with me here while considering that?'

She stiffened. 'The moment I make any marriage vows, I intend to keep them.'

'But haven't you made a promise already? Isn't that what an engagement is?'

'I'm not engaged to *anyone*,' she declared hotly. 'I'll do that at the time required. Until then, *everything* is my own.'

He suddenly leaned his shoulder against the wall next to her, facing her, *watching* her. 'You're using semantics. You're twisting it to get what you want.'

'Well, why shouldn't I get what I want for once?' She lifted her chin. 'I'm prepared to do everything for my country. I'll sacrifice my personal life to perform my duty.' She threw her shoulders back. 'But I've not yet made that promise to King Leonardo. Not him or any other man.'

'Would it be a very convenient marriage—with you both having affairs on the side?'

'I can't speak for anyone else. But if *I* ever marry, I have every intention of maintaining my vows.'

'You'd settle for a sexless life?'

She was burning with mortification at his relentless questioning. 'I've gone without sex up until now—I'm confident I can go without it for decades.'

But something went cold inside. Only now did she realise the gravity of her future choices.

'Wow. You're quite the willing martyr.' His eyes flashed. 'But you won't expect that from your husband?'

'I'd expect him to live with his own decisions, as we all must. And I don't intend to hold any of his decisions against him. I understand the sacrifice we must both make.'

'That's the biggest load of horse shit I've ever heard in my life.' Alvaro straightened, only to step closer still. 'So you're going to calmly turn a blind eye to all his affairs? You're going to let him parade his lovers in front of you?'

'Leonardo is not a monster. He cares about his kingdom and if he wanted to...to...' She trailed off, hating to even think of Leonardo in any kind of sexual way. He was like distant family to her. 'I'm sure he'd be discreet. We both want what's best for both our countries. We would come to an understanding.'

'Some understanding,' Alvaro scoffed. 'He gets to do what he wants while you get to die of boredom.'

She glared at him. 'I don't think that sex is the be-all and end-all of a fulfilling life.'

Alvaro laughed and she lost it.

'Look, if I desperately want an orgasm,' she snapped, 'I can give myself one.'

His jaw dropped. 'Sure,' he almost wheezed. 'Of course, you can and should...frequently, I would hope.'

She was mortified that she'd stumbled into this subject so blindly.

'But...' He cocked his head. 'You know how they say a trouble shared is a trouble halved?'

She nodded, mildly confused.

'They also say a pleasure shared is a pleasure doubled.'

'No one says that.'

'Maybe not, but that doesn't mean it isn't true.' He took a length of her hair, looped it around his fingers and leaned closer still. 'And you don't know that yet, do you?'

It was a whisper of a kiss, a brush so light and tempting that all caution slid from her again. And then there was another kiss—all temptation, all gentle, sweet tease. He was so hot. But beneath that tender touch, there was the promise of fire—that unleashed passion he'd swept her into only minutes before. She wanted both kinds—*now*. And when he lifted his mouth a millimetre from hers, she couldn't stay silent.

'Show me, then,' she breathed.

'So that's what you want, Queen Jade?'

'You? Yes.' She swallowed, but now her desire outweighed her embarrassment again. 'I don't know why it is. Part of me wishes it wasn't you…there's that cute guy who delivers the post—'

'Vito?' Alvaro lifted his head and barked. '*Not* for you.'

She exploded too—in pure frustration. 'I'm attracted to you. I like kissing you. And I want to explore—' She hauled back her self-control, trying to explain herself. 'But I understand if, given everything you've just learned, that's not what you want.'

'You understand?' Alvaro drew a sharp breath and swivelled to stand right in front of her again. 'You understand nothing, Queen Jade. Not a damn thing.'

'Enlighten me, then.'

He pressed his fists against the wall either side of her head and stared into her eyes. 'I can't sleep with a woman who's going to marry another man.'

'Surely most of the women you meet are going to marry another man some time,' she argued. 'Are you the marrying type yourself?'

He froze. 'No.'

No. She didn't think so. He had that air of the loner about him—the distant leader who inspired huge loyalty but remained isolated... Yes, she understood his type very well.

'We've already established that *if* I ever get married, it's not going to be a normal one. I'll do what I'm expected to do, at the time I'm required to. But what I do with my body *before* then? I want to lose my virginity to someone I actually *want*. At a place and time of my choosing. *All* of these things are *my* choices.'

He still loomed over her and his voice was a thread of steel. 'And are you saying your choice for all that is *me*?'

It was impossible not to answer him honestly when he was right before her, gazing right at her, seeing right through her. But asking? She was suddenly so afraid of his answer.

'Obviously you don't have to,' she muttered helplessly. 'I can't order you. I am not *your* queen. And I apologise if I misinterpreted your interest. As we've already established, I'm not especially experienced in such things.'

His jaw slackened for a few seconds and then he smiled. 'In "such things"?'

She'd just propositioned a man she barely *knew*. What on earth had come over her? 'If you'll excuse me, I'll go—'

'No. I won't excuse you.' He leaned closer. 'Won't let you leave.' He gazed down at her. 'Not yet.'

But he didn't kiss her as she wanted him to, and his fierce expression didn't lighten. In fact, the longer the silence grew, the more remote his expression became.

Her breathing quickened as every doubt mushroomed. She was so embarrassed. She never should have said anything. Never should have wanted.

'I apologise,' she muttered in an agonised whisper. 'I shouldn't have wanted—'

His harsh inhalation silenced her. 'You shouldn't apologise for wanting someone.'

She could feel that horrible blush burning across her skin. Worse was the horrible feeling rotting inside. Regret.

But then he smiled. 'You do realise you've invited a tiger in, don't you? Hell, Jade.' He breathed out. 'You must know I wouldn't mind if you ordered me to do what you really want.'

Her mouth dried and she just gazed up at him, unable to say another thing. All courage stolen by the promise in his eyes.

He lifted a hand from the wall beside her and lifted that lock of her hair again. 'You know what you need?'

She shook her head mutely.

'Food.'

Startled, she giggled.

'I'm serious.' But he grinned at her, transforming into a teasing, good-humoured hunk. 'You can't make important decisions on an empty stomach. And I've been watching—you've only had a couple of coffees and one sandwich from the lunch platters I specially ordered. I'm hungry on your behalf.'

Was it wrong to be pleased that he'd been watching?

'I'm starving,' she admitted.

'Then why the hell aren't you exploring all the cafés in the neighbourhood? Isn't that the point of this stupid switch? So you get to eat corndogs from street vendors?'

Now he knew, she couldn't help confessing everything to him. 'I don't even know what a corndog is.'

'What?'

'And I can't get Juno's money card to work.'

'You *what*?'

'I don't have any cash.' She tried to laugh about it. 'Never have. I know that's ridiculously precious, but—'

'You don't have any money.' He wasn't smiling any more. 'And there's no food in the apartment. Why didn't you *say* something?'

'I didn't want to bother Juno. I wanted to manage alone—without assistants and security...'

'What about a friend?' He pushed back from the wall, dropping his arms so she was free. 'Come on.'

'Where to?' She almost had to run to keep up with him.

'To get the best meal in Manhattan.'

He didn't look at her as he repeatedly pressed the button to summon the elevator.

'Don't you need a jacket?' she asked.

'Oh, no,' he said. 'I could do with the cold air.'

A minute later he guided her out onto the street; glancing down, he led her swiftly along the pavement. Less than five minutes later he ushered her into a tiny pizza parlour in a side street just down from the office building.

'Is this the best meal to be had in New York?' Amusement bubbled out of her.

'There are so many meals. But when you're starving, this is a good one to start with. Plus, it's fast.'

'It needs to be fast?' Her heart raced.

'It does.'

He ordered a couple of enormous slices of pizza. There weren't table or chairs for them to sit at, so instead they slowly walked back to the office and ate on the way. Jade smiled as she licked her finger. She wasn't just breaking every palace etiquette rule, she was throwing caution completely to the wind.

'Good?'

So good, she couldn't reply, her mouth was too full.

His sudden smile was so stunning she couldn't have spoken anyway.

'I am so damn glad I am not your employer,' he muttered beneath his breath.

She swallowed and grinned impishly at him. 'So I shouldn't call you *Boss*?'

'Absolutely not.'

She chuckled.

'But I am going to advance you Juno's pay,' he said. 'In cash.'

'I don't want—'

'Consider it a loan. You know you need money for food and to do things,' he interrupted bluntly. 'Don't worry, I have the feeling you're good for it.'

She was. But she truly appreciated the offer. 'Thank you, that's very kind of you.'

He shot her a sardonic smile and half bowed. 'It's my pleasure, Your Highness.'

She winced inside. 'Don't…'

'Then don't "polite me" off.'

'It was basic manners, nothing fancy,' she said defensively. 'Boss.'

There was a pregnant pause in which she wondered just what he was about to do. Every cell overflowed with anticipation.

To her disappointment, he just huffed out a tense growl.

'Come on, I've ordered you a car.' He nodded towards the black sedan now waiting outside his building. 'I'm not driving you. Not tonight.'

Crushed, Jade almost stumbled. So he'd declined her other—unmentionable—invitation? Given her some pizza to soften the blow?

But then he took her hand in his. 'We can have one night, if that's really what you want.'

'One?' Her heart leapt.

'Neither of us need complicated.'

'So we don't see each other after?' She nodded. 'That's good.'

His eyes widened slightly, then narrowed. 'So to clarify, we're going to have a one-night stand in which we do almost every possible carnal act, including you giving me your virginity, and then we'll never see each other again.'

His blunt description of the plan scorched her sensibility, leaving her with nothing left but excitement and acquiescence. 'Yes… I…you…'

She couldn't finish. Couldn't articulate what it was she wanted him to give her. It felt, not forbidden, but too *greedy*.

'Yes,' he confirmed. 'You do. I do. We do.' He rolled his shoulders and walked her nearer to that waiting car. 'You've finished that report, right? So don't come in tomorrow. Take the day. Then I'll pick you up and we'll have dinner.'

'We just had dinner.'

He brushed her hair back from her face, letting his fingers linger on her jaw as he did. 'We'll have another dinner. Most people need them every day.'

Heat swept over her again at the light caress and she couldn't resist turning to the slight cup of his hand. 'You don't want to just—'

He stroked her jaw gently but the blaze in his eyes was all erotic warning. 'I'm not settling for anything less than a *whole* night with you, Jade. Start to finish. I want drinks and dancing and privacy and all the hours there can possibly be in one damned night.'

Her legs trembled. 'Where?' She swallowed nervously. Drinks and dancing could mean cameras. There could be cameras even now and she'd been so mesmerised by him she hadn't even *thought* of them.

'My place,' he answered swiftly and released her. 'But now you leave. Now you have the rest of this night to decide if this is what you really want. You need to be sure, Jade. And I'm not touching you again because if I do…' He drew in a sharp breath.

The sensations swirling deep within her now were so hot and exciting…how was she supposed to wait? But her training—that insistence upon emotional control—finally came to her aid.

'Okay.' She stepped away from him.

'Tomorrow, I'll come and you'll either get into my car, or you won't. Let me know your final decision then.'

Her mouth dried at a horrible thought and she quickly turned back. 'What if you change *your* mind?'

CHAPTER SIX

As if he would ever change his mind?

At work the next morning Alvaro tried to stay so busy he didn't have a second to think. It didn't work. The only thing going round in his head was *Jade*.

Jade the tempting. Jade the innocent. Jade the literal freaking *queen*.

Jade, who lived on the other side of an enormous ocean, who had endless responsibilities, obligations and duties that he would never really understand, and who faced intensely unique, challenging pressures. No wonder she wanted her three weeks of freedom.

She'd embarked on a totally crazy caper with her sister, risking so much if either of them got caught. Yet she'd wasted almost a full week of it struggling to succeed in something she knew little about, to save her sister's job. Chancing discovery to an even more massive extent. No wonder she'd plugged in her headphones and stared into that computer screen for hours. And she'd pulled it off... until the moment she'd blurted the truth to him.

Jade not Juno. Stranger instead of employee.

The relief had been intense, before the uncontrollable urge had slammed into him and stolen his reason. He'd barely slept last night, his brain kept wildly awake by the constant recollection of those frantic few moments in the office and the resulting tension in his body.

Her confession. His kiss. Her killer response.

He hadn't given her the tender first-time kiss she should've had—that he would've given her if he'd known. He'd been so wound up he'd lost it the second he'd realised they weren't bound by workplace restrictions. He hadn't just unleashed, he'd all but lost his mind as he'd done what he'd wanted to do for days—kissed her to total satisfaction, subduing the desire that had been straining between them both since they'd first clashed last Monday morning...while stoking it higher at the same time. Their chemistry hadn't just been combustible, it had become an out-of-control inferno in seconds.

Then her second confession—of such complete innocence? And her barely whispered request for him to help her with that?

Yeah, his eyes had been wide, wide open for hours.

Because this was wrong. So wrong. Wasn't this worse than sleeping with an employee? To seduce a virgin queen—didn't that go against every one of his own rules?

No drama, remember? Certainly, no *dreams*...

He'd needed to get away from her. Not only to ensure her certainty and his own, but to prepare himself for the pure torture of her—he knew her gorgeously eager body would devastate his.

Not going to do that. Not going to rush this, or rush *her*.

He should've said no. But never had anything been as impossible as saying no to Queen Jade Monroyale. But while he couldn't resist, he could control the event and its outcome. He wanted it to be good for her and he was arrogant enough to believe he could make it so. He'd felt her shaking in his arms, he'd heard her moan in pleasure and felt her restless movements as she'd sought more...

It seemed her life had been almost completely prescribed, but she was mostly happy to go along with that. Even insisting she would eventually marry whomever was the best political match for her country. Irritation flared the length of his spine. He loathed that idea—which was ironic, because he never gave the idea of marriage a thought. It wasn't for him and wouldn't ever be. He valued his independence too much. So she was right, who she chose to marry later on was no concern of his. At all.

He gritted his teeth. She wanted what she wanted with whom she wanted. And frankly he was absurdly privileged to be her pick. He knew this wasn't simply opportunity. She could have found other times, other ways, other men, if she'd so wanted—she'd proven herself a resourceful survivor at heart—but until now, she hadn't wanted to.

So who was he to deny her all she wanted in her few weeks of freedom? Or say whether she should or shouldn't? Especially when he badly wanted the exact same thing?

He paced through the office, wishing time would speed up as long as it then slowed down once he got to her. He picked up a copy of the free daily paper that someone had left in the chill-out area. The international section slid out— the second he saw the lead picture, he knew why. For there 'she' was. 'Queen Jade' with King Leonardo—monarchs of the neighbouring nations of Monrova and Severene. They were dancing together at the Monrova Winter Ball, Juno looking up at the King while he was as intently focused on her.

Alvaro studied the image closely, seeking to spot the differences between the sisters. Juno's hair was tied up, masking the shortened length, and her face was slightly fuller, her smile wide, her skin a touch more bronzed. The real Jade appeared slightly more physically fragile than this. Yet she wasn't weak. She was strong and controlled and very determined. But she was also lonely. He recognised her isolation and her raw need for physical connection reverberated someplace deep within him.

He felt it too. It was exactly why he couldn't deny her. It was also exactly why he *should*.

One night. What harm could come from one night?

He glanced at King Leonardo again and his hackles rose. That was not a man who'd ever be willing to commit to a sexless marriage. Frankly Alvaro didn't know anyone who would—male or female. Jade shouldn't be so glib about making such a sacrifice either.

But the way Leonardo was looking at the woman he was dancing with? Alvaro tensed. Did the King know this *wasn't* Jade?

In the end he sent the remaining office staff home early. It was Christmas after all.

It was a little after five when he leaned against the car, eyeing her apartment building and pretending he was chilled. As if. He'd sent the text two minutes ago. Would she reply in person or by phone? Yes or no? The door opened. He folded his arms tightly across his chest because it was the only way to hold himself back as she walked towards him. She'd left her hair loose and now he saw just how stunningly long it was. It hung in a gleaming sweep of loose chestnut curls all the way to her waist. His jaw dropped yet every muscle tightened. Her green eyes were usually back-lit by a banked fire, but the smoulder in them now sucked all moisture from his mouth. It was as if he'd swallowed sandpaper. Her smile was shy, but her lips were glossed and pillowy and he wanted a first kiss do-over. Her black dress wasn't slinky, but demurely fitted—belted at the waist only to flare and finish mid-calf. It was sexier than any he'd seen. Those stupidly thin high-heeled shoes were on her feet again and she'd slung a black leather jacket over her arm and he could no longer breathe.

'Is everything okay?' she asked.

It took him a moment to realise she'd paused a couple of paces away and was watching him warily. Apparently, time had stopped for him but not for her, and he'd been staring in silence for too long. Yet even now he wasn't able to speak. His tongue was sealed to the roof of his mouth and his throat was so tight it hurt to nod. He straightened and had to consciously tell his arms to unfold so he could open the damn car door.

'Shall I get in?' Colour washed across her fine features, but a small knowing smile curved her luscious lips.

Vixen.

He pulled away the second she'd fastened her seat belt. That soft vanilla had arrived with her and he struggled to steady his breathing.

'Was your day okay?' she asked softly.

'They missed you,' he croaked, trying to think of normal things. He belatedly realised he'd not given her the chance to say goodbye to them even though they had no idea she wasn't Juno and wasn't coming back after the Christmas break. But no doubt she met people all the time, mostly briefly, with no permanency or long-term relationship ever developing. He was just another person to pass through her life too.

'What did you do today?' he asked, distracting himself from the unwelcome sensation at that thought.

'I went for a walk...'

As she trailed off he glanced and registered how tense she was too. Instinctively he reached out and covered her tight fist with his hand. A sizzle zinged up his arm at the small contact, but she tensed beneath his hold and he immediately loosened his grip. But she didn't pull away, instead she flipped her fingers and laced them through his. Alvaro had never held hands with anyone. Ever. But for the first time all day he felt as if he could breathe.

'I'm really glad you came for me,' she said softly.

Alvaro's gut clenched as that too-sweet sentiment plunged him into a vat of scalding oil—the images her words conjured up were too graphic, too inappropriate. He needed to rein in his own sexual impulse around her, because she'd not meant that double-entendre. She was too inexperienced and this night was such folly. But he couldn't force himself to turn the car around. He simply couldn't stop.

'I wasn't sure what to wear.'

She could've worn a sack, she'd look stunning regardless. But he did love this outfit, he did love the fact that she'd thought about what to wear for him. But his customary facility with compliments had fled. Hell, his whole brain seemed to have blown.

The relief when he pulled into the basement of his building was immense, but he could still barely speak as he led her into the elevator and keyed in the code to unlock access to the penthouse. He tossed his keys and wallet onto the nearest small table and breathed deeply.

'You have amazing views up here.' She walked through to the large lounge.

The penthouse overlooked the Hudson River, but she'd turned her back on the vast windows and was studying the apartment itself. Her avid curiosity made him smile.

'What does the décor tell you?' He relaxed enough to tease her. 'Any insights you can glean about me from the room?'

That colour washed back into her cheeks and she touched her tongue to her lips in an unconsciously nervous, yet provocative gesture that made him harder than he'd been in his life. But it was imperative he go slow. That he give her every chance to change her mind. Hell, *he* still wasn't anywhere near sure this was a good idea.

'It does tell me a few things, actually.' Her smile was suddenly impish.

'Oh?' He stilled. 'Such as?'

'You like comfort.' Her smile widened as she ran her hand over the soft woollen throw on the arm of his massive plush sofa. 'You're a sensualist, for all your outward discipline.'

Heat pooled in his already aching body. Because—at least as far as she was concerned—she was right.

'What would the palace tell me about you?' he asked huskily.

'It would tell you everything about my family going back eight hundred years or so. Before then, there was a fire and we lost those very valuable records. But the art and antiques collection that has been amassed over the centuries is amazing.'

'But what about your room?' he pressed, keen to know something more of her. 'Do you not get to choose your own pink fluffy cushions Princess Palace-Style?'

'Never,' she giggled. 'That wouldn't do. The décor has remained mostly the same for ever.'

But wasn't she the Queen? Didn't she get to dictate—demand fulfilment of her every whim?

'That's a shame,' he commiserated lightly. 'You should get to choose your own cushions. I like cushions.'

'I can tell.' She laughed as she gazed at the plump pile of them on one low shelf.

'Home should be welcoming,' he said, unafraid to admit it.

'Well, I don't know that you could call Monrova palace *welcoming*. I mean, it is amazing and stunning and beautiful but—'

'Not very comfortable?' He frowned. 'If everything is ancient, won't the seats be too small? Doorways too low?'

'Oh, the doorways were built for giants, but that has meant it's been challenging to heat.' She ventured deeper into his lounge, studying the spines of the books lining the shelves. She paused at one point. 'Is this your mother?' she asked.

Of course, she'd spotted his one personal photo in the whole penthouse.

'I don't have a mother,' he said.

She turned to face him. '*Everyone* has a mother,' she said gently. 'It's basic biology.'

'Biology?' he echoed. Then he could keep this straightforward and factual. 'Okay, there was the woman who gave birth to me. Then there was the woman who supposedly adopted me. And then there was the woman who saved me. Which would you say is my *mother*?' He couldn't help the bitterness in his tone.

And when he summoned the courage to look directly at her, he saw her jade eyes glimmering with an emotion he didn't want to identify.

'The one who saved you,' she said.

She was right, of course. The nearest he'd had to a mother. The woman he owed everything. Alvaro never discussed his personal life or background. But he understood Jade's curiosity because he felt the same about her. So for once he offered just a little.

'Her name is Ellen.' His gaze rested on the photo briefly and he couldn't help a small smile because Ellen *hated* that picture. 'She's still alive and I see her regularly.' He looked back to Jade, but her eyes were still filled with soft compassion. 'Come on,' he growled and strode through to the open-plan kitchen.

'You're cooking?' Jade studied the preparations he already had under way on the large wooden bench.

'I'm fairly competent,' he teased at her surprise. 'Are you willing to risk it?'

'Of course,' she rushed to answer with that cut-glass courtesy, but that delicious flush swarmed her cheeks again. 'Thank you for going to the trouble.'

'I don't think cooking is the trouble here,' he muttered, barely holding himself together. She got to him in ways other than the one he expected. 'Do you think we can be civilised for a few more minutes?'

'Is that what we're trying to do?'

'Yes.'

'Why?'

Oh, she was going to be the absolute death of him. He braced both hands on the bench and let out a helpless laugh.

'Given I know how rubbish you are at keeping regular meals when left to your own devices, I don't want you running out of energy any time soon.'

'So, it's purely for biological reasons?'

'No,' he growled. 'It's because you need time to be sure.'

'I wouldn't be here if I wasn't,' she replied with determined ease. 'It's only...'

'Sex?'

That colour stormed into her cheeks.

He gazed at her, grappling with his conscience. That was how he'd always thought of it, but he wasn't sure that *this* time it was. He didn't feel guilty about taking what she was offering, but he wanted it to be *better* than 'only sex' for her.

Suddenly he couldn't resist touching her. He walked over and lifted her chin with just a finger. She tilted instantly, willing and welcome. Slowly he pressed his lips to hers in a tentative, gentle touch—truly first-kiss-worthy. Her response was instant. Her soft, sweet mouth surprisingly mobile, she teased him back and made him forget about first kiss anything. She knew what she wanted and he wanted it too. He'd always worked like a dog until he got it. So he'd do the same now. And there was *nothing* he wanted more in the world in this instant than Jade Monroyale's total satisfaction.

But as she moaned, he broke the kiss and made himself step back to the bench.

She stared at him—her green eyes gleamed like jewels lit by an inner flame. And her expression was ever so slightly resentful.

'Food first, remember?' But his voice was hoarse and his resolve weak and he was a little too glad she felt this need as keenly as she did.

'Can I help you at all?' she asked after a moment.

He pressed his hands back on the bench, desperate to

regain focus and not drag her straight to bed. 'Do you cook in the palace?'

'No,' she confessed with an adorably guilty smile. 'It wasn't considered a necessary part of my education, which I know is terrible. It's a life skill.'

'That it is.' He picked up the knife and took his frustration out on the herbs.

'Whereas you were obviously taught well.'

Actually, he was self-taught. It had been that or go hungry. But he wasn't giving her any more of his sob story. 'Can you grab a couple of tomatoes from the pantry?' He aimed for diversion.

'Of course.'

Her heard her opening a couple of doors behind him and glanced back. She'd paused in front of the pantry and was taking in the well-stocked, perfectly ordered shelves. 'You live alone, right?' she asked.

And this was why he rarely had house guests—why he didn't open the cupboards to anyone, so to speak. Because it only invited questions he had no desire to answer. 'Always.'

She nodded but her eyes were wide.

'I imagine your palace pantry is far better stocked,' he pointed out dryly. 'But from the sounds of things, you wouldn't know.'

'I admit I wouldn't.' She reached for a couple of tomatoes and gave the pantry a final glance before closing the door.

'Cooking is a stress release for me. Plus, you know I need a bit of feeding.' He paused; he never explained himself to anyone but somehow a sliver of truth escaped. 'But I can't bear the thought of not having food in the house because endless hunger is a vivid memory that, unfortunately, I can't forget.'

She faced him. 'I'm sorry you suffered that.'

For a second the emotion that cascaded through him

was almost too strong to contain. He was glad he had to concentrate on the searing-hot grill.

'Do you think you can you manage to open a bottle of wine?' he asked, unable to look up from the hot plate and into her eyes. He needed anything to divert them from this moment.

'Of course.'

She chose a bottle and poured two glasses from it, taking a seat at the table from which to watch him as he sizzled two steaks on the grill. With the herbs and tomatoes, the salad he'd begun earlier was now complete. Fresh and simple.

'Shall we eat in here?' He took the chair opposite the one she'd taken.

She stared at the plates with admiration. 'It looks amazing.'

'And yet you're not eating.' He sent her a laughing glance. 'You need fuel or you're not going to survive the night.'

'Not *survive*?'

Her laughter bubbled but at the same time he saw anticipation light her face. She was curious, his petite queen. And hungry.

'You don't think I'm serious?' he teased.

'Perhaps I have more stamina than you give me credit for.' She spoke with such regal preciseness, but it was pure challenge and they both knew it.

'Oh, you do?' He attacked his steak with the fierce passion he was trying to stop himself using on her.

'Yes, I do. I might not feel the need to work out every morning and night like you, but I do exercise. And I do— generally—eat well, and rest.' She glared at his smothered snort. 'I think I'm fit enough to handle you.'

Happily, it wouldn't be long 'til he found out. He just had to hang onto his sanity long enough to make it good for her. 'I think you should stop talking and start eating.'

She loaded up her fork and tasted the salad, briefly closing her eyes as she did. 'You want all the feedback, don't you?'

'Damn right I do.'

'It's good.' She took in a breath. 'It's better than good.'

'It's fresh produce,' he demurred. 'Can't really screw it up. So, come on, what exercise do you prefer?'

She lifted her nose primly. 'I endure a variety of activities. Treadmill. Circuit. Laps of the pool. Gymnastics.'

'You *endure* them?'

'I've never really got that endorphin high,' she admitted. 'I blame my trainer—she's a dragon.'

'You have a female drill sergeant?'

'Well, it was never going to be a *guy*.' Jade laughed but that blush battled its way back into her cheeks. 'My father would never have allowed that.'

'He was that strict? You had no men around you at all?'

'In a way it was good—they were aspirational figures, right? My old governess was a former university professor. My trainer is just in cahoots with the palace physician. They conspire to make life hell.'

'You're the Queen, Jade, can't you just tell them to leave you alone?'

'There are expectations I must meet. It is part of my duty. Spent so long training for it—language lessons, politics, history, philosophy, ethics, manners, meditation and a boring exercise regime.'

'Meditation?'

'To master emotions.'

Wow. What a regimented, prescribed life.

'Don't feel sorry for me.' She smiled at him. 'I was a privileged princess through and through. Thoroughly spoilt.'

He wasn't entirely sure he believed her.

'Anyway, they're right. I need to exercise more.' She grimaced. 'The crown is too heavy. It doesn't sit right.'

'You don't believe you can hold its weight? Because you can,' he said reassuringly. 'I saw you single-handedly disarm thousands of angry emails. Trust me, you can handle the crown.'

Her mouth hung open for a second and then she smiled and blushed concurrently. 'No, I mean it's literally too heavy. It weighs a tonne. Gives me a headache five minutes after I put it on.'

Oh. He laughed. But he'd meant what he'd said. 'Have a new one made. I'm sure you can afford it.'

'I couldn't do that.' She stared at him in amazement. 'It's a *tradition*.'

'Make a new tradition.' He shrugged.

'You make it sound so easy.'

'That's because it is easy. Just choose what you want. Say it. Do it.'

'Is that what you did? Was it all that easy for you?'

He paused. 'I came from a position of far less power and privilege than you, Jade. So no, some things were most definitely not easy. But in a way, I had more liberty to do what I wanted. Because no one knew and no one gave a damn and no one was ever going to try and help me or require me to do something "their" way.'

'I'm sorry, I didn't mean to be—'

'Don't apologise, I'm glad you didn't face the struggles I did.'

'So how did you overcome them?' she asked. 'How did you do it all alone?'

She was so genuinely curious, he found himself telling her a snippet of history he'd not mentioned in years. 'My first plan to gain financial freedom was to be a professional sportsman. It didn't matter to me which sport—I'd got a full ride through sport into a good school. I was captain of both basketball and football teams and I'd decided to do which-ever paid me more to get through college. I trained my ass off. But I tore the muscles in my knee and that ended that. No more captain. No more sports teams. No more school.'

She looked shocked. 'They took away your scholarship?'

He nodded. 'I was a nerd as much as I was a jock, but they wanted me for physique, not physics.' He shrugged. 'I don't know why, but math just came easy and I had ideas and I sure as hell had nothing to lose. Only my own time. So, working around a bunch of hand-to-mouth jobs, I developed that fitness app. It grew very popular, very quickly. I leveraged it while hustling other work on the side, earning however I could, investing in small, then larger projects. There was a lot of luck and timing.'

'And effort.'

'Sure.' Maximum effort, all hours and every weekend for years. Hell, he still worked more hours than not.

'I can't imagine being the CEO of a huge conglomerate.'

He laughed. 'Yes, but a CEO of a private company can be directive and bossy and not give a damn about what other people think. I can't imagine what it would be like being Queen of a country where you're like public property. A figurehead, a role model who everyone looks to for guidance on everything from fashion to foreign affairs.'

'There's a parliament, my people vote. I don't make all the rules myself.'

It sounded to him as if she didn't make any. 'And you get a Sovereign Grant, I know. But you still give official assent, right? You're still the overseer of good governance.'

Jade had spent her life being trained to understand good governance. To understand *being* good, full stop.

'Do you have good advisors?'

'They're very experienced,' Jade murmured evasively and took the last bite of the tender meat.

'And they want you to marry that Leonardo guy.'

She shot him a glance.

'It must've been hard to be separated from your mother and your sister,' he added. 'Even with all your women mentors, you must have missed them.'

'Juno and I stayed in touch as best we could. She visited each year for a while...' But then Juno and their father had fought and Juno had left. 'Juno hasn't been back in years, not 'til now.'

'What about your mother?'

'I never saw her again after their divorce.'

His eyes widened. 'You were how old?'

'Eight.'

He looked at a loss. 'Pretty harsh way to deal with a difficult situation.'

His quiet response made her chest ache. She never discussed this, but Alvaro had got under her guard.

'My father didn't want to put in the work to find a new way of working as a separated family. He just cut her out, like a cancer or something.' It had devastated Jade and she knew it had been even harder on Juno. 'He was so rigid, he refused to even consider—'

She tried to catch back the fear and the pain it had caused her, wanting to shove it back down deep. Thinking about this was pointless; there was no changing it.

'I know he was hurt too,' she muttered. 'Badly. That's why he reacted so harshly, but...'

She shook her head. She'd *never* shared this. She couldn't trust anyone—that had been drilled into her.

'Why didn't it work out for your parents, do you know?'

'Maybe because she wasn't a princess?' Jade said sadly. 'She was Hollywood royalty, so she was used to some similar pressure... But I think maybe they were too different. And too quick to rush into it.'

'Is that why you think some arranged marriage with a prince would be better for you?'

'I…' She stared at him, her breath stolen. But then she lifted her chin. 'Maybe. I think my country deserves stability within the Crown.'

'Your country deserves that?' He watched her. 'What do *you* deserve?'

'My few weeks of freedom,' she said softly. 'And then?' She shrugged. She didn't want to think about it any more. Not tonight. 'Every family has its quirks, right?' she muttered glibly.

Alvaro's smile twisted. 'My family is a doozy,' he offered, as if recognising her regret at revealing any of this. 'I got some of that "cut-you-out-like-a-cancer" treatment too.'

The woman who gave birth to me…the woman who supposedly adopted me…

What did that mean, 'supposedly'? And was that when he'd been afraid he wouldn't have enough to eat? Had he not just gone hungry, but been starved of all those other necessities too? 'I'm sorry, Alvaro.'

He closed his eyes momentarily. 'What is it you're doing here, Jade?'

One truth spilled. 'Not having people watch my every move. Or have cameras trained on me every time I leave my home. I'm eating all the cheap chocolate. Soaking up the bright Christmas lights.'

'You don't have Christmas lights in Monrova?'

'They're very refined fairy lights. Traditional and dignified.'

'You want neon party lights?' He half smiled.

'Glow-in-the-dark reindeer? Yes, I do. Why not?'

'Surely as Queen you can make your own Christmas traditions? Demand all the fluorescence you can stand?'

One might think so, but it wasn't that easy.

Alvaro's expression grew serious again. 'What are you really doing *here*, Jade?'

She swallowed. 'I don't know,' she admitted from the

bottom of her heart. 'I just know there's nowhere else I want to be right now.' She didn't know why she was whispering, but she couldn't seem to breathe any volume into her voice.

'Me neither.' He reached out to caress her cheek, sliding his hand to cup her jaw. 'But you know this is madness.'

'It's my time for madness.' But her heart puckered at the swirl of emotion clouding his eyes. 'You're not doing this out of pity, are you?'

'Pity?' He half choked. 'No. Not pity.'

'You'll have a good time too? It's not all about pleasing me, is it?'

'Why shouldn't it be?'

'People try to please me all the time. It can be awkward. They don't quite know how to act around me. They get nervous and it's… I don't want this to be like that.'

'Not going to lie, I'm a little nervous, Jade. I don't want to hurt you and I do want you to have a good time. But honestly, I'm being more selfish now than I've ever been in my life. And I'm a pretty selfish guy.'

She didn't believe that about him.

'But I'm not awkward around you. And I think we're past getting hung up on our respective jobs and titles.'

'No one's ever yelled at me the way you did the other morning,' she confessed with a wry smile.

'And you snapped right back, which, I admit, doesn't usually happen to me. But I'm guessing you don't usually do that?'

'Not usually, no,' she acknowledged. 'It would be rude and abusive of my position. I know I have more power than most people, I need to be mindful of that.'

'Not with me. Not then. Certainly not now. I'm not awed by your crown, Jade.'

'I know you're not.' She half laughed.

'I'm glad you're not too polite to yell at me. I don't want you to be polite or hold back from me in any way. Not at any time. Understand?' He stepped closer and she battled to stand in place. 'So if you don't usually, if you master your emotions, why did you yell at me? Why did you lose your cool?'

'Because I was tired, and you were half naked, and I couldn't get my brain to work.'

'So to get absolute honesty from you, I just need to strip down and wear you out?'

His smile lifted and all she could do was stare at him. It was impossible, how beautiful he was. And she realised, with slight shock, that he could do anything he wanted with her.

'I'm going to make love to you, Jade.'

His rough, low promise devastated her.

She swallowed hard. 'I thought we were having sex.'

He shook his head and the serious determination in his eyes melted the last of her mind. 'If this is the one night that you get, with a man you actually want, and who you're giving your virginity to, then you deserve to be worshipped and adored. You deserve to have the best possible experience. So no, we're not having sex. I'm making love to you.' He stood up from the table and held his hand out to her. 'Okay?'

She couldn't possibly speak now. But she put her hand in his and rose to meet him.

'Jade?'

She was trembling. Aching so much for his touch. The kiss was everything she needed. A luscious sweep of passion and security. She slung her arms around his neck and heard his pleased little grunt as he caught her. He stepped her back until she was braced against the kitchen wall. She loved it like this with him so big before her.

'Jade?' He pulled back to look into her eyes. 'I want to know what you're thinking, what you're feeling, whether you're okay. I need to know that, sweetheart.'

But as he spoke, he worked the buttons down the front of her dress free and pushed it from her shoulders, leaving her in just her green silk slip. He fingered the thin straps on her shoulders, tracing one down to the seam at the neckline, and looked. His smile made her so grateful for the support of the wall behind her. 'Why, Queen Jade,' he mock-reproved. 'I do believe you're not wearing a bra.'

She laughed, finally able to answer. 'It's hard enough to breathe around you,' she muttered. 'I didn't want anything constricting my ribs and making it even harder.'

His gaze shot to her face again and he seemed oddly touched. 'You know you can say "when" any time.'

'That doesn't seem fair,' she breathed.

'Life isn't always fair. I think you and I both know that already.'

She didn't want to think about that right now. She lifted her chin and pressed her full, pulsing lips to his again. Her toes curled in her shoes when he kissed her back. His hands shaped her curves beneath the silk, eventually sliding under the hem and up to the lacy panties she'd specially worn. She gasped as he grazed the strip of silk at the front.

'I'm a big guy, sweetheart, you need to be ready,' he said softly as he kissed down her neck and across her collarbones. 'Getting you there is my job now.'

A wave of anticipation swamped her and she moaned as he skated his fingers across the dampened silk again.

His little laugh was low and searing. 'You like that idea?' He growled and nipped her gently. 'Do you want to know just how big?'

'Yes,' she breathed. She wanted to know everything about him. And she ached to feel *all* of him.

But her eyes closed and she could only lean against the wall for support as he skimmed over her secret parts. And as he kissed her deeply she unashamedly drove her hips against the sinfully tormenting touch of his hand.

'Please,' she begged but he kept strumming her so lightly, while his hot mouth softly kissed her sensitive skin and breathed even hotter words against her.

'You want me inside you, Jade?'

'Yes.' Desperately. So desperately. But he still didn't press harder where she wanted him to. And it was deliberate. The man was an impossible tease.

'We have all night,' he promised.

'That's…not…long,' she breathlessly complained, pressing harder against his wicked hand.

'One night is made up of many, many moments.' He finally flicked his fingers that touch harder. 'And this is a moment now, sweetheart. Take it.'

She slammed her hands on his broad biceps for balance, crying out as the orgasm shuddered through her—leaving her body so weak she couldn't stand.

Alvaro swiftly picked her up and carried her from the kitchen. She revelled in the heat of his chest and the ripple of his muscles against her as he strode with leashed purpose. She took in sharp details, like snaps captured in millisecond moments. Cotton and comfort, white linen contrasted with grey walls and heavy curtains, woollen rugs on wooden floors. Lit by the only lamp on a table beside his bed, his bedroom was large and sumptuous. She wasn't surprised by that this time; his whole apartment revealed a predilection for sumptuousness. Of his enjoyment for plush, soft furnishings. Like a caveman's den filled with soft skins—all for warmth and safety and sensuality.

He placed her on the bed, bunched the hem of her emerald slip and lifted it. She lifted her arms and it was gone in a second. Then he pushed her onto her back and slid her panties down her legs, then the shoes from her feet, so at last she was naked on his bed.

He sucked in a breath with a hiss. 'Do you know what I am awed by, Jade?'

She shook her head.

'You. Like this.'

Before she could reply he kissed her—brought his body on hers. For the first time she felt the weight of him and it was so, so good as he ground her into the mattress beneath that she cried out.

'Soon,' he promised. 'Soon, sweetheart.'

But he pulled back to only straddle her. Tenderly he cupped her breasts in his big hands, teasing her taut nipples and laughing when she became breathless all over again. He took his time. Gentle, not so gentle, gentle again. The teasing licks of his fingers, hands and lips were like waves creeping further up the shore of her arousal. That sensation grew closer. That desperation a deeper ache within. This time it wasn't his finger teasing her sensitive, private place. It was his tongue.

She shivered, her knees instinctively rising because this was so personal, so intimate. 'Alvaro…'

'Let me,' he rasped.

And she couldn't resist the carnal plea in his voice, not when it echoed her own so completely. Her legs splayed and her reward was the slide not just of his tongue, but of his fingers again. Only this time, this time, he pushed one inside her. She gasped and then breathed for more.

'You're so tight, sweetheart,' he growled.

She lay, stunned to stillness as she adjusted to the sensation of having someone so intimate with her, doing *that*. 'Alvaro…'

'I like the taste of you, Jade. I like all of you.'

Heat and delight burnished her entire body, because his words felt more than merely playful. Slowly he worked, in and out and again and again as he softly licked her most sensitive point with relentlessly gentle stokes. Inexorably, his focused care overcame her self-consciousness and the sensations tumbled faster and faster and faster within until she totally tensed. Her hands spread wide and she gripped the sheet. She drew so taut, her hips arched high off the bed. Yet still he plundered and tasted and utterly tormented her until suddenly all she could do was scream.

Endless, timeless moments later the orgasm left her limp and devastated in a splayed heap in the middle of his bed. Yet despite that overwhelming pleasure, she still yearned inside. She still *ached*. Because she wanted all of him and now she could barely move.

'Alvaro,' she called to him with a plaintive moan.

'I'm here.' But he stood back from the bed. For a moment he just looked at her, that satisfied twist still on his lips as he blatantly studied her pinkened parts from where the rub of his fingers and the rasp of his stubble had gently scoured her skin.

His muscles bunched. Her mouth dried and she propped herself up on her elbows to watch with fascination as he slowly stripped for her. First his shirt. And it wasn't only her appetite returning, it was her energy too. And he knew. He knew as he maintained that teasing eye contact and slowly unfastened his belt. Jade's breath stalled in her lungs as he undid the button of his trousers, half laughing as he had to do a shimmy of his hips to release the zipper given the strain it was under. But Jade could only then stare at the muscular thighs he'd just revealed. She dragged her gaze back up but only made it as far as his black knit boxers. He stepped closer to the bed and reached for something on the table. She watched as he slowly rolled the condom down the straining, rigid length of him. She swallowed and unconsciously rubbed her hands down her tense thighs.

'Do you want to touch me?' His voice was hoarse.

Somehow she was kneeling up on the mattress. She'd not even realised she'd moved. And she'd certainly not realised she was audibly panting. But she didn't care any more. The exhaustion from those earlier orgasms was obliterated by the yearning raging through her blood now. She wanted to touch him, to taste him, to test him. She wanted to discover everything she could—about him, with him.

He didn't move as she reached out. Indeed, he seemed to be braced, his feet planted wide apart, his magnificent body strained to take her touch. His jaw clamped but a groan escaped regardless as she bravely planted both palms on his broad chest and began a slow sweep of pure, fascinated inspection. He flinched beneath her touch. She felt the heat, the rise of sweat in his body.

'You said you were big,' she breathed. 'You're also beautiful.' And there was a dampness between her legs, an excitement in her pulse that emboldened her more.

She lifted her head. She had so little time. And the desire sluicing through her was so very strong, so very hungry.

His lips twisted as he read the need in her eyes. 'Tell me,' he said.

'Take me, please,' she asked simply and wrapped her hand around his throbbing girth. 'I want all of you.'

He put his hands on her waist and lifted her back onto the bed, finally coming to lie with her. She wriggled, relaxing against the mattress and lifting her arms to welcome him against her. He kissed her again—lush and deep and she was so excited.

He gently pushed her legs wider apart, teasing her again with his fingers. He lifted his head and their eyes met. He didn't ask if she was sure, if she was ready, he already knew. For a moment there was only agreement and pure anticipation between them.

He finally moved, aligning his hips with hers, his breath with hers, his heartbeat with hers. And as he set his lips to hers he met her intent with his in a slow, inexorable slide of possession that made her gasp deep. Instinctively she threw her arm around his neck, holding him near even as he hesitated.

'Jade?' he asked.

She saw the strain in his body as he tried to be gentle and go slow with her. But the pressure within, the drive for more, grew until it became undeniable.

'Kiss me.' She didn't wait for his answer. She kissed him, moving her hips against his, breathing hard as she embraced the pleasurable pressure-filled waves of his deepening possession.

Sensation soared as he buffeted against her and she began to understand, began to meet him back, stroke for stroke as she discovered how fantastic this felt, and how she too could drive this. With a smothered growl, he pushed his palms against the firm mattress beneath her and levered up, driving deeper in a surge of unfettered passion. She let her hands slide, gripping his forearms, feeling his muscles work beneath her, against her. She gazed up, awed at his power and strength as he fiercely pushed as hard as he could into her and enjoying the utterly exquisite ride. She couldn't form words, only sound as she gasped with astounded pleasure and he was the same. Grunting now with every pulse, every pound. And then he collapsed again, holding her more tightly than she'd ever been held, trapping her while at the same time imprisoned within her. She held him so fiercely. They were both shaking, almost violently convulsing as ecstasy overtook both mind and muscle.

Alvaro made himself gather the strength to lift away; he'd suffocate her if he stayed where he was. Her long drawn-out sigh in response almost brought him to his knees again. He'd tried to stay gentle, tried to take the time…but she'd come apart around him and he'd charged headlong into the fire with her like a man who'd lost it completely. But now she needed more again. He read it in her eyes and he heard it in her breathlessness.

'I like it when you hold me,' she whispered. 'I like it when you surround me so completely.'

Yeah, he liked that too. He liked the lock of her arms around his back and her thigh hooking over his hip so he could surge deeper. He liked being so close to her that there was no getting closer, but trying anyway with bared skin and salty sweat and sweet pleasure. She'd arched and he'd thrust, over and over until he was drowning in the heated, silky prison of her body, until that pleasure hit, until there was nothing like this satisfied exhaustion in all the world.

Now her long hair was a tangled mess, knotting them together, and her face was flushed as she gazed up at him. Amazement gleamed from her pleasure-bruised eyes and he had never seen anyone as shockingly beautiful in his life.

'Alvaro.'

It was a whisper that ricocheted through to his soul. 'I know.'

She was tired, but she needed another kind of closeness. And for once, so did he.

'You feel so good,' he muttered as he rolled onto his back and pulled her limp form to rest over his.

'I'm so tired, but I want—'

'I know. We will. Soon,' he promised. Because so did he. 'It's not even nine o'clock, Jade.' He chuckled. 'We can take our time. We have all night.'

Only it didn't seem like long enough already.

CHAPTER SEVEN

JADE SLOWLY WOKE in a relaxed, comfortable heap, tangled in soft cotton sheets, soaking up the heated strength of the man curved behind her. It was her strangest, yet best ever way to wake.

They'd snatched only a couple of hours' sleep at most last night. After that first time, Alvaro had run her a bath and revived her with a fistful of cheap chocolate—all the commercial bars and wacky flavours that had been long banned from her diet by that zealous palace physician.

'No royal rules here,' he'd teased. 'And it's treat night, right?'

The whole night had been a decadent, delicious, pure lustful treat. Now, her pulse lifted, her aching body still seeking more.

'You must be used to getting breakfast in bed,' he murmured.

'I have a maid who brings me a coffee in the morning.'

'With cream and sugar, right? I'll get it.'

His warmth was gone before she had the chance to answer. She sat up. So it was over already?

For a panicked moment she couldn't believe what she'd done. What if there were cameras outside? What if she was caught somehow and everyone found out?

Would it matter?

Her father wasn't alive to judge or punish her. It wasn't an external threat troubling her. It was Alvaro himself. How did she face the man who'd touched her with such profound intimacy? It had felt beyond physical.

It's not.

She was feeling biochemistry—oxytocin, serotonin, dopamine. Her body's biology was encouraging her to stay and mate again. All animal instinct. And that adrenalin fix? The rush of the unknown and the unexpected?

That was everything Alvaro had treated her to last night.

But it was over, and she needed to get out of there. Her composure was suddenly shockingly precarious and she'd *never* lost her composure before this week. She'd never lost her virginity either. Until Alvaro.

Memories swept over her, invoking a real, raw response from her body. She shivered. She couldn't let him distract or delay her departure. Self-preservation insisted she end this now. If she stayed it would soon become a whole other day and a whole other night and that would become too intense. And impossible to walk away from. She couldn't let that happen. It wasn't what he wanted. Or what she wanted either.

She needed this time on her *own*. Wasn't *that* why she was here?

She quickly hunted about for her panties and pulled on her slip before finding her way from his bedroom back to the kitchen—desperately scooping her black dress up off the floor from where they'd left it last night.

He'd glanced up as she walked in and put down the cup he was holding. A glint kindled in his eyes as he watched her back away with the crumpled dress in hand. 'Not staying for coffee?'

Silently she shook her head. So awkwardly she darted back into the hallway and quickly pulled on her dress over her slip. She was desperate to escape.

'So what now?' he asked softly when she stepped back into the kitchen. 'You've no more work to worry about. You're free to do anything. What's your plan?'

She didn't really have one.

'Neon lights?' he prompted.

'Sure.' She'd focus on those external adventures. Seize on them as a means of avoiding the awkwardness rippling through her and that ache for intimacy welling inside. 'Ice skating at the Rockefeller centre. Eating doughnuts or a pastry outside Tiffany's or something, right? Times Square.' But her smile slipped, and she scrambled to think of more. 'Art galleries. All the exciting, fun things a tourist ought to do in New York in December.'

'Sounds like you have quite the list.'

'Yes.' She was determined to make the most of every one of *those* iconic experiences too. '*Christmas* in New York—it's my one and only chance.'

'But isn't Monrova all snow and sleighs and bells and warmly spiced Christmas baking?'

'In some homes, I'm sure it is.'

'But in the palace?'

'Just another day. Normal lessons continued. There was no extended family gathering. I had dinner with my father in the dining room as I did every night. And received the usual lectures.'

'But last night you told me you were spoilt.'

'I was. Just not especially at any of those kinds of things. So this year, this once, I want the full Christmas.'

He blinked. 'The full Christmas? What even is that?'

'I don't really know.' She began to smile. 'Like something from the movies?'

His jaw dropped. 'The movies?'

'Yeah, you know. All those good ones where people go the extra mile to find that one perfect present for their child, or they get through the snowstorm against all the odds to be with their loved ones…'

'It's not really like that, Jade.'

'No?' She glanced at him.

'Those movies make you think everyone is having the best time. They're not. I don't think *anyone* is.'

'No?' What had Christmas been like for him?

'Never. People set their expectations *way* too high. It's

distant family stuck together for too long, drinking too much, and every time it gets so ugly…' He shuddered.

'You're cynical.'

He lifted his hands. 'It's how I see it.'

'You mean how it was for you?'

'You know I didn't have a normal family structure, so Christmas wasn't any of that for me, either.'

'You never had Christmas with family?' She was shocked. 'I'm sorry.'

'Not your fault, Jade.' He breathed out. 'Not mine either.'

But that throwaway comment weighed heavier than it should.

For the first time she didn't think he was being honest. Not with her, but with *himself*. And the tension within his muscular frame now? She shouldn't pry when she had no right. This was just physical. A one-night stand. She'd forgotten that fact so quickly. Yet she couldn't stifle her curiosity completely.

'So what did you do on Christmas Day? How do you know so much if you weren't with—?'

'I worked.'

'You what?'

'Christmas Day is an opportunity, Jade. There are *very* big tips to be got from large unhappy family parties. Ellen worked it every year, as did I, as soon as I was old enough.'

She stared at him. 'Do you still work on it?'

'Absolutely. It's a strategy day. I plan the year ahead.'

'Christmas is a *strategy* day?' She choked with an outrage that she didn't even need to exaggerate. 'That's even worse than *my* dreary day.'

He laughed. 'How is it worse? It's super productive. I like the peace and quiet. I achieve a lot.'

As she gaped at him she heard a familiar buzzing sound. It was Juno's phone. Startled, she whirled to hunt out her bag. But her phone stopped ringing before she could answer it. She glanced at the screen.

Jade.

Which meant *Juno* was trying to phone her—why?

Jade knew why. She'd seen it yesterday in a newspaper left on a table at a café she'd stopped at for lunch. Juno had been photographed with Leonardo at the Winter Ball in Monrova—and their shared glance wasn't one of two near-strangers being very proper and polite with each other. The way Leonardo had been looking at Juno? And then there were more photos of the two of them in Severene?

Jade knew Juno had wanted to talk to him. She'd been unusually concerned that Jade was considering a political union with him. She'd told Jade not to trust him. And yet—from those pictures? The media was salivating over an imminent engagement. Only problem was, they thought Juno was Jade.

'Everything okay?' Alvaro was watching her intently.

She grabbed Juno's leather jacket. 'I'd better get going. I need to return that call.'

'You could—'

'I need to go.' She was suddenly desperate to get away from him while she could. Thank heavens for Juno—she'd literally been saved by the bell of her phone.

'Sure.' He let her go.

But just as she reached the door he grabbed her arm.

'You're okay?' he asked.

She paused. That one touch was a reconnection that pushed aside her embarrassment to the joy still bubbling below.

'I'm so much better than okay,' she confessed. It had been amazing. 'I hope you are too.'

He stilled, his expression softened, his hold relaxed. And she took her chance to escape.

She quickly got out of the building into the crisp air.

People were going about their daily business. It seemed as if nothing cataclysmic had happened in anyone else's world. Only hers.

She couldn't believe she'd slept with her sister's boss. No one could ever know. Ever. Not even Juno. It would make things weird for her at work and that was the last thing Jade wanted to happen. So she couldn't tell her sister. Not ever.

Drawing in a breath, she returned her sister's call.

'Juno, it's so good to hear your voice,' she whispered as she walked along the pavement, struggling to pull her thoughts together. 'Sorry I couldn't get to the phone straight away… It's… It's pretty early here.' And she was wearing the same clothes she'd been wearing last night. And she'd just left Juno's boss half dressed. And she'd *slept* with him. She drew in a deep breath of wintry morning air. 'I thought we agreed we wouldn't contact each other, just in case?'

'Jade… I… It's wonderful to hear your voice too.'

Jade stilled, hearing a tearful breathlessness in Juno's voice. Had something happened? She paused on the pavement, that press photo she'd glimpsed at the café yesterday popping back into her mind.

'I'm sorry I woke you up,' Juno added. 'And I know I'm not supposed to call, but…'

'Juno, what's wrong?'

'Something, something's happened, Jade. Something… I really did not expect…' Her sister's voice trailed off again.

Intuition rang loud in Jade's ears. 'Is this about Leonardo, and your state visit to Severene?' Jade tackled it directly. 'You make a great couple.'

'We're not a couple,' Juno answered so instantly that Jade had to smother a smile.

'Are you certain?' she queried gently. 'You look really happy together in all the press coverage. And by the way, you're doing a stunning job impersonating me. Better than

I could do myself.' Juno looked more at ease with people than Jade ever felt.

'That's not true, Jade. I'm just good at faking it,' Juno said.

While Jade didn't know much about relationships, she didn't think that obvious chemistry with King Leo could be faked. 'You're not faking anything, Ju, you're a natural,' Jade said wistfully. And it wasn't just that sizzle, it was those smiles with those people who'd come to greet them in Severene. 'I always said Father was wrong not to consider you as his successor, and now I get to say I told you so.'

There was a moment of silence. 'Aren't you angry with me?' Juno asked.

'Why would I be angry?' Jade asked, amazed. She was delighted to see her sister in her rightful place.

'Because I'm not supposed to be in Severene? Because this swap was never supposed to get this complicated? Because I could end up completely screwing up Monrova's relationship with her neighbours.'

Jade thought for a moment, then answered calmly. 'No, I'm not angry about any of that.' Because it had got complicated for her too, so quickly. 'I've come to realise, seeing the press reports of you two, that Leonardo and I were never meant to be together. I'm really glad you persuaded me to come to New York.'

She'd realised she needed to slow down on that decision making. She was still young. She had time to think things through.

'It's been an eye-opening experience for me,' she added. 'I've discovered so much about myself and there's so much more to learn.'

There was so much she wished she could learn with Alvaro. But she'd had her one night and it hurt to remember it was over. So instead she focused on her sister. 'I also think it's super cute that there seems to be something developing between you two.'

'There's nothing developing between us. Nothing permanent anyway,' Juno murmured. 'It's just... There's a lot of chemistry between us and I like him more than I ever expected to.'

'Are you sure there's nothing more between you?' Jade asked softly. 'From the press reports I've seen, he looks at you in a way he's never looked at any of the other women he's dated.'

'No. There's nothing more,' Juno said, but she sounded unsure. 'Jade, I just... What I need to know, the reason I called, is... If Leo and I jump each other tonight. I mean, he's asked me and I... I really want to go for it. Because, you know, chemistry.' Juno drew in a breath.

Jump each other? Jade chuckled inside at her sister's choice of words. She guessed she'd 'jumped' Alvaro last night.

'We've agreed it won't mean anything beyond the physical. That it won't have any political implications. That the marriage is a whole separate issue.' Juno continued her rapid explanation. 'But if you'd rather we didn't... I mean, I don't want to mess things up for you... With Leo.'

'Juno, you're not serious—what possible claim would I have on Leonardo?' Jade almost laughed.

'Well, you know, you were considering marrying him a week ago.'

Jade did laugh then. A cold marriage of convenience now seemed appalling. Now she understood what the sacrifice would be if she were to marry solely for political reasons. She couldn't believe she'd actively been considering it—why on earth had she? And then she remembered. 'The marriage was always just about securing a trade relationship and uniting our two kingdoms.' Her ancient advisors had wanted it as a neat and tidy option. But it had been a way of avoiding personal uncertainty as well. 'I can't believe I ever thought that would be okay.'

'Jade, you don't sound like yourself.' Juno asked, 'Are you sure everything is going okay in New York?'

'It's… Yes, it's been really transformative in a lot of ways,' Jade said, trying not to let all her crazy thoughts explode out of her. 'I'm discovering things about myself I didn't realise. Not all of which I like.'

Her naivety. Her recklessness, tolerance, acceptance, her silence…and her *selfishness*.

'What things?' Juno asked. 'There's nothing about you not to like.'

'I used to think the same thing.' Jade laughed but she didn't feel it. She'd thought she'd been so good, so dutiful… whereas really? She was a coward.

'If something's happened, Jade, you can tell me, or we could swap back. Now.'

'No. I don't want to swap back, not yet,' she said swiftly. She didn't want to end it for Juno already. And she needed to straighten out her own head before she headed home. She *needed* this time. So much more than she'd realised. 'I'd really like to stay until New Year's Eve, like we agreed. Plus, I don't want you to miss your chance to jump Leo,' Jade added with a choked laugh. 'Unless you need to…'

'No, I don't want to swap back yet either…' Juno admitted.

'Listen, Ju, I've got to go.' Jade made herself get moving before she confessed everything to her sister. 'I've got a busy day ahead of me,' she fudged. It wasn't a complete lie; it would be a busy day recovering from the night of her life. 'But whatever you and Leonardo do, or don't do, you have my blessing. Okay?'

Her sister deserved some fun. Jade desperately wanted her to be happy.

'Okay.'

But Juno had said she and Leonardo had agreed it wouldn't be anything more than physical, that it was just chemistry, and now Jade knew that wasn't as easy as it sounded.

'But do me a favour,' she added swiftly before ending the call with Juno. 'Don't underestimate your feelings for him. They might be stronger than you think.'

Because that was the fear gnawing inside her—that the reason she'd told Alvaro she was 'so much better than okay' was that *it* had been so much *more* than physical. And now, the desire for more with him still tempted her to risk everything all over again.

But she was Queen and she *couldn't*. She could only be grateful that she'd had the night she had. Now, she needed to focus on *herself*. That was what Alvaro had shown her. She needed to speak up and strengthen her own damn spine.

Liberation swept over her. She and Juno had endangered themselves with this switch. But if she could time travel she'd choose to do the same again. No regrets. By the sound of things, Juno had none either. They could sort out any resulting mess once Jade was back home. But one thing was certain and it had been certain from first thing Monday morning. There was no way Jade was ever marrying King Leonardo or any other suitable prince her advisors recommended...

But she couldn't marry for love either. Her parents had tried and look how that had worked out. They'd fallen in love so quickly and out again only a few months later. They'd come from different worlds. And the mess it had made of their lives? Now, she knew there was nothing to be gained from a reckless, passionate relationship. Fortunately, the fact that she couldn't go ten seconds without thinking about Alvaro Byrne wasn't anything to do with love. It was lust. Simple, basic, bone-deep lust. And what had happened between them was perfect. Finite and perfect.

Honestly? She didn't think she'd ever marry *anyone*.

CHAPTER EIGHT

ALVARO PACED AROUND his apartment. She'd wanted immediate escape. She'd turned as soon as she could, trying to leave without drama, her face aflame in awkward embarrassment… But when he'd stopped her something else had emerged. Not the deeply ingrained politeness, not the ex-virginal embarrassment, but a pure, personal, simple admission.

She'd said she was 'so much better than okay' and then, *I hope you are too.'*

That sweet wish for him had glued him in place—but he'd been unable to admit the same. Frankly he'd been unable to even breathe. Not before she'd already left.

She'd required no post-mortem. Apparently had no regrets either.

But that was good, wasn't it? He'd wanted—needed—her to go, too. He too wanted nothing, no last words, to spoil the perfection of their night together. And it would be spoilt eventually if they saw each other again.

He'd spoil it. Somehow.

He knew a moment in time was all they could ever have.

But he hated how empty his home suddenly felt. How desolate and vast his bed now was. He'd loved the curling length of her hair, the creaminess of her back, the narrowness of her waist and the flare of her hips…slender but sweet and soft. Irritated, he scratched the back of his neck and headed to the shower.

The next day he went out of town on a totally unnecessary field trip to sign the deal that had been under discussion for so long. It didn't matter that his own office was closed, he never stopped working. And the distance meant seeing her was impossible.

But that didn't stop him thinking about her. And in the end he couldn't resist phoning her.

'Alvaro? What's wrong?'

He winced. Did there have to be something wrong for him to phone? 'I'm checking up on your Christmas spirit. Have you been ice skating yet?'

'You should have seen me. I nailed it.' Her laughter was literally like bells.

Too much Christmas thinking. Too much missing...

'You've probably been skating since before you could walk.'

'I did find the rink a little small and crowded for my triple axel,' she joked.

He couldn't stand the thought of her ice skating on her own around that damned rink. 'And you saw the tree?'

'It was awesome, yes.'

'And how many lights?'

'Lots. Really good window displays too.'

Window displays? Wow. It all sounded ridiculously sad to him. 'What else?'

'Are you living vicariously through my Christmas experiences?' she teased. 'You don't even like Christmas.'

'I never said that,' he protested. 'I said I *work* Christmas.'

'You said Christmas was distant families getting drunk and miserable.'

'You've seen otherwise?'

'I've seen lots of family groups in restaurants. They look happy to me.'

'You only got a glimpse. You've got to see them at the end.'

'Well, I'm hardly going to stand around for hours outside, peering through the windows and watching them like some stalker.'

He grimaced at the image. Yeah, she was isolated. She shouldn't be doing those things alone. She should have family or friends with her to enjoy it with. But she had none. The only person who knew the truth of her life right now was him.

He returned to Manhattan two nights later. He stripped the bed. Even bought new linen—midnight blue, anything to make it different from how it had been when she'd been there with him. But he still couldn't sleep, couldn't stop seeing her smiling and her pretty form supine and the soft stretch of her creamy skin with the dew of sweat and the stain of colour in her face as he'd aroused her. So slow, so delicious, so worth every precious moment. The slippery sweetness of her taste. Being with her had been the hottest experience of his life and the ache of desire in his body now was enough to send a man insane.

But that wasn't what was really messing him around. It was his conscience. That sense of having done something wrong. But the mistake wasn't having had her, but in leaving her alone since.

That had been no ordinary night. And she faced no ordinary week. And he was flooded with something so much bigger than regret.

He woke early and went to the gym, desperate to burn off his frustration. It didn't work. That jaded, irritable feeling within only grew. He stalked to the coffee shop and got a triple shot. Waiting for it to be made, he glared out of the window, then his gaze dropped to the table beside him, and the paper spread on it. He flicked through a couple of pages, knowing what he'd find. Sure enough, there were more pictures of 'Queen Jade', aka Princess Juno, and King Leonardo, gallivanting around Severene, doing royal walkabouts and other feeding-the-media-frenzy things.

Jade had said there'd been some speculation about that stupid possible marriage—but these weren't whispers, these were screaming headlines and they sparked Alvaro's fury. Had Jade seen these pictures? What was her sister playing at? Was Jade seriously still contemplating some kind of political marriage? Was that why she'd been so keen to leave him so early the other morning? Was this all part of some crazy plan?

No. That wasn't Jade. She was too straight. And she'd been so determined to fix her job for her sister. So determined to be good. To not offend *anyone*. She was dutiful to the point of damaging her own future.

She'd said she wanted a few weeks of freedom. Some space to do the iconic Christmas things… Alvaro had never had the most abundant or joyful of Christmases, but he thought he'd actually had more than she had, even when he'd worked all day.

Fairy lights and fir trees…she'd had restrained decoration but never heartfelt detail. Not the closeness and comfort of family or even friends…those fun times that he too had seen in so many Christmas movies or season specials of nostalgic TV shows.

At the end of a long Christmas Day, he and Ellen had at least had each other. She'd tried her best to give him something even small. So now he gave her all he could in return.

If Jade wanted to experience some real Christmas joy, maybe he could help her. Maybe they could both do something a little better than their usual Christmases?

By Thursday he couldn't stand it a second longer. He couldn't stop thinking about those pictures of Juno with King Leonardo and his anger at Jade being all alone bubbled. What the hell were they all playing at? Jade's apparent docility regarding that so-called dutifulness infuriated him. Why did she have to sacrifice every element of her life for her crown and country? This wasn't the fifteen hundreds. People were allowed private lives. People were allowed some *fun*.

She was used to having an austere Christmas. So was he. And usually the thought wouldn't bother him at all. But the point of this time away was for her *not* to have that. She should have something more than aimlessly walking around city streets alone—even if it was Manhattan with all the bright lights it had to offer. He could do better than that. He wanted her to have more non-royal duty time. More fun. And for that she needed...if not family, then a friend.

After all, there was no reason why they couldn't be *friends*, was there?

His conscience told him exactly why.

Alvaro wasn't used to being a friend. Or having one. He was happy to be that loner who knew precisely what his value was to others—on the sports field back when he was a youth, as an entrepreneur, an investor, as a boss... and yes, as a lover. And if he didn't deliver, then he was no longer valued. And definitely not wanted.

The affairs he had never became anything more than a few weeks' fling. He gave into the lust, got it out of his system, moved on. It was only sex, after all. But that wasn't what he and Jade had done. Which was exactly why they couldn't do it again. She was more forbidden now than when he'd thought she was working for him. Not just because she was vulnerable. But because he was afraid he was too. But he couldn't resist phoning her once more.

'Alvaro?'

It wasn't right how happy he was to hear her carefully modulated tones again. Nor was it right how much he liked to make her breathless, to make her forget what it was she'd been going to say. Only right now *he* was the one who'd forgotten what words he'd meant to utter.

'Boss?' she teased.

And that was it. The moment he knew. He gripped the phone more closely and grabbed his car keys. 'Have you been on the eggnog already?'

He finally knocked on her door and then she was there. Slim jeans, thin sweater, wide, wide eyes. His body seized.

Don't kiss her. Don't kiss her. Don't kiss her.

'Alvaro?' She stood back from the doorway. 'What are you doing here?'

'Not kissing you,' he said brainlessly. Then he flinched and hustled to pull his head together. 'Just getting that out there first up,' he clarified more softly. 'I'm not here for that.'

'Okay.'

But that crestfallen hint in her eyes hit him like the thinnest, most deadly of blades. He could kick himself for his lack of tact. He couldn't admit how much he wanted to now. It would mess things up for her, wouldn't it? And that damn political marriage she was going to have to agree to some time in the next decade or so.

'I thought you'd be out already, doing all the things. It's after ten.'

'I'm just…' She drew a breath. 'Why are you here?'

'I don't want you to be alone for Christmas.'

'I'm quite used to being alone, Alvaro.' She went to close the door on him. 'It's not your concern.'

Her pride was back. Her politeness. Her refusal to express her emotions and her desires. *Queen Jade* herself.

'I'd like to show you some things.' His mouth felt as if it were stuffed with cotton wool. He was making such a mess of this.

She folded her arms across her chest. 'What things?'

'Just…things.' He realised this wasn't going as well as he'd thought it would. What had he expected? 'I mean—'

She was growing chillier by the second. 'I thought we weren't going to see each other again.'

'I think that was unnecessary caution on my part.'

'Caution?'

'I don't believe you'll fall in love with me just because we had sex and might spend a few days together.'

'Was *that* your concern?' Her jaw dropped and there

was a glint in her eyes and he just knew she was thinking he was an arrogant jerk.

She was right. He had been.

'I don't wish to interfere in your life's plans,' he said.

She actually smiled but it was all queen. 'Nothing comes before my duty to my country.'

'I realise that now. I'm sorry. I was arrogant before.'

'Before? You're not any more?'

'It's possible I might relapse,' he said cautiously, watching for Jade to return.

'Would it be terrible for me to fall in love with you?' She studied him carefully.

'Yes. It could never work out.'

'It wouldn't work out with just me? Or with anyone?'

'Anyone,' he answered immediately and irritably. He had no idea how they'd got onto this. 'But especially not you.'

'Because of the Crown.' She actually nodded. 'I think it's best that we don't sleep together again. Definitely.'

'You do?'

'Once was a considered risk. A thrill, of course. But more than once wouldn't be rational. It would be reckless stupidity.'

Being with him again would be reckless *stupidity*? The stupid thing was that even though he'd decided there was no way they could be intimate again, now that she'd said the same thing he instantly wanted to fight back. And fight hard.

You always want what you can't have. And what would be so, so bad for you.

It was the human condition, wasn't it? That weakness, that failing…to be consumed by transient, addictive desires. That was the kind of thing that ruined people's lives. His didn't matter, but he wasn't ruining hers.

'Come on, you need to pack a bag.'

'You want me to leave with you now?'

'As I said, I don't want you to be alone for Christmas.'

'It's not Christmas.'

'It's close enough.' He offered her a grin. 'Don't be a grinch. It's the holiday season. Go pack enough for a few days. We'll be back just after Christmas.'

'You're inviting me to spend all of Christmas with you?'

The temptation to lean close and kiss her almost overwhelmed him. He'd convince her quickly enough that way. But distracting them both with sex wasn't allowed. Not this time. They'd even agreed on that.

'Go pack your bag.'

'I get no choice? You're abducting me?'

And damn if she didn't look as if she liked that idea.

'I think of it as more of a rescue than an abduction. You want to stay home in a tiny apartment all by yourself for Christmas Day?'

Her expression flickered and he glimpsed the loneliness he'd recognised in her before.

'You wanted some other kind of Christmas, Jade. I can't promise everything, but it might be better than usual.' His lips quirked. 'It'll definitely be different. No palace. I promise.'

He watched her green eyes widen but she was silent. So silent, even when he could see the acquiescence, the *want* in those eyes. And he sighed.

'Abduction it is.'

CHAPTER NINE

IMPOSSIBLE MAN. Impossible to ignore. Impossible to resist.

Jade pulled an old carry-all down from the top of Juno's wardrobe. It was larger than her little flight bag and she quickly stuffed warm clothes into it, somehow stupidly afraid that if she didn't hurry, he might change his mind and leave without her.

Her heart skipped as she snatched up her toiletries bag and tossed it in as well. She'd been close to saying no, stupidly hurt by that barrier he'd instantly put between them when he'd arrived. But then her inner recklessness had whispered again. The same whisper that had seen her say yes to her sister's switch plan. She had so few days left, why shouldn't she enjoy them?

Honestly, she'd absorbed all the Christmas window displays she could stand and had breathed in the holiday mood as she'd passed restaurants and bars and convivial people celebrating. But night fell earlier and earlier and the crowds on the pavement with their hats and coats and bags of shopping had brushed by her as they'd scurried to be where they were needed or wanted. And it had left her too aware of those others like her, the ones on the edges. Alone.

She'd come back to Juno's apartment and filled the fridge with sugary snacks. All the things her father would have totally disapproved of. But the chocolate bars had reminded her too much of the midnight recovery snack she'd had with Alvaro Byrne.

And now he was back. But not for *that*. Yet she'd glimpsed fire in his gaze and guessed that he was battling temptation too. She wasn't the only one still feeling it. And suddenly that became part of the fun ahead—the challenge, the sparks that had flown between them from the first moment they'd met? It was exhilarating. Being around him made her feel *alive*.

Yes. He was impossible to deny.

Minutes later, he glanced at the green jacket she'd shrugged on over the top of her thin sweater and jeans, then reached forward and took the carry-all from her. He turned and led the way without a word.

'Not the sports car this time?' she asked as he remotely unlocked the large black sedan parked right outside.

He didn't reply.

'Where are we going?' She tried again once they were both seated and belted and he'd already turned on the ignition.

'The coast.' He put the car in gear. 'But we're making a couple of stops along the way, okay?'

'You're the boss.'

He stiffened and she smothered her smile. Yes, he wasn't as unaffected as he liked to make out.

Alvaro wasn't slow in getting them out of town. Jade stared resolutely ahead, defying her inner desire to simply stare at him. In the black turtleneck jumper and dark blue jeans he looked all moody muscle and appallingly mesmerising.

Companionship for Christmas. That was all he was offering. *Not* kisses.

That arrogance of his annoyed her intensely, but as he drove she slowly relaxed and a bubble of pleasure broadened inside. She was glad to get out of town and see something—*anything*—new. The changing landscape was the perfect distraction.

'We're heading to New Haven,' he suddenly said in a clipped voice. 'We'll stay there the night. We need to visit someone tomorrow morning and in the afternoon we'll head to my place.'

Her curiosity roared. 'Who's the friend?'

His hands tightened on the steering wheel. 'Ellen.'

Jade remembered, she was the one whose photo he had, the one he'd said saved him. She glanced at the tension in his hands. 'You grew up in New Haven?'

He shook his head. 'That's where she lives now. And she's still working Christmas, she takes in all the waifs and strays she encounters, so she's providing lunch for a random bunch of people.'

She picked up on the frustration. 'You don't approve?'

'Of course, I do.' He sighed. 'But she does too much. She's older now and she doesn't have to…'

'How many people come to her lunch?'

'Half a dozen maybe? I never know the exact numbers. She cooks up a storm and serves the leftovers to the ones who drop in for days after.'

'She sounds amazing.' Jade smiled. 'People want to be around her?'

'Yeah,' he muttered. 'I guess they do.' He suddenly turned off the main road and wove in and around a few streets before pulling into a car park.

Jade stared out of the window. He'd stopped in the centre of a coastal village at the town green. It was festooned with gorgeous fairy lights and a small Christmas market with green and red bunting on the very pretty stalls. It looked delightful.

'Are we there already?' She followed his lead and got out of the car.

'No, but I feel like you need food,' he said shortly.

She laughed. 'I feel like you're projecting.'

'Probably.' He rubbed his hand across his stomach as he leaned to the side to stretch out the kinks in his back. 'Come on, they have the best pastries here.'

Jade focused on the small market ahead, refusing to wish it were *her* hand skimming over the washboard abs she knew were beneath the soft wool. Alvaro headed like a sweet-seeking missile, straight towards one stall, and she heard him order coffee and pastries.

'You've got to try one.' He held out the cardboard tray to her two minutes later.

She picked up one of the spheres of fried dough; it was drenched in honey and sprinkles. Sticky, sweet, so hot and one was simply never going to be enough.

He grinned as he watched her chew. 'Good, am I right?'

'So much better than good.' She sighed.

As they walked around the market, the warmth inside Jade wasn't from the small sweet pastries or the smell of Christmas spices, it was the company, the easing of the tension between them. Alvaro was clearly familiar with the market and the goods available—or at least the edible ones.

'You call in here every year?' she asked when he made a beeline for another stall—fudge this time, in an assortment of mouth-watering flavours.

'Absolutely.'

She liked that he had his own little Christmas tradition, even if he insisted on working the actual day. They took their time weaving along the stalls, admiring the decorations and hand-crafted garments for sale. She lost him briefly, when she paused by one trestle table, taken by an incredible display of miniature treats—gingerbread houses, Bundts and Christmas puddings.

'Are they edible?' she asked the woman behind the stall in amazement. They were so *tiny*.

'Of course.' She smiled. 'You're welcome to try a sample.'

'Thank you.' Jade beamed. Back home she'd never be allowed to eat market food without it being tested first. She'd only ever been offered pre-selected, triple-checked tastes. Here she could try anything she wanted to. And she did.

'They're so perfect, they must have taken so long to make,' Jade marvelled.

Those very particular edible presentations on tour were always fine and fancy, but the intricate piping on these tiny structures utterly amazed her.

'Could we take some of the houses to Ellen?' She turned to Alvaro when he walked back to where she'd lingered. 'For her Christmas dinner?'

'Sure, that'd be nice.'

The stallholder delightedly boxed up a dozen. Ten minutes later Alvaro carefully stowed them in the trunk of the car and then slammed it shut.

'Which did you prefer, by the way?' he turned to her to ask. 'The sweet dough balls or the fudge?'

'They were both delicious,' Jade answered.

Laughter lit his eyes and he shook his head. 'No. You can have only one. You have to choose.'

'Why do I have to choose?' She smiled. 'They were both amazing.'

His eyebrows lifted. 'Why is it so hard to pick a favourite? You must have an opinion on them.'

'Well, I don't.' She shrugged.

'Don't or *won't*?' The gleam in his eye was sharper now, not as amused. 'You're allowed your *own* opinion, Jade.'

'I am.' She nodded. 'But I'm also aware that I can't share it much.'

'Pardon?'

'Look,' she huffed. 'I know this might sound arrogant, but I have influence. And with that comes responsibility. I can't be seen to endorse one product over another. So I don't choose. I never choose.'

Alvaro theatrically glanced up and then down the path. 'Jade, I'm not sure if you've realised, but we're currently *alone*. No one is paying any attention to us. There are no cameras, and no one around for you to influence, other than me. And I won't be overly swayed by your opinion, I'm confident in my own tastes and desires.'

Her lips twisted. 'I'm aware of that.'

Truthfully, she was still getting used to the fact that there were no cameras on her when she went out. It wasn't normal not to have them. It had been drilled into her all her life—that any moment could and probably *would* be caught on camera. Remembering that horrible fact stopped her from doing things she shouldn't. Like challenging him to kiss her right now.

'You truly won't say which you prefer?' he asked.

'It's how I've been trained.'

His eyebrows shot up. 'So do you say you just like everything?'

'I can find something *positive* in everything,' she replied.

'Wow. So even if you hate something, you'll find something about it to bestow your approval on?'

She glared at him as her annoyance grew. 'You make it sound as if that's a bad thing.'

'It is. It's dishonest.'

'No, it's not. It's just…judicious. It's being kind.'

'Kind?' he scoffed. 'It's cowardly. You have to be able to admit when you don't like something. You have to have that freedom. That choice. Otherwise you just end up… bland. And in the end no one can trust a word that emerges from your mouth.'

She was suddenly hurt. 'I don't lie.'

He straightened up from the car and stepped closer. 'But you don't fully express yourself either.'

Horrible, hot resentment built within her at his judgment. Because she had with *him*. She had been so honest, so vulnerable, so exposed. And he knew it.

'I dare you to say what you like.' He stood right in front of her, his whisky-amber eyes hot and hard as if he were even angrier than she. Impossible.

'Tell me what you like,' he said. 'Tell me *one* thing you

absolutely love and can't get enough of. That you'd do every day if you could.'

There was fire in her hurt and fury now. But she wasn't being provoked into saying something she *knew* he wanted her to admit.

'What do you want, Jade?' he pushed. 'Tell me one thing you really want.' Passion now burned in his eyes as well. 'You're allowed to say. You don't need my or anyone else's permission. Why is it so hard? You did with me once already.'

'That was different,' she muttered through clenched teeth.

'How?'

'Because it *was* once. Once. One night.' She didn't want to say it again. She didn't want to let him have that victory. But then it wouldn't be only his win, would it? It would be *hers* too.

So she stepped closer, unable to ignore the craving any more. 'I want you to be quiet,' she whispered furiously. 'I want you to stop goading me and start doing something else instead.'

'Something else?' He towered over her but still didn't touch her.

'You know already,' she growled at him. 'You want it too. You're as dishonest about that as I am. You didn't come back to kiss me? That was *such* a lie, Alvaro.'

'But *you* agreed it wouldn't be wise.'

'And it wouldn't.' She nodded, never more sure of that than she was right now.

This entire trip wasn't wise. Because she was so tempted by him and it was utterly impossible. Getting close to him again? Exploring that magic with him again?

She couldn't. Because it *hadn't* been 'just sex' for her. He'd made her want so much more.

'I'm supposed to be considering marriage to another man,' she said, reminding herself more than telling him.

Never mind that it was no longer the truth, it was a viable reason to make herself *step back*.

But the look in Alvaro's eyes flared and he stepped forward. 'Was that ever a serious consideration? And now? After...' He frowned as she coolly met his gaze. 'Wow. Is it seriously still on the cards for you?'

She suppressed a shiver and stood her ground. If there was one way to put their chemistry on ice, this was it.

'I haven't ruled it out. But I need to see what he wants,' she fudged, regretting bringing the subject up.

'What *he* wants? So if he wanted to proceed, you would?'

'It's my duty—'

She broke off as he made a sound in the back of his throat.

'It is my duty,' she repeated, 'to do what is best for my country. Nothing and no one can come before my duty to the Crown.'

'You really believe that?' he softly, lethally questioned, leaning far, far too close. 'You really think that what *you* want comes second? That you have to sacrifice your life because of some duty you think you owe just because of some stupid birth order?'

She glared up at him, because she did believe exactly that.

'You're using it to hide,' he savaged her. 'Because you're too scared to stand up for yourself and for what you really want.' He drew in a jagged breath. 'I get that your father was strict, but you don't have to do as he says any more. You don't have to do as *anyone* says. You can be your own woman.'

'I'm the Queen of Monrova, Alvaro,' she said bloodlessly. 'I can *never* be my own woman.'

He pulled a torn piece of paper from his back pocket and

shoved it into her hands. Jade stared at him a few seconds longer before dropping her gaze to unfold what he'd wanted to show her. It was torn from a newspaper—a spread of photos that she barely glanced at before holding it back out to him. 'I've already seen photos of Juno and Leonardo.'

'When?'

'The other day.' She'd seen those ones from the Winter Ball where they'd been dancing.

'Before we were together?' Alvaro's gaze drilled into her.

She hesitated and looked down again, smoothing out the paper he'd not taken back. 'It was after I'd asked you.'

'But did this impact on that decision?' he probed.

She shook her head. 'I did what I wanted.'

But now she stilled as she scanned the other pictures of Juno and Leonardo in this paper. Her sister looked *happy*. They were on a walkabout and Juno was bent, talking to a small child. She looked more relaxed than Jade ever felt on such an engagement and the obvious chemistry between them had columnists frothing at the mouth. And it certainly wasn't based on nothing. A wave of tenderness swept through Jade.

'Does he know?' Alvaro asked.

Jade couldn't bear to think about that. The press and the rest of the world thought that was her—*Jade*—with Leonardo. That this was the beginning of a great romance and the world was now anticipating a royal wedding to end all royal weddings. It would be an absolute fairy tale. It certainly would be fiction. How could they possibly continue with this when she returned to Monrova and they switched back? They wouldn't, of course.

'He knows she's Juno, right?' he asked again.

Surely Leonardo did. Jade trusted Juno; she was sure this would work out. Juno had been vehemently anti Jade's possible marriage of convenience with Leonardo. There were obviously feelings there that Jade hadn't been aware of. Maybe Juno hadn't been fully aware of them either.

But Jade could feel Alvaro watching her now. 'Stop trying to analyse me.'

'I'm trying to figure out what you're feeling.'

'What I'm *feeling* doesn't matter.' That wasn't relevant to her role as Queen.

'It matters to me.'

The soft anger with which he said that broke something inside her apart. 'Stop feeling sorry for me.'

'Why shouldn't I?' That anger in his voice built. 'I thought you just said you were still considering marrying this guy. Aren't you hurt by this?'

'Of course not,' she argued. 'I'm many things, but I'm not hurt.'

'Then *tell* me the many things. Tell me even *one* of them.'

'I want Juno to be happy,' she snapped. 'She *deserves* to be happy.' And she hoped more than anything that she was reading Leonardo's expression right.

Alvaro nodded. 'And you don't deserve that?'

'It doesn't need to be a comparison all the time.' Jade shook her head. 'Just because we're twins.' She hated that and knew Juno did too. 'It's okay for me to consider her without thinking of myself the next second. I want *her* to be happy.'

'Okay.' Alvaro paused. 'But I'm interested how this impacts on you. On what you want for yourself.'

She closed her eyes briefly. 'I want to do what's best and what's right for Monrova.'

'And what's that?' he kept pushing her. 'As if who you marry is going to matter?'

'It's *not* going to matter,' she exploded at him. 'Because I'm not marrying *anyone*.'

'Finally.' His stance eased and his anger ebbed. 'You've

finally seen the light. Now let's get going before it gets too dark and cold.'

But Jade's anger hadn't fallen—suddenly she was furious with him. For a few days there she'd been fine about abandoning any arranged marriage plan. But now? Now it felt as if he'd left her with nothing. He'd made her face how alone she really was. And how was she ever to meet someone? Who would ever want to join her in the extraordinarily proscribed life she led? Not him, that was for sure.

A silent hour's drive later Alvaro pulled up outside a hotel. The receptionist's eyes widened when they walked in and Jade knew the woman had recognised her—hopefully as Juno, not Jade, so she remained quiet when Alvaro signed them both in.

'She recognised you,' Alvaro murmured as he declined a porter and carried their bags himself. 'Which is why this is your room here, while mine's a few along.' He paused at the door and passed her bag to her.

'That's the only reason we have separate rooms? For the look of it?' she asked as lightly as she could through gritted teeth. 'I thought you didn't bring me along to kiss me.'

His gaze intensified, drilling through her. 'I think we ought to eat out. I'll knock on your door in half an hour.'

Food? Again?

She half groaned, half laughed, and let herself into her room. Maybe eating was the perfect displacement activity for them both.

She tossed Juno's carry-all onto the bed and unzipped it to find a fresh sweater to wear. But given she'd packed in a hurry, she ended up tipping the entire jumbled contents onto the bed. As she went to lift the empty bag away, she felt a hard object in the interior pocket. She frowned, not remembering what it was she'd put in there. She unzipped it and paused when she saw the sheaf of papers. She *hadn't* put this in there.

Her blood chilled as she realised these documents must be Juno's. Jade had thought the bag was empty. But curiosity had her in its claws, because she'd caught a glimpse of photos in there, and she'd recognised the name on the top corner of one of the papers.

Alice Monroe.

Jade pulled out the pile before she could guilt herself into stopping. Because this was personal and private and she shouldn't…but why shouldn't she, when this was her mother, and her sister?

It was the photograph that consumed her first. Juno must've been about fifteen and she was standing. The defiant tilt to her mouth contrasted sharply with the sadness dulling her eyes. Jade recognised strain and pain and a world of things she shouldn't have had to face. Not alone. Not cast out.

Because the thin, worn woman she was standing next to at a slight distance? Their mother—Alice. That formerly beautiful, once celebrated actress. In this wretched instant-print snap, she was holding a glass at an angle and her addiction on her face. All the vitality she'd once had, sucked out of her.

But she'd known so little about her mother and of the world that Juno had grown up in. And seeing this discharge form now? From a city hospital where her mother had been briefly admitted to 'rehydrate'?

Jade had grown up in an abnormally strict world, but Juno's simply hadn't been safe. She'd been alone and dealing with adult things from such an early age. Because there it was—her sister's handwriting, filling in the utilities forms when the banks were foreclosing. These few pieces of paper revealed so much.

Jade almost snatched up her phone. But she and Juno had vowed not to make contact unless there was a crisis. And this could hardly be called a crisis.

But her heart ached for her sister. For everything they'd missed out on together. They'd not been able to support each other the way they should have.

She thought about Juno's reasons for wanting these weeks in Monrova—they'd been layered. Juno had looked after their mother. And now she'd wanted to look after Jade regarding that marriage of convenience. But she'd not told Jade these details from her life here. She'd not confided in her.

Jade had been protected for so long. Jade, whom Juno still wanted to protect—from the big bad wolf she'd seen King Leonardo as.

As if Jade couldn't make decisions for herself?

And she'd not. She'd done everything her father had told her to. She'd only been considering that stupid marriage contract because of her father.

Why? Because she'd been too scared not to. Because she'd always been too scared.

No one seemed to think she could manage on her own. That she could handle these decisions. They all wanted to guide her, to protect her. To have her as Queen, yes. But only ever a dutiful one. Because she'd not been vocal enough. She'd not *said* what *she* wanted.

Not the way Alvaro had encouraged her to. Not in any aspect of her life. Except the most intimate now. He wanted nothing more than for her to scream her desire. He wanted to please her, but not in the same way as so many others in her life wanted to please her. Not as Queen and servant, or Queen and subject, or as Queen and someone simply curious. But as equals.

He'd dared her to be open and honest about the littlest of things and she'd struggled with that. She'd spent her life being careful not to upset anyone—trained to be the ultimate diplomat.

Or was that *doormat*?

A low anger throbbed within her.

She loved that her sister wanted to care for her, but she didn't need her to. She didn't want Juno to feel that she had to protect her. *That* was the problem—that there was this assumption that Jade was somehow rarefied...more fragile, or more precious than other people?

Of course, she wasn't.

She'd been a coward. She should have stood up to her father years ago when he'd been awful to Juno, awful to her mother, awful to her. She should have challenged his old advisors. If she'd only had courage. Regret swamped her. The horrendous feeling of failure submerged her in acid. She presented this facade of capability, of being a perfectly studied monarch, when she was so far from it. When she was a far less than perfect person.

She'd not been *naive* in her consideration of a political alliance. She'd known what it would have meant and only a couple of weeks ago she'd been willing to accept discretion—to turn a blind eye while having no lover for herself. But what she'd said to Alvaro this afternoon was her truth now. She didn't want to marry. She *couldn't.*

That you could fall in love quickly? That was possible. She was horribly sure of it. It was about the only thing she was sure of right now.

The knock on her door startled her. Alvaro. She couldn't face his all-seeing eyes like this. She couldn't hide the truth of her heart.

But he knocked again. 'Jade?'

She could hear his concern. She couldn't ignore him— he'd have security up here in a heartbeat.

'One second,' she called out as she got up and went to the door. She opened it a fraction. 'I'm sorry—'

His gaze narrowed instantly. 'What's wrong?'

He'd pushed her door wider and stepped into the room before she had the chance to answer. His gaze hit the scat-

tered papers on the floor—and that awful photo of her formerly glamorous mother and her strained-looking sister.

Jade knelt to gather the papers, but her hands were shaking. He was beside her in less than a second, helping her—
emotionlessly, so politely not even looking. But she knew
he couldn't avoid seeing it.

'The carry-all is an old bag of Juno's. I didn't realise
it had anything in it,' she explained quietly without looking at him.

She put them back into the bag. She'd explain to Juno
that she'd borrowed the bag, and she'd seen the hidden contents by accident.

'I once looked it up on the Internet,' she muttered on.
'My parents' romance was all so well documented. She was
a famous actress, he was a handsome king…you know, the
stuff of fairy tales.'

But not long after their marriage her mother had grown
miserable, unable to cope with royal life in Monrova. And
then, after the split, when sent away with one of her daughters, she'd been unable to cope with her 'freedom' back in
the States.

Suddenly, to Jade, a life swamped in duty seemed safer
after all.

'I had no idea how bad it was for Juno with our mother,'
she said. 'I wish she'd told me.'

'Could you have done anything if she had?'

She shrugged. 'I don't know…but I didn't even get the
chance. She should have confided in me,' she said sadly,
leaning back in a heap against the end of the bed. 'She
shouldn't have had to deal with all that on her own.'

'You dealt with things on your own too.'

'Not the same, Alvaro.' She shook her head. 'So not
the same.'

'You can't beat yourself up for not knowing what she was
dealing with. You were on the other side of the world, you

had limited contact and you were barely an adult yourself. You didn't have much power to help either of them, Jade.'

'I could have been a support to Juno,' she whispered. 'But she didn't want that.'

He was silent a while. 'She probably wanted to protect you.'

'I don't *need* protection.' She hated the thought of people thinking she couldn't cope or that she wasn't wise enough to make her own decisions. Or didn't have something to give other people besides a smile and a polite wave. 'She didn't need to do that for me.'

'You want to protect her too,' he pointed out with a wry smile. 'That works both ways, Jade. She feels that you have burdens of your own that she'd wished she could ease for you…the Crown, for one thing.'

She shook her head again. 'I had it easy compared to her.'

'Did you?' He sat next to her on the floor, his leg running the length of hers. 'You were left with an unloving father who didn't bother to get you anything for Christmas. Let alone anything more meaningful. You were probably terrified that if you messed something up, he'd boot you out too.'

She stared at the floor, her eyes stinging with tears. Because it had been exactly that. She'd been terrified of stuffing up. Of him yelling at her the way she'd heard him yell at Juno. Of being banished the way her mother had.

She'd worked so hard in every way to do and be all that he wanted. And he still hadn't noticed, hadn't softened… hadn't cared.

'Jade?' Alvaro cupped her face with his hand in that careful, tender way and turned her to look at him.

She couldn't speak, couldn't push past that lump in her throat as she gazed into the warmth of his eyes.

'Is that how it was?' he asked.

She was so stiff with agony, she could barely nod.

'I'm sorry,' he muttered.

'I...' She breathed in a hard breath. 'I just wish she'd talked to me.'

'It can be the hardest thing to say something painful...' he said softly. 'Even to someone...'

She nodded again. She knew.

That was how it was for him, wasn't it? Impossible to say something personal, even to a friend.

The silence between them grew as she gazed into his beautiful, beautiful eyes and wished for other things to be different too.

'Jade...' His voice was strained. 'We really need to get out of this room.' He lifted his hand and ran his fingers through his hair.

She glanced up at him and attempted a feeble joke. 'You want to go to the gym?'

His face lit up at the thought she truly hadn't meant for real. 'Now that is an *excellent* idea.'

'I wasn't serious.' She really, *really* wasn't serious.

But he was already on his feet. 'There's one on level three.'

'You know that? Oh, my...of course you know that.'

'Come on.' He extended his hand to her and, heaven help her, she took it.

'I thought you wanted food,' she groaned.

'We can get something after. There's a Christmas carnival down the street. They have flashing lights, I promise.' He opened the door and went out into the corridor. 'I don't know about you, but I need to burn some energy.'

Five minutes later Jade found herself facing Alvaro, who'd already whipped off his sweater to reveal a tee that hugged that masculine vee of his body. Too well did she remember the heated wall of muscle that was his chest.

He danced in front of the boxing bag and winked at her. 'Spar with me.'

'You cannot be serious.' She lifted her hands in surrender instead. 'You're way bigger than I am.'

'I'll keep one hand behind my back.'

'And hop on one foot?' She shook her head and walked over to the equipment rack, leaving him to it. 'Not going to happen.'

But he was trying to make her laugh and it was working.

'There are things I could do with that skipping rope, Jade, if you don't want to use it in the usual way.'

She shot him a look and his laugh was low and sexy and then he turned and took a couple of playful swipes at the bag. She stared at his pure graceful strength and athleticism.

'You're not being fair,' she softly complained.

All the emotions he'd made her feel in the last twenty minutes?

'And you are?' he countered quietly. 'Look at you… just…'

'Just what?'

'Standing there.'

Warmth flooded her. He made her feel so wanted—at least in this one way.

'We both agreed the rules,' she breathed. 'We both understood them.'

'But you've broken other rules already this week, Jade. If you've done it once you can do it again.'

'Or perhaps I've learned my lesson.' She stepped back. 'And all I've eaten today are some pastries. Let's go get something more substantial, shall we?'

'Oh, fine,' he growled.

Two hours later they walked back to the hotel. Jade hadn't laughed as much in years. Alvaro had unleashed his ultra-competitive side and she'd been unable to resist the challenge. With his apparently bottomless supply of quarters, they'd thrown darts at balloons for far too long before eating unidentifiable meat on a stick and piping-hot fries. She'd refused the neon cotton candy because she didn't need the sugar high to make her heart pound faster.

They'd talked of nothing serious. Nothing of her past or her future, only whether or not they should do the rifle range first or the big six. She'd loved watching his enthusiasm emerge. He had a dynamism like no one she'd ever met. Not recklessness—he was incredibly disciplined and energetic regarding his work, but he had a controlled zest that, once released, was infectious. And killer competitive spirit. In the final tally he won the most—offering her the obligatory oversized ugly plush toy alligator that secretly Jade was sure the operator gave him only because he'd spent so much money on the damn games.

'Not going to fit in my cabin baggage, sorry,' she'd demurred.

He'd laughed and given it to a family passing by.

And now, back in the hotel, he paused by her door.

'Let me know if you need anything,' he muttered.

And who was being unfair again now?

She stared up at him and that ripple of desire—of promise—made her shiver again. But she'd deny it still—not even say it to herself. 'I think I can manage everything fine on my own, thanks.'

Amusement and appreciation flared in his eyes. 'Maybe there'll come a moment when you can't,' he whispered, teasing retribution. 'Watch out then, Jade.'

And she couldn't resist responding, 'Is that a threat?'

He opened her door for her only to then step away. 'More of a promise.'

He'd meant it only as a joke, another little lightening of the atmosphere after her earlier emotion. But for her, it was all warning.

CHAPTER TEN

'IT WON'T TAKE LONG, but I need to check on her.'

'Of course.' Jade didn't mind how long it took, she was fascinated to be meeting someone who'd had such an impact on him.

But Alvaro had been quiet on the drive and now they'd pulled up outside a suburban house, his tension was even more palpable as he checked his phone with a frown.

Jade hadn't bothered even turning her phone on. The morning was too gorgeous and she was too intrigued. Now, as they got out of the car, she scooped up the box of tiny gingerbread houses and carried them up the path. Alvaro had no other gifts with him, which surprised her a little. But he'd just lifted his hand to knock on the door when it opened and an older woman stepped out. She gazed up at him for a moment then nodded. 'Alvaro.'

'Ellen.'

It was the briefest hug before the woman turned to scrutinise Jade with sharp interest. 'Have you brought a friend with you?'

Her audible amazement sent warmth flooding through Jade. She felt outrageously pleased that a woman with Alvaro was an obvious rarity.

'Ellen, this is—' Alvaro shot Jade a quick query.

'PJ,' Jade swiftly stepped in.

But she didn't want to lie to this woman. She'd discovered how much she *hated* lying. 'It's a pleasure to meet you, Ellen.'

Warmth—and avid curiosity—swirled from the slightly stooped figure. Ellen was older than Jade had expected, but she guessed the lines on her face were hewn not just from hard work, but from smiles too. Because it also took only a split second for Jade to see that Ellen absolutely adored Alvaro.

Of course, she did.

'Come in.' The elder woman hustled them. 'It's too cold to loiter out here.'

Jade glanced at Alvaro's bent head and saw the crooked smile he gave Ellen even though she'd already turned to lead them into her lounge.

Inside Jade didn't know where to look first. There were shelves stacked with books and board games—not ancient battered editions, but new ones covering every genre, and a wide variety of non-fiction. There were puzzles too. The place had a literal warmth to it, with a cosy fire heating the large room and thick coverings on the floor. She caught Alvaro's eye and saw his quick wink, heard his low murmur. 'And the décor says…?'

That Ellen liked to welcome a wide range of people to her home. Jade had expected to like her—this was the woman who'd somehow 'saved' Alvaro—but seeing this, meeting her? She liked her all the more.

Jade held out the box of pastries to her. 'We've brought a few—'

'Alvaro,' Ellen turned and scolded him. 'You know that's not necessary. You've given me far too much already.'

'Don't look at me.' Alvaro spread his hands in mock innocence. 'These are from PJ.'

Ellen swivelled towards Jade. 'You'll forgive me, but finding places to put all the things he's sent me is impossible.'

This was clearly a source of ongoing banter between them, but Jade could play along.

'These are miniature cakes, Ellen,' Jade answered gently. 'They are *most* necessary.'

Ellen stared at her for a second, then laughed. 'Alvaro, you've found an ally.'

He just grinned. 'What do you need me to do, Ellen?'

'You couldn't just sit down and talk to me?'

'No.' He'd already pushed up his sleeves. 'Is that fire-wood delivery properly stacked?'

'Oh.' Ellen laughed again. 'Go on, then, I know you have to see it with your own eyes.'

He glanced at Jade. 'Want to come see—?'

'Of course, she doesn't,' Ellen swiftly answered before Jade could. 'We'll find a place to put these pastries.'

'I didn't bring her here to be subjected to an inquisition, Ellen.' Alvaro looked to Jade. 'You don't have to answer any questions, there's no penalty, just so you know.'

Jade felt absurdly shy but followed Ellen through to a large kitchen. She met people all the time in the course of her duties, but this sharp-eyed woman was important to Alvaro, even if he was reticent to admit how much. And that made her nervous.

'You've known Alvaro long?' Ellen asked.

'I met him through work,' Jade replied, smiling as the inquisition instantly began. 'He's been a good friend to me.'

Ellen's gaze sharpened. 'Has he?'

Jade maintained her smile and went for immediate diversion. 'Where would you like me to put these? I don't think they need refrigerating or anything, so I could just tuck them on that shelf over there?'

There was the smallest space because the shelves, like those in Alvaro's own kitchen, were incredibly well stocked.

'You see what I mean?' Ellen laughed.

'The wood store looks good.' Alvaro reappeared sooner than Jade expected.

'They're good lads.' Ellen nodded. 'They did it in record time.'

Alvaro washed his hands before checking the contents of the pantry and giving a satisfied nod. 'I'll get under way.'

'He comes every year to help with the preparations.'

Ellen sighed to Jade, but pride was evident in her voice. 'He makes the Christmas butter.'

'The Christmas butter?' Jade laughed as she glanced across the table at him. 'Alvaro?'

He shrugged as he reached for an apron. 'It's the best and, no, I won't share the recipe. I have my own secret blend of nuts and spices.'

'It is the best.' Ellen nodded. 'I'll give him that.'

Of course, it was. Because Alvaro was the world's most competitive person in everything he attempted.

'It doesn't take long,' he said gruffly.

But Jade didn't want Ellen thinking she was making him cut this visit short.

'Can I help? Please let me help.' She rubbed her hands together nervously. 'Anything that doesn't require skill, that is.'

'You don't cook, PJ?' Ellen asked.

'Not really,' Jade mumbled apologetically.

'I'm sure you do other things,' the older woman said with that oddly brisk kindness. 'Not everyone can excel at everything, like that overachiever there.' She gave Alvaro a warm glare.

Alvaro had been looking thoughtfully at Jade. 'We can make a start on the potatoes for you, Nel. I know you hate peeling.'

'What I hate is the arthritis I get when I try.' Ellen grimaced. 'So, yes, thank you. You ordered far too many, even for us.'

Jade watched Alvaro gather equipment.

'I'll peel, you chop, okay?' he said.

'Sure.' She was just relieved she didn't have to stand there uselessly any more.

An hour passed swiftly as they slipped into a natural rhythm. Jade listened to the banter between Ellen and Alvaro—each ridiculously quizzing the other. Alvaro visibly relaxed and teased more. Once the potato mountain was peeled, he moved on to his famous butter—chopping a massive pile of nuts and dried fruit.

'Will you stay for lunch?' Ellen asked.

'You know we can't stay this time,' he said instantly.

'This time?' Ellen rolled her eyes and gruffly scolded him again. 'You flit in and tear up the place getting everything done and the second it is, you're gone. You never stay.'

'And you know there's always the next job to be done...'

'It's supposed to be a holiday,' Ellen grumbled before she turned to Jade. 'Come and admire my Christmas tree, PJ,' she ordered. 'So chef here can maintain the secrecy of his recipe.'

'It won't be long,' Alvaro reminded them as Jade dutifully followed Ellen to the dining room.

The tree was in one corner, but the room's real draw were the two large rectangular tables. Set end to end, they took up almost the entire space. An assortment of chairs was stacked in the corner while heaped on the end of the nearest table were packets of table decorations, Christmas-themed plates and tinsel. The courier sticker was still on the packaging of one and the name on it caught Jade's eye—Ellen Byrne.

Jade stilled, surprised. Alvaro had taken Ellen's surname? So for how long had they been in each other's lives? When had they met? And in what way had Ellen *saved* him? It was obvious they were close, and yet...

'You do this every year?' Jade sought to relieve some of her less intrusive curiosity.

'Yes, and Alvaro arrives every Eve to help.' Ellen straightened. 'It's not enough that he *pays* for everything.' Her expression tightened. 'He's always paying...'

'You don't like him to?' Jade asked.

'I wish he didn't feel that he has to,' Ellen muttered.

'And so much. Look at that pile of decorations. What am I supposed to do with them all?'

Jade chuckled. 'People like being able to do things for those they love. I guess this is something he can do?'

'He ought to understand that the Christmas butter is enough. But every year he sends more and stays less.'

Jade had been surprised that he'd arrived seemingly empty-handed but of course he'd already provided the *things*—the food, the heating, the whole house. All those vital, *practical* things. But then he left. Jade couldn't help wondering what it was that made him feel as if he couldn't stay. Why didn't he want to? Because it wasn't for lack of welcome. Ellen obviously would like nothing more.

'He doesn't like to be a burden.' Ellen sat in a chair at the table and softly offered her opinion on the questions Jade hadn't even voiced. 'He doesn't understand that he never was that to me.'

'What was he?' Jade asked.

'Everything.'

Jade nodded. She could understand how that might be so. But then she heard Ellen draw a breath and she just knew a question was coming. A personal question she had no good answer to. So she got in first to avoid it. 'There are a lot of decorations. Would you like me to see if I can do something with them?'

Ellen took her measure for a long moment. Then she smiled. 'Unlike Alvaro, I never say no to an offer of help. You go for it.'

'Great. Then you go have a coffee with him.' Jade smiled and looked back at the packets of printed paper plates. 'And leave me to this. It'll be fun.'

It *was* fun—because there was an insane amount of Christmas decorations and Jade had never got to do Christmas decorations before. She set the chairs out, having seen the way footmen and maids prepared tables for formal receptions at the palace. She knew the sort of thing that was required. But this was better with all the whimsical little ornaments and snowy glitter to scatter everywhere.

'Uh, Jade?'

She looked up, suddenly self-conscious, and realised Alvaro was standing in the doorway, an odd expression in his eyes.

'I just need a few more minutes,' she said apologetically, glancing down at the table. She'd not realised how extraordinarily colourful she'd made it. 'I'm not quite done yet...'

Had she done an okay job? Or was this...too much?

'Sure thing.' He nodded slowly. 'Come back to the kitchen when you're done. It's looking amazing.'

But he wasn't looking at the table when he said that.

That betraying warmth scalded her cheeks and she looked back down at the paper serviettes. Truth was she'd started off slow purely to give Ellen time with Alvaro, but she'd truly lost track of time. It had been a bigger job than she'd realised.

When she eventually went back to the kitchen she found Alvaro standing, his jacket already on, and teasingly tapping his watch.

'Are you finally ready to leave?' she teased and met his stare limpidly.

'As if it's my fault we're leaving late?'

As Jade walked ahead to the car she heard Alvaro's soft query to the older woman.

'You're okay?' he asked her.

'I'm always okay. But I'm always better for seeing you.'

Jade knew just how she felt.

Alvaro couldn't bear to look at Jade, yet couldn't tear his gaze away—his damn body betrayed him every time. Her stunning hair hung in those half-curls down her back and that emerald jacket with its warm, woolly lining brought out the sparkle in her eyes and the roses in her cheeks. He wanted to grab the lapels, tug her close and taste her again. She looked like a fresh-baked treat—glitter-dusted by all those ludicrous decorations. He wanted to haul her to his hideaway and keep her all to himself like a selfish treasure-hoarding dragon.

And, for just a few nights, he was going to.

He got into the car and waited for her to fasten her seat belt. At least the darkening sky was doing him a favour—he wouldn't be able to see her as she sat beside him. Leaving Ellen's almost two hours later than planned shouldn't matter. He should be relieved to have less time completely alone with Jade and be pleased to have spent more time helping out Ellen. But Jade had had more time with Ellen too and her super-polite reticence had almost instantly melted, revealing her innate warmth and humour.

'Thanks for being so patient with Ellen,' he said gruffly.

'Why wouldn't I be?' Jade sounded surprised. 'It was a privilege to meet her.'

He found he couldn't say anything to that. Ellen was the most important person in his life. But he was deeply private and protective towards her. So someone seeing, someone knowing? But Jade wasn't just someone. And she was precious too. Even when he didn't want her to be.

'Did you think I would find it a chore?' Her voice cooled.

An ache bloomed in his chest. He'd not meant to offend her. 'I figure you have to meet people all the time. It must get tiring.'

'I might not find it naturally easy, but I do try.'

Oh, she did. And whether she found it easy or not, she was good at it. She listened and set people at ease. 'You were lovely with her.' He forced himself to smile and lighten the mood. 'But dressing the Christmas table, Jade?'

'I thought you and Ellen might like some time to catch up without me.'

Yeah, he'd suspected she'd fiddled about with those decorations as a stalling tactic so Ellen could talk with him longer—asking everything but those questions that really mattered. They both knew to avoid those. But Jade had wanted more time for them. Because Jade was very sweet.

'You didn't need to do that,' he muttered, a little hoarse. 'Ellen and I understand each other perfectly well.'

'It was fun,' she parried lightly.

Yeah, she *had* enjoyed it. He'd seen that when he'd gone to find out what was taking her so long—he'd been unable to resist quietly spying on her. She'd taken such care and such sweet joy, becoming self-conscious only when she'd realised how long she'd taken. She'd joked about making origami animals from paper towels, but he'd seen the pleasure she'd found in setting out gaudy dollar-shop decorations and hanging tinsel as if she'd never touched it before. And she possibly hadn't—not up close, not to play with herself. Even in their poorest moments Ellen had found a string of tinsel from somewhere and Alvaro never let her go without yards of it now. Ellen had struggled on her own for so long and he owed everything to her. And for once it was easier to talk about her rather than think about the other woman currently sitting beside him.

'I've tried to get her into a new place,' he said. 'But she won't move. I changed her appliances though. Haven't heard the end of it. Her baking has suffered ever since, apparently.'

Jade chuckled.

'She's useless at accepting help.' He smiled fondly. 'Fiercely independent, to the point of frustration. But she worked so hard for so long and never got ahead. It wasn't her fault. There just weren't the hours in the day and by the time she took me on, she was tired. In my early teens I realised that getting her out of that hand-to-mouth cycle was down to me. She was worn down from all those years working all those hours to support others. Her own family. Her mother. Her brother. Then me.'

She should've had someone who'd helped her long before him. And he'd been part of the burden holding her down for too long already.

'And you did that, right? She doesn't have to work any more if she doesn't want to.'

She still did, of course. He nodded.

'You keep her house maintained, you stock her pantry.'

'She gives most of it away. She takes in all manner of waifs and strays and I worry she'll get taken advantage of again.'

'Again?'

That 'family' of hers had more than taken advantage. They'd used her up, literally worn her out. It had only been when she'd taken Alvaro that she'd finally fully escaped them. When she'd seen what they'd done to him.

'She gives too much,' he said in vague explanation.

'Is that possible?'

'When it's at your own expense—yes.' It had cost Ellen—her youth, her time, her health, her own future.

'So you only see her on Christmas Eve,' she said softly. 'You don't go to her dinner on the day?'

'I don't want to add to her load. It's really just another job for her, only this time the restaurant is at her home. I don't understand why she still does it when she doesn't have to. Why she wants all the work of cooking for a bunch of people she doesn't really know. You'd think she'd want a break.'

'Maybe she appreciates the break from the financial stress, sure. But perhaps there are other things she gets out of it? Being needed…caring for someone or something. That's important to a lot of people.'

'Not to me,' he muttered. He refused to allow it to be. 'I owe Ellen and I'll always support her and I'll support my employees. But beyond that?'

He needed his space and his freedom. He glanced sideways and saw the pure scepticism on her face. 'You don't believe me?'

'I don't believe for a second that you don't care.'

'Well, you're wrong.' As he rejected her notion a bitter bubble formed right below his ribs and forced him to challenge her back. 'Who do you care for?'

'My country.'

His lips twisted. 'One person's not enough for you? You need a whole nation?'

'Apparently,' she answered lightly.

'You and Ellen,' he murmured softly. 'She won't say no either. Does all things for all people. She won't give up on someone no matter what, and she'll forgive almost anything.'

'Do you forgive?'

That bitter bubble burst, sending that acid through every cell. 'What do you think?'

'I think you forgave Juno's mistake.'

He grunted dismissively. 'I'm not talking that kind of thing. That was nothing.'

'What kind of thing can't you forgive, Alvaro?'

He glanced at her. She'd swivelled in her seat and was studying him too closely. And as he saw the seeking emotion in her eyes he blanched inwardly. He could never tell her all of it. He could never tell anyone. This whole conversation had to be over.

'You should rest, we have quite a drive yet.' He pressed the sound system on the car and sleigh bells rang out.

Thankfully, she took his cue. 'Christmas music?'

'Uh-huh. Cheesy Christmas music. That's what we're doing here, right? Christmas.'

'So you're not working tomorrow?' she asked.

'Guess not.' He swallowed.

He didn't want to think about tomorrow. Or yesterday.

Or any time ever. He'd give anything to distract himself from her right now. Because having her here with him, wanting her to like where they were going…holding onto her company longer than he should… It all *mattered*. And he really, *really* didn't want it to matter.

A couple of hours later she saw it and broke the silence.

'Is that a lighthouse?' She sat upright in her seat and stared hard at the building they were heading towards.

He nodded. 'Reactivated after it was restored a few years ago,' he said, glad to focus on something that wasn't personal. 'There are a few private towers along the coastline here—this is one of them. It's not neon, but it is a flashing light. A pretty big one.'

'Is it *yours*?'

'Yeah.'

'That's amazing.' Her face lit up before the lamplight even got to it.

But that bitterness swirling inside him had lodged deep. 'You're not just finding something positive to say?'

'No! Alvaro, this is the coolest thing ever.' She looked back at him and all the light a man could ever want shone in her eyes. 'It's beautiful.'

'It is not a palace, Jade.' He half laughed. But her excitement broke through and pleased him an inordinate amount.

'I don't need a palace. I've spent too long in one of those already.'

And she would be going back to it soon. At least she wasn't going to marry some unworthy aristocrat now. But he half wished she were—that would make her completely forbidden again.

He gripped the wheel, glad of the cover of darkness.

'It's beautiful,' she muttered again softly, leaning forward to see better as he drove down the narrow private road. His road. And for the first time, he wasn't travelling it alone.

The beacon guided him. It had always been a source of peace—like a sanctuary. And it had been gut instinct to bring her with him—that undeniable certainty that she shouldn't be alone this Christmas. Even though he had little to offer her really. But to make up for that, he'd arranged a couple of Christmassy things that he couldn't face right now.

But the *reason* why he couldn't face them was the truth he needed to *avoid* even more.

He couldn't bear to think any more. Or talk. Or do anything other than survive. Because as he parked the car, finally home, he was barely hanging onto his self-control.

Jade walked to the lighthouse cottage beside him, aware of a terrible tension within him and not understanding why it had suddenly sprung. In silence he swiftly unlocked the door and ushered her in. Aside from the beaming beacon itself, the only other light was from the Christmas tree at the end of the short hallway, so she still couldn't see his face properly. She really needed to see him. But before she could say anything, he caught her hand.

'Come up to the tower,' he muttered.

She followed him up the curling staircase that had been tucked to the left of the door. Around and around she climbed higher, her pulse rising too with every step. It was narrow up there, but—

'This is *incredible*,' she breathed as she took in the bright lamplight and the darkened, wide windows.

There was the sound of sea hitting shore, but the space was otherwise silent. That regular swirl of light offered a sense of strength and safety. It was the ultimate in serene isolation.

But when she turned, she was finally able to see his face and she realised that her sense of safety was very *wrong*.

'Alvaro?'

He stood still and silent and so strong.

'Alvaro?'

'Don't,' he muttered. 'Don't say anything.'

But how could she not say anything when he'd just stripped off his sweater, together with his tee, leaving him bare-chested? How could she not when he moved towards her with such intent?

'What are you doing?' she asked, even though she knew. Even though she wanted it with every ounce of her being. 'I'm leaving soon.'

Her heart pounded as she said it to remind herself too.

'I know,' he muttered. 'That's good.'

'Is it?' She shook her head with a sad little smile.

'Jade…' His voice was rough and gravelly. 'You know I'm right. You know that this can't…'

'I know.'

'And you know we can't not do this now.'

In the sweep of light from the beacon, the intensity in his expression was revealed. She swallowed. The lighter sexiness of that first night had been replaced by something stronger. There was almost ruthlessness in his intent—as if the hunger had deepened and the resulting, revealed pain needed to be assuaged. This time would be different. This time, she truly feared for her heart.

It's too late already.

She closed her mind to that secret whisper. It didn't matter. Because it *was* too late. And because it was too late, there was no denying this now. She lifted her chin and he stepped close to meet her, to cup her jaw in his large, gentle hands. She closed her eyes at the first kiss. She'd missed him. And now she breathed him in—that musky scent, the heat of his body, the surety of his touch.

They barely undressed. They barely had time. There were too many kisses to enjoy and it didn't matter. In the swirl of light that swept over them every other second, they glimpsed all that was needed—desire, willingness, need.

'Please,' she whispered, her arms tight around his shoulders.

He hoisted her into his hold, pressing her back against the wall. Leaning so close she ought to be crushed. Instead she was elated.

'Don't be polite, darling,' he begged. 'Demand what you want from me.'

'What word do you want to hear, if not please?'

He groaned against her and then uttered a command. It was blunt and coarse, yet he whispered it gently in her ear. That was him. An impossible contradiction of demand and patience.

'Do you have any—?'

'Of course.' He slammed the condoms on the wall beside her head. 'I wouldn't hurt you for the world, Jade.'

She was saddened for a second that he considered creating something magical together would be so destructive for them both. But he was right. And then her need overruled everything. 'Hurry, then.'

Because denying him. Denying herself. Was impossible.

Moments later he groaned her name—a long sigh of searing need and looming satisfaction as he slid home.

'You're so ready for me,' he added in an awed whisper.

'I've been ready all week,' she confessed.

'Why didn't you say so sooner? Wasting time.'

'You went away.'

'Ran fast as I could,' he growled and pressed closer still. 'Stupid.'

'Why did you?'

'Because it's like this,' he said simply. 'Too good.' He stared into her eyes as if seeing her for the first time in so long. 'You should get to have all the fun, Jade.'

Did he think so? Right now, *she* thought so too.

'Give it to me, then,' she asked softly.

The flickering light fell on his gorgeous face, his expression burnished in the alternating lamp light and shade of night. They were alone in the world. There was only them, only this. And Jade was utterly lost, utterly captured in his arms, deliciously lost in his intensity, in his tender passion and the brute strength of his body.

CHAPTER ELEVEN

JADE OPENED HER EYES to a beautiful winter's day—the wide window showing the gorgeous blues of the wide ocean and sky. Last night he'd carried her from the tower straight to this big bed. They'd made love for hours. Not had sex—that was not what it had been for her. She'd loved him as hard as she could for as long as she could stay awake. Now she took in the coastal blue and creamy white paintwork, the warmth of natural wool rugs and the worn wooden floor and that low-burning flame of the cosy fire.

It was perfection. And she told herself she could suppress the yearning inside—she'd suppressed pain for a long time before. She could live with an aching heart. She wouldn't let it ruin this couple of days.

'Good morning.' In just black boxers and nothing else, he was a gift.

But he'd brought her coffee too; she could smell the invigorating strength of it and see the steam curling from the blue mug.

'Merry Christmas,' she whispered, curling her toes at the sight of him.

'Shh.' He bent and gently silenced her with a touch of his finger to her lips. 'Not yet.'

'No?' She frowned.

He shook his head and laughed. 'First we start with an Easter egg hunt.'

'A...*what*?' She raised herself up on two elbows as he sat on the edge of the bed beside her.

'Easter egg hunt.' He looked at her blandly.

'You...' She cocked her head to study him more closely. 'It's *Christmas*.'

'Yeah, but I figure, if you didn't really get a Christmas,

I bet you didn't get Easter either. Or Halloween. Obviously not Valentine's Day…'

'Obviously…' Her heart thudded and she couldn't help but slide into the warmth of his smile.

'So. We might not do them in the exact right order…but an Easter egg hunt.'

His playfulness astounded her. So did the lighthouse's cottage. In the course of the hunt for gold-foil-wrapped chocolate decadence, she discovered the other decorations gilding the beautifully refurbished cottage. So many decorations. There was Christmas in the kitchen. Valentine's in the bathroom—champagne and a giant heart balloon above the bath, which had that amazing view across the ocean. She peeked in to discover Halloween in the study with a witch's hat and a cauldron and a carved pumpkin jack-o'-lantern on the side table next to a plush reading armchair. At each of these small decorated settings sweet treats were stationed. The effort and thought he'd gone to put a lump in her throat.

'Alvaro…'

'Silly, I know.'

'Not silly.' She faced him and slung her arms around his neck. 'I love that there are themed snacks in every room for us to refuel.'

'Holiday candy can't be beaten.' He tugged her closer. 'And I'm glad you got my plan. Season's Eatings.'

But she didn't eat. She kissed him. Lazily and playfully and with such sweet gratitude—showing rather than saying how his gesture made her feel. He'd put in so much effort. Already the fires were lit in the bedroom, kitchen and study, making the whole cottage gorgeously warm.

'This must have taken you ages.' She hugged his arm as she gazed around again in absolute awe.

He laughed. 'I'd love to take the credit, but it only took me a few phone calls. I have a person who checks on the place and he got a party company to deck it out. I had to hide most of it from you last night.' He shot her a look. 'I paid them very well given it is the holiday season, but they didn't seem to mind.'

'I bet they had a blast.' Who wouldn't want to come to this magical place?

After the hunt, as they snacked on the Easter eggs they'd found, he pointed out the two stockings hanging on the Christmas tree that she'd not yet noticed.

'Alvaro…' She suddenly felt dreadful; she had no gift for him.

'Don't panic.' He chuckled as he caught the distressed look she shot him. 'This isn't from me. It's from Ellen.'

Jade's heart beat a flood of warmth around her body. She reached into the felt stocking and pulled out a gorgeous soft green winter hat.

'Knitting is her hobby—though she's slower now. She has a collection she chose from.'

'I love it.' She was so touched.

'She chose well,' he said softly. 'It matches your eyes.'

'What did you get?' She peered eagerly.

His was a matching soft wool hat, only in dark grey.

'It looks good on you.' She giggled. Especially with just the boxers he had on.

'Why don't you go into the study? I'll be there in a moment.'

She'd already decided the study was her favourite room—aside from the bedroom, of course—with its stunning views of the ocean, and the cosy comfort of its whitewashed walls, bookcases and plump, soft furniture.

Two minutes later Alvaro appeared carrying a tray, on top of which was a gorgeous chocolate cake and a single lit candle.

'What's this?' She stood to meet him.

'I thought, if the main festival days were impersonal,

what were birthdays like in recent years?' He looked at her gently. 'I had a hunch that maybe not all queens got to eat cake?'

Her heart melted all over again at his astuteness. And his consideration.

'No.' Her birthday had barely registered on her father's mind.

She'd missed her sister and her mother so much at those times. Once they'd left there'd been nothing personal—a brief greeting from her father, a signed book, and a reminder to stay calm and study hard.

'So we're having cake for breakfast?' she asked. 'Because it's a treat day?'

'Why not, right? It's Christmas.'

It certainly was. Jade's heart filled as he sank into the big armchair by the fire and watched her, a smile on his face as she blew out the candle.

'Did you make a wish?' he asked.

'I'm not telling,' she teased. She carefully cut into the cake with the enormous knife he'd brought with him and marvelled as a mountain of candy-covered chocolate pieces cascaded out, spilling all over the pretty plate. A couple of pieces even hit the floor.

'Oh, wow!' She giggled. 'That's awesome.'

She could see the chocolate cake itself was rich and decadent and then with that mess of colour in the centre?

'It's the birthday cake I would have adored as a kid,' he said softly.

Her heart burst and she turned to face him. 'Would have?'

Alvaro shrugged as he watched Jade carefully put a slice of cake on a small plate. The flush in her cheeks, the smile that hadn't left her face since she'd woken, they were the best presents he'd ever had. She didn't cut a second slice, instead she came with the plate and fork and, with a wriggle of her hips, wordlessly asked to sit on his lap. She was the sexiest thing. He teased the thin strap of her negligee as she settled over his thighs and offered him a bite. How could he resist?

'You like?' she asked.

Somehow it had flipped, as if he were the one receiving the gift—yet he wasn't quite comfortable. He should be pleased and at ease. He'd checked on Ellen, he'd come to his sanctuary, he had Jade back in his bed and she'd loved his little 'festival of festivals'. Now he had cake and warmth and the most beautiful woman in the world on his knee.

Yet the strangest wall of emotion slammed into him—hitting him so off track, he couldn't even figure what it was. As it sank beneath his skin, he felt exposed and somewhat mortified that he'd done this at all. And now? Now she was looking at him with gleaming eyes and a smear of chocolate just below her sweet lower lip and—

'It's gorgeous,' he muttered.

His body ached and it shouldn't. It ought to be sated and in some soporific state of recovery, yet now he hungered for things more than physical. It hurt. His chest, his gut. It really, really hurt.

'You didn't ever get a cake like this?' she asked gently as she offered him another bite.

'You know I didn't,' he said huskily.

A frown gathered in her eyes. 'But I'm sure Ellen did something?'

He heard the curiosity in Jade's voice, saw it in her eyes.

'Ellen did her best. Always.' He couldn't say anything more.

Ellen was a carer; she'd taken in the most unwanted of unwanted things. More than stray dogs or waifish children, but the absolute rejects. She'd been tough but she'd had to be. They wouldn't have survived otherwise.

Jade was watching him. Sure, the basic details were

out there—he'd been given up for an adoption that hadn't worked out and Ellen had taken him in. But the specifics hadn't been that straightforward. He didn't ever go into those. And yet here those details were, cramming in his head—memories of birthdays and Christmases gone by in which there'd been…anger and hurt and rejection and such loneliness.

He wanted to tear his gaze away from her. He wanted to clear his throat. He wanted to escape…yet he couldn't move. And he certainly couldn't speak. He couldn't tell her the whole of it. He'd never told anyone. Not even he and Ellen had discussed it. It was in the past, long, long buried.

In the end Jade glanced away, faint colour running under her skin. She caught sight of the whiteboard on the wall above his desk and seized on it. 'You were serious about this usually being a strategy day?'

He rested his head back on the chair and gently stroked her back, unable to resist the contact. It soothed him even though every time he touched her it was as if his vital organs got an electric shock.

'Companies don't run by themselves,' he said. 'I need to check direction, and there's inevitably some crisis or other to prepare for…'

'Yet you continue to expand?' She turned back to face him. 'You don't think you have enough?'

He half smiled at her as he shook his head. It wouldn't ever be enough and, no, he couldn't ever rest.

'Do you worry that one day you'll wake up and it'll all be gone?' she asked softly.

He stiffened. He'd worked hard for what he had and he wasn't about to lose it. 'I'm not really that much of a risk-taker, Jade.' He'd had to be to begin with, but not any more. 'You've seen it yourself. I keep my safe reserves.'

And he was always, always hungry. He didn't really mean for food or indeed sex. But for that security. Because he always felt that threat looming. He had to keep winning. He knew what happened when you lost. When you no longer had any tangible value.

He picked up the fork and fed her a piece of the cake to stop her asking another question. Yet stupidly he couldn't help from admitting the tiniest truth to her.

'When I was little, my birthday was never celebrated. It was nothing to be celebrated.' Back then he'd only known what day it even was, thanks to Ellen. 'Ellen made me a cupcake once, when I was nine.'

He remembered it clearly. And the repercussions when the others had found out.

Jade was very still on his lap; he could feel her sudden tension. But her eyes had such light to them—they were so clear and vibrant and he couldn't look away from her even when it seemed that she was looking right into him and seeing the gnarled lump of nothing inside. 'You knew her then?' she prompted so softly.

'I've known her all my life,' he admitted simply and the long-sealed vat of poison bubbled up, bursting through the crust he'd thought indestructible. And he couldn't stop it. 'My birth mother was young. Her very uptight parents were horrified and the only reason I was even born was because by the time my existence was discovered, it was too late for me not to be.' He rested his head on the high-backed chair. 'She was so young she didn't even realise she was pregnant. Not too young to have a boyfriend from the wrong side of the tracks, though. A boy her father couldn't have disapproved of more. So, I was given up.'

'Adopted?'

'Not through the usual channels unfortunately. My grandfather didn't want anyone to know, so they sent my mother away and the second I was born they gave me to Nathan and Lena. Nathan had once worked for him—so it was a private arrangement. They were paid to take me, on

the condition that there would never be any communication
between my birth family and me. Certainly, there would
never be any contact between me and my mother. My connection to the whole family would be denied.'

Jade's jewel-like eyes softened. Of course, she understood the pain of that—she'd experienced similar in her
life with her own mother.

He knew she hated being kept in the dark. And she'd
shared her secrets with him. What did it matter for her to
know she wasn't alone? And it was because of that—and
the softness in her expression—that more spilled from him.

'My birth wasn't even registered at the time. But later
on, there was contact,' he said wryly. 'Because Nathan
and Lena only took me for that monthly pay-cheque. They
weren't interested in *me*, I was just a complete pain. Nor
were they interested in working… They only wanted their
next fix. They both left all the cooking and cleaning and
caring for me to Nathan's older half-sister.'

It took her only a moment. 'Ellen.'

'She did everything. She had done all her life. Everything for everyone. She'd left school early to care for her
mother, who got unwell after Nathan's birth, so she didn't
get a decent education. When their mum died, Ellen struggled to raise Nathan. He took huge advantage of her for
years. Lena then did the same—they treated her like their
slave. And they used her to look after me. And she was
so…worn, so downtrodden with years of that awful treatment, she just accepted it all.' It had frustrated the hell out
of him. 'But then the monthly money to cover my costs
stopped coming. So one day, when Ellen was at work, Lena
and Nathan took me back to my grandfather's house to
find out why.'

The bitterest, smallest details spilled out. 'It was my
ninth birthday when I met my grandfather for the first and
last time.'

Jade sat so still on his lap he didn't think she was even breathing. He wasn't sure he was either. He couldn't—because every pulse point in his body hurt.

'He wasn't interested, of course. He was irate. Yelling that he didn't want to see them *or* me. He'd screwed up some investment. Screwed up his marriage. Sure as hell screwed up his daughter. In the end he just slammed the door. As far as Nathan and Lena were concerned, if there was no money, they didn't want me any more. So they left me there—outside his locked gates. My grandfather didn't open them. So I was alone.'

He'd been terrified, because the only people he'd known there had driven off, leaving him in some city miles away from the one person who'd ever shown him any kindness.

'What happened?' Jade asked.

'Ellen came when she realised what had happened.'

'How long were you waiting?'

'I don't know,' he muttered. 'Hours. She didn't have a licence let alone a car. She had to bus and then walk and she'd only found out after she'd been at work all day. When she'd forced it out of a drugged-up, barely coherent Nathan.'

'You must have been terrified.'

'Cold and confused and starving.' The memories twisted inside. 'Ellen had made me that cupcake in the morning, but Nathan saw and before she left for work, he raged at her for wasting an egg on me. I was nothing but a drain on them then, you see. He smashed it in front of me after she'd gone. He was just so bloody *mean*.' Alvaro had hated him. 'But then, when it was dark, she came.' Finally, finally, he'd been too relieved to even cry. 'We never went back. She walked out on Nathan and Lena. She was finally furious enough to get past her own fear. Not for what they'd done to her. But to me. You should have heard how they used to talk to her. I'll never forget it.'

'And how did they talk to you?'

Yeah, he didn't forget that either. How unwanted he'd been. How useless. How, if he wasn't bringing them money, he wasn't worth anything.

'Ellen worked every job she could—taught me how a work ethic enabled a person to survive. Cooking, cleaning, picking crops, bussing tables, stocking supermarket shelves in the small hours…and she wasn't young then, Jade. And it was hard and some days there was nothing much to make a meal with. And I was so hungry.'

'So you worked hard too.'

He nodded. But he'd been on his own a lot—learning to cook as best he could, not just for himself, but for Ellen too. So she had something to come home to.

'My birth mother had been a kid who made a mistake. But her parents? They were wealthy and they could have afforded to do the right thing. They could have gone through a proper adoption agency or something. But they were too obsessed with their own perfect image. So they passed her little mistake—*me*—off to someone else—never taking responsibility, let alone any kind of care for anyone other than themselves.'

'What happened to her—your birth mother?'

'No clue.' He shrugged.

'And her boyfriend?'

'Apparently they paid him off too. My grandfather told me he took the money and didn't look back.'

'You've never tried to trace him?'

'I don't want to know,' he said bluntly. 'I don't need that rejection all over again. Ellen and I got through—we got out of it. I've never seen any of them again and I never, ever want to.'

'Alvaro, I'm so sorry.'

'I'm not,' he said, meaning it completely. 'Not any more. I don't need people like that in my life. People who only want to use you? Who're only interested when you have something to offer them—like money. Or status. People who can't stand there and take responsibility for their own damn actions.'

Jade looked upset and angry and he shouldn't have told her. But once he'd started he'd been unable to stop and now she was…

'They should have been more to you,' she said with a broken voice. 'They should have been there for you. They should have supported you.'

He shook his head. 'Having it hard made me better. Made me fight in a way that maybe I wouldn't have if everything had come easily. It made me appreciate Ellen and work my ass off to get her what she deserved.'

'What you deserved too.'

Yeah. Becoming strong, becoming independent, had been everything. He'd refused to be a 'burden' to anyone any more. He would repay Ellen a million times over. And he would always make his own way with full independence. And he would never, ever *need* anyone again the way he'd needed someone that day when he'd been abandoned.

Only now Jade was watching and to his absolute horror a need deep within him was unfurling…for *her*. He needed her. Right now.

To lose himself in, right? To find that mindless obliteration in sex with her. Because he didn't want—*couldn't* want—to need her any other way.

But he couldn't seem to move; his body was leaden. And his damned head hurt. Not just his head. His heart too. Everything. It all still hurt.

She carefully took the plate from him and picked up the black witch's hat that had been placed there as that stupid Halloween decoration, putting it on her head to make room for the plate.

He nodded, because it was perfect. She did bewitch him. And that was all this was, wasn't it? An ephemeral thing that wasn't even real. She was like a beautiful witch. She looked at him unlike any other woman he'd known too. There was heat certainly, but tenderness too. None of that avariciousness in her eyes, no awareness of any kind of quid pro quo, it was almost an innocence. It was, he finally realised, an authenticity. And now she curled into him, wrapping her arms around him, holding him in an embrace that he couldn't help returning. Enfolding his arms around her, feeling her soft skin and warm body, her gentle breath on his chest and the regular beat of her loving heart.

He should move, but he couldn't. She was like an anchor in his lap. Not letting him leave. Giving him something to hold onto. Herself. Just to hold, here and now. And suddenly he was so very tired. He'd kept all that in, all his life. And now?

He'd never been as exhausted. As aching. And as *okay*. It was the strangest feeling of release.

'Do you know what you are?' Her whisper was so faint he had to concentrate hard to hear her. 'All my birthdays and Christmases, rolled into one perfect present.'

Oh, but that was what she was for him. Unburdened by her crown, she was just Jade. And her gift to him was just herself. Not just her body, but her care too. He felt it flowing from her now. Everything.

'No,' he muttered as that most vulnerable part of his soul shrank from the burn of her tenderness.

But she rested her head on his shoulder and wouldn't let him go. 'I won't hurt you,' she whispered.

He should have scoffed at that soft promise, should have teased—*as if she could?*

Instead he closed his eyes and wished he could believe her.

CHAPTER TWELVE

ALVARO SLOWLY STIRRED the risotto, taking the time to make it creamy and rich and telling himself everything was just fine. It was only Christmas. Only a day in which there'd been a few smiles, a lot of sex, few words spoken. And what were words, after all? Mere moments that vanished with the next breath.

But he couldn't believe the words he'd uttered today. He never thought about his past, let alone raked it up and told someone else of that miserable, lonely rejection. But, he rationalised as he swirled figures of eight with the wooden spoon, she was about the one person in the world he could trust. A queen—keeper of total calm and self-containment. She was ultra-discreet in her own life and so wary of exposing anything to anyone for fear of it being splashed across the media. She was resolute. And he respected her for that even though it annoyed him on an intimate level. But he knew he didn't need to worry that she wouldn't keep his past private. His knowledge of her true identity was the secret that bound them both to confidence.

So it wasn't a fear of someone else knowing. No. The mistake he'd made ran deeper than some mere switch or even some mere affair. And it was more dangerous. Somehow her knowing, her seeing him, her *soothing* him had struck a vein within. And now that vein wanted to bleed even more.

The raw exposure was hideously uncomfortable. The irony was he'd *wanted* to tell her at the time. At the time it had actually felt good. He'd felt a deep peace after for all of…what…*all of the time you had her in your arms.*

For the first time in his life he'd fallen asleep on Christmas Day—slept half the afternoon away, like a damn baby.

Cuddling her. And when he'd finally stirred, she was still there. She'd lifted her head and smiled at him and he'd done the only thing he possibly could.

He'd kissed her. Silencing, not just her, but the voice in his head telling him he didn't deserve it…that he shouldn't allow it…because that other part of him, that long-ignored, tiny, tiny part was more desperate than anything for it to happen. For him to take what she offered. All she offered. Again and again like a glutton, because he'd been deprived too long. Like the damaged, undeserving man he was.

And for as long as he was touching her, it had been okay. But now? Now there was something akin to panic. But he couldn't suck it back. He couldn't *untell* her everything. He couldn't cut off the connection that had somehow been forged.

It doesn't matter.

Because she was leaving. And this would end. She was the queen of a small country on the other side of the world. They would have nothing to do with each other again after she returned home in only a few short days. This was merely an interlude for them both.

But now, as he reminded himself of that, his panic magnified.

He should end it now. But he couldn't. He shouldn't have let any of this happen and yet he still couldn't resist, still couldn't refuse himself these moments.

He carried two bowls of the risotto up to the tower. She was curled in a chair up there, looking out at the coastline as the sky began to darken and the beacon began its work. Her smile was quick when she saw him and he desperately needed distraction before he sank to his knees and spilled out the rest of his soul to her. Somehow she knew. She made light jokes about the juxtaposition of cheap candy and rich chocolate. And in the end there was nothing he could do but haul her close again. He was determined to expend every ounce of this desire. But no matter how many hours he spent with her in his arms it deepened still. Even when, beyond exhaustion, he still wanted her close.

It seemed the guy could do everything. He wasn't just strong and skilled, he was thoughtful—treating her to gourmet cakes and trashy take-out food, then cooking her a beautiful dinner. Making her move, making her laugh. And finding out the heartache he'd suffered had only made her appreciate his strength even more. The loneliness and the rejection that had given him such drive made her ache to her bones.

But he'd built a world for himself. He had not just a career but a whole company and ambition beyond. He'd made this his sanctuary, his security. She understood he needed freedom and independence. But in reality, he'd cemented his own isolation. Having glimpsed his background, she understood why. The problem—and it was *her* problem— was that she'd fallen in love with him. Deeply, completely in love with him.

She waited for a while—letting herself float through the next two days—hoping this emotion was just a wave of hype and hormones, a feeling that would pass like any other given enough space and time. Jade was used to managing emotions, she knew how to live with deep ones, how to keep them secret, how to mask them.

But this? This was too big, too raw, too unwieldy. She couldn't contain this; couldn't stop this; couldn't cope with it for too much longer. And while she knew he wanted her, he didn't *need* her. And she certainly didn't think he loved her. He was too controlled for that.

And even if he did, this couldn't go anywhere.

She needed to do what was best not just for her country. But for him too. And in this instance, yes, her own desires had to come behind his.

She couldn't ask him to live a life of restriction and duty in the way she had to. She couldn't ask him to sacrifice so much. He'd resent her eventually—as her mother had resented her father. And no way could they maintain a long-distance relationship either. She'd lived through separation with Juno and it was too hard to have someone you loved so far away for so much of the time. It would hurt her heart too badly.

So it was better to be over completely. And as soon as possible.

The conversation between them stayed light, but terribly fragile. It was as if he, too, was determined to make the most of these moments here. They walked on the beach, laughed about little unimportant things. Mostly they made love like wild animals every moment they could.

And the next morning, it happened.

'Do you mind if we don't drive back to Manhattan?' Alvaro said.

Her bruised heart lifted. 'What did you want to do?'

Did he want to escape somewhere else? Or stay here for ever? Either way she'd have said yes in a heartbeat.

'It's faster if we fly,' he explained.

Her heart plummeted. So stupid. She'd *known* it was coming. Because despite their physical connection, she'd felt him pulling back personally. She had too. They'd had no discussion of his past since Christmas Day, not hers either.

Light and easy. Remember? Light and easy and so very fragile.

It wasn't a long drive to the nearest town and a helicopter charter service there. It wasn't long in the air either. But every second passed like sixty—amplifying the time she had to think. And all the while certainty sank like a lead stone in the lake of her churning stomach acid.

There was only one course of action. She had to go home. She had to say goodbye to him now. Anything difficult was best done sticking-plaster-style—ripping it off in one swift motion. In this case, she decided, it was the *only* way.

From the helicopter port, Alvaro collected a car. She didn't know if he was planning to take her back to his apartment or not, but she knew she had to speak up. Now.

'Can you take me back to Juno's?' she asked as he started the engine. 'I have a couple of things there that I need.'

'Sure, we can go now. It won't take long.'

His easy-going accommodation of her request made her grit her teeth. The drive was familiar now. Her heart raced but she remained cool on the exterior.

As soon as he'd pulled over opposite Juno's apartment she drew in a deep breath.

'Alvaro, I'm going home.'

'You are home.'

'I mean to Monrova. Tonight.'

He killed the engine and swivelled to face her, his eyes wide. 'You're leaving New York tonight?' He looked stunned. 'I thought you had another couple of days—'

'I need to get back to Monrova. Something has…'

She trailed off; she couldn't bring herself to lie to him completely.

'Something has…?' he prompted. 'What something? It's not like you've had any calls—' He gazed at her intently.

She glimpsed emotion in his face. A flash of anger, swiftly smoothed by determined acceptance.

'That's it?' he said. 'That's all you can say?'

But she saw the bitterness of self-blame in his eyes. It was as if he'd expected it all along. And of course he would—she was always going to leave.

But not this soon.

They both knew that. And he took the reason, she realised, to be himself. That this was somehow his fault. She understood why he'd think it—it was what she would think too. Two people who'd been hurt before. Who'd blamed themselves before.

Regret burned the back of her throat. Too late she realised she'd just hurt him. In a way that hadn't needed to happen. He'd done nothing wrong; it wasn't *him*. Suddenly she couldn't leave without telling him her truth. Couldn't let him think she didn't care. Because she did.

Alvaro had been right when he'd said she needed to put herself first sometimes and say what she wanted. But really, he'd meant in sex. He'd not meant for them to become *emotionally* intimate. But they had. And in that too she needed to be brave.

More than that, she needed to do what was *right*.

She gripped the car door handle. She had to *tell* him. She couldn't let him think he wasn't wanted. And she couldn't hold back her own truth. Even though it would change nothing that could happen, it might help him understand. There would be the slightest soothing of her soul too—and hopefully his—just from the power of knowledge.

'I can say more,' she said tightly.

He didn't respond; he just stared at her as if he'd seen Medusa and been turned to stone.

'I have more to say.' Courage began flowing through her veins. 'I have to go now, Alvaro. You want to know why?'

'You've already said why. It's *something*.'

She nodded. 'It's you.'

His eyes dilated.

'Well, to be more correct, it's my feelings for you.'

He was utterly still but already she saw it in his gaze— the denial.

She'd always put duty before desire; protocol before the personal. But her reticence in sharing anything, in admitting anything, in asking for anything, had been more than so-called *duty*. In essence she'd always been afraid. Scared that if she said what she really wanted she'd lose what she loved most. That she'd be sent away—as her mother and her sister had been. But she was leaving now anyway. And speaking her truth wasn't just for him, but for herself too.

'I've fallen in love with you,' she said, amazed at her own calmness. 'I know you joked it might happen. But you weren't being arrogant, in fact you were selling yourself short. You're very easy to fall in love with.' She ran her tongue over her suddenly dry lips. 'You don't have to worry. I'm not proposing. I'm not asking you for a future. I know that's impossible. But I'm telling you how I feel. That's all. I'm trying to be *honest*.'

'No, Jade. I...' He actually looked sorry. 'I don't think this is true.'

'I'm doing the one thing you've encouraged me to do. I'm picking my favourite. And it's you.' Her equilibrium began to tilt. 'Only now you decide you don't want to hear it?'

'You're...' He shook his head. 'You've been very sheltered.'

'Are you about to suggest that I shouldn't trust my own feelings?' She glared at him.

His jaw clenched but he forced a breath. 'I'm about to suggest that you're inexperienced in these things.'

'And you aren't?'

He laughed. Short, bitter, *biting*.

'When did you last have a long-term relationship, Alvaro?' she challenged. 'When did you last open up to anyone?'

His smile vanished.

'Emotional intimacy is something you dodge like a vampire avoiding sunlight,' she snapped.

He stilled, silenced.

'Nothing to say to that?' she asked.

She didn't even want him to say anything now. She just wanted to run away. She didn't know what she'd thought would happen. As if confessing this would *help* in some way? That he might *appreciate* what she'd just *given* him?

Yeah, so wrong on that.

Anger bubbled—like none she'd ever felt.

'So your plan now is to leave?' He shifted in his seat. She could feel the tension streaming from him. 'Yes.'

'Why?' His cold gaze sliced through her. 'Why leave early when you've suddenly realised your feelings for me? Why miss out on the few days we have left? Are you too scared to see it through, Jade?' His accusation burned. 'You still don't really believe in your choices yet, do you?'

Why was he being so cruel?

'Because it's going to hurt me,' she said. 'And if I stay 'til the end, it will hurt more.'

'So, you'll admit love in one breath, but run away in the next?'

'It's not like you're perfect.' His antagonism riled her. 'You act like you have it all together. Like you're cool and all in control. You think you have your life just the way you want it and, sure, it's pretty good. To a point. But you're as much of a coward as I am. In fact, more so.'

'How do you figure that?' he snapped.

'Your awesome "independence"? Your whole refusal to be a burden to anyone? It's a cover, so you can hide and not open up, not let anyone in. Because if you let someone in, if you let someone shoulder what you've got going on in there…'

'Then what?' He dared her to say it, frigid rage on his face.

'Then they might leave you.'

He visibly withdrew. That iron anger hardened his amber eyes. 'I think that's *your* fear talking, Jade.'

'Sure. But it's *your* fear too. You choose to be alone. You choose isolation. And it's hurting you. You should find someone and make your own family.'

'You sound like Ellen.'

'She knows you better than anyone. And she's right,' Jade said. 'You deserve happiness and you should have it all with someone. You shouldn't lock yourself away the way you do.'

'I don't lock myself away. And I don't want a family.'

'Because you don't care?' She shook her head. 'That's *all* you do, Alvaro. *You* are the lighthouse. You're tall and strong and you care for people, you protect them. Like Ellen. Like your employees... But you don't just keep "safe reserves", Alvaro. You also have rocks around you, just like that lighthouse. They're your defence—warning people to stay away from you. Keeping you isolated. But lighthouses aren't fully automated machines, they still need care and attention. They still need a keeper to refuel them. They still need that source of power, at least that *one* person to keep them switched on. *You* need that.'

And so badly she wanted his one person to be her.

'And the irony is,' she said sadly, 'that bright light attracts us all. We're like moths. We want to be around you. To love you. Only you won't let anyone in.'

He didn't just look shocked. He looked horrified.

'Jade...' He paused for a moment, clearly searching carefully for the right words. 'I can't give you what you want.'

And they were the wrong words.

'This was only ever an affair,' he added. 'This wasn't meant to...'

'Become something more?' She knew that this was meant to have been nothing other than an escape for them both. But that didn't explain everything. And, heaven help her, she couldn't stop herself from asking. 'I can't walk away from you without being honest, Alvaro. And I won't allow you to do that either.'

'You won't allow it?'

'*You* encouraged me to speak up for my own desires. To demand what I wanted from you. So tell me.'

'Tell you what?' he suddenly exploded. 'And for what purpose? What *possible* benefit is there to this?'

For all his demands of her, that encouragement of her, *he* didn't talk. And now she was furious.

'*Why* did you do it?' she yelled at him.

'Do *what*?'

'Christmas Day on steroids. Why?'

He gaped. Then breathed. 'I didn't. I told you. I just phoned up a company and they set it all up.'

'At *your* suggestion,' she pointed out, her emotions slipping away again. 'But *you* thought of it. You went to that expense and the effort, because you took the time, you had the consideration. Why did you want to do that for me?'

He glanced away then. 'Maybe it wasn't for you. Maybe it was for me.'

'You?'

'You know I never had those things either.' Frustration ripped out of him. 'We have more in common than you might think, Jade. You had everything, but not the treats. I had nothing, and certainly not the treats. I figured we could both have them for once.'

'And that's all it was?' She didn't want to believe him. She'd wanted it to mean more. For it to have *mattered*.

'You only had three weeks, Jade,' he said, almost plaintively. 'Only a few days. It was your one Christmas of freedom. I wanted to make it good for you.'

'So you only took me there because you knew I was leaving?' she asked. 'You wouldn't have bothered otherwise? With any of it? So, really, it was pity?' He'd done it all because he felt *sorry* for her.

'No. It was a gift.'

A gift? Something nice for the poor, little rich girl? Christmas Day had just been a favour, a benevolent, charitable act? Hell, it had basically been a *job* for him. And sleeping with her in the first place had been a favour too.

Bitter disappointment broke her heart. *He* broke her heart.

And then she saw it on his face—the apology. She didn't want his *apology*. She wanted his love.

'Jade—'

'It's time for me to leave, Alvaro.' She tried to open the car door but it wouldn't open.

'Jade.'

'Now, Alvaro.' She *needed* him to let her leave.

And this time he listened. The car door locks unclicked. The door swung open. And Jade escaped.

CHAPTER THIRTEEN

THE SALON IN Monrova's Palace Monroyale was still decorated with tall fir trees dressed in scarlet and gold satin ribbons. The same way it had been decorated for the month
of December for decades—or at least, for all of Jade's life.
Everything was the same—as if she'd never been away or,
indeed, never been there at all. She passed the antique furniture knowing she should feel pride in their craftsmanship,
their preserved glory...instead they stifled her.

Jade wheeled her trolley case herself, smiling at the foot-
man's astounded expression as he held the door for her.

'Good morning.' She smiled tightly.

'Your Highness.' He blushed as he bowed.

She walked towards the west wing, where her private
apartment was situated within the palace.

'Your Highness.' Major Garland halted midway along
the wide corridor, a perplexed look wrinkling his very high
forehead. 'I thought you were—'

'In Severene, I know.' Jade kept walking. 'I apologise
for the confusion.'

'But—' His eyes had bugged almost out of his skull.
'You *are* in Severene, right now. With—'

'Clearly, I'm not,' Jade said crisply. She wasn't about
to waste time debating her identity with this supercil-
ious advisor who'd always seemed to sneer at her. 'The
princess who is currently in Severene is my twin, Juno.
I am Jade.'

Major Garland's mouth hung open for an unflattering
few seconds. 'But—'

'No buts, Major. It is truly me and if we need to get
the palace physician to verify it we can, or you can just
take me at my word. Juno and I switched places for a few

weeks but I've returned a couple of days earlier than we originally planned.'

'You…what?' A purple hue tinged the expanding frown on Major Garland's face. 'You switched places? As if you're twelve?' He straightened to glower down at her from his full height. 'May I remind you, Princess Jade—?'

'You may not,' she interrupted him. Because calling her 'Princess Jade' revealed exactly what he thought of her. That she was still a child. She wasn't. She was the Queen. And she was also tired and devastatingly heartsore and she grasped for the control expected of her. But, she realised, control didn't mean meekness and mildness. This was a time for honesty and assertiveness and getting what *she* needed—which was support and clarity. Neither of which, she finally realised, she was probably ever going to get from Major Garland. 'I'm the Queen, Major Garland, and I know what my obligations are and I do not need you or anyone else to tell me what I should or should not have done in the past, be doing now or, indeed, do in the future.'

His eyes widened and his mouth hung ajar for another moment. 'But—'

'I need you to gather my senior staff,' she said firmly. She raised her eyebrows at him when he didn't move. 'Now, please, Major.'

'Uh…' He swallowed. 'Of course, Your Majesty. I shall assemble everyone in the Rose Room.'

The Rose Room was a large, cold, uncomfortable conference space where her father had always met with his pompous advisors sitting before—and literally beneath— him at unfriendly rectangular tables. The hierarchy of the palace had been defined by the seating positions. The King himself had sat like some despotic dictator at his own table on a raised platform above them all. Jade had always hated sitting up there for them all to talk to her as if she were still two. 'Actually, I'd prefer not to use the Rose Room for this meeting, thank you, Major.'

His expression puckered as if he'd sucked on something sour. 'But—'

'It's too large and too cold for me. I'd prefer to meet everyone in the dining room.'

'The dining room?' He looked thunderstruck.

She would have laughed if she weren't so cold and tired.

'Yes,' she said, drawing in a calm response. She could keep calm and courteous, she was the *Queen* and she would not shout at any of her people. 'The table is large for us to all fit around. Let's meet in half an hour. We need to summon my assistant back from Severene.' She frowned thoughtfully. 'Actually, leave that to me. I'll sort that when I speak to Juno.'

Minutes later in the privacy of her apartments, she pulled Juno's phone from her pocket and finally turned it on. She'd avoided the task while she'd travelled home. Now she stared at the screen, but there was nothing. No ping, ping, ping of incoming messages. There wasn't even one—let alone any from the one person she wanted to hear from most of all.

Drawing a breath, she touched the keypad and called her sister.

'What's this about you being back in Monrova?' Juno asked instead of even saying hello.

'You've heard already?' Jade shook her head. Major Garland was *very* efficient. 'News travels fast.'

'Is everything okay?' Juno asked.

'More importantly, is everything okay with you?' Jade questioned. 'I heard…'

'I did something stupid,' Juno said quickly. 'But I'm fine. In fact, I'm better than fine…'

Jade gripped the phone, listening closely to her sister's effervescence as she confessed that she hadn't just 'jumped' King Leonardo. She'd fallen in love with him and he had with her. The joy was something Jade hadn't heard in her sister's voice in so long and she loved it. They planned to marry as soon as possible, meaning Juno would become the queen that Jade had always known her sister was capable of being. It was perfect and *everything* that Jade needed right now.

'You're going to live near.' Jade's eyes filled with the sweetest relief. 'You're going to be my neighbour.' It was a balm soothing her own devastation.

'Jade?' Juno suddenly paused. 'Is everything okay?'

'Better than okay.' Jade made herself nod. 'It was just time for me to come home. I'm ready, Juno, really ready to be here and do this the way I actually want to. I had a great time away. It was so good for me.'

None of that was a lie. She couldn't regret a moment of it. But she heard Juno's hesitation and her intake of breath and knew she was going to ask something difficult and unavoidable.

'Now, when's the wedding going to be?' Jade spoke again quickly to head off Juno's query.

She knew her sister could hear something in her voice. Even when they'd spent so many years apart, they could tell—there was no real ability to lie to each other. To conceal, yes, but not outright lie. So she had to distract. Fortunately, Juno fell for it, her happiness swamping her— making it impossible for her not to answer and share her joy.

Jade listened with pure delight and then they quickly made plans to front up to the press. The only way forward for them both was with honesty.

The irony that everything she'd done to save her sister's job was now rendered utterly pointless wasn't lost on Jade. She didn't even need to *tell* Juno about anything that had happened in New York. Certainly nothing about Alvaro. She couldn't anyway; she didn't want to say anything that would cause Juno to worry about her. She would let nothing diminish her sister's much-deserved happiness.

Juno and Leonardo the couple came as no real surprise. Jade had suspected there was something between them from the moment she'd seen those photos from the Monrova Winter Ball. And now, listening to Juno, she knew they brought the best out in each other. Some things were just meant to be.

She and Alvaro, however, were not.

He'd caught her eye from the first second—he was compelling and magnificent. But then, when he'd let her in? Let her really see him? Not just feel him, not just touch him, but be with *him*—his intelligent and laughing, protective and vulnerable, utterly passionate self?

But Alvaro hadn't argued, hadn't begged her to stay, hadn't really said anything when she'd told him she loved him. And he certainly hadn't wanted to hear what she'd finally been brave enough to say. And that hurt her deeply. She'd never said that to *anyone* before.

While on the one hand he'd given her so much—a joie de vivre and an inner confidence she'd been missing—he'd also devastated her. Because she wanted everything else from him too. She wanted *him*. And for the briefest of moments, she'd thought he wanted her too.

But he didn't.

The afternoon she returned to Monrova—having liaised with Leonardo and Juno, and with her assistant back by her side to help—she read her prepared statement to the teleprompter. She'd watched King Leonardo make his statement and then take a couple of questions only moments before her live cross. Beside him, Juno had looked beautiful—she was literally glowing. It was the only thing that got Jade through the broadcast.

What got her through the next couple of days was pure grit. She called on Serena, her assistant to work through switching up her daily schedule and her long-term commitments, finally changing some of the routine that her father had imposed on her life for so long. Finally, she felt liberated and able to make her own calls. Hiring a new personal trainer was going to be one of them, she laughed at herself. Calm but nervous, questioning herself but with growing confidence in her own choices, she began. *She* was going to be okay—eventually. Because she'd found her own voice.

But at night her mind wandered and she remembered things that were so wonderful, but so bad for her. She'd asked for what she wanted from Alvaro. Repeatedly. And he'd given it to her. He'd listened. He'd not minimised her desires as the irascible wishes of a spoilt princess, but seen them for what they were—the real, secret desires of a lonely woman who'd wanted to *feel* something for once. Who'd yearned to be wanted in return.

She'd been such a fool about that bit. He'd just been giving her the fairy tale for a fortnight. Because, for just a fortnight, he could. He could deliver every desire, every dream…because it was finite and it was only physical. Because there was not and never would be a future in it. And that was safe for him, wasn't it?

But the second she'd suggested that there might be a future?

That was when he'd pulled back. Because he hadn't meant any of it. He *had* just been indulging her. *Spoiling* her. Like the poor little rich royal she was.

For the first time she understood why people did such stupid things for lust. It fogged the mind and got so far beneath your skin, it made you reckless. It felt so good, you didn't care about possible dangers or consequences or repercussions. She imagined it was like a drug.

Jade hadn't been an addict before. Hadn't craved anything the way she craved physical contact with Alvaro.

His touch. His kiss. His care and attention. She missed it. He'd so arrogantly teased her that she'd fall for him. But it wasn't *him*, was it? Wasn't it just his body? The way he could make her feel? A physical response?

But it wasn't. Because the physical frustration she could survive. The tear in her heart and in her soul?

She liked herself more when she was with him. Being around him, she felt free to say what she wanted, without having to be polite about it. People had looked at her all her life. They'd stared—endlessly. But no one looked at her the way he looked at her. As if he really saw her—the soft, secret, most vulnerable, most human part of her. And no one had wanted to listen the way he wanted to either. She'd trusted him. And in the end, she'd trusted him with everything. She'd trusted him with her heart.

That was when he'd let her down. But even then, when she was honest with herself, she knew he hadn't. It wasn't his fault he didn't want to carry that burden. She'd been wrong even to ask him. Hadn't she seen how terrible it was for someone to be caught here—in the palace—when the relationship wasn't right? And it had been less than a fortnight—to be irrevocably changed by one person?

And even if he had been—even if by just a fraction of the way she had? It made no difference to the inevitable impossibility of *them*. His company was everything to him as her country was everything to her. There could be no compromise. It wouldn't be fair on either of them.

But as it was, he'd *not* been changed. At the end of the day, he didn't care for her the way she did for him.

He had not fallen in love with her.

Alvaro's phone rang. He glanced at the screen and grimaced. This was one call he couldn't decline.

'Hey, Ellen.' He braced for incoming attitude.

'I've just seen that friend of yours on the television.'

Yeah, he'd seen it too. Over and over. But Ellen had obviously only just caught up with it on the late-night news show.

'She's a queen, Alvaro. You didn't tell me that.'

'I know.'

He didn't want to talk about her. Didn't want to think about her. But he'd been unable to do anything else for hours. Seeing her at that press conference—all regal in the palace courtyard—she'd looked so different, so distant. Monrova was a whole world away from him.

Ellen was quiet. Yeah, they didn't talk about the things that hurt. What was the point?

'How was Christmas dinner?' he asked heavily. 'All those potatoes get eaten?'

'Every one.' Another long pause. 'Alvaro?' Ellen mumbled. 'Are you okay?'

She'd named him, this woman. She'd raised him. She'd protected him. She'd done the best she could, as he had for her. It sure as hell hadn't been perfect. But after their escape, at least, it had definitely been better than okay.

But no. He wasn't okay now. He was angry. Jade had turned everything upside down. Jade had made him want. She'd made him wonder. And she'd made him dream.

Distant, unattainable, *impossible* dreams.

And he couldn't even go to the lighthouse to escape any more.

'I'm fine, Ellen,' he lied. Because there was no way he could burden her with the truth. Not when she'd done everything she could for him already. This was his own agony to endure. 'I need to go. I have a meeting I can't miss. I'll call you later.' But there was one thing he suddenly realised he needed to admit—one fact she deserved to hear. And had deserved to hear for years. One thing neither of them ever admitted.

'Thanks for calling.' The words choked in his throat. 'I love you, Ellen.'

There was another silence. 'I love you too.' She sounded as rusty as he had.

Alvaro ended the call and pressed his phone to his aching chest and figured maybe Jade would've been pleased.

And maybe he could get used to saying such things.

CHAPTER FOURTEEN

'I WOULD PREFER the trinity tiara, Major Garland.'

'Are you sure? Your father, the King, preferred—'

'The crown of Monrova is too heavy for me on a sustained walkabout.' She already had a slight headache; she didn't need to make it worse. She saw the Major pause, but she spoke again before he could. 'I'm sure you'll agree.'

'Of course, ma'am.'

'Thank you.'

Within half an hour the tiara was delivered to her suite from the Royal Jewel House. Jade sat patiently as her maid styled her hair around it. The waiting crowd was larger than usual this year. They were curious about the twin switch. There had been some criticism in the press, but she'd had a swathe of public support online as people defended her right to have a private holiday away. And everyone was entranced by Leonardo and Juno—their happiness simply radiated all the way here from Severene. They were the perfect fairy tale.

But today marked the end of Jade's holiday period and her royal obligations resumed, beginning with the New Year's Day message and a brief walkabout just beyond the palace gates. It was the first chance her people had to see her since that media conference of a couple of days ago.

When it was time, Jade took a minute to calmly breathe before stepping out beyond the palace wall and into the small arena in the centre of her city. Immediately the crowds cheered. Their sonic wall of warmth lifted her spirits. She squared her shoulders and her smile came naturally—more openly with the more people she greeted. Finally, she settled in.

'Thank you for coming out in this cold.' She spoke softly

to well-wishers while her assistant gathered their offered bouquets.

'Lovely to have you back, Queen Jade.'

'It's lovely to be home.' She beamed, appreciating how true her response was.

She was here, doing what she'd been born to do. And she would do it her way. She walked along the barrier that had specially been erected, taking the time to talk to as many people as she could.

Towards the end of her time a prickle of awareness skated over her skin. Turning, she scanned the crowd, having the oddest sensation of being watched.

Duh. Of course, you're being watched.

But it felt as if *Alvaro's* gaze were upon her. That electrified sizzle swept over her skin. But he was so tall, he'd literally stand above most others and she'd spot him—wouldn't she—if he were here?

No. That was the stuff of films and fantasies—pure wishful thinking. He was on the other side of the world, working on his strategic plans, all alone in his lighthouse. Right where he wanted to be. So she smiled again and, with a final wave, allowed her security team to sweep her back inside.

She swiftly returned to her private apartment. Later this afternoon she'd arrange a meeting to reorganise her schedule. She'd felt briefly invigorated from that interaction with the public, and she wanted more of it. But right now, she was eager to get out of her dress and tiara and have a moment to breathe again.

She didn't get it. Her phone rang a bare three seconds after she'd dismissed her maid and closed the door. It was her own mobile phone—she'd had Juno's one couriered back to her, not wanting to stare at it in the hope Alvaro might call. And it was her twin ringing now.

'Juno?' Jade answered briskly. 'Is everything okay?'

'Why must you think something's wrong every time I phone?' Juno joked. 'But in truth, I have just been in touch with palace security.'

'Oh? Why?'

'You need to go to the Rose Room now,' Juno said.

'Why?' Jade hated the Rose Room.

'I haven't time to explain, but trust me, Jade. Go there now.'

Her sister ended the call before Jade could ask anything more.

She didn't want to go. She hadn't even had the chance to get changed. Feeling a little sorry for herself, she hoped it wasn't Juno's idea of something fun. She wanted to curl in a ball, cuddle a hot-water bottle and hide.

Step. Up. You're the freaking Queen of Monrova.

Alvaro Byrne had to admit, he was intimidated as hell. And damn if he didn't feel sorry for Jade right now. The palace was stunning but definitely designed to awe and humble the average person and this room was the worst. It looked like something from a movie set in medieval times—a throne on a dais, dust motes hanging in the gloom, despite those magnificent stained-glass windows. All it needed was an executioner in a suit of armour waiting with his axe…or maybe that was just how Alvaro was feeling on the inside. As if he were about to beg for mercy—plead for his life, from the most powerful person he'd encountered. And that wasn't anything to do with her crown.

He'd been unable to admit it—not for days and least of all to himself. He'd thought he was invincible—that he had everything he wanted and needed and was happy enough. But the happiness he'd felt in those few days with her?

Whole. Other. Level.

He'd tried to blame it on euphoria—on an ephemeral spell of sex and hormones.

Bull. Shit.

The soul-destroying gap in his heart—in his life—as she'd walked out, taking away the one thing he'd wanted most of all before he'd even registered how desperately he needed and wanted and, yes, loved her.

Today he'd watched her on her walkabout from across the road, leaning against the corner of a building at a safe, unrecognisable distance. The crowds had been huge and had rushed that flimsy-looking fence when she'd appeared. But they'd been respectful. She'd taken her time—shared smiles and said how delighted and excited she was for her sister. Easily sidestepping questions about what she'd done in Manhattan during her switch. She'd managed to avoid any mention of him and he'd convinced his staff to say nothing about 'PJ' to the press. To his pleasure, they'd all agreed. And he knew it wasn't to please him, it was to support her. In such a short time she'd earned their respect and loyalty—and yes, their sense of protectiveness.

He'd got the same vibe from the throngs gathered here. Watching her on the walkabout, he'd decided it was because of the quiet kindness that was somehow so obvious, despite her restrained, almost demure appearance. She'd looked beautiful in a long-sleeved, pretty-patterned winter gown in green, a short cape keeping her shoulders warm. She'd had no problems in high-heeled boots on those old cobblestones. Her hair was half up, half down, intricately entwined somehow in that gleaming diamond tiara with its trio of emeralds. She couldn't have looked more picture-perfect regal—graceful and elegant, dignified and remote. Yet those eyes of hers had been so filled with emotion. She was, he knew, so very human.

He also knew he wasn't worthy of her. But he couldn't stay away. He couldn't stop himself from being selfish. Only she'd say he wasn't, she'd say he *deserved* it—happiness. Well, so did she.

The double doors suddenly swung inward, two liveried footmen attending each. Alvaro braced. Nothing like a dramatic opening. He stood where he was, in the centre of that vast room, as the Queen of Monrova walked in.

The doors sealed shut behind her. The quiet thud of their closure reverberated around the room. The Queen stopped just inside the room and stared at him.

She didn't smile, instead she turned paler and paler.

'Jade—' He broke off as she flinched.

Every muscle chilled and he couldn't move. But she visibly pulled herself together.

'Alvaro.'

Hearing his name on her lips jump-started his brain.

'Getting into this palace is a challenge,' he said. 'I tried to phone you. I got Juno instead. But she was helpful.'

'Why are you here?'

He half smiled; she had a good brain. But sometimes, even good brains couldn't figure out the blindingly obvious right away—especially when there was fear involved. He knew that one personally. Fear stopped normal function. Fear made people freeze. And she'd frozen right now—just as he had. But he was breathing again. And he could win this. Yet suddenly another emotion rose in him—and it wasn't the one it ought to have been. It was anger.

'You think it's okay to tell someone you love them and then just walk away? Walk out with no intention of ever returning? Ever getting in touch again? Of leaving for *life*?'

Jade's heart thundered at his sudden flare. She was still grasping the fact that he was here—that somehow her inner radar had got it right. And he'd come to…*yell* at her? Absurdly, that didn't upset her, because she was suddenly too furious herself.

'I thought that's what you wanted,' she snapped back at him.

'You didn't give me a second to know what I wanted.'

'You didn't know already?'

The banked heat in his gaze exploded. 'You didn't even try to fight. For the last few days...' He dragged in a breath, visibly trying to calm down. 'I've been so angry. Too furious to think straight. But then the fury died and I was left in hell.' He shook his head and slowed himself down. 'It was only then that I began to think.'

Jade stared at him, her own fury evaporating as swiftly as it had risen.

'And I realised you did fight. Just by telling me how you felt about...' He trailed off, his expression softening. 'That was you fighting. Speaking up? That's big for anyone, and huge for you. But I said nothing. I'm sorry, Jade. I was so stunned—not just by what you said, but by you. And I was so scared I couldn't think. Even when, yes, I knew the answer already. It terrified me.'

Her chest tightened under strain, as if her ribs were shrinking or her heart were getting bigger.

'Do you know, it's so damn hard to get anywhere near you? You say I'm isolated—some people might think this is a *prison*.'

'It's my home,' she said, fierce pride enveloping her. 'It's not a prison to me.'

'No.' He nodded. 'I watched you today, and this is where you belong. You shine everywhere, Jade. But most of all, here.' He stepped closer. 'And it's why you left me, isn't it? Because you thought there was no way this could work out.'

Her poor heart broke all over again. Because that was true.

'But you can't give something like that only to then take it away again.' He actually waggled his finger at her.

'I wanted to leave it with you. I wanted you to treasure it.'

'So you didn't mean it?'

She drew breath to stave off the sharp stab of pain. He took advantage of the second to step closer still, only he was smiling.

'Do you think you could give me a second chance, Jade?'

Of course. Always.

But her only response was to tremble.

'The problem is,' he explained quietly, '*that* memory isn't enough for me. I want more. I want to wake up with you every morning and to go to bed with you every night. I want to have as many moments of as many days together as we can. I don't want us to be apart, Jade. You know why.' He finally reached her, finally put his hands on her waist, grounding her here in reality to hear him. 'Because I love you.'

All she could do was blink, trying to clear the blurring tears so she could see properly…because she was trying to *believe*?

His lips twisted. 'It's hard to trust, isn't it?' He lifted his hand to touch her hair. 'Hard to believe that someone might accept you, want you, love you…just for you, just as you are. That even if you have nothing, were no one, even if you didn't do the things expected of you…that you would still be loved. I didn't just find it hard to believe that someone could feel that for me, it was impossible. That's my problem. Believing. Trusting. Even though it's the thing I want more than anything else in the world, from the person I want more in the world. I'm sorry I let you go. I'm sorry I let you down. I'm sorry you ran so quickly before I could think. But I've done nothing except think since. And do you know what I've realised?'

Impossibly overwhelmed, she shook her head.

'Wanting love. Wanting fun, friendship, laughter and, of course, fantastic sex…all those things shouldn't be out of the ordinary for anyone. It shouldn't just be a "treat day" thing. And we shouldn't have to feel excessively grateful for getting something we *all* should have. We all deserve.' His hands tightened on her waist—energy passing through his skin to her. 'It's too close to feeling *guilty*, Jade. As if we don't deserve it in some way. As if we should feel grateful for crumbs… I want the whole damn cake. Why shouldn't any of us get a cake? Jade, you should have a cake. So should I.' He lifted one hand and cupped her face with his big strong palm. 'I love you. Every beautiful thing about you. What do you say, sweetheart?' He brushed away her tear with his thumb. 'Say something. Anything.'

'I love you too.'

His smile was slow and still nervous and so heartfelt. 'I was really hoping you'd say that.'

The skim of his lips over hers was like a gossamer graze. The gentlest gift—not *tentative*, but as if he too were still slightly wary of believing this was real. Like a swimmer dipping only a toe in the water rather than diving straight in, in case the depth was deceptive. She kissed him back as softly—it was so rare, this connection. And then the emotion overwhelmed her so much she shuddered—she'd missed him so much. And then his arms were tight and his mouth hungry and the kiss was everything—all the passion absolving all the absence and her heart soared.

He released her suddenly, breathless and hoarse. 'I have something for you.'

Her heart thundered as he put his hand in his pocket. His smile curved as he pulled his fist out. She knew he held something small and suddenly everything was moving too quickly.

'Alvaro—'

He flipped his hand and unfurled his fingers so she could see what sat in his palm. A metal ring, yes. But it was a key ring. A single house key was attached, together with a silver charm of a little lighthouse. She instantly understood that it was a key to his cottage. He wanted to share his sanctuary with her.

'You can go there any time,' he muttered, still breathless. 'I'll always meet you. I'll always share everything I have with you.'

Her heart melted but at the same time an agony of uncertainty slammed into her. *How* was this going to work? 'I want this. I want you. But...'

'You're worried about protocol? Because I'm not a prince?'

'You're a prince to *me*,' she said sadly. 'But you don't understand what this world is like.'

'That's true.' He laughed as he looked around the stuffily ornate room. 'But I'll learn.'

'You need time.' She felt terrified. What if he hated it? What if—?

'*I* don't need time, sweetheart, but I understand that you do.' He cupped her face again. 'We'll take it slow.'

How could there possibly be slow? Once people—the world—found out she was in a relationship, the pressures that would come on them would be immense.

'You live on the other side of the Atlantic,' she fretted. 'You run a massive company that's been your life... I can't ask you to give that all up.'

'Do I have to give it up?' Smiling gently, he slowly shook his head.

'The politics and business...' she muttered. 'It gets complicated.'

That soft amusement in his eyes deepened. 'Do you know what I do, Jade?'

'Buy companies. Develop them.'

'Actually, mostly I just problem-solve. I like complicated. I like challenge. And you problem-solve too. You're good at it.'

But there were problems, and there were *problems*. And

surely this was impossible. 'I can't ask you to move here.' She shook her head sadly. 'I won't ask that of you. It won't work. It won't last.'

'You're thinking of your parents.' He put his broad palm on her spine and drew her to rest against him. He was her tower of strength. 'I know you've been stuck in your palace a bit, darling, but times have changed, and technology with it. If I can work from my lighthouse, I can work from here when we're ready.'

She wanted to believe him so very much.

'But it worries me that they're going to hound you. So what if we steal some more time together before anyone has to find out about us?'

Her heart fluttered and she lifted her head to look into his eyes—warm amber shone at her. 'You want to be my secret boyfriend?'

'Desperately.'

'I want you to myself.' Just for a while. And then? Excitement suddenly poured through her body as she suddenly realised this was all real. All true. 'I want you for ever,' she confessed. 'So much.'

His expression lit up. 'Well, why don't you show me your secret passages, then, my lady?'

With a giggle, she grasped his hand. 'You'll have to follow me.'

His fingers curled tight around hers. 'Gladly.'

She led him along the still, quiet corridor to her private apartment.

'Oh, this is…better.' He glanced around her lounge.

'I've ordered new cushions,' she assured him.

'Fantastic.' He laughed and hauled her into his arms. 'I can be patient, Jade.'

But his hands and body said the absolute opposite. Jade simply swooned against him.

'We'll do the proper protocol,' he promised. 'Whatever

your palace people want, but only when *you* want, your timeline, sweetheart. Because you're worth waiting for and this is your call. Whenever, however, this has to be, then I'll be here. I'm all in.'

'You don't mind all the hoops?' Her eyes filled again as he moved against her with such powerful passion. 'There'll be so many hoops.'

'As long as you don't mind stealing away to the light-house with me sometimes,' he whispered, his breath lost. 'That's my wish.'

'Mine too.' She shuddered. 'I would love that. Because I love you.'

She moved with him, their breathing aligned, their hearts beating in time.

He held her close and tight, the way she loved, and his smile, his love, shone down on her.

'Then that's what we'll do.'

CHAPTER FIFTEEN

New Year's Day, one year later

JADE GENTLY SQUEEZED Alvaro's hand twice as they stepped away from the woman and young child—their pre-agreed wordless signal that she was finally ready to finish. This walkabout had taken even longer than last year's, but Juno and King Leonardo had arrived from Severene to attend as a special surprise. The crowds had roared ecstatically, constantly calling questions to the couple about their sweet daughter, Alice, currently fast asleep in Monrova palace.

The second they were back within the palace walls, Leonardo wrapped his arm around his wife's waist to bring her closer. Watching, Jade melted inside. She'd never seen Juno so happy, nor Leonardo so demonstrative. He visibly adored his wife and child and it filled Jade with such satisfaction.

She glanced up and saw Alvaro's gaze on her—his smile tender and teasing and so knowing.

She smiled back. 'I'm happy for her.'

'I know.' This time his hand tightened on hers. 'It's time for us to refuel, yes? Because that took longer than anyone was expecting, right?'

Well, that was because everyone had wanted to see *him*. After getting over their delight at seeing Juno and Leonardo, the crowds had been momentarily stunned to see Alvaro step forward beside Jade. Until today he'd hung back at official events, happy to accompany her but remain 'in the shadows', as he'd put it. As if he ever could be anything like invisible. And for ages now, the public had been asking to see and hear more from him. So she'd been thrilled when he'd agreed to join her today.

They'd had almost six months to themselves at first. Stealing away, solidifying that passion and playfulness that had sparked from the moment they'd met. Then, of course, the press had found out. Alvaro had begun visiting Monrova 'officially' and eventually 'palace sources' had confirmed he was the Queen's consort. Another six months later, he'd been proven right again as they'd problem-solved their way through constitutional traditions, so now it was accepted that he was with her here in Monrova more often than he wasn't.

But they'd gone to the States for Christmas. In early December they'd invited Ellen to visit Monrova and attend the Winter Ball as Jade's special guest. It had been the best ball ever because of that, in Jade's opinion. Then Jade and Alvaro had accompanied Ellen home and actually stayed at her house for Christmas dinner for the first time—with Alvaro's special butter and no work whatsoever. Then the two of them had headed to the lighthouse for their own private Christmas night.

Now Jade glanced at the dining table in her private apartment and turned to Alvaro. 'What's this?'

'Just a little something delicious.' He shrugged carelessly, but the warmth in his gaze was a total giveaway.

The chocolate cake was glazed in a shiny, rich ganache and looked so gorgeously lickable that it gave Jade a few ideas. 'It's not my birthday,' she teased with a slow blink.

'Can we only enjoy cake on special occasions?' he asked, just as sweetly innocent.

Her smile turned a little wicked and her mouth watered. Jade picked up the knife. The cake looked dreamily indulgent, but as she cut into it the blade skimmed over something hard in the centre. She shot Alvaro a suspicious glance. He merely raised his eyebrows.

She tried again and this time, when she removed a

wedge, she discovered not a cascade of candy inside, but that a small box sat in a hidden centre cavity.

She stared for a split second, then her heart sprinted and her lungs tightened. Because she knew what was going to be in that box. She had to drop the knife on the table because her fingers were suddenly nerveless.

'Jade?'

Her eyes were already watering.

He reached out and took her hands, turning her to face him. 'Marry me,' he said simply. 'Be my queen.'

Exhilaration flooded her even as those tears trickled.

'Does this really come as a surprise to you, sweetheart?' He softly wiped the tears before gently kissing her. There was such promise and such truth in that kiss.

She drew a shuddering breath and pressed closer, overwhelmed with longing and an urgent need to love him completely. It was her only possible answer at that point.

He rapidly shifted, understanding her need as always. In record speed he got her on the sofa—and as searing need stormed through her he caressed her, as unleashed as her in moments.

'I've got you.' He held her tightly and kissed her burning skin. 'I'm here.'

And he was—with her, around her, in her, not just her anchor but her lighthouse—protecting her, here for her. And as he enveloped her with his strength and size, she couldn't hold him tightly enough. He was her everything and he gave her everything—all of himself. She arched to meet him, straining to gift him the same, until she could no longer contain anything and she crumpled completely in an explosion of love.

When she could finally open her eyes, his lips curved in a twist of that old arrogance. 'Aren't you ever going to answer me?' he teased as he gazed into her soul. 'I've been patient so very long…'

She smiled—as if she hadn't answered him already? But she knew that he needed words as much as he needed touch and action, just as she did. And, as always, he was impossible to deny.

'Yes,' she breathed as her heart burst with fullness. 'Always and for ever, *yes*.'

* * * * *

STOLEN TO WEAR
HIS CROWN

MARCELLA BELL

To Eileen M. K. Bobek and the Romance Rebels.

CHAPTER ONE

MINA ALDABA SMOOTHED her palms over her hair as she took a deep breath. The motion wouldn't do anything against the strengsth and determination of her curls to frizz—even if there was enough moisture in her palms to give it some hold—but it felt purposeful. On the other side of the ornately carved door in front of her sat the men and women of Parliament—the people whose decision would dictate whether or not she finally kept her promise to her father.

Like her hair, she was determined and untamable. She had done everything she could, with a full heart and to the very best of her ability—and that had carried her to this side of the door, inches away from the chance to achieve everything she had ever wanted.

The rest was up to the men and women inside.

The thought set off a series of stuttering palpitations in her chest—and not the kind that could ever be confused with excitement.

This next part was up to fate. The only thing she could do was be herself, trust her knowledge, and hope that that would carry her through. Unfortunately, faith wasn't one of her stronger virtues. She hadn't gotten to this side of the door by wishing. She'd done it by force of will and desire, continuous studying and practice, so she would be ready to deliver when the opportunity came.

Now was that opportunity.

She could steel her spine even if she couldn't calm her stomach.

She wore her usual black pantsuit and white blouse. Selecting one size up and choosing a square cut lent her hyper-feminine figure some much-needed gravitas. The hard lines of the design concealed any hint of curve—which she appreciated, given her very round derrière and rather Rubenesque chest. Dressing her figure for academia—or, more accurately, concealing her figure for academia—was a challenge that she hadn't anticipated when she'd decided to become a scientist at twelve years old.

Still, one had to accept what one had.

She would never forget the day a female colleague had taken her aside about it, though.

"You're going to have to do something about all of that."

Her fellow doctoral candidate had spoken blithely as she'd gestured in a vague circle toward Mina's jeans-clad rear and her breasts with a long red fingernail.

"It's just too much," she'd added. *"You'll never be taken seriously."*

At the time, the words had stung, but Mina was grateful for them. Her colleague had been right. The thin old uni sweatshirt she'd been wearing that day had stretched across her full chest, and her jeans had been form-fitted. She'd looked like the student she had always been, rather than the professional academic she was becoming, and the world she'd been about to enter was cutthroat, old-fashioned, and antagonistic—especially if you happened to have been born with female anatomy.

As soon as she had transformed her attire, her work had begun to garner more attention. Her male colleagues, it appeared, had been able to focus on it, rather than her.

Thankfully, she had mastered those ropes long ago—so well, in fact, that she was now in line to reap the highest professional reward: an interview for the appointment of an adviser to the King of Cyrano.

In preparation, her dense chocolate-brown curls had been ruthlessly brushed back from her face, heavily gelled, and confined into a thick French braid. Today—a day in which when she couldn't afford to have even a single hair out of place—she had used nearly double the amount of product to tame the springy, indomitable mass.

She had learned long ago to avoid putting her hair in a bun. Too many academics harbored sexy librarian fantasies.

The combination of the suit and the braid created a no-nonsense image—that of a serious academic. It was precisely what Mina wanted to project. Especially since she was the youngest candidate ever to sit for a parliamentary interview—and only the second woman ever nominated.

The door cracked open, and a page popped his perfectly coiffed head out.

Standing too close to the door, Mina jumped back with a quiet squeak.

The page lifted an eyebrow. "They'll be ready for you in just moment, Dr. Aldaba."

She nodded, replying, "Thank you," but the young man had already gone back inside.

Mina took another deep breath, her mind spinning. *It's almost time, Papa.*

She felt, rather than heard, the ghostly whisper of his reply: *"Cyrano is counting on you."*

Though he was long gone, her father's words were as alive as ever in her heart and mind. He'd said the same thing before every one of the significant milestones he had been alive to witness. That had amounted to thirteen years' worth of first places, gold stars, and academic honors. And then no more.

Mina shook her head, trying to clear it. There would be time for bittersweet melancholy later. Thirteen years might not have been long to have a father, but it had been long enough for them to develop a shared dream—one that she was determined to see to fruition today.

She had gone over potential interview questions for ten hours the previous day, digging up and scouring over old questionnaires from dawn until dusk, taking only short breaks for meals.

She had gone to bed at a reasonable hour, awoken early, and eaten a balanced breakfast, and then spent another hour in preparation before leaving her apartment for the interview.

The door opened again, this time fully. The page stepped into the hall and gestured for her to enter. "They are ready for you, Dr. Aldaba."

Her stomach lurched, but this time she merely nodded to the page with a confidence she didn't feel. "Thank you," she said, her voice steady and strong despite the butterflies rioting in her gut.

She walked in.

If all went well, she would walk out into a new future.

"Members of Parliament," she said, once she stood beside the interview seat. She had settled on that form of address after practicing every single acceptable salutation listed in Cyrano's official protocols. Giving the appropriate formal bow, she added, "I am honored to be here before you today."

She sat in the provided chair. It had a plain wood frame and legs, with leather cushions studded onto its seat and backrest. To its left sat a small side table, set with a microphone and a bottle of water.

Years of declining invitations and losing friendships for the sake of study flashed through her mind—as well as the exhaustion of her constant efforts to cultivate her academic image. To get here had required near-continuous drive, laser-like focus, and every ounce of passion she had. She had lived with singular tunnel vision, blocking out the rest of the world, for this moment.

And then the vetting began.

Two hours later the open question session ended, followed by a five-minute break before the voting.

Silence and time stretched on while Mina waited, stiff-backed, wrung-out, and entirely at their mercy.

Five minutes and an entire lifetime later, Parliament returned and the vote began. First, in the far upper right of the assembly, a green light flickered on. Then, in the middle of the room, another. Then, like a sea of green gently flashing to life, every light in the room turned green.

A tingling sensation filled her body, running the length of her skin and making her feel as weightless as if she were flying through thin, icy air, with the wind brushing against her skin, her mind scattered and light.

She had done it. She had just been appointed advisor to the King of Cyrano.

The prime minister stood and the rest of the people in the room rose from their seats, Mina included.

"Congratulations, Dr. Aldaba," he said. "Your appointment has been approved. We know you will be a credit to Cyrano and advise our King wisely."

There was no stopping the wide smile that broke across her face as she bowed, saying, "Thank you, Members of Parliament, it will be my honor to serve."

In her mind, she screamed, *We did it, Papa!*

And then the thick antique door came crashing inward, slamming onto the tiled floor with an earsplitting crack.

Men in riot gear rushed into the room—a wave of Kevlar and gunmetal-gray that tackled Mina to the ground before she could suck in enough air to scream.

An officer yanked her arms back, pressed a knee into her spine, and secured zip ties around her wrists and ankles.

"What is the meaning of this?" the prime minister demanded. "You cannot barge into Parliament like this!"

One of the officers responded, "King's business, sir."

Another representative shouted, "Excuse you! This is the House of Parliament. Our business takes precedence here!"

Even so, Mina was lifted none too gently and trundled away from the nightmare that her greatest dream had become.

After a dizzying series of twisting hallways and stone passageways, she and her captors arrived at their destination. At least, she deduced it was their destination when they deposited her on the floor in front of another large wooden door, this one just as thick, but humble compared to the door of Parliament. They cut her free from the zip ties.

"You are to go inside," one of the men in riot gear said.

Mina stood, did her best to straighten herself out, and reached a shaking hand out to touch the door. When her fingers touched wood, it was as if the world turned over. Her heart tumbled with the sense that a different reality lay on the other side.

Sucking in a slight gasp of air against sudden vertigo, she pressed her palm against the door. It slid open silently at the slight pressure of her hand, revealing an intimate room. The scent of fading incense filled her nostrils as her eyes adjusted to the dimmer light inside.

A red-carpeted center aisle with pews along either side led to a slightly raised dais in front of an ornate altar. As the image came into focus the details coalesced in Mina's mind: flickering candles, thick velvet, pews... She was in one of the castle's many chapels.

A cluster of figures stood on and below the dais, and they were all staring at her.

"Go on then," the officer said from behind her, giving her a nudge in the back.

Mina took a few halting steps into the chapel before once again squaring her shoulders.

No one spoke.

Even the administrative clip of her sensible heels was muted by the aged red carpet of the aisle.

As she neared, the cluster of people became more defined. Two men stood on the dais: the taller dressed from head to toe in midnight-black, the shorter one, older, dressed in bright white vestments. The Archbishop of Cyrano. Four others stood below the dais, arranged in front of the two men in a crescent pattern. Two men and two women—each of them wearing the indigo uniform of the Royal Guard.

Which means the man in black is the...

Mina's gaze darted toward the man to find his eyes already waiting for hers.

His were violet and smoldering, confirming the descriptions she had read in magazines and dismissed as fluff. His jaw was clean-shaven, his caramel skin smooth enough to run her fingers along. The thought was so un-Mina-like, it startled her from the spell of his face.

His stare was unwavering. His eyes bored into hers. His jaw was clenched and tense, as if carved from living granite, but she was no longer so enthralled that she couldn't take in the additional details of his expression.

Faint lines of displeasure creased either side of his mouth, and a slight line formed between his sword-straight thick black brows as he took her in. His eyes held heat, but there was no welcome in their warmth.

Mina had imagined her moment of meeting the King countless times over the years. It had been a core component of her greatest dream for so long that the image was virtually woven onto the back of her eyelids.

In her imagination, she executed a perfect bow and rose, somberly accepted as his newest advisor.

In reality, she was the worse for wear, for having been

dragged before him by Cyrano's version of a SWAT team, and very much in doubt as to her welcome.

Circumstances couldn't always be ideal, however. So, gathering together the shreds of her dignity, Mina once again straightened her shoulders, steeled her spine, and then dropped into the flawless half-bow of a royal councilor to the King.

As she rose, tendrils of the King's scent swirled around her—a mesmerizing combination of leather and oak, mixed with something smooth and expensive that caught her attention even through the years of burnt incense in the chapel. It slid like silk along her senses—a flavor, a temperature, and a color all at once—and it was all she could do to remain steady as she came upright.

One look at the monarch's face, however, told her that something more than her unusual reaction to his presence was wrong. Instead of the coolly cordial distance she'd always imagined the King would exude upon their meeting, he radiated a furious intensity that almost took her aback.

He wasn't merely bothered by her. He was angry.

Holding back the frown that wanted to crease her own brow, she addressed him. "Your Grace…"

Without a smile, he replied, "It's Your Royal Majesty."

His voice was a smooth baritone that stirred something deep in her core, which was likely why it took her longer than usual to process his rejoinder.

As she did, her frown broke through her hold on it. Keeping her voice controlled, she said, "Excuse me?" She tilted her head to one side, ever so slightly.

The King looked bored. "The proper address is Your Royal Majesty. And it's customary for a woman to curtsy, rather than bow, before the King."

Her frown deepened. He was correct—the exception to the rule being female Members of Parliament and members of the King's advisory council.

For reasons she did not fully understand, rather than attempt to smooth the situation, she decided to point it out. Tersely. "Apologies, Your Royal Majesty. As a newly appointed member of your advisory council, I chose the more standard salutation."

Rather than looking chastened, as she'd expected, the King scoffed, adding casually, "You're fired. Effective immediately. You may go down in history as having had the shortest ever tenure on the advisory council."

His words, tossed out so cruelly, hit her like a bullet in the chest. She felt the telltale pressure of tears forming in the back of her eyes but refused to allow them free. Fate, it was becoming clear, would not be satisfied until it had trampled every last piece of her dreams into the dirt.

She wasn't supposed to meet the King for months, and when she finally did, it was supposed to be in the comfort of the council chambers—not a cramped chapel with the Archbishop, politely ignoring their exchange, mere steps away.

And, while she had never expected friendship—he was the King, after all—she had at least expected basic professional decorum and respect.

Instead, he had insulted her.

"Of course," he went on, after taking her in from head to toe, with a faint flare to his nostrils, "a curtsy would have been ridiculous in that suit. You deserve credit, at least, for selecting the path of least clownishness. Given your...presentation, I imagine that must be a challenge."

Mina quietly gasped, her mouth dropping open at the same time as her eyebrows drew together.

Years of effort and sacrifice flashed before her eyes— all of it gladly given for the opportunity to advise the arrogant man who now stood before her.

Her father's words echoed again in her mind: *"Cyrano is counting on you."*

If this was the King, there was little she could do for Cyrano.

It had been naive of her to imagine a paragon for a monarch. She should have known better. Vast wealth and privilege weren't known for instilling integrity and character into individuals, but for some reason she had always imagined the King would be the kind of man who listened.

She had been mistaken. But she'd encountered enough bullies throughout her career to know when it was time to stand up for yourself.

"Well," she said, "if you brought me all this way to fire me, consider your goal achieved. If you don't mind, I'll take my leave now—*Your Royal Majesty*." She was proud of the amount of scholarly disdain she infused into the words.

The King remained unfazed. "In fact—unfortunately—I did not. If it were that simple I would have sent a note. You are here because we have been searching for you for some weeks, to no avail. Only to have you stroll into the castle of your own accord."

"That's absurd. My interview was scheduled six months ago, and I am by no means in hiding."

A part of her took note of the fact that she was arguing with the King, and in front of an audience no less, but that part wasn't strong enough to pull in the reins.

The King's nostrils flared. "The error has been corrected. We may move on."

"Move on with what?" Mina asked, unsure if she even wanted to know the answer.

"Our wedding."

He broke their visual connection for the first time since he'd established it to look at his watch, and Mina felt the absence as a physical experience—though his words overwhelmed even that novel experience.

"Our wedding…?" she croaked.

The King tsked. "Reports of your intelligence seem to

have been greatly exaggerated. Look around you. This chapel is certainly not where I meet with advisory council members."

Mina's mouth dropped open once again, and he observed her with a mild grimace.

"The papier-mâché box of a suit is bad enough. The fish look doesn't improve it."

Mina's mouth snapped shut, and her eyes narrowed.

"Are you nearsighted, as well? We can have that fixed… though the recovery will be long. That might be for the best, though. Give you more time to acclimate. Glasses make you look older than your age, you know."

He said all this matter-of-factly, more akin to a man examining livestock he'd just purchased than a king speaking to his…to his what?

Confusion crinkled Mina's forehead even as her eyes stung at his words. And, yes, she *did* know—though she wasn't vain or naive enough to blame it on the glasses.

At thirty-six, she wasn't young.

She had skipped being young to secure her disastrous interview before Parliament.

Closing her eyes on a sigh, Mina brought her fingers up to rub her temples. None of this made any sense.

"I think there has been some mistake," she said. "My name is Dr. Mina Aldaba. Six months ago, after applying for review, I was invited to interview for a position on your council—"

Taking a step down from the dais, one step closer to her, the King cut her off with a raised hand. "We know who you are. Dr. Amina Aldaba, only daughter of Ajit and Elke Aldaba. And, while there certainly has been a mistake, it is not ours."

His eyes chilled momentarily, and Mina realized she preferred his fire to his ice.

As if he could read her thoughts, he once again captured her gaze, his eyes warming.

She couldn't look away.

Lost in a sea of violet, she felt electric tingles ran up and down her spine, her entire body aware of the narrow distance between them.

His nostrils flared and his eyes darkened, some new emotion wrestling for dominance with the irritation that had simmered in them from the moment they'd met.

But he merely said, "There is no mistake—and you're late. Let's get on with this."

The King turned to the Archbishop, whom Mina had all but forgotten in the intensity of their exchange.

Her cheeks heated in embarrassment at behaving like a fawning teen in front of the holy man, but the archbishop only emanated an aura of kindness and acceptance.

There, at least, things were as expected.

His voice threaded with iron, the King turned to the older man and said, "Archbishop, are you prepared to begin?"

"Begin?" Mina interjected.

The Archbishop gave Mina a look of apology, but nodded to the King. "Yes. *Your Royal Majesty.*"

Mina felt a little jolt of triumph at the censure in the holy man's tone. At least she wasn't the only one appalled by the monarch's behavior.

"I, Archbishop Samuel, solemnly consecrate the agreement entered into by King Alden of Cyrano, and Ajit Aldaba, declaring their intent that their two families be joined through the sacred bond of marriage." He turned to the King. "Zayn Darius d'Argonia, King of Cyrano…"

The King said nothing.

"Welcome Amina Elin Aldaba as your wife and Queen. Care for her, treat her as your equal consort in all ways, and your union will blossom, a blessing to all of Cyrano."

Mina broke out into a cold sweat from head to toe.

Consort? Queen? Wife?

He had said "wedding," but that was absurd. They had never even met before.

The Archbishop continued, his words swirling around in her mind, spoken in her native tongue, yet completely incomprehensible.

She was supposed to be an advisor to the King. Not his wife.

The Archbishop turned to Mina, and the room reeled. King Zayn steadied her elbow with his large, firm hand, the heat of his skin burning through the thick starched fabric of her suit jacket, his eyes on her, pinning her in place like a butterfly with the needle of his violet gaze. The pressure of his touch was gentle, though, even if his expression was mocking.

"Amina Elin Aldaba. Grace smiles upon the woman who looks to her husband as her King. May you ever look to your husband as your King, with your eyes filled with love. Honor and support him, and in turn you will honor and support Cyrano. Before God we celebrate this fruition of the promise your fathers made, joining your families, for evermore, in holy matrimony. May your union be one of love and laughter. May your marriage be blessed with children, and may your reign be long and fruitful."

Mina shook her head in denial. Hearing her father's name on the Archbishop's tongue had set off an explosion of memories, the soundtrack of her father's steady voice forever repeating: *"for the good of Cyrano..."*

Suddenly it all made sense.

It wasn't their shared dream that she become an advisor to the King. She had been the one to misinterpret that. That was *her* dream. *Her* mistake.

Her father had wanted her to become Queen.

The room spun as her perspective on her entire relationship with her father shifted.

His insistence on her studying, his absolute refusal when it came to the subject of dating… His incessant litany of, *"Cyrano is counting on you…"*

He had meant it literally.

The familiar phrase morphed into a menacing phantom swirling around her mind, taunting her as everything she'd ever known about the world went up in flames.

The King knelt, and everyone in the room followed—except for the Archbishop and Mina.

Mina stood frozen.

The Archbishop whispered, "Kneel," and she knelt, her obedience to a direct order automatic even through her shock.

The Archbishop continued with the ceremony. "When you rise, you rise together as King and Queen of Cyrano. Joined in marriage for the betterment of the nation."

And if we stay down here?

The thought bubbled up in Mina's mind—a deranged joke as her world ended.

The King stood, capturing her elbow his hand with a secure grip, drawing her up beside him.

So much for that, she thought wistfully.

The Archbishop bowed to them, the movement acknowledging them as co-monarchs. The King released Mina's arm to embrace the Archbishop and then lead the older man out.

Mina stared after them, absurd thoughts bouncing around her mind like senseless pinballs: *I was married by the Archbishop of Cyrano… Papa would have been so proud… Papa…*

There was a neon sign in her mind, flashing in bright, desperate alarm.

Her father had married her off. To the King.

An arranged marriage. People didn't do that anymore.

She was a scientist, not a queen.

Her knees buckled, but the King, having returned to the dais, once again steadied her, casting her a frosty glare as he did so.

She turned away from the glare, desperate for something else to focus on, knowing on some level that she couldn't escape, but looking for a route nonetheless.

Again, the King read her mind. "There's no way out."

She shook her head. "There has to be. An annulment. A divorce."

He gave a firm negative with a shake of his head. "It is an edict of the King."

"You're the King."

"I wasn't then. There is no getting out of it. I have exhausted every possibility."

His words stung, even though she was just as desperate for answers.

"This can't be real," she said. "Cyrano is a modern European nation."

As if he were arguing with a toddler, the King's eyelids fluttered closed, and a small sound of exasperation slipped from his lips. "We are. And, like in many modern, *civilized* nations, it is easier to put a law on the books than it is to get it off. Though it pains me to admit it, breaking our betrothal would require a constitutional amendment."

"But you're the King."

His eyes narrowed, a different kind of disappointment entering them. "A king is not above the law. I shudder to think of the counsel you would have provided as advisor, given that I have to remind you of that fact."

She would have thought that by this point in the day she would be numb to something so minor as a casually thrown verbal barb. Instead, his words cut right to her heart.

Hadn't she been thinking along the same lines about him just moments before?

Before they were married.

"I would never suggest that." She didn't bother to keep the snap out of her voice. They were married now, after all. She added sarcastically, "Forgive the implication. I'm not at my best. It's not every day that I am arrested to attend my own surprise wedding."

Something that might have been compassion flashed across his eyes, but it was gone before she could be sure. When he spoke, he said, "Obviously we will go over terms more formally in the coming weeks, but in the immediacy of today know this: out of respect for my father, you will be Queen, with all the associated rights and requirements. That includes a private guard, access to the Queen's suites in the palace, and an annual salary. Planning and hosting the Queen's Ball will be your first official duty, and it will also serve as your debut."

"But that's just two weeks away."

"As I mentioned, it took us longer to locate you than anticipated."

Mina almost laughed. He made it sound as if it was her fault. The only reason she held back a snort was the fear that she would deteriorate into mad cackling if she let it out.

Cyranese custom held that the Queen hosted an annual ball, inviting the entire aristocracy of the island, as well as Members of Parliament, representatives from media outlets, and other illustrious members of society to attend. The tradition had begun a century before—one savvy queen's method of diverting angry lords from violence—but had not taken place in the two years since King Alden's death. The first year the widowed Queen had been too deep in mourning. The second year Zayn had been crowned and the country no longer had a queen.

Traditionally, the ball took place on Queen's Day—two weeks away.

Mina had never planned a party in her life.

Again, the unbelievability of this narrative struck Mina.

A person didn't go from being ordinary one moment to being Queen the next. The Archbishop had conducted the ceremony, but there had been no judge present, no license signed. Surely even the King needed a license and a judge for a marriage to be legal?

But the King had moved on.

"Your guards will be…" he scanned the row of guards "…Moustafa and d'Tierrza."

Two blue-clad figures stepped forward. Both were women. One wore her long brown hair pulled back into a braid nearly as tight and controlled as Mina's. The other sported a swoopy silver-blond pixie cut.

The blonde guard's voice was a low rasp, infused with humor, as she executed a bow and came up saying, "Your Royal Majesty…"

Without missing a beat, the other woman followed, and Mina found herself nodding to them with a genuine smile on her face, amused and slightly grateful at their military manner. It reminded her of her father.

Her father who had secretly arranged her marriage.

Mina pushed the thought away. She wasn't ready to untangle that knot quite yet.

Instead, she focused on the women in front of her.

The blonde woman's name was revealing. The d'Tierrzas were one of the oldest aristocratic families on the island. The family was currently headed by a daughter, the mother scandalously passed over in the father's will, who was infamous for her scandalous appointment to the Royal Guard.

And now she was Mina's guard.

"There are several other matters we need to discuss…" the King's voice cut into Mina's thoughts "…but that will have to wait. I have an appointment. Your guards will escort you to your rooms."

He spoke as if he were working through a to-do list, rather than parting from his new bride. He was so casual about it all that Mina wondered if he had always expected his marriage to be like this—sudden, rushed, and painful.

For once, however, he seemed to be unaware of her train of thought, continuing with, "Meet me in my office tomorrow at eight a.m. We will go over the rest."

Then he was leaving, with the rest of the guards pouring out after him.

Now she was alone with her new guards the small chapel felt colder, the emptiness of the space more profound for its lack of the King.

Her husband.

Mina shivered.

"Your Majesty?" Moustafa asked.

It took Mina a moment to realize the woman was addressing her. When she did, she grimaced. "Please, call me Mina."

The woman nodded. "Mina. Would you like us to escort you to your rooms?"

"If by that you mean my apartment in the city, that would be wonderful. Can you do that?" Despite everything, she couldn't keep the wistful thread of hope out of her voice.

D'Tierrza laughed out loud. "You certainly deserve it. But we can't—at least not until we've swept and secured the premises." She added the last with a wink.

Mina felt an answering smile grow on her own face as she took a closer look at the other woman. D'Tierrza's rich alto voice and confident demeanor, coupled with her creamy skin and line-free face, as well as the startling clarity of her sapphire-blue eyes, were completely at odds with the danger coiled in her frame. The woman was beautiful—

but Mina got the distinct impression that that fact didn't matter to her in the least.

Moustafa had her own stern beauty, with her dark coloring and angular bone structure. Her face was all high cheekbones and slashing brows, and it suited her perfectly. Her surname was common, and she lacked the insouciant ease the island's aristocracy seemed born with. Both facts confirmed the impression that she had made it to the palace the same way Mina had: through hard work and a fierce refusal to give up.

Her guards would make good friends in the palace.

Accepting that, if nothing else, Mina said, "Please lead the way."

Moustafa and d'Tierrza turned, and Mina followed them out of the chapel.

The hallways they took her through were dim and quiet, clearly not open to the public. Low-wattage bulbs provided just enough light throughout, and beneath them the marble floors sparkled.

"These are the residential corridors. You'll eventually figure them all out," d'Tierrza said after the they'd taken a third turn. "They're the fastest way to travel the palace and the grounds and are well guarded and surveilled."

Mina almost laughed. It would be some time before the security of the premises became a concern of hers. She was a scientist, not a dignitary. Or she had been.

After a long walk, they finally stopped in front of another wooden door and Mina flinched. Her day at the palace had become a nightmare of Monty Hall problems.

So what monstrosity lurks behind door number three? she wondered as she pushed it open.

Only this time is wasn't a nightmare. It was a paradise.

The room was all wide-open ivory walls and floors and creamy marble. There were several open archways leading into other spaces, all of which encircled a large sunken sitting room that was comfortably appointed with plush furniture. The upholstery was smooth buff suede, and there were pillows and throw blankets everywhere one might want to reach for one.

As Mina entered, d'Tierrza stopped her with a hand on the shoulder. "For the Queen's Ball, call Roz Chastain. She'll take you because you're new. Let her have her way on everything."

She took out a pen and paper and scribbled a number down.

Mina nodded, a sense of relief penetrating her for the first time since she had learned she had landed the Parliament interview months ago.

"Thank you."

D'Tierrza grinned. "My money is on you. I've never seen anyone affect him like you do. He completely lost his cool—and that can only be good for him."

With those enigmatic words, she gently nudged Mina inside before taking her position outside the door.

Moustafa took her position as well, leaving Mina to wander in and out of each room.

The wing included a bedroom, a bathroom suite with a tiled hot tub, a large-windowed office with a stunning view, and an enormous balcony overlooking the sea.

The bed was lush, and freshly made with bright linens and fluffy pillows. The towels were the thickest she had ever felt, and a gorgeous robe and slipper set was hanging outside the double-headed waterfall shower.

Interestingly, while the suite was stunning—indeed, the most elegant accommodation Mina had ever been in—there were signs that the wing had not been updated in at least a few decades. Rotary phones graced the side tables in the bedroom and the sitting room, three nineteen-fifties era television sets that Mina was sure would not connect to Cyrano's digital cable network rested on sideboards in multiple places, and there wasn't a computer in sight.

All it needed was a laptop and decent Wi-Fi signal, though, and it would make the perfect location for a research sabbatical.

Not for her, of course.

After the fiasco of her arrest and then her firing, her career was ruined. Academia was quick to condemn and slow to forgive. The only thing for her to do was fade into the shadows quietly.

A feat that would be more challenging now that she was apparently Queen.

Her academic reputation was tarnished.

She was Queen of Cyrano.

It was her wedding day.

She was alone.

Walking into the bedroom, weary in a way she never imagined she could be, she collapsed on the bed without taking her clothes off or loosening her braid. The SWAT team had done a good enough job of that last bit.

She hadn't harbored many of the fantasies common to young girls. Weddings, babies—none of that—but she had still vaguely imagined that she'd marry. Probably not until the autumn of her life, and likely only then to a warmly regarded colleague. But she'd pictured it. Even in that tame picture, though, she hadn't gone to bed alone on her wedding night.

Rolling over onto her back, she stared at the bright ceiling, no longer able to hold back the wave of emotion.

She was the Queen of Cyrano and her greatest dream was a warm pile of smoking ash.

For the first time since her father died, Mina cried herself to sleep.

CHAPTER TWO

SOME MEN WERE driven by passion, acting on their instincts without thought or strategy. Much to his late father's chagrin, Zayn Darius d'Argonia, the youngest ever King of Cyrano, was not that kind of man.

It was the old man's own fault, though. After all, he had been the one to raise a young prince with an ironclad sense of self-reliance and an unwavering commitment to forging his own path. Early on in his life, he had decided that his was the path of careful study and planning.

To give his father credit, he had, on most issues, steadfastly supported Zayn in whatever approach he chose, saying, *"Each man is his own. It does the world no good to try to walk the path of another."*

His father had believed this self-reliance was a vital characteristic for a king. Of course, neither of them had imagined that Zayn would become King so soon. Nor that, in that transition, his inner compass would be the only thing that saved the country from near governmental collapse, economic depression, and an attempted coup in the immediate and ugly aftermath of the King's assassination and the ascendance of a young, inexperienced monarch to the throne.

But any self-flagellation for lack of foresight on the matter was a pointless waste of time—a luxury a working king could not afford.

Some believed that Parliament ran things. They were mistaken.

Cyrano's monarchy had given its people a powerful voice through their elected officials, and more power still through the Parliament-selected advisory council, but the royal family had retained control and rule of the country—through centuries and countless plots against them.

Zayn would not be the one to jeopardize that—not through poor planning, not through acting rashly, and not through marriage.

And that was just one of the many reasons the shock of his betrothal still stung.

Filling the position of Queen was to have been one of his most potent bargaining chips—a lucrative lure to play to Cyrano's strategic advantage.

The woman who would be Queen had to be cut from a particular cloth—intelligent, quick-thinking, compassionate, determined, unflappable, steel-coated, perfectly presented, and always poised. And she needed to bring something of real value to the Crown—money, trade, connections…something tangible.

She could not be common. She could not be unfashionable. She couldn't let her feelings show in her beautiful green-gold eyes every time someone was frank with her.

His greatest bargaining chip was now a virtual throwaway, offering nothing advantageous to the nation and burdening him with a softhearted academic unprepared for the sharp edges of public life in the process. That his father had been the one to hamstring him like this made it all the worse.

It didn't make any sense. Up to the very end, his father had done everything he could to support him.

Zayn had already considered the obvious—that Mina's

family had somehow blackmailed the late King—but it didn't pan out.

While his father had been no angel, Zayn was sure there were no skeletons in his closet so monstrous that he would sacrifice his son. Nothing had mattered more to King Alden than his family. It didn't add up—especially given the old King's feelings on marriage.

While he was alive, marriage had been the one point of disagreement between them.

Never one to keep his opinions to himself, Alden had tried his damnedest to turn his son around to his thinking.

"Your Queen will be your greatest helpmeet and partner. She will be the difference between a legacy of success or failure. Finding her, falling in love—and soon—that is your most important duty."

Fresh from his second year at university, and riding high on the thrill of finding his passion in the philosophy and study of governance, Zayn had merely rolled his eyes at his father's hyperbole.

His father had persisted. *"I'm serious, son. I don't want to hear any more of this 'strategic alliance once you take the throne' nonsense. I want you to fall in love, and fast."*

"Regardless of this mystery woman's status or fitness to rule?" Zayn had replied, not bothering to rein in the sarcasm in his voice.

King Alden's eyes had briefly darted away that day, and Zayn had counted the point as his victory, but now he knew better. His father hadn't met his eyes that day because he had been playing the hypocrite.

And therein lay the rub.

Why go to the trouble to wax on about love and marriage when he'd already given his son away?

Perhaps his father had been more strategic than Zayn had given him credit. Maybe he'd owed someone a favor for his good fortune, and Zayn had been the repayment.

That kind of *quid pro quo* was the norm amongst the ruling set. The logic was clean.

But Zayn didn't believe it for a minute.

Logical though it might be, the idea was uncharitable to the man his father had been, and about as far out of character and respect to the relationship they'd shared as this whole betrothal fiasco was in the first place.

Whatever the circumstances had been, his father had not conned his way onto the throne. King Alden and Queen Barbara's had been a great love. The intensity of it had gone so far as to be a frequent distraction from rule, in Zayn's opinion. But his father had insisted that their passion set the tone for the nation, energizing its transition from a European backwater into the next most-desired off-the-beaten-path destination.

It was hard to believe that the same man would—either strategically, or under threat—bargain his son away.

So how in God's name had he ended up married to a stranger? And why had his father kept the betrothal from him?

The betrothal agreement was dated just weeks before Zayn's birth, witnessed by the former Archbishop, Henry Innocence, and signed by both Zayn's and Mina's fathers. Curiously, their mothers' signatures were absent.

With nothing more to offer than that, the current Archbishop, Samuel, had raised his palms pacifyingly and said, "I'm sorry, Your Majesty. The late Archbishop made no note about the betrothal in his diary entries. I scoured the entire year's worth myself."

Nothing about the situation made sense, and no one could explain. Indeed, logic had taken its leave of the situation from the moment Zayn had approached Archbishop Samuel with his list of prospective brides.

Each of those women would have brought something of advantage to Cyrano.

Daphne Xianopolis came with access to excellent Mediterranean Sea trade routes. Françoise La Guerre was a princess in her own right, and marriage to her would have opened up the potential for stronger diplomatic ties to continental Europe. And Yu Yan Ma would have been the most fabulous prize. Connection to her father would have given him power enough to propel Cyrano into the world of international trade.

Zayn had merely intended the Archbishop to vet the list for any potential religious challenges before he made began making approaches. Instead, he'd learned that he was otherwise engaged.

"What do you mean, I'm 'already taken?'" Zayn had demanded.

The Archbishop had smiled, as if the situation were a delightful joke, and repeated, "You are affianced, Your Majesty. You have been since before you were born."

"That's impossible!"

But it had not been impossible. The archbishop had shown him the official document, signed, witnessed, and filed—binding in every way—and Zayn had been forced to acknowledge the truth.

Dr. Amina Aldaba would bring nothing of value to Cyrano. As far as he could discern, she was nobody. She came from simple people of Moorish descent. Her father had been eighth generation Cyranese and had first a soldier, then a farmer—not the kind of man who entered his unborn child into a royal betrothal.

Like all natural-born Cyranese men, her father had served in the military for mandatory service at eighteen. Unlike most, he had re-enlisted for another three terms of service, earning enough money to purchase a small villa at the edge of the city. City permit records showed that he had then converted two courtyards into farm plots and taken to life as a vendor at the city's famous daily market. A few years later he'd married Elke Meyer—a woman who had arrived in Cyrano on a student visa.

The couple had married in the courthouse and had one child. They'd lived as a family until the father's death thirteen years later. Nowhere in that timeline was there any record of their family's path crossing with the royal line. Not in service, not in friendship—nothing that would suggest a closeness that might brook the future joining of their families that was constitutionally binding.

And so Zayn had Dr. Amina Aldaba for his Queen—a woman who had spent her life absorbed in academia, developing no practical skills for queenship.

She would need to learn everything from scratch, and there was no way he could keep her out of the limelight long enough for her to master the ins and outs of public life. Undoubtedly, she would embarrass the Crown along the way.

With her over-starched headmistress aesthetic and easily ruffled feathers, it was obvious she was better suited to that scientific advisory position on the council than the throne. At least in that role she would have had something to recommend her. Zayn had scoured her research and found her work insightful. He could see why Parliament had approved her interview.

In the role of scientific advisor, she would have been perfect.

There was nothing to recommend her for the role of Queen.

A protest against the thought rose from some vague, primal part of his mind. She didn't exactly have *nothing* to recommend her. That much was clear, even with the atrocious packaging.

Her eyes were astonishing—a shade of green that Zayn had never seen before, falling somewhere between that of the sage that grew in the dry upper reaches of Cyrano's hills and the new spring grasses that grew in the meadowlands.

And her gaze had depth—enough that it was easy to fall into it, like a moss-lined crevasse in a mountain forest.

Her skin, too—a satiny brown that glowed warm and bright wherever the light touched it—was notable. Smooth and clear, it virtually demanded to be caressed.

Like her skin, her hair, too, hinted at softness, even shellacked and tightly braided as it had been. The color of her hair had reminded Zayn of the brown beaches of the island palace, its chocolatey brown and natural highlights calling to his mind the island's long stretches of pristine coastline, dappled with dancing ribbons of sunlight streaming through the woods.

Her eyebrows were a shade darker than her hair, thick and fierce over her magnificent eyes.

Her coloring was that of the Mediterranean landscape, come to vibrant life in the form of woman. He sensed that the rest of her—everything she hid beneath her over-sized and over-starched office wear—would be just as vibrant and bountiful.

There were hints of it even with the camouflage. Her lips were full and defined even naked of lipstick, as they had been. They were naturally rose-colored, lending her mouth a naughty allure that she didn't even bother to hide.

Her utter lack of effort to accentuate her beauty only seemed to emphasize the truth of it.

Her nose was straight-bridged, with a rounded tip, lending her expressive face an element of forthrightness that offset any urge to write her off as merely pretty.

Instead, she was earnest. Pure. *Untasted.*

That last thought was unlike him.

And, at thirty-six years old, it was highly unlikely that she remained untasted.

But, shoving that thought to the side, he was willing to acknowledge that it wasn't fair to say she brought *nothing* the table. She would be lovely when adequately dressed.

Unfortunately, "lovely" was usually only as exciting and useful as the time it took to secure a taste of it. "Lovely" wasn't reason enough for most common men to marry, let alone a king.

Zayn glanced up at the wall clock in his office to note that she was five minutes late. She didn't even have the sense to respect the demands on his time. They had a great deal they needed to discuss concerning the terms of their marriage and he didn't have all day.

He watched the ticking passage of another two minutes before she walked in, head high.

As it had been the day before, her armor—or, more accurately, her schoolmarm disguise—was in place: controlled braid, no-nonsense posture, and a direct stare. Though by now, day two, her suit was beginning to lose its crisp edges. This morning she looked more like a wilting librarian than a roughed-up rigid professor.

Zayn gave her a once-over before saying, "Your clothing is ridiculous. You'll need to work on that."

Hurt flickered across her gaze, but she schooled her expression.

She'll need to work on that, too, he thought.

A queen needed thick skin.

Taking her in, he mentally sighed. Her eyes were slightly puffy and swollen—a telltale sign that she had cried the night before. A queen needed to be prepared for long, thankless days and constant smiling, for being bombarded with hate and never revealing whether she was hurt, tired, ill, or angry. Mina might as well have been a projector screen for the way she broadcasted her feelings to the world.

Zayn added, "As Queen, you are expected to dress at the height of fashion and always be well presented. You have a budget for that express purpose, as it is considered part and parcel of your royal duties."

Her cheeks darkened but she made no comment to his

remark, so he gestured for her to sit down at the desk across from him. The desk had been his father's before his, and his grandfather's before that. The very room itself had been the King's office since the palace's construction.

And now it was his.

Mina sat, looking around the office as she did so. For once, her expression did not give away her thoughts. Her posture was ramrod-straight as she sat at the edge of the chair, legs primly pressed together, hands in her lap.

It was a small blessing, and, observing her, he could at least find no fault with her there. When his eyes finally moved back up to meet hers, she cleared her throat and opened her mouth.

"I'm not the Queen. We're not married."

The words, abrupt and inelegant, hung in the air between them.

Zayn closed his eyes and took a breath before answering. "We are."

It wasn't that he hadn't been expecting her to say something along those lines. He'd merely hoped she would be smart enough to understand that if there had been a way out of the situation, he would have found it.

She shook her head. "There was nothing legal about that ceremony."

"I assure you, our union is legal and binding."

"That's ridiculous," Mina insisted. "You didn't even know who I was the day before yesterday."

"Not true. I've known who you are for exactly three weeks."

She looked taken aback by that fact, but pressed on. "You can't force a woman to marry you. You said it yourself: 'The King is not above the law.'"

"No. But fathers can apparently still force their children to marry."

"So, this is real?"

She sounded so desolate he was tempted to take pity on her—but she was the Queen now, and making it easy on her wouldn't be doing her any favors.

So he didn't, instead saying, "It is. So, if we may continue?" He inclined his head toward the stack of forms sitting at her right hand. "There are several legal statements you must sign. You are to select one to three, but no more, causes to champion. These will then inform your outreach activities."

Her expression suggested that he'd grown another head, but she said nothing so he continued.

"Your attendance is expected at all official state functions. A personal secretary has been assigned to you to manage your calendar, your discretionary budgets, and personal affairs."

Zayn noted that her color was fading, but she remained upright, present, and attentive. It would do. He sensed there was more going on inside, but overnight she seemed to have managed to gain some control over her constant emoting.

At least she was a quick study. She would need to be. There were those who would use her every emotion against her, and he wouldn't always be around to protect her.

"Your diplomatic functions will include acting as royal hostess, overseeing entrainment for visiting dignitaries, and representing Cyrano whenever abroad."

At this, she brightened, once again broadcasting her feelings, transparent as glass. He'd given her credit too soon.

"Politically, should anything happen to me, you are to take my place as ruler, working closely with the advisory council—"

She sucked in a pained breath at his mention of the council, and he felt another twinge of regret. Not for firing her from the position. That had been a given. The Queen did not have a seat on the advisory council. But he could find sympathy for her obvious disappointment.

Continuing, he said, "In readiness for such an emergency, you are to keep abreast of the status and scope of my duties as well as your own. This is considered a royal duty, and you will be allotted time for review in your official schedule."

Here was another duty she felt an affinity for, judging from the ease she radiated.

For the thousandth time he wondered why his father had chosen her—and for the thousandth time he brushed the thought away.

Speculation was a waste of his time.

"Other duties will be assigned as they arise, but you will be informed well in advance. I mentioned that you would receive a wardrobe budget. In addition to that, you will receive an administrative budget and an annual salary. You will get three months of vacation per year, and six months of maternity leave—"

Mina made a choking sound in the back of her throat, and the energy in the room took on a new edge.

They had not yet discussed heirs.

Heirs—or at least the attempt—would be one of her essential duties as Queen. It was literally spelled out in the position's description.

As Zayn took her in now, a burst of color masquerading as a deflating cardboard box, he was surprised to feel heat stirring in his gut.

Unlike the women on his list, Mina bore none of the traits he found attractive in a woman. She was tall, whereas he liked petite, serious whereas he valued humor, and, he suspected, she was curvaceous under her suit—more like a proud Valkyrie than a woman with the willowy frame he preferred.

His father couldn't have selected a more inappropriate woman for him had he tried.

And yet...

Zayn cleared his throat. "Out of consideration for our heirs, and the continuation of the d'Argonia line, both parties are prohibited from extramarital relations until the union has produced three children who have lived past the age of five."

Mina's face, having darkened when he began, was a mortified mask of purple by the time he'd finished.

"That's oddly specific," she squeaked.

He would have called it distasteful, but essentially he agreed. This conversation was crude. All this information was included in the marriage contract, usually reviewed by each party privately before the wedding. However, there was nothing usual about this marriage.

"Once we have produced the requisite number of heirs, we are free to explore or return to other relationships." He found himself frowning as he spoke, oddly as insulted by the idea of Mina taking a lover as he'd been intrigued by the idea of producing an heir with her.

"Perhaps we can take it slow when it comes to heirs," she suggested, her voice coming out scratchy and uneven. Her cheeks were still red-tinged, and she had pushed her seat back, away from the opposite side of the desk.

Unbidden, he had a distinct impression of innocence from her, followed by a strangely conflicted dual surge of interest and frustration. He chose to focus on the frustration. Training a prudish virgin scholar in bed was the last thing he wanted.

The answering rush of heat to his groin, however, said otherwise.

Ignoring it, he nodded at Mina. "Certainly. Everything is spelled out in the marriage agreement." He tapped the thickly bound stack of papers on the desk. "Copies are filed here, as well as in your own office and with the state office. I mentioned the Queen's Ball yesterday... As your first official duty, your work on it must reflect the quality and standards of the Crown. The royal steward will inform you if you've achieved that. Now, if you don't have any questions, you may take your leave."

The phrasing was open, but his dismissal clear.

Instead of taking her leave, though, Mina opened her mouth.

"I've certainly got questions. Let's say that I believe this impossible situation is irreversible, for the sake of this conversation. If that's the case, what about my things? I have an apartment and a car in the city, as well as a storage unit filled with my research. My laptop and phone were confiscated outside Parliament. I will need those returned if I—"

Zayn held up a hand to stop her. "You will be given new encrypted devices, and your belongings are being seen to by palace staff as we speak. Your car has been donated to charity. As Queen, you will not need a vehicle—and you are, in fact, not allowed to drive."

"That's absurd!" Mina protested.

"Regardless, it is true."

"I have rights as a citizen of Cyrano."

Zayn shook his head, ruefully. "You are no longer a citizen of Cyrano. You are the Queen of Cyrano."

"And if I refuse?"

"There is no refusing."

"It's not right."

Zayn stared at her for a moment before slightly inclining his head. "I agree. But it *is*. And it is more important than you or I."

Mina frowned. "Your cavalier response to an obvious injustice leaves a bit to be desired."

"As does your reaction to the acquiring of new and unwanted responsibility. It seems we both have room for growth." Zayn's voice was even, but no less cutting for its collegiate tone.

Her green eyes narrowed. "Do not presume to know the first thing about me, *Your Royal Majesty*."

She was right. The fact that her words were valid only added to the acid sting of them. He knew nothing about her—and yet she was his wife.

"I do not. Neither, however, should you make assumptions about me. Aren't we lucky that it appears we will have many years together to learn?"

And how does any of this prove your point, Father? he wondered.

How in the world did marrying him to a stranger prove how urgently important it was that he find a wife to love and cherish? His father had contradicted every single one of his words to his son about love and marriage before he'd even said them in the first place, betrothing him to a stranger and never giving him the chance to come to know and love her.

Zayn had at least known the women on his list socially. Some he had known a bit more. That had to make a stronger foundation upon which to build love than no knowledge whatsoever.

And if a love match had been King Alden's hope for his son, why had he taken the choice from him? If he had truly believed a partner must be a helpmeet, why hadn't he prepared this woman for her future role? Or even informed her of it, for that matter?

Unfortunately, there were more questions than answers, and no time to spend on them—especially now that he had a stubborn and inept queen sitting in his office.

It didn't matter that the issue burned in him all the more for being the one subject that he and his father had never seen eye-to-eye on. No. All that mattered was the future of Cyrano.

And Cyrano would weather this—just as it had endured

the loss of its King, two years of turmoil, and a century of war and technological transformation before that.

That kind of continuity was more significant than his feelings, his father's and his wife's combined.

Turning back to the woman across the desk from him, he noted that while she had no retort for him, neither did she appear to be any closer to leaving.

"Is there anything else, Dr. Aldaba?" he asked.

Her color was high and bright, but not the dusky rose of her earlier embarrassment, and she looked as if she was casting about for a reason to linger. Frustration poured off her, and Zayn was momentarily comforted by the return of his ease in reading her.

Finally, she said, "When can I expect my new personal devices?"

She was grasping for power and control over something, and they both knew it, but instead of irritating him, the pointless effort stirred something like pity inside him.

He glanced up at the clock. "They should be waiting for you in your office, along with your new secretary, by the time you return there."

Again, the dismissal was blunt—and again she stayed where she was.

"You're certain there's nothing we can do?" she asked after another long pause.

He almost didn't hear the quiet question. The note of defeat and vulnerability in her voice called out to him, but he reminded himself that pity did her no favors. A queen had to be impenetrable.

"I am certain. Now, I suggest you return to your office. Please select your causes soon, and inform your secretary so that we may update the royal website. And, please, for the love of God, assign someone to your wardrobe immediately."

As he'd intended, she pursed her lips and narrowed her

eyes into outraged green slits. Gone was the air of fragility, replaced with the heat of anger and the spark of determination he'd seen her muster so many times in their brief interactions.

She stood stiffly and he almost smiled, relieved to see the fire radiating from her. She was going to need fire like that if she was going to make it as Queen.

CHAPTER THREE

"*AND PLEASE, FOR the love of God, assign someone to your wardrobe...*"

A week and a half later, standing in front of her new closet, staring at the same old four black cocktail dresses she owned, the King's words still stung.

It was the morning of the ball and, while she might not have taken his advice in the time since their meeting, she had taken d'Tierrza's.

Like a fairy godmother, Roz Chastain had turned out to be everything Mina hadn't known she needed.

Roz wore a uniform that consisted of a long-sleeved boat-necked black shirt with black skinny jeans and leopard print loafers. Her mind was as sharp as a sword, and—a fact Mina could personally attest to—her tongue even sharper.

Mina could scarcely believe the day of the ball had arrived as she settled on the sleeveless dress. The dress's design was plain, but suitable, as were the simple black ballet flats she would wear with it. Both had served her well through years of parties, publication celebrations, and galas.

With the task of choosing her ensemble complete, she glanced at the clock. It was early—just past seven in the morning—and, after Roz's efforts and hers, she had the whole of the rest of the day to relax before the big event.

Grabbing her mug of tea from the side table where it

rested, she made her way onto the large wrap-around balcony of the Queen's Wing and considered trying her mother's phone again.

Since her father's death, her mother had run the family farm business on her own, ferociously protecting Mina's study time by refusing to allow her to help—even if that meant working from dawn to dusk to maintain the thriving business and the house in support of the dreams of her daughter and her late husband.

In anticipation of how busy Mina would be, preparing for her parliamentary interview, her mother had taken a rare trip back to Germany. They were to reconnect when she returned in late summer.

But what would she say to her? *Hi, Mom. I got married.*

She would be heartbroken—not just because she had missed one of the most important major milestones of her daughter's life, but also for the same reason Mina was. Her father had kept this secret from both of them. Of that fact Mina was of no doubt. There was no way her mother would have kept her betrothal from her. She knew her too well to leave her that unprepared. And now, in addition to swallowing her daughter's marriage and becoming Queen, her mother would also have to reckon with her husband's great secret.

It wasn't something Mina was willing to do over the phone. No, it was better to wait until her return and to break the news gently, in person.

So instead of calling her mom she took a deep breath of sea air.

Overlooking the stunning Mediterranean, the smooth architecture of the balcony was timelessly elegant, although it was a bit chilly. Mina wore a pair of slouchy boyfriend jeans, wool socks, sandals, and a knit sweater, and still the sea breezes found their way to her skin.

Her long braid, dangling down the center of her back

now, had loosened over the past nine days. It was just one of many signals that her life as a scholar was over.

The thought brought an ache to her chest.

Looking out to sea, she wondered what, if anything, her colleagues had learned of her humiliation.

The ball was to be her debut as Queen, so no information about her identity had been publicly released. Neither had she found anything about her dramatic parliamentary interview online, or in any of the city's newspapers. Not that she had had much time to look, ensconced with Roz in event-planning as she had been.

Their efforts had been well worth it, though. It was amazing what could be accomplished in a short amount of time when one had limitless funds and access to a ruthless genius event-planner.

A knock on the door startled a jump out of her, and tea sloshed over her sweater sleeve. It served her right. She had been about to lose herself in thoughts about the King. It was enough that he was devastatingly handsome. She didn't need to compound the situation by developing Stockholm syndrome.

Moving as quickly as she could, while also steadying the mug, Mina hurried to the door and opened it to find Roz standing in the hallway.

Without a word, the older woman pushed the door open wide and Mina to one side.

"Out of the way, dear," she rasped.

Mina frowned. The other woman's behavior was not unusual, but it was unexpected. As far as Mina had understood, they'd had no plans to see each other until the ball tonight.

A young woman also dressed all in black had followed Roz into the room, wheeling a large beauty salon chair and vanity unit in front of her. Another woman sporting an extreme asymmetrical haircut and a color block dress followed. A heartbeat later, a bald man with a salt-and-pepper beard, thick black glasses, and a thin gray sweater entered. The last to come, and the shortest of the lot, was a woman with a face so perfect it looked like a painting. She shut the door behind her.

Mina looked around the suddenly crowded room. "Roz. Everyone… To what do I owe the pleasure of your company?"

Before answering, Roz conversed with the first young woman about where to place the salon chair. Then she replied, "We're here to fix you, my dear."

Mina laughed. "I wasn't aware that I was broken—but, thank you, Roz."

Roz gifted her with a stare utterly devoid of patience and, much like the vacuum of space, of life itself. Roz did not like to repeat herself.

"I did not put together the event of the year in a single week to have it fizzle out at the finale."

Mina set her tea on a side table and wrapped her arms around herself protectively. "And how does that relate to me?" she asked.

Roz's eyebrow inched up, setting off alarms in Mina's head. She had seen that look before.

"You are the finale, dear, and as it is now you simply won't do."

Mina frowned. "What's wrong with me?"

"Nothing. Other than the fact you plan to wear a depressingly square department store cocktail dress to my ball."

Heat came to Mina's cheeks even as she shook her head in denial. The dress hadn't come from a department store. It was from a boutique that had been going out of business. And it was not square.

Reading her mind, Roz said, "Everything you wear is square. Off with it all. Put this on." She held out an ivory silk robe.

Shoulders slumped, Mina took the robe and turned toward her bathroom with a sigh.

Roz stopped her with a commanding click of her tongue. "Where are you going?"

Mina turned around slowly, feeling as guilty as if she had tried to disobey her mother. She winced. "To change?" she said, the question in her voice acknowledging that it was obviously the wrong answer.

"Not in the bathroom." Roz shook her head. "Right here. We need measurements."

The woman with the asymmetrical hair nodded.

Mina shook her head. "No."

Roz tsked. "Don't be stubborn, Mina. You don't have anything that everyone in this room hasn't seen a million times before."

The woman with the perfect face smiled encouragingly, adding in a soft, wispy voice, "It's true."

With her inherent modesty now being represented as immaturity—at least in the eyes of this roomful of strangers who were waiting to see her naked—Mina gritted her teeth and pulled her sweater over her head. She followed it with the rest of her clothes, until she stood shivering in the bright morning light wearing nothing but her underwear.

"Good figure," the woman with the perfect face commented.

"Bad underwear," asymmetrical haircut added.

Mina's cheeks heated uncomfortably.

Roz agreed. "Horrible. Get rid of them."

Mina started to shake her head, but realized there was no point. Roz always won in the end.

Face aflame, she quickly removed her undergarments until she stood naked in the room. The woman with asymmetrical hair darted over and began taking measurements, calling out numbers to the young woman in black, who took notes.

When she'd finished, Mina quickly shrugged the robe over her nakedness, just before the woman gave her a little push toward the bald man and the salon chair. Then she took the notes from the younger woman and hurried out of the room.

Staring at the chair, and the man who stood behind it, Mina heard her practical German mother's voice rising in her mind: *"Never trust a bald hairstylist."*

But there was no getting out of it.

Sucking in a deep breath, Mina sat in the chair.

The man spun a cape around her and secured it at her neck. In one swift motion, he slid a pair of scissors out of the pocket of the apron at his waist and cut the elastic that held the end of her braid.

Mina reached up with lightning speed to place her hand on his wrist. Turning to meet his eyes, she said, "Please don't cut too much off. I've been growing it for over twenty years…"

Since her father had died.

The man grimaced, as if her statement explained everything, and then waved her words away with little flicks of his hand. "Don't worry, sweetheart. I'm going to make you look divine."

And then he moved behind her and made his first cut into her bone-dry hair.

Her stomach knotted as he worked. No one had ever cut her hair dry before.

She winced at every thick slice, each one a visceral reminder that scissors were now shearing their way through years' worth of growth in curls that were slow to grow and quick to frizz.

She took a deep breath.

It was only hair.

Hair that hung past her rear end when it was wet.

Hair that she hadn't cut since her father had died because

he had seen the stubborn curls as a reflection of her inner strength and determination.

Her heart squeezed, but she didn't move in the chair. She was strong enough to endure a haircut.

By the time the stylist moved to the front of her head she wasn't so sure.

Not only had he taken off inches and inches of length all over her head, he'd done the unthinkable for a curly woman—added multiple chunky layers. A pained moan bubbled out of Mina's throat, and her eyes teared as he continued, oblivious. He completed his massacre with a flourish and two swipes of his scissors, saving the worst horror for last: a set of frizzy, puffy bangs.

He had turned her into a nineteen-eighties poodle.

Then he barked, "Washbowl!"

The girl all in black ran over, pushing a portable sink and that had appeared in the room sometime when Mina wasn't looking. Raising Mina's seat with the foot lever, the man tilted her back and began washing her hair.

The light, fresh aroma of the shampoo, combined with the relaxing pressure of his fingers massaging her scalp, lulled her mind away from the monstrosity he had made of her head.

A haircut is temporary, she mentally repeated to herself.

The mantra was easy enough to believe with her eyes closed and strong hands massaging her skull. When he sat her back up and she heard the distinctive sound of foil crinkling, though, all sense of ease evaporated.

She opened her eyes in time to see him painting a dollop of white cream onto a wet curly clump, and slapping a piece of foil on top of it. He made quick work of a second and a third, before the first squeak escaped the frozen O of Mina's mouth.

Without pausing in his application, he said, "Relax— you'll hardly notice it."

Heart beating rapidly, Mina tried to breathe. She had never colored her hair. She had always heard that color was the death of curls.

In far less time than she felt it should have taken, the stylist had her whole head foiled. He stood back and admired his handiwork while Mina's stomach churned.

Roz smiled. "That's good for now. Someone call for lunch. We will eat and then continue working while the color sets. Time is ticking."

Food arrived moments later, and the group ate efficiently, quietly talking amongst themselves. All except for Mina, who took robotic bites of food and stared woodenly at the clumps of her hair littering the floor.

And then round two began—not with the hairstylist, as Mina had expected, but with the woman with the perfect face.

Upon closer examination, Mina could tell that the woman's visage was the result of careful and precise makeup application. She had used lighter and darker colors to alter the dimensions and shape of her face like an artist with paints on canvas.

"I'm excellent. I know."

The woman's voice was wry when she spoke, and Mina stopped staring long enough to make eye contact. "My apologies," she muttered.

"None needed," the woman said. "Be still."

And then she set to work.

An hour later, she stepped away from Mina and handed her a mirror.

Mina's mouth dropped open at what she saw—only it wasn't her mouth. It was the lush, deep, red-wine–colored mouth of a siren. Or, set against the bronzed sheen of her golden-brown skin, it looked like the mouth of an ancient Egyptian goddess. In that vein, Mina's large hazel eyes were lined in thick black, and her lashes curled and darkened to match. Her eyelids shimmered with shades of gold, drawing out the similar specks floating in the depths of her irises.

She looked…arresting, even with a head full of foils.

The short woman said to the man, "Don't wash any off when you finish her hair. You'll owe me three-hundred and twenty-five crowns' worth of product if you do."

Mina swallowed. Three hundred and twenty-five crowns for one coating of face paint? She had only ever spent that much of money on rare texts when she'd been unable to secure them through the university library.

The man merely snorted before tilting Mina's chair back. His busy hands made quick work of the foils, and soon his strong fingers were once again massaging her head in the sink.

After using another lovely-smelling product in her hair he gave it a light rinse, before tilting her upright and pulling out a strangely shaped hairdryer.

Mina closed her eyes, dreading the frizzy mess her hair would be when he'd finished with her. Her hair did not take well to blow drying.

While he set to work, Roz addressed the room. "Where are the clothes?"

Someone ran off. Mina did not see who it was.

After what felt like a lifetime of blow-drying, two sets of feet shuffled back into the room.

"You give me no time, but I still work miracles."

Mina recognized the lyrical voice of the woman with the asymmetrical haircut.

"Yes. Yes. Get over here. She's ready," Roz rasped.

The man spun Mina in the chair to face Roz.

"Stand," Roz commanded.

Mina did.

The woman handed her undergarments first—though Mina wasn't sure there was enough fabric for the underwear to be considered a garment. An impossibly thin and seamless black thong—a tiny triangle of material—slid on like silk and felt like a cool nothing.

Mina had never worn a thong.

Scholars did not wear thongs.

The woman then reached out her arm for the robe. Mina looked around, frowning. The whole team of five watched expectantly, again with no patience for her modesty. Reluctantly, she shrugged the robe off her shoulders, leaving herself exposed before them, this time topless in nothing but the thong.

The woman crouched in front of Mina with a creamy liquid gold piece of fabric that put a warm glow into the bright room.

As was clearly expected of her, Mina stepped inside its circle.

The woman pulled the garment up over Mina's hips to cover her body.

The fabric was as thin as the thong and softer than a rose petal. It whispered against her skin as the woman fastened the clasp behind her neck. The cut was a very deep halter and the fabric an exquisite silk, clearly of the highest quality. The design was simple, as elegant as it was revealing. It was virtually backless and fit snugly around her hips and rear before falling gracefully to pool around her feet.

Mina squeaked when the woman's hand darted under the dress to place a small adhesive cone over one nipple. Ignoring her, the woman repeated the process on the other breast and then stepped back to look at her handiwork.

A fierce and prideful light had appeared in the woman's eyes. Roz gave a satisfied nod, and Mina knew that whatever their goal had been, they had achieved it.

"Shoes!" Roz barked.

The girl in black ran over with a pair of elegant pumps in the same gold color as the dress. The heels were three inches, if they were anything, and Mina had never worn anything over an inch and a half.

She sighed. Of *course* there would be heels. She had never quite mastered the balance and the shifting of weight required to walk in heels with any grace. Walking around in these would be a nightmare. But as she wrapped her fingers around their bright red soles and slid her foot inside she was surprised to find them comfortable.

Roz said, "Turn around."

Mina did as she was told, and gasped when she saw the creature that stared at her from the full-length mirror that had been dug up from somewhere.

The woman in the mirror was not Dr. Amina Aldaba, only daughter of Ajit and Elke Aldaba. *That* woman wore a severe braid and boxy suits.

The woman in the mirror was an art deco goddess in a perfectly fitted dress of luminous golden silk. Her skin gleamed a warm brown, as if it had been buffed and polished like a pearl, and her hair exploded around her head and shoulders like a starburst of bouncy hydrated curls, every one defined, their dimension magnified by gorgeous highlights.

She looked like the kind of girl who danced all night and slept through lectures, rather than the sort of girl who had not gone to a single social event during the entire course of her university studies.

She looked confident and…and busty. Very, very busty.

The low cut of the dress and its snugness around the hips highlighted her figure, rather than hid it, and she fleetingly wondered what King Zayn would think. It was indeed a change from her suit.

When she finally spoke, her voice was a thin croak, pathetic even to her ears. "I'm stunning."

"Of course you are, dear. Would you expect anything less of my grand finale?"

Mina laughed, her eyes glistening, though she would never let a tear fall and mess up her makeup. "Certainly not, Roz," she said.

Roz's team started packing up their tools, and Mina tore her gaze away from a mirror to check the time. The whole process had taken the bulk of the day, but there were still two hours until the ball began.

She tottered over to the chair that sat near the window, overlooking the sea. Her current novel sat on a table beside it. Her thought was that she would not muss herself if she just sat and read, but Roz barked at her even as she began to bend.

"Stop! No sitting. Practice walking instead. We haven't much time to get you proficient. You might look the part, but it will all be for nothing if you fall flat on your face when it is time to take your mask off."

Roz deserved an award for her way with words, but Mina only snorted.

The whole team guided her in practice for an hour and twenty minutes, and then retouched everything.

Five minutes before their departure, Roz cleared her throat and the entire room stopped.

"It is time for the mask."

The girl in black and the one with the asymmetric haircut scurried out of the room, while the woman with the perfect face clapped her hands together and the bald man smiled.

Mina's stomach sank. The mask. She would wear it until midnight, at which point she would remove it and reveal to Cyrano their sham of a queen. Roz and her team could make her look the part all they wanted, but she would never truly be the stuff of queens.

The two women came back into the room, carefully carrying what looked like a small sun.

It was Mina's mask.

Fitting snugly around the top half of her head, it was made out of soft yellow-gold fabric, with long beams jutting out from it in a haloed crown of rays. It wasn't a mask that was about disguising the Queen until the big moment as much as it was a mask about identifying where to look when the time came.

It gave off its own light, for goodness' sake.

It was a spectacular creation.

Between the dress and the mask, no one would be able to take their eyes off her.

Words rose up and got trapped in her throat.

Between the gown and the mask, she would be the center of attention—Roz's grand finale.

It was all too much.

The stylist carefully placed the mask over her head, securing the latch that would hold it in place until she pressed the release button.

As she did so, the woman with the perfect face hissed, "Careful with my masterpiece."

The bald man hurried over to adjust individual curls once the mask was in place, and then stepped back with a smile.

Mina looked once more into the mirror.

The beautiful creature that stared back was made of living, breathing gold—exuding class and style despite the shine.

Tonight, the sun would set on Mina the scholar and rise on Mina the Queen.

CHAPTER FOUR

RATHER THAN CHECK the alert when it buzzed through on his phone, Zayn checked his watch.

There was still an hour and a half until the start of the ball, and the car that would drive him was not due to arrive for an hour.

He could be getting ready. The timing was not unreasonable. In fact, his assistant had been anxiously glancing at the wall clock for at least twenty minutes.

Zayn ignored both of those observations. He was determined to finish reviewing the pair of trade agreements in front of him before he allowed Mina and her ball any more space in his mind. She had been a constant presence in it over the past week and a half, despite the fact that Zayn had expended actual time and energy to ensure that she would not be in his presence.

His wife.

He would not spend his time lost in thought about his wife.

Not when there was work to be done. He refused. He was not his father, who had not been above putting off his royal responsibilities to spend time with his wife.

Zayn would not be that man. Nothing came before Cyrano. His time of being irresponsibly carefree and open had ended the day his father had been shot. As King, he had no time for brown-skinned women with moss-colored eyes who lingered in his thoughts.

He refused to waste any time on leisurely preparing his attire, like some kind of old-fashioned dandy. He might have been born into royalty, but his father had instilled in him a sense of proportion.

He turned his attention back to the agreements, his will an iron wall around his mind, defending it from the obsessive onslaught of green eyes and wayward thoughts.

Forty minutes later he was nearly two-thirds of the way through the second agreement when his phone vibrated again. Once again, he ignored it.

"Your Majesty."

Frowning, he turned his attention to his assistant. "Yes?" he asked tersely.

"I think you should see this." The man held up his phone, a slight tremor in his arm.

The headline read: *All Hail Queen Midas!* Below it was a full-body picture of Mina who, unveiled in her ball attire, revealed a body that indeed looked sculpted from gold.

She had even more curves than he'd imagined. Heels lengthened her impossibly long legs, which were clearly outlined for the first time since he'd seen them by garments that actually fit. She held her shoulders straight, her posture holding the same determination he'd witnessed her summoning for him, and the effect only enhanced her high-breasted glory.

Her mask was immense, its rays stretching out to create an invisible bubble between her and anyone who might get too close to her radiant form.

She wasn't merely gorgeous.

She was the force of gravity at the center of the universe.

And she was walking the red carpet early.

Without him.

He pulled out his phone at the same time as its buzzing

began in earnest. Alert after alert—curated courtesy of the fact that he'd set a news alert to monitor mentions of the Queen—popped up on his screen.

As images of her loaded, blood rushed in his ears, and he acknowledged to himself that he was not going to finish the trade agreements.

Pushing his chair away from his desk, he stood and stepped around the heavy furniture.

His assistant, still scrolling through images himself, started at the King's sudden movement, but quickly followed as Zayn strode out of his office.

As they walked, Zayn instructed him to have his closet man prepare his clothes and his barber meet him in his parlor.

It was time to get ready for the ball.

His clothing arrived in his room at the same time as he did and he dressed quickly, appreciating the ease of perfect tailoring. One never had to worry how one looked when one's clothes were made for one's body.

Commissioned for the event, the tuxedo was entirely black, made from thick Chinese silk. Each element of his attire, from the jacket to the butter-smooth button-down shirt, was perfectly coordinated and fitted to his body alone. Nothing about anything he wore spoke of it being a costume, and yet when he placed the midnight domino mask on his face there was no mistaking him for anything other than the King of the night himself.

The unforgiving black of the silk absorbed all light that touched it, calling to mind a dark moonless night in the dead of winter.

How convenient that Mina was the sun personified.

Ten minutes later he was in his car, on his way.

His driver pulled up and cameras flashed as he stepped out onto the red carpet.

His arrival had disrupted the flow of other prominent

citizens, but he didn't slow for photos, reaching the entrance stairs quickly and taking them two at a time.

The lobby of the grand theater had been transformed, though he had little attention for its grandeur as he cut through the parting crowd.

Inside, all of the seats had been removed and temporary flooring installed, creating the impression of walking upon a vast expanse of space. In fact the entire lower half of the large room had become the night sky, brought indoors. Taking advantage of the theater's classic gilded ceilings, the upper half of the room was an homage to daylight. Balconies had become starbursts and sunbeams. And the stage was the meeting of day and night—a twilight alcove, romantically furnished, clearly the resting place for the stars of the evening: the King and the Queen.

But she was not there.

Instead, she stood across the room, engrossed in conversation with the French ambassador.

Zayn's brow crinkled in irritation. The ambassador was a lecherous middle-aged man who had no business standing so close to the Queen of Cyrano—especially not with that appreciative light in his eyes.

Not that he could blame him.

She was divine. And she was the true meaning of the word "radiant" as a petite woman dressed all in black led her along the outer edge of the ballroom.

Moustafa and d'Tierrza followed at a close distance behind them.

The theater was crowded, with barely enough room to move around. Even this early in the evening elegantly costumed couples spun around the dance floor in the center of the room, while other partygoers milled about anywhere there was room. Wait staff carrying trays laden with champagne flutes and hors d'oeuvres wove through the crowd, handing out their wares.

For a moment, Zayn simply watched her.

Awareness of his presence, however, soon spread through the crowd, bringing a hush to the group despite the fact that the music continued.

Slowly the people parted, opening a pathway between Mina and himself. She did not notice—perhaps because she had moved on from the French ambassador and was now involved in what looked like an intense conversation with the Minister of Agriculture.

Zayn approached her without her knowing, observing as he neared that the lines of her back, revealed and accentuated as they were by her astonishing gown, were obviously the shared creation of heaven and hell.

Her spine was a graceful indentation that slid and flowed between her slim shoulder blades, drawing his gaze to the generous swell of her hips. If there was ever a reason to burn all the trousers in the country, it would be because Mina had once used them to commit the sacrilege of hiding her glorious backside.

The dress did sinful things to her legs, too. Seeing her clothed in garments that actually fit, he could now see that her legs were the true source of her above average height. And tonight she was even taller than usual—a tall golden bouquet of curves and curls.

And there was another surprise.

Freed from the severe braid, her hair was riotous—sensual, soft, and mesmerizing. He fought the urge to thrust his hand into the vibrant cloud of her hair, palm the back of her hand, and bend her face back towards his. Instead, he curled his fingers around the soft exposed flesh of her upper arm, running his thumb along the buttery-soft smoothness of her skin.

Up close, the thin film of her dress seemed so viscerally alive it was as if he felt it shiver along with the rest of her body at his touch. His senses zeroed in on her further, taking in the flush beneath the glow that hadn't been there moments before.

The music still continued, but all eyes in the room were on the King and his unknown Queen.

She turned slowly, forcing him to release her arm.

His eyes burned over her body like a grassland fire as she rotated, taking in the curve of her hips and indentation of her waist.

The front of the dress was even more of a revelation.

A full-grown woman had been hiding beneath all that oversized clothing.

He felt her with his gaze as he raked it upwards, spending extra time on her proud breasts before finally letting it make its way up to meet the wide-stretched green eyes behind the mask—eyes that had haunted him since the moment he'd seen them in the chapel.

Her breath caught, but she held her composure, giving a small vertical curtsy and murmuring, "Your Majesty." Her voice was cool, but as taut as the rest of her body.

He inclined his head, addressing her with the same cool tone. "Your Majesty."

Mina opened her mouth to speak again and Zayn felt his pulse quicken, waiting for what she would say, but the petite woman in black had stepped from behind her, holding a milky stone circlet out to him.

Her voice cracked out like a dry whip. "You're late, Your Majesty. Put this on."

Zayn's spine straightened at the familiar rasp, his hand automatically reaching out to accept the offering—obedience to this particular individual had been drilled into him since childhood.

"Roz." He inclined his head to her respectfully, before looking at what he held. It was a black circlet inlaid with moonstone. He put it on without comment.

Roz had been his royal etiquette instructor throughout

his childhood. Now she was the most sought-after event-planner in the kingdom. She was also his godmother.

A number of things about the evening made abrupt sense.

"Please join us in making the rounds, Your Majesty," Roz said.

Beside her, Mina stiffened.

Roz's request had been more order than invitation, but she was one of the few people the King still deferred to.

"It would be my honor, Roz."

He reached an arm out to the older woman, but she gave a small shake of her head. Telling himself he was doing as he was told because it was Roz, rather than because he wanted to get his hands on the silk that was Mina, he smoothly took her arm in his.

As their skin touched her scent rose up and wrapped around him—fresh and floral, with just a hint of something wicked. He closed his eyes, resisting the urge to bend his head to her neck and breathe deep.

Her flush deepened and he felt the heat of it emanating from her body. Rather than stop himself, he leaned in a fraction of an inch closer to her and breathed in her heat and her scent. Her eyes widened into mossy pools beneath her mask and her mouth opened slightly in surprise, her body frozen by his gaze.

His impact on her was obvious. The power and thrill that came with it, however, was unexpected. He was used to power. He was the King, with power over millions of souls. And yet this power… He had a feeling his power to affect this woman was somehow singular.

Roz cleared her throat loudly, saying, "If we may…?" And the moment evaporated.

Like good little soldiers, he and Mina turned at attention, in unison, but out of the corner of his eye he could see that wherever there was skin visible Mina had blushed a deep red.

Fixing him with a long stare, Roz led their trio toward another diplomat—this one from the United Kingdom.

A distinguished older man, Charles William Henry was a minor aristocrat in his home country. As its official ambassador to Cyrano, however, he held a high enough status to warrant a personal greeting from the King and Queen—Zayn credited that fact with his seeking of the position in the first place.

"Your Majesty…" The man oozed over Mina's hand with an enthusiasm that grated on Zayn's ears. "It is truly a pleasure to finally make your acquaintance. I must say it was worth the wait, however. You are more radiant than the sun. Apollo must bow when you enter a room."

Zayn didn't know which was more grating on his nerves: the man's abysmal poetry or the way he extended every syllable in his exaggerated posh accent.

Below her mask, however, Mina smiled. It was the first true smile Zayn had ever seen her wear, and it spread across the lower portion of her face, showing too many teeth for a proper queen's smile, but all the more bright and breathtaking for it. It cut through him as if he were a storm cloud and she a literal ray of sunshine.

Only the fact that it had been a rain of asinine compliments that had somehow managed to make her glow kept him from falling under the spell of the smile himself.

"You are too kind, sir. I understand your family owns property in the South of England? I have always heard the country there is lovely."

Both men started when she spoke. Her English was clear and understandable, if slightly North-American-accented, and Zayn found himself perversely pleased that, wherever she had learned the language, it had not been Britain.

"You speak English, Your Majesty!" the ambassador

exclaimed. "When I learned you were native to Cyrano, I did not expect it—most citizens don't, as you know," he said, insulting their country with mock abashment. "Indeed, Your Majesty, I *am* from the south of England. Thank you for noticing. And, yes, there is nothing quite like it. It would be my honor to host you there. I am certain I could give you a proper English time."

A muscle in the back of Zayn's neck twitched as the man's words grew bolder with each passing moment. Establishing a bond between the two kingdoms had been one of Zayn's many coups. Great Britain was a global power. The fact that it would acknowledge Cyrano as anything more than a Mediterranean backwater had been unprecedented.

However, now, as the ambassador undressed the Queen with his eyes, his voice dripping with suggestion, Zayn found himself wondering how necessary that diplomatic relationship really was.

Resisting the urge to put the question to the test, Zayn simply put himself between the other man and the Queen, responding for her, his voice as soft as velvet as it wrapped around the English words.

"Of course there will be tours in the future. However, I plan to keep my new bride to myself for as long as possible. Newlyweds—I'm sure you understand."

He guided Mina away from the man with Roz following.

"Very subtle and diplomatic, Zayn," she observed.

The humor in Roz's voice eased the tension in his neck as if he were slipping into well-worn leather boot, gently reminding him that he was acting like a fool.

Rather than respond to that, though, he said, "I assume you're behind Mina's transformation?"

"Well, hello to you too, Your Royal Majesty."

Mina's voice matched Roz's for dryness. Zayn shuddered to think what else she might have picked up from her time with the older woman.

"You were late," Roz observed.

They were ganging up on him.

Zayn smiled, "And I thought you were early."

Again, Roz snorted. "A queen is never early."

She started to guide their group forward again—Zayn imagined to make more introductions. But he found he did not care to continue the rounds, filing away the name of each and every single man who stared overlong at the Queen, when he could have the golden star of the night all to himself.

Roz pointed them toward a cluster of popular musicians, but Zayn shook his head. "The Queen is wilting." He nodded toward Mina who, if anything, glowed with her own inner light.

"I'm fine, thank you," she said, irritation threading through her voice.

He shook his head distinctly, negating her statement. "You are a dimming sun. It's time for you to set. You can't be used to standing in heels for so long."

Mina's mouth dropped into the O of outrage he was so familiar with and he smiled. Roz lifted her eyebrow at being crossed, but gave a short nod, watching their interaction closely. She could add it to the list of transgressions he was sure he would hear about from her later.

Leaving her to act as hostess, he led Mina to the stage and helped her into the seat that had clearly been designed for her dress. She didn't sit, exactly, as much as recline regally. A subtle golden spotlight beamed down on her where she rested, maintaining her haloed image even as a very human sigh escaped her.

At her side, of the same height as her unique chair, was a dark, high-backed throne, obviously intended for him. She would look like a celestial sphinx stretched out next to a dark midnight king. Even sitting, the royal couple would remain the center of attention—and conversation—for the night.

Roz had considered every detail.

Rather than simply letting the old devil have her way, though, he remained standing. Mina stared up at him, her eyes glowing especially green in the light, and he had to fight the urge to dive into their mossy depths. This close, he was caught in the web of her scent and temperature, mesmerized by the thin silk of her dress, which seemed to reveal more and more to delight his eyes the longer he was near her.

He sucked in a deep breath.

The effect she was having on him was a manufactured thing, created by Roz, and yet knowing that did nothing to dampen it.

Pulling his attention away from her, he lifted his hand in a signal for refreshments.

In an instant a quintet of servers arrived, their heavy platters laden, offering each option on the floor.

He reached for two flutes of champagne and offered her the first selection. Taking the glass, she thanked him before choosing a small cracker dressed with some kind of cheese and slivers of tomato and basil from one of the trays. She ate delicately, for all that her morsel disappeared in one bite, and he watched her do it, arrested by the series of movements in her eating, from the parting of her full lips to the contraction of her throat muscles as she swallowed.

He shook his head lightly. He needed to get away from her. He would leave immediately after the unmasking. Until then, he would remain in the place Roz had clearly assigned him, as a king on full display.

"Roz outdid herself tonight," he commented.

"She did." Her words were clipped and close.

He felt irritation rising in his blood. She was wary. *Of him.*

"Admirable of you to admit it," he said dryly.

Instead of rising to his bait, Mina smiled. "It would have been a disaster without Roz." She waved her hand toward the room, adding, "Instead, it's the sun and the moon."

"She knows how to throw a party," he agreed.

This time Mina laughed, and the honest clarity of the sound went straight into his blood, as energizing as it was agitating.

"That's quite the understatement," she said, when she could speak.

The corners of his own lips lifted of their own accord, and behind her mask her eyes widened.

His chest heated with pure male satisfaction. He wasn't the only one caught up in Roz's mirage.

With a nod, he said, "The woman is a force of nature."

As if sensing their conversation, Roz appeared on the stage, accompanied by a tall, slender older woman in an elegant blue gown and a peacock feather mask.

Zayn rose and gave the woman a bow. "Aunt Seraphina."

The woman nodded to him with a smile, "It's supposed to be a mystery, Your Majesty."

"My apologies. You look lovely."

Seraphina d'Tierrza, his maternal aunt, shook her head with a mild reprimand. "Flattering an old woman when you have your beautiful Queen beside you?"

Her voice was as warm and as gently teasing as it had been when he was a little boy, caught climbing trees with her daughter.

Zayn offered Mina a hand, their fingers exchanging a mild electric shock upon contact, and when she stood her scent once again wrapped around him, capturing his complete attention, even if for only a moment.

Mina reached a hand out to Seraphina. "It's so wonderful to finally meet you. Your daughter has been heaven-sent."

Her voice followed the model of her scent, its warm tones enveloping him in her spell.

"I'm glad you think so, Your Majesty. Not everyone has the sense to appreciate her as you do. We are very proud of her being a member of your guard."

"More than that." Mina smiled. "She is a friend."

His aunt beamed beneath the new young Queen's words and Zayn frowned.

"You are truly the gem my Helene claimed you to be." His aunt's voice sparkled.

Surely his aunt—the sister of a queen herself, and the nation's only remaining duchess—could see how unsuitable Mina was for her new role. Yet here she was, extending a warm familial welcome to the cuckoo in the nest.

He'd always thought of his aunt among the least sentimental of the bunch. Of course, Mina *had* just complimented her child. Every mother had a weak spot when it came to flattery of her children.

Roz led Seraphina away after a few more pleasantries, only to return with someone new. The woman was obviously determined they circulate, even if she had to bring people to them. The observation brought with it a mischievous spark he hadn't felt since he and his cousin's days of scheming to evade Roz "the dragon lady" and her plans.

As it had then, Zayn's mind bent itself to the creative task as Roz led away her latest guest to exchange him for another.

Turning to Mina, he smiled, drawing her into the game that had only ever belonged to him and his cousin. "We're going to dance," he said.

Unexpectedly, Mina shook her head in a fast and firm negative.

"You can't tell me you are enjoying this introduction train?" he asked imperiously.

Mina swallowed, but she held her ground with another slight shake of the head.

Out of the corner of his eye he saw Roz making her way through the crowd with the Dowager Countess of Redcliff. Their progress was slow, as the one-hundred-and-four-year-old Countess moved rather...deliberately.

"You must," he commanded, holding out his hand to assist her.

If she did not take his hand it would be in the news tomorrow. He wondered if she'd realized that yet.

Fortunately, she did not put it to the test, taking his hand with a sigh.

"We're not going to dance," she insisted.

And then he understood. And, like the spark that had had him leading her to the floor, a boyish thrill shot through his veins.

"You can't dance."

It wasn't a question.

She blushed, but gave a sharp nod.

He laughed. "Of course you can't."

Mina winced, but his grin only grew.

"Don't worry, Mina mine. I am an excellent lead."

"You're something, all right," she muttered.

He led her on, riding high on the strange cocktail of youthful excitement and lust stirring in his blood. They passed Roz and the Dowager Countess as they made their way to the floor. Roz's eyes narrowed at the King, and their glances were exchanged in the knowledge that she knew exactly what he was up to.

His grin stretched wider, and even the indomitable Roz was affected, the firm lines of her glare softening.

But softening was not the same as disappearing altogether.

Catching Zayn's arm in her bony talon as they passed, Roz hissed, "The unmasking will happen at the end of your dance! You'll have to take the mask off for her—there's a clasp in the back."

Then she let them go.

Zayn led Mina to the dance floor, a pathway clearing before them. Other dancers left the floor as they approached the center, a warm spotlight finding them as they came to a stop, facing each other.

He wasn't sure whether it was due to the rush of success in dodging Roz, or simply the primal effect of Mina's radiant glow in the spotlight, but although they were surrounded, the rest of the room slowly disappeared as he looked at her.

Reaching out his arms, he took her by the waist and pulled her body flush against his. As tall as she was in the heels and the mask, her head still came only to his shoulder, allowing him to rest his cheek on the smooth front of her mask, his own expression shielded by the emanating rays.

Her dress was a warm second skin beneath his palm and her lush curves pressed against the hard planes of his own body. Heat and blood rushed to his core as if this were the first time he'd ever drawn a woman close on a dance floor.

Her palm came to rest softly at his shoulder while he stretched their arms out, hands gently clasped. She sucked in a breath, her breasts brushing against his chest in the process, the sensation stealing his own breath.

The orchestra struck up his favorite waltz.

He had no idea who the performers were, but they knew his favorite waltz.

It was good to be King.

Zayn drew her into the dance, and for first time since he'd met her she gracefully followed his lead.

The floor had cleared completely by this point, and he took advantage of the space to set them a double-time pace, leaving her breathless and clinging to him. Smile wide, she seemed too focused on holding him to be nervous. Scientist that she was, she gave in to the momentum of their bodies, allowing her hips to press into his naturally, reminding him exactly why this dance had been banned during his country's more conservative historical eras.

So focused was his mind on the press and heat of her that it took him some time to realize that the joyful notes weaving their way into the music were the sound of her laughter. Bubbling around them, it wove its way into his blood like the finest champagne, silky and reserved for an exchange of goods that cost far more than money.

He slowed down as the familiar chords came to their conclusion until they stood together in the large warm spotlight, chests pressed close and lifting in unison, eyes locked on each other.

Conversation in the room fell silent.

As if compelled, she lifted her hands to the sides of his face. Zayn closed his eyes as her fingertips trailed through his hair, seeking and finding the thin leather straps that held his domino mask in place. He felt a small surge of power as her eyes widened when she removed the mask. She would never be able to hide her reaction to him. Somehow he knew that.

He pulled the mask from her hand and dropped it to the ground without a glance, then drew the pads of her fingertips to his mouth, to place small kisses on each one. Then he drew her closer to reach his hands around her neck and find the clasp at the back of her mask.

He pressed the release and the mask unlocked.

With two hands, he lifted it from her head slowly. Two servers appeared at his side to carefully carry the solid gold creation away.

Bright curls exploded around Mina's head, replacing the mask to bathe and halo her face in light.

Her face was even more of a masterpiece than the mask. Gold flakes sparkled in the emerald of her irises, and the creamy golden brown of her skin glowed in the light. She was all sparkling eyes and slightly parted plush lips, and there was nothing for him to do but thrust his fingers into her hair, cup the back of her skull where it met her neck, and possess her.

Her breath caught as their lips met, etching the moment into memory through all of his senses—taste, touch, sight, scent, and sound. Her lips were velvet-soft and plump as she leaned into him, returning the kiss, as lost as he was to the current sweeping over them.

The crowd erupted into cheers, abruptly grinding the madness to a halt—he was the King and this display was unseemly—and yet he still broke the kiss gently, unable to rip himself away from her despite his horror at what he had just done.

Her eyes fluttered open, clouded still with the haze of their kiss, and, fighting the urge to pull her back to him, he acknowledged that forgetting decorum seemed to be one of the results of proximity to Mina.

Slowly, but with a flourish, he spun her out to his side and raised her arm, the smooth flow of his movements smoothing over his breach of etiquette and giving him some distance from its cause at the same time.

Another cheer rang out from the crowd. Cyrano loved its new Queen. Now Zayn just had to figure out what to do about it.

CHAPTER FIVE

A MASSIVE POUNDING shook Mina from a heavy sleep and what she was sure had been a pleasant dream. Warm lethargy lingered in her body and almost had her rolling over to try to find it again.

Unfortunately, the pounding continued.

Groaning, she sat up—only to realize that not all the noise was coming from *outside* her head.

And here, she'd always heard that fine champagne didn't have consequences…

Lifting the weighted comforter in order to get up, she was startled to realize she wore only the thin strip of cloth that the styling team all seemed to agree was underwear.

To her horror, the golden dress lay in a puddle on the floor beside the bed, alongside the heels that had had her feet aching by the end of the night. She realized she had no idea what had become of her mask.

The sheets were smooth and slick where they touched her bare skin, which should have been a soothing counter to the pounding in her head, but as she typically slept in an oversized T-shirt rather than *au naturel*, the sensation only served to accentuate the sense of unfamiliarity.

Once covered, she answered her suite door.

Moustafa and d'Tierrza stood on the other side, the latter grinning like a fool.

"Good morning, sunshine! You've been summoned."

Her brow crinkling, Mina's voice was a dry croak. "Summoned?"

D'Tierrza rolled her eyes. "His Royal Majesty has commanded your presence at breakfast."

Mina frowned. Not once in the time since she'd been at the palace had Zayn requested her presence for a meal. Of course, that had been before he had kissed her in front of the entire country.

The memory of it flooded her senses as she stood in the doorway.

He'd kissed her on the dance floor, in view of everyone in attendance, and then there had been too many toasts to count, as if they were celebrating the dawn of a new year, rather than a new queen.

Mina groaned and squeezed her eyes shut. Now, at least to the rest of the world, their marriage was very real.

Dressing quickly, she met her guards at the door, flashing her best determined smile and saying, "Lead the way."

The two guards led Mina through a new series of twisting hallways and corridors until they came to yet another set of high wooden doors.

Moustafa and d'Tierrza pressed them open for her and Mina walked in, her head high. She would face the King this morning with dignity—even if she had no idea how you faced someone you had kissed.

The King sat at the end of a long table, face hidden behind his newspaper. It occurred to Mina that the length of the dining table and hall seemed particularly excessive when one was slowly approaching one's mercurial husband who had kissed one the night before.

A staff member in crisply starched attire rushed forward to pull out her chair as she neared, and the King finally lowered his paper.

As always, his beauty struck Mina like a physical blow.

In the fresh morning light the darkness of his hair and the deep violet of his eyes were so pure she could drown in them. As usual, he wore all black. This morning his clothing consisted of a perfectly tailored black button-up shirt with a sheen to it, and trim black pants that appeared to flow with the line of his leg like water.

The table was set with breakfast for two, and it crossed Mina's mind that her presence had been assumed. Summoned, indeed...

The King cleared his throat as the breakfast server pushed her chair in for her, and his brows came together in a frown as he took in her appearance.

"They're calling it a love match," he said.

"Excuse me?" she choked out.

"The nation's media outlets are quite abuzz about it this morning. They say I fell madly in love with a commoner. The story is currently the most trending topic online in Cyrano."

Mina's stomach twisted. "Should we correct them?"

At the King's decisive shake of his head she felt some of the tension ease in her. She didn't know what that reaction said about her integrity, but the thought of clarifying the nature of their relationship for the public was more than she could bear.

"It serves no purpose. However, I prefer that my personal life not be the nation's most trending topic. Therefore, we're going to the summer palace, in order to give the public time to find something else to fixate upon."

"We are?"

"We'll leave by the end of the day. The Champions League finals begin in three days. That should be enough distraction to supersede any gossip about us. We will be gone for five days, as we must be here in attendance for the Ambassadors' Dinner on the fifteenth. Are you going to eat or simply stare at your plate?"

"Yes…" Mina said, reaching to serve herself from the platters of fruit and pastries and fluffy golden eggs laid out in front of her—though she wasn't sure she was hungry, and this was the first she was hearing about the Ambassadors' Dinner. Her secretary probably thought she had enough to deal with before then.

"We will leave here at five p.m. We'll have a late meal at the summer palace, and then enjoy the island. The Ambassadors' Dinner is one of the less glamorous royal engagements. Returning for that should keep any mention of us to the government pages, rather than the front page of the culture section."

He indicated the paper he'd set aside earlier, and Mina noticed the picture for the first time.

It was her and Zayn, their bodies molded to one another, lips pressed close—the very picture of a man and woman in love, or at the very least in lust.

Her cheeks heated, flushing beet-red through the brown of her skin.

The passion between the couple in the photo was undeniable, and yet none of it was real. Her husband was a stranger who could barely stand the sight of her. He certainly didn't harbor any passion for her.

Her stomach churned again, threatening to upend the few bites of breakfast she had managed to swallow.

The King appeared indifferent, as if being discussed in the newspapers and photographed in such a personal embrace was a common occurrence for him. Though, come to think of it, it probably was. He had likely been photographed kissing women more times than he could count—whereas she could say with certainty that she had never been photographed anywhere so near *in flagrante delicto* as this.

It was easy to be certain when you had only ever had one kiss in your whole life. And now hers had been immortalized on the front page of the "Arts & Culture" section of the *Cyranese Times*.

She wondered if this was what her father had had in mind when he'd given her away to the King. He'd certainly been vigilant in protecting her chastity.

"Boys? Sss! No boys! You have no time for boys. Not when you must work. Work hard, my Princess, for the good of Cyrano."

She hated it that what had seemed like memories of normal fatherly protectiveness had come to take on such a cynical nature now. And it wasn't just her memories. It was her entire life.

She had been so proud of her accomplishments. It hadn't been easy to become the youngest female scientist ever nominated for the King's council. But the years of sacrifice, the endurance, the at times cruel reshaping of herself—now she couldn't figure out exactly why she had done any of it.

She had thought it was because it was the one thing she had left of her father—the final living ember of a love that she had thought as transparent as it had been absolute. But she had been wrong—so wrong. All of it had been done so that rather than being a private miracle, her first kiss could be the stuff of headlines.

The thought was like a rock in her stomach.

She ate without noticing flavor or texture, her mind churning over the photo and the kiss. It seemed Zayn wasn't going to mention it at all. Was a front-page kiss so commonplace to him that it didn't bear remark?

Looking at him surreptitiously out of the corner of her eye, she imagined that, once again, the answer was yes. A kiss wouldn't mean much to a man who looked like him— let alone one who had grown up as the heir to the throne and then become King. She imagined women had been throwing themselves at him since long before it had been allowed according to the Cyranese age of consent laws.

He ate deliberately, clearly feeling no need to fill the silence that stretched between them. In the absence of conversation, the sounds of their eating filled the quiet morning—however, instead of feeling awkward, the experience of eating breakfast with the King was somehow more intimate for its lack of forced chatter.

Mina was reminded of the mornings of her childhood, the details of individual days blurring together to emphasize what had been commonplace: her mother and father moving in sync through the steps of their morning routine with the practiced familiarity of a long marriage.

The memory was a painful twist in her chest. The silence of those mornings had been companionable, unlike the quiet that enveloped her and the King now, and yet the comparison lingered in her mind just the same.

She and the King shared no loving glances, and their eyes were not full of the previous night's memories and plans for the day ahead. Neither of them reached toward the other with small caresses or touch points. And yet they were still a man and a woman—husband and wife—sharing a meal. She certainly hadn't shared the experience with any other men in her life.

The realization was both revealing and sad. It was becoming more and more clear to her that she should have gotten out more. She hadn't needed to sow her wild oats, but it wouldn't have hurt her or derailed her career to go on a date once in her life. And it would have certainly gone a long way toward her not being the kind of woman so starved for companionship that she was finding it in a stilted meal with a stranger.

"Where is the summer palace?" she asked, both to break the silence and to stem the internal tide of self-recrimination.

Turning the full power of his attention to her, the King replied, "Cantorini Island."

She started. She'd heard the name of the famous private island, but had had no idea it was tied to the royal family. "I've heard it's beautiful there."

The King smiled, his features softening in the process, making him look almost boyish. "It is. It's private, of course, and remote. The only structures on the island are associated with the summer palace compound. It's a wonderful escape from the constant observation of the capital."

Between his smile and the open warmth of his tone, Mina's heart stuttered. He had no idea how dangerous he was.

"There are supposed to be multiple species endemic to the island," she said, inwardly cringing at this offering to the conversation as soon as it was out.

But the King's smile grew. "That's right. Most of the island is vegetated, and it provides excellent habitat for a number of native species. We occasionally allow groups of biologists and students access, for observation and data collection."

The corners of Mina's lips lifted in response. "That's right! I considered applying for the trip between my junior and sophomore years of college, but I was selected for a fellowship in the Galapagos instead."

"Well, as you have the opportunity to visit now, it appears you made the right choice at the time."

The stiff response hung between them, effectively cooling the warmth that had grown.

"Yes. Well…" Mina searched for a smooth exit but, finding none, settled on, "I have some coordinating to do in order to be ready to leave this afternoon, so…"

Telling herself that the fact that the King looked mildly relieved at her words stung only a little bit, Mina rose as he said, "Yes, of course. Five o'clock, then."

Mina nodded, excusing herself from the long dining room and letting out a sigh only after shutting the door behind her.

Moustafa and d'Tierrza stood to attention on either side of the door. Sensing them, Mina took a breath and straightened her shoulders. She never would have guessed it could happen, but she was actually coming to find comfort in the constancy of their presence.

With a half-smile, she said, "Well, ladies, it looks like we're going to the summer palace."

D'Tierrza started, before quickly catching Moustafa's eye.

Mina was immediately uneasy. "What?"

Moustafa opened her mouth to say something, only to close it again. On her second try, she got out, "Guards are not allowed at the summer palace."

Mina's eyebrows came together. "That doesn't make any sense."

D'Tierrza took over. "The summer palace is a retreat for the royal family—a place for them to go to feel normal. The staff there live in residence year-round, are heavily vetted, and are all military trained. With them around, members of the royal family can be free to go about their day safely, without guards."

"But that means it will be just the two of us…"

Moustafa winced at Mina's forlorn tone.

D'Tierrza let out a bark of laughter and began to lead them back towards the Queen's Wing. "You'll love Cantorini. Just make sure to have the staff pack some books…" D'Tierrza narrowed her eyes at her Queen "…and a swimsuit."

Nine hours later a chauffeur opened the back door of a sleek black SUV and Mina got in, her bags long-ago stowed and packed by someone else, filled with mysterious clothing items selected by her staff. She imagined there was a swimsuit somewhere in there…

The thought brought a smile to her face—which was

more than could be said for the King, who had followed her into the car before the chauffeur shut the door behind him.

Though he'd said no more than a few words to her in greeting, his presence had dominated her senses from the moment they'd met outside the palace at one of the many private entrances.

Like her, he wore the same clothes he had at breakfast. Unlike her, he remained as flawlessly put together as he had been that morning.

As spacious as the vehicle they were enclosed in was, his fragrance still enveloped her, throwing her back to the sensation of being wrapped up in him, his lips pressed against hers.

Mina's breath caught as she tamped down the memory. That was most certainly not the thing to think about while traveling alone and in close quarters with the King.

"Was the rest of your day productive?" she asked, hoping shop talk would do the job of breaking the tension between them.

Swinging his gaze lazily to capture hers, he let his eyes pin her against the seat. Her breath caught. His nostrils flared slightly and she felt herself lean forward, drawn toward him despite the danger obvious in his regard.

A spark lit in his stare at her movement, the corner of his mouth lifting slightly, and she realized he knew the effect he had on her. Something wild and indignant in her demanded she break free of the hold, but he was too strong.

His words were drawn out, slow and languid in a way she'd never heard him speak before, when he asked, "Do you really care how my day went?"

And although her body shivered at all the unspoken things in his voice that showed what he thought she really cared about, Mina found herself surprised by the truth in her words when she replied, a tad breathlessly, "Yes."

Something in her reply took him aback, though she

didn't know if it was the honesty that had surprised her, or the unspoken invitation to talk about statecraft itself.

He shrugged and sat back, snapping the tautness between them as he traded a bit of languid grace for upright alertness. Mina found herself regretting the loss.

"I secured two new international trade agreements, resisted a foreign power's overreach into Cyranese affairs, and set the stage for establishing an official diplomatic relationship with the Kingdom of Montenegro."

Mina's breath caught in her throat. The fact that he had answered—and not facetiously—felt somehow more important than it probably was. But it was what he'd said, the casual mention of allegiances and world politics, which shook her to the core. He was the King. His days were comprised of the stuff of nations.

And what were *her* days comprised of? Royal summonses and waiting for others to coordinate her luggage. Falling softly back against the seat, she mourned the loss of her old identity once more.

Queen Amina's days were idled away. Dr. Mina Aldaba's days had been spent in research and study, her mind applied to the most pressing concerns of modern science.

But she had asked the King a question, and she was being rude in dwelling on herself. "That sounds like a very productive day," she said.

He smirked at her. "Where did I lose you? Trade agreements?"

Mina frowned. "Of course not. I understand how important advantageous trade agreements are for a small nation like ours."

His smirk blossomed into a real smile, and Mina realized he'd deliberately worked a rise out of her. Her own lips stretched wide, unconsciously imitating his light expression, and as they did so his face changed, as if he were suddenly transfixed.

How long they would have stayed that way, staring at one another, Mina had no idea, but fortunately the car came to a stop, breaking the moment.

Seconds later the door opened and the chauffeur offered her a hand. Stepping out onto Tarmac, Mina deduced that they must be taking the small plane that waited about six meters away, its rounded door open, a stairway lowered.

Attendants ushered them quickly to the plane. On board, the King checked the safety equipment before showing Mina the amenities. About halfway through the mini-tour, Mina realized the plane was his private plane, and that he loved it.

"The flight is short—just forty-five minutes in the air—but it's the safest way to get to the island at this time of year."

His posture had lost some its characteristic rigidity since they'd boarded the plane, and his voice had taken on a note of youthful excitement that hinted at the kind of man he might have been before his father's death.

The idea filled Mina with the strangest urge to have known him then—before he became King. She didn't know where it came from, but she couldn't shake the sensation that he must have been different—lighter, more joyful.

"I've never taken such a short flight," she said, although the scientist in her was frowning somewhat at the impact this small flight might have on a delicate eco-system like Cantorini's.

Reading her mind, the King said, "The benefit of a plane this size is that we've been able to retrofit it to run on completely renewable energy. In fact, the entire summer palace was updated six years ago, to achieve a net zero impact on the island. The technology isn't scalable for all of Cyrano yet, but at this point it's just a matter of time."

She was impressed. While wealth like the royal family's

made such experimentation infinitely more possible, not many who had the capacity also had the will.

"That's wonderful. Your parents must have had excellent forethought to do that. So when do we take off?" she asked.

But the King shook his head. "It was my idea. I pestered my father until he was willing to do anything to shut me up."

His eyes lit with the memory, his smile turning into a downright grin, and Mina was enchanted. "It must've cost a fortune," she said.

His grin stretched. "It did. Well worth it to know the future of the island is safer, though. I've always loved going there."

"I can imagine. A place to run around like a normal child... That had to be precious to you."

His face softened as he nodded. "It was. It can be a challenge to be a prince and a child at the same time."

Her heart reached out to that boy with the pressure of a nation on his shoulders. Her own childhood had been bright and free, even though she now knew that her father had arranged for her to be a queen before it had even begun. Her dreams and his encouragement had pushed her to achieve, but for all the striving she'd still been a normal girl. Her parents had ensured that.

"I'm glad you had a place to escape."

He turned to face her at her words, searching her face for something, and even though she didn't know how she knew, she could sense it was genuineness. Her heart broke for him. He was adored and idolized by an entire nation, and yet starving for everyday acts of compassion.

She had the feeling he didn't have many people he could talk to.

"Me too," he said. "I was fortunate that Hel was a member of the royal family as well. Otherwise there would have been no other children to play with."

"D'Tierrza? You two are close?"

He nodded. "We always have been. A cousin makes a convenient best friend."

"It's good you two had each other."

He laughed. "I won't argue with that. Without my steadying influence, who knows where the woman would have ended up?"

Mina snorted. As Helene d'Tierrza had flouted every aristocratic convention and continued to cause controversy by holding her position in the Royal Guard, she had to wonder indeed.

The King smiled. "And, in answer to your earlier question, we take off when I get in there." He angled his head toward the cockpit.

She started. "You're flying us?"

The grin that flashed across his face at her astonishment was pure and light and worth every iota of uncertainty resting in her gut about putting her fate in the hands of a hobby pilot.

Anxiety stood no chance against the cocky ease in his expression. Its spark was like a snapshot to the past, undoubtedly more familiar to older versions of himself. Her heart thudded even as the right side of her brain demanded she collect more information.

"When did you learn how to fly?" she asked. Somehow it didn't seem politic for the nation's future King to have engaged in such a risky recreational activity.

His grin stretched wider, and she had the distinct impression that she was going to be even more shocked by his response.

"When I was fifteen."

"Fifteen?" Mina sputtered. "That can't be legal!"

He shrugged, obviously enjoying her shock, before asking insouciantly, "What's 'legal' to the King?"

"I should hope a lot. And you weren't the King then," she pointed out.

He shrugged. "What's legal to the Queen?"

"The Queen let you fly planes at fifteen?"

He laughed at the incredulity in her voice and nodded. "She did. Insisted, in fact."

"That doesn't seem very safe…"

Zayn tsked. "That's awfully judgmental of you, Dr. Aldaba."

She shook her head. "Reasonable. You were the only heir to the throne."

"As you are about to entrust your health and wellbeing to my flying, I'd have to beg to argue that it's incredibly safe. I never would have imagined that you, Dr. Amina Aldaba, youngest scholar ever nominated for the King's council and barrier-breaking pioneer, were so old-fashioned."

Instead of stinging, his words brought a smile to her face. He wasn't throwing her lost dreams in her face— he was teasing her. The idea filled her with an unfamiliar feeling of warmth.

"I am an excellent pilot, if you're worried," he added.

She looked up to meet his violet gaze, saying with complete honesty, "I have no doubt you are excellent at everything you do."

Her words hung in the suddenly charged air between them. She hadn't meant them as anything but a straightforward observation, but somehow, in the atmosphere of it being just she and the King together, the words throbbed with innuendo.

Clearing his throat, the King said, "Glad to know I have your confidence. Now, if we're ever going to arrive, I'd better get this bird in the air."

He left her in the cabin with a nod, heading into the cockpit and closing the door between them with a decisive click.

Mina took her seat and clicked the seat belt, though there was no light to indicate she needed to do so in the luxurious interior. Alone, without the presence of her husband to absorb her focus, she had more time to examine every element of takeoff.

Fortunately, their transition from thousands of pounds in weight of land-bound metal to weightless flying creature was buttery-smooth. Better, she had to acknowledge, than any commercial flight she'd ever been on.

The first twenty minutes of the flight were smooth and clear, with the island soon coming into sight. Sooner than she would have imagined. Given the height and angle of the plane to the island, and the lack of any visible infrastructure, she was surprised when they banked toward a gorgeous long stretch of sandy beach.

Her geometry was rusty, but a frown came to her brow as they began what felt like a descent right on to the beach. There was no runway in sight.

She entered the cockpit to find the King ramrod-straight in the pilot's seat, gripping the wheel with what was surely an unnecessary amount of muscle. His neck was tense and his entire being was focused on guiding the plane toward the beach ahead of them.

She looked once more from the King to the beach, and then back to the King again.

"We're having to make an emergency landing on that beach, aren't we?" she asked as if she had been asking about the weather. Her nerves felt strangely numb as she took in the situation, while her mind, well-muscled and rigorously disciplined, processed the data.

"We are."

He didn't look at her. He shouldn't and she didn't really want him to. She wanted him to land the plane. With all her heart, as it turned out. It took only one stark moment for her to realize that she wanted her life—even if it consisted of tattered dreams and ill-suited roles.

"I was afraid of that." She was far too calm for the situation going on around them. She recognized that, and knew that it suggested she was in shock. In a mild haze, she asked, "What can I do?"

He shook his head. "Nothing. It appears our engine has stalled, so unless by chance you have some knowledge of aerospace engineering, I suggest you sit tight." He spoke sarcastically, though his forearms flexed against the plane's yoke.

Mina nodded. She did not, so she sat calmly in the copilot's seat, closed and adjusted her seatbelt, and was still. Searching for something to hold on to, her hand found the King's thigh, and she squeezed as she watched the rapid approach of the long beach of rich chocolate-brown sand.

At what felt like the last possible moment, he straightened the plane, lifting its nose just enough to bring the wheels into jarring contact with sand, rather than the front end of the plane. They skidded to a halt, the plane's front end digging huge tracks into the beach but miraculously holding its shape and integrity.

"Are you all right?" the King asked, once the noise and dust had settled around them.

After her breath returned, Mina nodded.

"Thank God." The words came out on an exhale, along with the unspoken message that he'd been far more uncertain about landing than he'd projected.

Taking a deep breath, Mina said, "I'm glad you know how to fly planes."

The King let out a shaky laugh. "Me too." But he was back to business quickly. "Now, I hope you're ready to walk. It's about a half-day's trek through the woodlands to get to the cabin, and then another couple of hours of pretty steep hiking from there to get to the summer palace, as the crow flies."

Mina nodded. After surviving an emergency plane landing, she could handle a half-day hike through gentle woodlands.

"Leave your luggage here for now—just worry about water. The cabin is stocked, as is the summer palace. The clean-up team will collect what's here."

"Won't they be looking for us at the plane?"

"I sent them a message in my SOS. They know we're heading to the cabin rather than waiting. This beach is inaccessible via land vehicle, and we do not have any ship large enough nearby to handle carrying the plane, so it will take hours for the crew to get organized."

He was up and moving, grabbing items from the cabin as he spoke, and soon Mina had no choice but to follow the King across the beach and into the woods.

CHAPTER SIX

"Take off the sweater," Zayn said through clenched teeth, waiting for an obviously overheated Mina to catch up once again.

While the wild woods of Cantorini were renowned in the region for their density, they remained Mediterranean woodlands, comprised of a mixture of oaks and mixed sclerophylls. It was an infinitely traversable landscape, even if the rocky terrain was brutal on the ankles. But not if one was wearing a wool sweater more appropriate for a winter evening by the sea than a warm summer walk through the woods.

"Excuse me, I will not," she insisted.

It was the same thing she'd said each time he'd made the demand, but this time he was going to make her do it. He was the King, after all. It was his prerogative to order people to do things.

Her cheeks had a rosy flush to them that had nothing to do with her reaction to him, and her skin glistened with perspiration. He wasn't having it. She had only a few more miles in her before heatstroke set in, and they had more miles than that before they'd reach the cabin.

Rather than repeat the order, he simply began to unbutton his own shirt.

Mina's green gaze widened. "What are you doing?"

"Giving you my shirt."

"What?"

"You're going to wear my shirt."

"I couldn't," she said, shaking her head.

"I insist," he ground out, his irritation at being resisted growing with every button he freed.

"Absolutely not."

"If it requires my tearing that atrocious sweater off your body with my bare hands, I absolutely insist."

"You wouldn't dare," she challenged.

"As that eyesore has been burning itself into my mind's eye since the early hours of this morning, I can assure you I would. Quite happily."

He said the last with a growl in his voice and Mina took a step back.

Fighting the urge to roll his eyes, he said, "I'm the King, Mina. Not a murderer. You're going to get heatstroke if you don't take off the damn sweater."

She stared at him mutinously and he prepared for another refusal, inwardly curious at the idea of making good on his word. The image of relieving her of her clothing, albeit with more finesse than she was likely expecting, lent itself to all kinds of intriguing conclusions.

But it wasn't to be.

"Turn around," she said.

He raised an eyebrow. "Really, Mina? We've just survived an emergency plane landing, we're alone in the woods, and we're married."

She set her jaw and nodded.

"You're a child," he said, turning.

Behind him, she muttered under her breath, "Just because I'm not an exhibitionist like everyone else around here…"

He found himself smiling. And that in itself was unexpected. After starting his day with the punch to the solar plexus that had been Mina fresh in the morning, and closing it out by crash landing his favorite plane on a heretofore pristine beach, he wouldn't have thought he could muster the mood for a smile.

Stealing a quick glance over his shoulder, though, he caught a flash of Mina's golden-brown skin before it disappeared beneath the black of his shirt and realized he could do more than smile. The glimpse was over before he'd barely had time to register it, and banally chaste at that, yet his mouth watered. The heat that raced through him was the same heat that had overtaken him when she had been in his arms the night before.

Had it only been the night before when he'd kissed her for the first time? He'd have to add bending time to her list of uncanny abilities, this stranger who was his wife. In the short time he'd known her she had been transformed, and yet he realized now that the packaging was entirely superficial when it came to this woman. The core essence of her remained, no matter what she wore, and at her core she was the same woman he'd encountered in the chapel at their first meeting.

The thought had him stealing another glance at her.

She walked deliberately, her eyes continuously scanning the scenery. His shirt was large on her, though her breasts appeared to be doing their best to fill it out, and it occurred to him that it wasn't fair to other women to have such a brilliant mind wrapped up in all that delicious packaging.

They fell into sync, making their way through the woodlands, walking side by side, with Mina occasionally stopping to examine a particular plant or sign of wildlife, and Zayn tolerating the delays long enough for her to make a quick note in her pocket memo pad before he drove them onward.

On one particularly exuberant occasion she stopped,

gasping and pointing a waggling finger over his shoulder as a series of strange squeals escaped her throat.

Zayn whipped around to catch a rustle in the underbrush and the sound of something scurrying away. Turning back to Mina, he waited for her to catch her breath.

"It was a brown-beaked warbler!"

He smiled. The brown-beaked warbler was one of the endemic species on the island. He'd seen them before, having taken countless trips to the island over the course of his life, but her excitement was catching nonetheless—like watching a child at Christmas.

"To just happen upon one!" she gushed. "What are the chances?"

Her color was up, and so bright that not even the black of his shirt could diminish her glow, and he realized that, despite the circumstances, he was enjoying this time with her. In a way he couldn't remember enjoying anything since becoming King.

It was hard to truly enjoy things after losing your father, learning that your uncle had been behind the plot that killed him, saying goodbye to your mother, because her home had become a house of mirrors filled with the ghost of her husband, hiding it all, and then assuming the throne—all within a year and a half. And yet here he was, enjoying himself nonetheless.

As they continued their hike Mina grew bolder, pointing out more and more flora and fauna as if she were leading a tour group. None of the information was new to him, the island having been in his family for the last hundred years or so, but her enthusiasm charmed him. With every step, the combination of her earnest exuberance and being back on the island seemed to shake off some of the weight of the past two years.

And she had no idea.

"What exactly is your field of study?" he asked, suddenly feeling the gulf of his lack of knowledge about her.

She frowned, eyeing him suspiciously. "I'm a biological systems scientist. Or rather, I was…" This last she'd added with a frown and a note of confusion.

The uncertainty in her voice roused in him an urge to conquer and destroy, but her identity crisis wasn't an enemy he could fight. She could thank their fathers for that.

"You are still," he said, trying anyway. "Becoming Queen does not negate your years of study."

She sent him a nod, accompanied by a vague smile, and he had the unusual experience of realizing she was humoring him.

"It doesn't," he insisted, more determined in the face of her brush-off.

"Of course not. I know that."

She put more effort into her smile, and it occurred to him that the expression would likely have fooled anyone who wasn't looking closely.

He *was* looking closely. "But…?" he asked.

She sighed. "But what does a queen need a PhD in biological systems for?"

He was still searching for an answer when she distracted him once again.

"Look! Another warbler. A female, I think."

He obediently turned in the direction she pointed and smiled when he caught sight of the small, unassuming brown head.

"Females are even more difficult to spot than males," she squealed. "We're lucky we're here at the beginning of the mating season."

"You know quite a lot about our little warblers."

She shook her head. "Not the warbler, actually. Just this particular bio-system. I was the only scholar at the university in over a decade to focus on Cyranese ecosystems. It was never as sexy as studying the famous ones, like the Great Barrier Reef or the Amazon, but my father always encouraged me to value my home and work for 'the good of Cyrano…'"

Her voice trailed off as they both followed the thought to its conclusion.

Her father's meaning and motivation were clear now, and they both knew that he had gone far beyond simply being an encouraging parent, but for the first time Zayn didn't resent the man.

"It certainly doesn't hurt for a monarch to have a deep understanding of the nation in their charge."

She cringed, saying, "You don't have to pretend when it's just the two of us. We both know I'm no monarch."

Zayn raised a brow. "I believe there's a small island nation which would disagree."

Instead of rising to his bait, she doubled down. "But we both know I'm a fraud."

"How do you come to say that?" he asked.

"I'm a scholar. Not a queen."

"As far as I understand, being a queen entails inheriting or marrying into a throne—the second of which you have done."

"I'm an imposter."

He didn't reply, scanning the scrub and the grasses that covered the ground around them, and smiling when he saw a cluster of the plants he was looking for. Four small stalks stuck out of the ground, each bearing leaves of shiny dark green, growing in sets of three. Crouching down, he reached toward the plants on the left.

Mina opened her mouth to protest and he stopped, his finger just inches from the leaves.

"The wax leaf sand thistle. Now, here is an imposter," he said. "As I'm sure you know, Dr. Aldaba, this plant nefariously mimics its companion here, the wax leaf sugar sap, growing in the same conditions and showcasing almost identical foliage. But, whereas the wax leaf sugar sap is both a delectable treat for the spotted fallow deer that live on the island, and an important nitrogen fixer for the soil, the wax leaf sand thistle is bitter to the deer and known for stripping the earth. It mimics the sugar sap for its own benefit—using the deer to spread its seeds, while offering them nothing but a stinging mouth in return." He rocked back on his heels before adding, "We don't know each other well, Mina, but I don't get the impression that you are a person out to take without giving back."

Leaning back further, to take her in, he noted the cracks in her inscrutable expression, her desire to believe him warring with her natural skepticism.

When her eyes widened and rounded, he thought desire had won out—until she shouted, "Watch out!" just before he felt a sharp stinging pain in the fleshy side of his palm as his hand brushed too close to the thistle.

The burn of it was immediate—another feature of the sand thistle was its shockingly powerful prick, often likened to that of a bee sting.

Mina acted instantly, dropping her pack to crouch down and begin searching the undergrowth. Zayn distracted himself from the swelling throb in his hand by watching her move. It didn't matter that he had no idea what she was doing, or that she wore baggy jeans and his shirt, there was something erotic about her in that position.

She found whatever she was looking for with an, "Aha!" and was at his side an instant later. "Give me your hand."

Her command was absolute. She had no thought that she might be disobeyed, and he found a silly half-grin lifting the corner of his mouth at her authority, even through the discomfort of obliging her.

She shoved the bunch of leaves he now saw she had collected into her mouth and chewed, before slapping the gooey mess on the place where his hand had made contact with the thistle.

Instantly the pain subsided. A small sound of pleasure escaped him, and he didn't know if the expressive slip-up had more to do with the sudden absence of discomfort, the fact that being on the island was like going back in time to an era when he hadn't had to manage his every move, or the fact that Mina had just made him feel good.

Her answering smile glowed with relief. "Systems science. Antidotes to the toxins that have evolved in a given environment can almost always be found nearby."

If she'd still been wearing her glasses, he imagined this would have been the moment she pushed them up the bridge of her nose, but there was no derision in the thought. Her earnestness wasn't the cluelessness of a sheltered academic. She was just genuine.

He came to his feet to hide just how that revelation hit him, and composed himself before offering her a hand. "And you said a queen had no use for a PhD in biological systems…"

After a slight hesitation, and looking at his offered hand for a beat too long, she accepted it, letting him carry some of her weight as she came upright.

"Thanks," she said, when they both stood again.

Her green-hazel eyes mirrored the color of the forest around them as she stared at him, revealing herself in the process, as natural and forthright as the woods.

She stole his breath, but she didn't seem to care that that gave her power—maybe she didn't even know it.

Heat was coming to her cheeks at their continued eye contact, and she cleared her throat. "Well, should we keep going?"

Watching her trying to hide her reaction to him filled him with an unfamiliar urge to beat his chest and let out a wild howl. And even though the movement wouldn't have been like any version of himself—not the island-exploring boy, not the passionate student, not the charming heir, and certainly not the King—he realized it came from the same place that made a man hunt and kill and die for his woman. It didn't matter what version he was of himself. This part was his real essence.

It wasn't a comfortable realization.

He wasn't, however, about to wallow in his mind's damning over-simplifications. The real world offered intrigue enough.

Unlike his present company.

The more time he spent with her, the more he realized she couldn't offer intrigue if her life depended on it. However her father had managed to secure a royal betrothal so long ago, his daughter didn't appear to have a machinating bone in her body.

"Tell me about your mother?" he asked, curious to know if her earnestness stemmed from another source.

"Do you know you're quite bossy?" she retorted, rather than answering his question.

He raised an eyebrow. "I ask about your mother and you resort to name-calling?"

She snorted with a little laugh, watching the ground as she walked, at complete ease, and he realized he couldn't remember the last time someone had snorted around him.

He tried again. "Will you tell me about your mother?"

She laughed out loud this time. "Even when you use the right words you can't really ask for anything, can you?"

She sparkled, and he marveled at her while she teased him as if he wasn't the King.

Glancing at him out the side of her eye, she asked slyly, "Don't you have some sort of dossier on me?"

Taking on the challenge in her question, he shrugged. "Of course. Your mother was born in Germany and came to Cyrano on a student visa. She dropped out of school and illegally outstayed her visa, during which time she met your father. They married, and through your father—who was a natural-born citizen and had been a military officer—earned her citizenship."

Her eyes had widened into small green gold orbs in her face and he laughed.

"But what is that? Facts? I want to know what my mother-in-law is like."

He really was curious about the mother-in-law he had yet to meet, but he couldn't remember the last time he had been able to laugh at his plans going awry. Mina, however, was unaware of that—completely oblivious to the fact that she and the island were drawing out parts of himself he'd thought long dead—and she laughed, the sound of it as bright as the sun overhead.

"When you put it that way…"

Her voice carried her smile with it, right into his chest, where it blossomed like a hothouse flower.

"She is a devoted mother, and so strong—she had to be after we lost my father—"

The ghost of pain in her voice was a quiet echo of the raw-edged thing that lived inside him, usually clawing its way up to the surface from the deep place where he had buried it the moment he let himself slow down, and in a strange way it was both comforting and hopeful.

"I could have easily fallen into a depression after that, but she wouldn't let me. She said that he was alive as long as I kept his dreams alive in my heart, and she encouraged me to keep getting up every day, to keep studying and trying, and not to just lie down and give up forever."

"Somehow, I don't picture that ever happening," he said, an image of her squaring her shoulders in the chapel coming to his mind. "You would have gotten back up eventually—though perhaps she was right to push you. Watching someone you love collapse in grief is…hard."

She searched his face before asking, "Your mother?"

Irritated by the pinch her soft question set off in his chest, he answered with a short nod. "For a time it looked like I might lose her as well as my father. Ultimately she had to leave, so it didn't matter that she'd got back up. I lost her anyway."

A thousand questions flashed across her eyes, but she only asked one. "What do you mean, she had to leave?"

Like a terrier, she had grabbed hold of the one thing he'd said with the greatest implication for matters of state. Matters that had not been made public and that he had no intention of ever making so.

And he'd thought her mind was only suited to science. She just might learn to be Queen after all. And, though he'd been enjoying the unfamiliar lightness of their conversation, he didn't resent this, her inevitable intrusion into his personal life, as it was an opportunity to test her as Queen.

Carefully, he said with casualness, "She was the true target of the assassination."

Mina stopped in her tracks, completely guileless in her shock. "What? Why does no one know this?"

"Many details around the assassination are classified."

"Did she leave because she was afraid?"

He laughed, "My mother? That woman has never been afraid a day in her life." He shook his head. "No. She left because ours is a small island. My father's memory was everywhere for her, and guilt and grief were killing her."

"I can understand… But this way it's like you've lost two parents at once."

Her eyes oozed pain for him and he frowned, not liking the way her empathy felt like a balm. "Now, Mina. Don't be maudlin. You know there is nothing like losing a parent but losing a parent."

The bite in his retort had exactly the effect he had been

going for. The sympathetic light in her eye dimmed, replaced with a hint of fire.

He continued, "But, as you now know the full story, you must indulge my desire to learn more about the new mother figure in *my* life."

Mina rolled her eyes, but it was a sham to cover up the heart pouring out of them. "I don't know how I would have made it through without my mother. We adore each other. I have dinner with her two nights a week, usually, and typically stay over on those nights."

"Interesting…" Zayn noted. "I hadn't observed that."

Mina laughed, once again righting the world with the sound of joy.

"Well, not lately. She's been wanting to take an extended holiday back home in Germany—my grandparents are getting older, you know—and when I learned of my parliamentary interview we both knew I'd be focused on preparing, so she decided to take her trip now. She's due back midsummer. We'd planned to take a spa weekend together, either to celebrate or soothe, depending on the outcome…"

Her voice trailed off and they both thought of what the outcome had been—something far different from what Mina and her mother had imagined.

Zayn vowed in that moment to make sure Mina's time at the summer palace made up for the spa weekend she'd missed. He couldn't reinstate her position on the council— a queen could not sit on the council—and he couldn't give her back her life as a professor and researcher, but he could at least give her back one of the plans her marriage to him had taken from her.

Her pampering would begin the moment they arrived at the summer palace. But they had to get there first.

"We're about thirty minutes from the cabin," he said. "We can make it there before we lose the light. From there it's less than two hours' walk to the summer palace, but for that we can wait for daylight."

Mina nodded. "I'm ready if you are."

Once again he set the pace, and Mina kept up, this time forgoing any observation notes, and as the last creeping tendrils of light faded on the horizon they stepped suddenly out of the woods into the clearing that housed the palatial log cabin.

Constructed of thick old logs, and large polished stones, the building was designed in a traditional lodge style, with large, scenic picture windows in the center of two outstretched, smooth-timbered wings. Two-storied, it was a commanding structure, made all the more so by the fact that it was the first evidence of mankind they had encountered in miles.

"The cabin is kept stocked with supplies at all times. But unfortunately, it has yet to be retro-fitted with satellite services, so we won't be able to call from it. It should meet our needs for the night, though."

Mina merely nodded as he opened the door, gasping when she stepped inside.

Smiling at her wonder, Zayn took in the large exposed beams of the ceiling, the plushly accented open spaces and the enormous central fireplace with nonchalance. "I always thought it was rather rustic and a bit too cozy myself..."

Mina laughed. "I'm sure. After all, no satellite services..."

She wandered round the expansive living area first and then the large kitchen, noting the locations of necessary items as she opened cabinets and drawers.

"Oh, and here's a can opener! Perfect!"

"A can opener?" He raised an eyebrow.

Mina's owlish look alone would have been comical, but when it was coupled with her next words he had trouble keeping a straight face.

"You *do* know that people eat food out of cans, right?" she asked delicately, and her attempt to disguise exactly what she would think about him if he answered no was almost painful.

Holding back, he nodded seriously. "I am aware."

Her sigh of relief was too much, though, and it broke the dam on his laughter.

When he could breathe again, he wiped the tears from the corners of his eyes and offered, "I may be King, but I still had my uni days."

She rolled her eyes at that. "I'm sure…"

"What's that supposed to mean?"

Grinning, she shrugged. "Somehow I imagine your late-night takeout and pajama days were a bit higher-class than mine."

It was his turn to shrug, his smile easy. "Probably. But caviar still comes out of a can."

This time it was she who couldn't hold back, and the laughter rolled out of her with a faint edge of hysteria to it—the only hint at the unusual day she'd had. He was impressed.

"Whether it's out of a can, or anything else, we should eat and then rest up," he said. "We can shower and change and set out early tomorrow. If we're lucky, we'll be at the summer palace before lunch."

Sobering, she nodded. "I don't have a change of clothes, but a shower sounds divine. Or, even better yet, a long soak…"

She virtually purred at the idea, her voice going husky and smooth, and despite crash landing his plane and an unplanned half-day hike, he felt his pants tighten in response.

"Ask and you shall receive," he said. "The summer palace is always stocked with spare clothing and the master bath is equipped with a state-of-the-art hot tub and, I believe, every kind of bath salt and soaking serum anyone could want."

Closing her eyes, she let out a long, contented sigh, before her eyes shot open again. "Do you know how to cook?"

He almost answered honestly—the question as ridiculous as her concern about canned food—but held back at the last second, curious to see how she would respond.

Keeping his face carefully blank, he said, "I know how a can opener works."

Frowning, she said, "That's not very self-sufficient— but unsurprising. When would you have had to cook? It's fine, though. I can put something together for us. It won't be what you're used to—I'm no chef—but we won't starve." She eyed him through the corner of her eye, apparently content with her own answers to her questions. "And it will be more than a heated up can of green beans…"

Not bothering to correct her impression, he smiled openly. "Wonderful. I can't say I was looking forward to green beans…"

He did, however, find he was looking forward to having her cook for him. He might be used to top-rated chefs, but something about the idea set off something hot and primal inside him.

"After dinner, though, that bath has my name all over it."

Her grin could only be described as wolfish, but he found himself attracted to its wild greed, wanting to see the same glint reflected in her eyes when she took him in. Preferably in the bath, her body naked and slick…

His body stirred again, and, with the direction his thoughts were taking, he decided it was time for a shower himself. An ice-cold one.

Entering the brightly lit and expansively marbled bathroom, he reflected on the fact that his concept of "cozy" was relative. At ten thousand square feet, the cabin certainly wasn't small, and it boasted every modern comfort. But, most importantly, it was private.

The time he'd spent here with his parents was the only time he could remember in all his life when they'd had no servants or staff dancing attendance. His father had insisted on it after the renovation. His son might have been a prince, but he was going to experience life without being waited on hand and foot.

Removing his pants and putting them in the hidden hamper, Zayn then turned the shower on. Steaming jets burst forth from the wall and the waterfall showerhead, stinging his skin as the water encountered the small cuts and abrasions he'd picked up from trekking shirtless through the woods. He hadn't noticed amassing them on the way. He had been too engrossed in Mina.

Electricity lit his veins at the thought of her. The two of them were absolutely alone, with no staff present to witness any lapses in decorum. Any uncontrolled response would be private...a secret shared between him and his wife.

With her downstairs, preparing dinner for the two of them while he showered, he could almost pretend they were ordinary people—a regular man and woman settling down for the evening, rather than a king and a queen with responsibilities to put their nation before their own happiness. He could almost imagine that they were united by common ground and shared desire, rather than by merely being the casualties of an antiquated contractual agreement.

He turned off the shower and pulled a plush towel from the tidily stacked pile to wrap around his waist. Exiting the bathroom, he was greeted by the scent of North African spices, drawing his attention to his gnawing hunger. Whether he was starving for sustenance or the woman behind the delectable combination of aromas, however, he wasn't sure.

He followed the scent downstairs and into the kitchen,

to find Mina standing in front of the stove with her back to him.

She still wore her jeans and his shirt, the hem of which hit her mid-thigh and hung loosely. The jeans beneath it certainly weren't cut to showcase the female form, yet the image of what lay beneath was so clear in his mind it was as if he could see through every layer of clothing.

More curls had escaped the loose bun she'd started the day with, but the effect sat well with her masculine attire, hinting at the vibrant femininity that lay beneath. And below that her dizzying intellect. What lay below that he could only guess at, though each layer he discovered seemed more powerful and awe-inspiring than the last.

He could spend a lifetime delving into her depths and never run out of new facets to explore… The idea brought unfamiliar warmth to his chest.

He knew the moment she became aware of his presence, though she didn't turn around. It was as if a pulse of electricity travelled through her body, until she thrummed with a kind of tension that invited him closer.

"The kitchen is really well stocked," she said. "We had everything I needed for my grandma's chicken tagine."

She kept her voice over-bright, and he knew she was trying to settle her response to him. Not wanting that, he stepped further into the kitchen, standing only a few feet away now as she continued to cook.

When he spoke, he let his smile spill into the words. "Definitely better than a heated can of green beans. Smells delicious."

And even though she kept her back to him he could sense the blush of pleasure that heated her skin. Could hear it in the catch of her breath.

"Thank you. You're lucky. It's about one of ten dishes I know how to make, and it is by far the best."

Warm laughter rumbled in his chest, rising up out of him

from a place far different from the presentational mirth he normally put on. Unbidden, an image of his father rose in his mind. Of the three of them, in fact—his father, mother, and himself—together in this very kitchen, his father at the stove, joking, he and his mother sitting at the counter, his rapt audience.

He was sure he hadn't recalled that evening since it had happened, which had to be at least fifteen years before, because there was nothing remarkable about it. And yet there the memory was, crystal-clear after all these years.

"Almost done here." Mina's voice shone through the bittersweet thoughts, and she said over her shoulder, "Do you mind setting the table?"

He almost laughed.

The question had been so natural and innocuous, delivered off-hand from one person to another. For a brief moment, at least, she'd forgotten that he was the King. It was a novel experience—one he rather liked.

She turned off the stove and finally turned around, opening her mouth to speak as she moved.

But whatever she had been about to say was lost when she abruptly snapped her mouth shut, eyes going wide. "I'm sorry. I didn't realize you weren't dressed. I'll set the table."

He did laugh this time, the sound low and heated. Still smiling, he said, "I'll get dressed after dinner. I'd be happy to set the table."

She licked her lips, and although his groin tightened in response, threatening the stability of the towel, he was certain she was unaware of the action.

Her cheeks had a rosy sheen to them, and there was a light in her eyes that hadn't been there moments before, but rather than take any steps down the path of seduction, she clapped her hands together and said in an overloud voice, "Great. Thanks." Before reaching for, and knocking over, the container of wooden serving spoons that sat on the counter.

Sure that his laughter would not be abating any time soon, Zayn decided to give her a break, gathering the silverware to set the table as his lady had requested.

CHAPTER SEVEN

IT HAD TO be shock. Shock that was setting in after a day that had begun with her first hangover, included a plane crash, and was now coming to a close with a disorienting coziness that felt almost normal—albeit on a rather larger scale than most people could afford.

Considering the last few weeks of her life, any hint of normalcy would be reason enough for her to go into shock. So that was what was happening. That was why her temperature had spiked when she'd turned to see Zayn's broad chest, clean and gleaming, a plush low-slung towel wrapped around his waist the only barrier between her eyes and his full naked glory.

Shock was why her breasts had gone heavy and tender when he'd stepped closer to her in the kitchen, and her imagination had supplied her with the sensation of his breath against the back of her neck, his body heat radiating outward to envelop her.

Shock was behind the growing heat at her core—not the King.

Her body was short-circuiting from a system overload, rather than due to the arousal the biologist in her demanded that she acknowledge. She was a mammal, after all. She couldn't help her body's natural response to being confronted with the perfection that was her King.

Golden and muscled, his chest was sprinkled with light hair that disappeared around his gorgeous pectorals and didn't reappear again until it formed the line that began below his navel and disappeared beneath the towel.

Mina swallowed.

She had seen the naked human form before, but never like this. Never so visceral and hot and alive. Never so commanding. Never so cut.

It had been hard enough to focus during their hours of hiking, when only his chest had been exposed. There was no way she would make it through dinner knowing he had nothing on under the towel.

What would her grandmother think of her wild thoughts? How could she sit at a table and eat her grandmother's recipe while her mind took off on a carnal tear, presenting her with crisp images of kissing a trail from his jaw all the way down his chest and along that oh-so-kindly marked path she'd observed.

She was going to combust while he laid out utensils on the table.

Human immolation was rare, but scientifically possible, given the right conditions. And the growing internal inferno that threatened to engulf her entire body seemed like the right conditions.

Shoving her hands into oven mitts, at this point more to protect the pan from her heat than the other way round, she carried the dish to the trivet Zayn had laid on the table.

"Mina…" His voice was a seductive caress. "That looks delicious."

Since it wasn't possible to blush any more than she already was, Mina tried playing it cool as she joined him at the table. "Thank you. It helps to have such high-quality ingredients."

Zayn smiled and her toes curled in her socks.

"My dad used to say the same thing," he said.

His dad. King Alden. She wondered if she would ever get used to such casual references to royalty. But to Zayn, the royal family wasn't the pinnacle of the aristocracy. It was just family.

"Your father cooked?" she asked, placing the serving spoon and turning to collect the rice and the teff. Zayn had chosen the small dining nook for their dinner, and Mina was grateful. The large table she'd seen in the dining room reminded her too much of breakfast.

"He did," he said. And after a beat, he added, "He insisted I learn as well."

Mina snorted. "You call heating up a can of vegetables cooking?"

He shrugged. "Your words, not mine."

She raised an eyebrow at him. "You're telling me you know how to cook?"

"Don't sound so surprised."

"What can you make?"

She couldn't picture Zayn in a kitchen outside of the image he presented now, sitting at the table, shirtless.

"Simple things. *Pesce al grappa, polle al grappa, paella, polle dominga, jamon e quez...*"

Mina was impressed with the list. It was classic Cyranese cooking, much of it considered common food, but all the more delicious for it.

But rather than tell him that she said, "Well, next time you're cooking, then."

He smiled, and in the intimate lighting of the nook it lit his face with ease. "Gladly. I would love to feed you."

His words carried promises far beyond those of a shared meal and Mina shivered.

"Did your mother cook?" she asked.

Zayn chuckled, shaking his head slightly. "No. The noble Singuenza daughters were not allowed anywhere near the kitchens during their formative years and later it was always beyond my mother. I imagine it's the same for Aunt Seraphina. She was never the rebel."

"I hear the sound of family stories there." Mina leaned in, observing her own ease for the first time she could remember in months—certainly since long before she'd learned of her parliamentary interview.

He lifted his hands, palms up to her. "You'll have to ask my mother yourself. Everything I know I learned second-hand from my cousin Helene, who learned it piecemeal from her mother. There are rumors that my mother was quite the wild child in her youth, though."

"Queen Barbara? Absolutely not. She is dignity personified."

Zayn lifted an eyebrow. "You buy the image? For shame, Mina."

She laughed. "Well, I'll just have to ask the source."

"What about you? Do you have any wild stories from your youth?"

She knew a frown flashed across her face at his words, but it was gone as soon as it appeared.

"Not me," she said, with a self-deprecating smile. "I really just studied. Nothing exciting about my past—I'm just your average citizen,"

Zayn snorted. "I find that hard to believe. You were about to be appointed to the King's council, you speak multiple languages, you've been to Ecuador on a research expedition. That's a lot more than the average citizen."

Mina smiled. "When you put it like that…"

He laughed, and she wondered if he knew that the low rumble of that sound was the key to the lock that kept the heat of her core at bay.

"I do," he insisted.

He was iron and charm, threaded together through both King and man, and the combination created a powerful magnetism.

Heat bloomed in her cheeks, her breath catching a bit as she said, "Well, it takes a lot of study to do those things, which doesn't leave much time for wild stories."

He raised an eyebrow. "In my experience, wild stories make time for themselves."

The heat in Mina's cheeks took on a different nature at his words. Wild stories, it would seem, had just purposely avoided her then—because she had none. She had stories of falling asleep with her nose in a book, and spending her rare free nights tucked away in her mother's living room. All to keep alive the memory of a man she apparently hadn't ever really known.

"Not even a love affair to distract from your focus?" he asked.

She shook her head in response. "Not even a love affair, I'm afraid. Just boring study, night after night." She blushed again. She hadn't meant to say that, emphasizing that her nights all the rest of the life she had spent alone. She took a sip of her water to wash down the knot of embarrassment lodged in her throat.

"It sounds like you're ripe for something wild, then."

His tone implied that he was open to being the one to introduce wild into her life, and she choked on her water before trying to brush it off as a chuckle.

"Ha-ha." She enunciated the sound as if she was new to the process of laughter, before adding, "The only thing I'm ripe for is a bath."

He shook his head, amusement alive in his eyes, but simply said, "I can handle the dishes, Mina. Go upstairs and take your bath."

She didn't wait for him to say it twice. Making her way into the living room, it was impossible for her to miss the gorgeous wide staircase that led to the second floor. Taking it, she wandered the hallways, every now and then stealing a glance down through the open-plan living room into the kitchen to see Zayn in his towel.

It occurred to her that the towel was the first thing she'd seen him wear that wasn't black. A bubble of laughter escaped at the thought, and the edge to its sound reminded her that, regardless of how relaxed things were now, she'd pushed her body past its limits over the course of the day.

Away from Zayn's temperature-raising presence, the aches and pains of the day made themselves felt. And why shouldn't they? She had drunk and danced late into the night the night before, been woken up too early, with a hangover, survived an emergency plane landing, and gone on a four-hour hike within the last twenty-four hours. It was a wonder she was even upright at this point. A hot bath and a date with a pillow were exactly what the doctor ordered.

Offset from the other doors, at the far end of the long upper hallway, was a pair of large French doors. The master suite, if she had to guess and, she suspected, the location of the hot tub.

Inside, the bedroom was bright, plush, and clean. A massive bed covered with a well-stuffed white duvet demanded attention, but it didn't begin to dominate the enormous room. Much like the Queen's Suite at the palace, small archways led form it to what she assumed were closets and additional rooms.

Moments later, she squealed with delight to find the bathroom.

She searched the cabinets, gleeful when she discovered a gratuitous selection of luxury bath salts and balms. She turned the water on in the tub while reading the package labels. Settling on a combination of relaxation and muscle-soothing, she added the salts and quickly peeled off her clothes, before stepping over the high edge of tub and into heaven on earth.

A moan slipped free from her lips as she sank in, feeling hot jets of water working her tender muscles the whole time.

The tub was everything Zayn had promised and more—deep, powerful, big enough to drown in—and she couldn't have designed it better in her imagination.

"Mmm…" Her hum of pleasure was unstoppable.

For the first time since she'd left her apartment for her interview, weeks ago, she was completely alone. The relief that came with that was more profound than she would have believed possible before meeting the King.

She closed her eyes and leaned back, thinking there was a real chance she might fall asleep in the tub. Slowly inhaling the lavender and eucalyptus combination of the bath salts, she bent her mind to the task of relaxing, beginning at the crown of her head and working her way down, part by part. By the time she reached her toes her mind floated in a Zen haze, lulled into stillness by aromatherapy and hot water.

In that state, Zayn's image formed in her mind.

A smile curved her lips.

In her imagination he rose from a steaming spring, the same broad chest she'd barely been able to tear her eyes from all day glistening with beads of heated water that begged to be traced with her tongue. As usual, his violet gaze burned, but this time the fire was fueled by desire—and all of it for her.

She shivered in the tub, despite the heat of the water. There was an undeniable thrill that came with the image. To have the King burn for her…

The bathroom door hinges creaked and Mina shot up, her eyes popping open, arms crossing in front of her breasts.

Zayn stood in the doorway, his movement halted mid-entry.

Their eyes met—hers wide and bright, and her cheeks

flushed from more than the heat of the water, his piercing and focused, entirely zeroed in on her.

He cleared his throat. "I apologize. I was looking for my clothes. They are not in my old room."

Swallowing, Mina nodded, not trusting her ability to find words.

Entering the bathroom, he made his way toward the closet in the corner with gentlemanly decorum, not glancing toward the tub as he passed, and though she didn't know what else she could have wanted, Mina was disappointed.

He turned to leave with equal restraint, a folded black T-shirt and black cotton pants in his hands.

Mina watched his back as he walked toward the door, a heavy sense of urgency growing in her chest. His hand was on the door handle when she called his name.

"Zayn."

He turned, meeting her eyes without a word.

Mina lowered her arms and the air left the room.

Time was transformed, racing as Zayn's eyes locked with hers to rip an irrefutable confirmation of her invitation from her at light-speed even while it slowed, going still as they sensed the invisible precipice they stood on.

And then he was moving toward her, a predator gone beyond stalking his prey, ready to pounce.

Her throat caught. She was suddenly nervous, but not enough. Not nearly enough. Not when they were alone in the cabin. Not when they were man and wife, their union not just sanctioned but sanctified. Certainly not when his eyes burned with an intensity that put her imagination to shame.

Her life's dream had been revealed to be a sham. Her academic reputation was in tatters. There was no more research to complete, no more grants to apply for. No more benchmarks to reach. She could make up no more excuses or distractions from taking a chance on real life—not when her husband was looking at her like that.

She stood, wearing only the water that ran down her skin.

The King stilled, not frozen but hyper-aware, his attention locked.

And then he was on her, closing the distance between them and cupping the back of her skull in his hands as he lifted her face towards his to take her mouth.

Her breasts pressed against the bare skin of his chest, her pebbled nipples exploding into sensation on contact. He snaked his arm around her waist, bracing her as he pulled her closer, pressing the hard length of his body against hers.

Held fast in his arms, she gave herself fully into the kiss, her senses wide open, etching each feeling into her memory. A hungry, desperate voice in the back of her mind was urging her on, warning her that this might be her only opportunity to feel this way.

Blood rushed through her, each vessel a river of heat coalescing at her core.

His hand found her breast, and the faintly roughened skin of his fingertips and palms against her skin was the most sensuous contrast she'd ever experienced. She arched into his grip, her breath catching in her throat.

The movement elicited a painful groan from him before he took her nipple between his thumb and forefinger. Rolling it gently, he experimented with pressure, watching her face intently as he set off mini waves of electric pleasure through her system.

She gasped when he replaced his fingers with his mouth, swirling his tongue around the sensitive hard bud. A moan of protest escaped her as he transitioned to the other breast, and she was bereft until he once again took her in his mouth.

Her fingers raked through his hair, thrilling in the silky

texture she'd wanted to touch since seeing its midnight sheen up close in the chapel, and she had the strong urge to lift her legs and wrap them around his waist, press the burning heat at the juncture of her thighs closer to him.

Reading her mind, he scraped a palm down her back, over the curve of her behind, then down along the outer edge of her thigh to cup the back of her knee, drawing her leg higher, her heat closer.

When he had her leg where he wanted it, he scooped the other leg up, lifting her with an ease that belied her height and weight. She wasn't petite. But he held her.

Her ankles locked behind his back as his palms found the rounded cheeks of her behind and dug in. As if she weighed nothing, he swung her around, catching her mouth with his again while walking them into the bedroom.

Mina was now grateful for the enormous bed that had seemed too much when she'd entered the room earlier. As it was, it took too long for him to reach it, where he laid her down, his eyes taking her in like a pillaging conqueror.

It wasn't hard to picture him that way. Her very own dark warrior with piercing violet eyes. His body was perfection personified—that of a man who obviously believed in hard work—a wall of well-defined muscles all the way down.

There was finally nothing left to the imagination, and for that Mina was intensely grateful. Her imagination had been woefully inadequate when compared to the real thing. The trail of fine hair began at his navel expanded into a wider, thicker plateau from which a manhood jutted that put every diagram and model she'd ever seen to shame.

Looking at him, her heart pounding, she began to truly understand that the urge to join was about far more than basic biology. It wasn't biology that had her lips parting, that filled her with the boldness to meet his eyes as she let her legs fall open, not hiding any part of herself from him.

He rewarded her action by devouring her with his eyes, the heat of their caress as physical as if it were his body leaning down to cover her. He brought his palms down to the bed, his arms bracketing her on either side of her head, his face above her own before he once again claimed her lips.

She pressed into his kiss, returning it with everything she had, their tongues dancing with one another. His hardness pressed hotly against her core, its temperature somehow registering despite her internal inferno, and she wiggled her hips towards his, instinctively seeking the angle that would bring them even closer together.

Smiling into their kiss, he said, "Patience, Mina *amora*. I want to savor you."

His words danced across her bare skin, leaving shivers in their wake. Bringing her arms up to wrap them around him, she traced patterns on his back with a light scratch of her nails, reveling in the unbridled access to the broad expanse of skin.

For this night, the King—no, Zayn—was hers and hers alone, and she didn't have to worry about whether she was Dr. Aldaba or Queen Amina. Here he was Zayn and she was Mina—a man and a woman in a dance as old as time.

Leaning close, he set a trail of light kisses at her jaw, then travelled down her neck and along her collarbone, along the outside edges of her breasts and down her ribs beneath, before circling around to find her nipple once again.

She arched her back to meet him, moaning as the heat of his mouth enveloped the tender tip.

Then he was pressing his lips against her sternum, and lower, in a path that would soon intersect with her navel and beyond.

A tremor shook her body when his lips reached the upper edge of the patch of hair at the junction of her thighs. Rather than continue in a straight path from there, as she'd expected, he took a detour, tracing feather-light electric kisses teasingly along the edges and her inner thighs. Her skin tightened, pulling taut with each press of his lips, her breath catching every time he exhaled against her skin.

Her hips lifted of their own accord, inner heat building as each breath was hitched, caught and released, no match for his sensory onslaught.

When his lips finally pressed against the seam that held her together she cried out with relief, the thrumming anticipation reaching a fever-pitch she knew would break her apart.

He explored her with gentle strokes of his tongue, slowly delving deeper into her core, traversing ground no man had ever walked before with an intimacy that should have left her shaking with nerves but instead threatened to undo her with pleasure. It rolled through her in waves, each one closer, tighter, more intense than the last. Moans escaped her lips with growing urgency, though what was so urgent she didn't know.

"Let me take you, Mina."

The hum of his words against her most intimate center pushed her over the edge. Shockwaves of sensation ravaged her system. She was arching her back as every muscle in her body tightened then released, leaving her to collapse into a tumbling shell against the bed, her mind dissolved.

But he wasn't done with her yet.

Kissing his way back up, he made quick progress until he once again hovered above her.

"Bend your knees and lift your hips."

The command was absolute. A king's will to be obeyed. And she didn't know if it was due to shock or desire, but she obliged him immediately and shamelessly. His groan at her acquiescence was almost reward enough for her obedience. Almost.

And then he positioned himself at the gateway of her

slick entrance and paused, drawing every ounce of her attention to the hot, pulsing point where their bodies touched. She gasped and he grinned rakishly, twitching the head of his shaft against her, teasing her with each flickering movement.

Leaning down, he kissed the hollow behind her ear tracing his lips down along her jaw, whispering as he went. "Do you like the way that feels, Mina?"

She answered with a moan, her body tensing, anticipation building once more. Again her hips wiggled toward him of their own accord, in an instinctive motion urging him to finish what they'd started.

Leaning slightly to one side, he freed his arm to wrap it around Mina's hips, holding her steady as he angled his body and pressed gently against the smoldering heat of her. Her breath caught, her attention zeroing in on the pressure of his hardness, stretching her open, and then he pulled her body closer, catching her mouth in a deep kiss, setting off a sensual onslaught on another front and overwhelming her ability to focus on any single sensation rising inside her.

He entered her slowly, pausing for her slick body to move past the sharp sting of his presence before he pressed deeper, inch by inch, his pace deliciously teasing, luring her to lift her hips and meet his as she stretched to accommodate him.

The thick pressure of him inside her was a wholly new experience, his heat a pulsing rod, radiating warmth from her core outward. Her heart beat in time with its pulse, and the rhythms of their bodies connecting and syncing threatened to dance her into oblivion once again.

She gasped his name and he increased his pace, sliding deeper and deeper into her with each stroke. The veins in his neck and arms were pressing taut against his skin, his own breathing becoming choppy and irregular.

Sensing he was nearing the same peak, she locked her

ankles around his back, angling her hips to allow him even deeper access, driven by primal instruction. He growled in response and the sound sent a wild thrill of possessiveness through her. Tightening her arms around his back, she dug her nails into him, marking him as hers even as he irrevocably claimed her body with each thrust.

"*Ay, Dio*, Mina!"

The words were ripped free from his lips, their strained tenor nudging her own system ever closer toward the edge they both teetered on. They moved in sync, drawn together by a kind of magnetism that had nothing to do with poles, their breath coming fast, their bodies slick with sweat.

A jumbled assortment of words rose in her mind and slipped between her parted lips. "Yes. Keep going. Don't stop."

He obliged, maintaining a pace that was driving her crazy with no sign of flagging, his endurance and stamina obviously a match for the demands of her body.

And demanding it was. Inexperience seemed to have no effect on its sense of entitlement to the pleasure she knew only he could provide. The bonds that held them together made this her right and, overtaken as she was by the sensations it set off, she had every intention of exercising it.

"Mina, Mina, Mina…" Her name was a chanted prayer on his lips, a desperate litany dancing torturously along her nerve-endings, each utterance a lick of fire.

Tension screwed his body tight and he sped up, no longer holding back the force of his own need. She felt the edge of his control in every cell of her body, its rigid urgency weaving them even closer together, binding them toward a fall that would obliterate them both.

"Zayn…" His name on her lips was its own form of begging—a plea for him to carry them into oblivion together.

He obliged, surging into her, plunging them both over the edge, until they dissolved into twin waves, each pulsing deep inside as he emptied himself into her, every heated jet shattering them both into millions of little pieces.

Undone, Mina fell back into the plush mattress she had only just noticed. Zayn dropped to his elbows, his arms still bracketing her, his body hovering just above hers.

A laugh bubbled out of her. She doubted laughing was standard pillow-talk, but the sound had escaped before she'd had the presence to be self-conscious enough to stop it. And it felt good.

Still smiling, she looked up at him and said, "You can relax. You're not going to crush me."

Something like hope flashed across his gaze before he bent down to catch her lips with his. This kiss wasn't the passionate demand of his earlier kisses. Instead it was a soft command, infused with warmth, that wrapped around her from the inside out and held her there.

When he pulled away, though, anything she thought she'd seen was gone, replaced by the charm of the practiced grin he flashed at her before collapsing on her dramatically. He rolled off quickly, then reached for her again as they settled side by side.

Still wondering at that look she'd seen in his eyes, she nestled closer to him, for the first time in her life unwilling to ask a question and risk breaking a moment in the name of curiosity.

Hints of that strange warmth were creeping back into her skin, and now that she'd seen where following sensation could lead, she wanted to follow where these took her as well.

"Are you sore?" Zayn asked.

The question had her cheeks heating, even after the experience they'd just shared. "I'm comfortable, thank you," she said, her voice taking on a prim note she couldn't seem to hold back.

Holding her as he was, she felt his low chuckle ripple

through his entire frame. "It's a reasonable thing to ask after a woman's first time."

Mina's body flushed a hot red. "Who's to say it was my first time?"

Laughing, he pulled her closer. "I am, Mina *amora*."

"Hymen lore is mostly that—lore," she said tartly.

"I don't claim any expertise in the mythology," he said, then paused before continuing in a dry voice, "But I felt yours."

"Oh." Well, she had *tried* to save her dignity.

After a long pause, he asked, "Are you embarrassed?" His voice held surprise.

Mina opened her mouth to deny it, but the automatic response seemed foolish, given the circumstances. Instead, she said, "A little. At a certain point virginity becomes a bit sad."

He shook his head. "No. It's not. You were dedicated to something bigger."

Something raw and jagged inside her began to knit itself together at his words, and while she wanted to think it was the result of being validated by someone other than her parents after all these years, she had a feeling it had everything to do with who was doing the validating.

Rolling over in his arms, she faced him, her head tilted to take him in. As always, his eyes locked on hers when given the opportunity, violet latching onto hazel like a missile on target. And, as always, the contact struck her, holding her frozen and breathless in its possession.

His expression lit with knowing as he held her, a naughty grin lifting the corner of his mouth as he squeezed her. "I like it. All mine."

His voice carried a note of surprise, as if he hadn't expected the truth of his own words, and she got the distinct impression that while it might not have been something he'd ever thought about before, he meant it now.

That realization came with its own thrill, and this time it was she who instigated their kiss, scooting up close to gently press her lips to his. He drew her tighter against his body and returned the kiss. Then, pulling them both more fully onto the bed, he turned her over so her back fit snugly against his chest, her rear end was tucked into the juncture of his hips, his arms wrapped around her.

Once they were settled, he turned the lights down and pressed a final kiss against the back of her neck. Quietly, he said, "Goodnight, Mina."

"Goodnight, Zayn," she whispered back, reveling in the feel of him all around her, on her lips, at her back, and deep in her core.

CHAPTER EIGHT

It wasn't the light that woke him—not with the thick curtains that covered the windows. Neither was it a discreet knock from a member of staff. There was no staff here at the cabin. No. It was the lush weight of warm breasts resting on his forearm, the rounded curves of female anatomy pressed tight against him, and the long shapely legs intertwined with his own that transitioned him from dreams into even more pleasant reality.

He couldn't remember the last time he'd woken up with a woman. Not since he'd been crowned. He had been with women, of course, but it just didn't do for a parade of women to creep in and out of the King's bedroom. His assignations were discreet, taking place in secret locations, and were more likely to include a nondisclosure agreement than a morning-after.

To make matters more unfamiliar, in this case it wasn't merely waking up together. It was having had breakfast and dinner together the previous day. It was a feeling of true relaxation and peace that, while he'd like to chalk it up to the location, he knew had to do with the company. It was a merging of bodies that had reached inside him and stirred things up, rearranging him from the inside out without his permission or regard. It was all that and more. And with his wife of all people.

It wasn't safe. If he'd learned anything from his parents' example it was that. Regardless of what his father had believed, a king must never allow anything to come between him and his country. Not even his wife. Especially not his wife. They'd all seen what could happen in the aftermath of that.

And so he didn't stay where he was, content in a way he couldn't remember being since he'd truly understood what it meant to be the heir to the throne, nestled happily with a woman he was bound by law to love and cherish. Instead, he eased his arm free from under her neck and head, unwound his legs, and slowly pulled away from her.

She murmured in protest, but didn't wake—not that he'd expected her to…the previous day had been enough to tax an elite soldier—and, even though he was tempted to return, to pull her close and place gentle kisses along the back of her neck until she heated and stirred, willing and ready to greet the day with him in brand-new ways, he resisted the urge. He forced himself to step away from the siren draw of the woman on the bed and search instead for the clean pants he'd discarded the night before.

Tearing his mind from her, he forced it toward the morning. They should leave the cabin immediately. Breakfast together would be far too intimate an affair after the night they'd shared. If they prepared food and sat down across from each other again at that small table, just the two of them, he knew that the deep ease that existed between them would be ever-present, even in the face of what would be her inevitable new shyness.

She was his now, in a way she was no other man's, now or ever.

The thought was more satisfying than it should be.

No, breakfast at the cabin would definitely be a bad idea. And if he felt a twinge of guilt at evading eating with her, he vowed to make up for it by ensuring she had a wonderful time on the island—including the full spa experience. But she would need something in her system before they set out on their short hike to the summer palace, and since she had made dinner, and he was in the mood to dote on her, he decided to put together a small bite to eat.

Satisfied with the plan, he executed it, putting the kettle on for Mina's tea before tossing two croissants in the toaster. He then cut two thick slices of deli ham, a peach and some strawberries, before grabbing some soft white cheese from a plate in the refrigerator. Now all he had to do was make a cup of coffee and wait for Mina.

Twenty minutes later she came into the kitchen, quietly but without timidity, and he was impressed. He imagined her steeling herself, squaring her shoulders in that way that was becoming familiar, before walking into his sight. The corner of his lip lifted. Her hair was pulled into a high curly ponytail and she wore clothing that fit her for once, fresh hiking gear that consisted of purple leggings that hugged her hips and long legs paired with a snug fitted windbreaker in light gray.

"There's tea," he said, nodding toward the mug that rested on the counter as she neared. He'd noticed at breakfast the day before that she had taken tea over coffee, with two sugars and cream.

"Oh, thank you, that sounds heavenly." The warmth of genuine pleasure filled her voice at the news, and he was glad that he'd gone ahead and prepared the tea for her, rather than wait to ask when she came down.

She took a big sip and moaned with delight and he couldn't help but smile again—both at her hedonistic enjoyment and her ability to gulp down the steaming hot beverage without regard for the temperature.

"I see where my real value lies in this marriage," he said. The word "marriage" must have reminded her of the night they'd shared, because her cheeks darkened, and a dusky rose tint overlaid her golden-brown skin.

"Oh, well. Good, then..." she stuttered lightly, obviously flustered by the images flashing across her mind.

He wondered what she saw. Was it him? Was it their bodies coming together, joining in the most primal way?

Picturing her mind filled with images of their love-making set his own body off, his blood heating as he too recalled losing himself in her, the complete release of everything, if only momentarily—even the fact that he was King.

That last thought was enough to shake the spell.

Stepping back, he said, "We'll have a real brunch at the summer palace. After that massages, soaking pools, salt wraps, and another massage. Think of our time here as the spa trip you missed out on."

Mina's eyes had lit up at the word "massages," and he was glad that he'd made the decision. They would spend the next few days together, enjoying the island and each other, free to explore the exquisite fit of their bodies as much as the island's beaches. And while they were doing all that he wouldn't need to examine why he felt at peace for the first time since his father's death.

He watched Mina finish her light breakfast, making small talk while eating himself. Once finished, he washed the dishes, as was his custom at the cabin, and they readied themselves to leave.

"The trail from here to the summer palace is a reasonable distance, but it's easy hiking the whole way, and doesn't take long. Its long enough to feel like you've accomplished something, but not so far it's a strain."

She grinned. "What are we waiting for? Massages are at the other end!"

And then she took off, without a backward glance. And just like that she made something as commonplace as a massage brand-new and exciting again.

Zayn followed briskly, eager for a change in scenery, though all he seemed to have eyes for was the woman in front of him.

"The summer palace is beautiful."

The words were out before he'd thought about them, an unconscious attempt to solicit one of her golden smiles.

She turned to him, a spark of interest brightening her eye. "I can't wait to see it. D'Tierrza said you spent a lot of time there, growing up?"

He nodded, remembering those days of running wild at the summer palace hiding away from the public eye. "I did. It gave us a chance to be normal."

Mina surprised him by laughing. "Normal children don't have private islands—but I understand what you mean. As normal as possible for a prince."

He smiled, giving in to the urge to touch her, caressing the back of the hand nearest him with a finger as he said, "You don't have much sympathy for your Prince."

Her cheeks darkened, but she didn't move her hand. "It's not good to be too sympathetic toward powerful people— it inflates their egos."

Not bothering to fight the wicked spark her words lit in him, he leaned closer, his lips near her ear and his voice low as he said, "It's so good for me that I have you to take care of my...ego."

Before his eyes, the slight darkening of Mina's cheeks blossomed into a full-bodied blush. As close as they stood, he could feel the heat radiating from her body. He was leaning in to take her lips before he knew what he was doing, capturing their plump fullness before the warning to keep her at a distance could go off.

She leaned into him without hesitation, opening her mouth to what was becoming the familiar dance of their lips meeting.

He took what she offered without hesitation, reveling

in the sensation of freedom she brought him: freedom to take, freedom to plunder his sweet prize without regard for propriety and decorum, freedom to unleash the force of his unvarnished personality and know that she not only had the full capacity to handle it, but would meet him with her own passion and intensity.

She returned his kiss with a new boldness. Her body was coming to understand the power it held over him even if her mind, new to the back and forth between a man and a woman, had yet to grasp it.

She made him forget himself each and every time, over and over, and he had the distinct impression that the experience would only continue—no matter how many times he came to the well, he would leave thirsting for more. She was dangerous, but he didn't pull away from their kiss. He couldn't.

When he did finally pull back, he looked at her, beautiful green eyes still closed, her face glowing and bright, and he locked the image tight in his mind, storing it.

She opened her eyes then, and they glittered like polished gems. He couldn't look away…entranced like a dragon with its hoard.

Less than an hour later they once again left the forest to enter a clearing—this one even more massive than the last. It opened into a large secluded bay, with a gorgeous dark brown sandy beach, arched cliffs, and there, like a bright white beacon, standing proud and timeless, was the summer palace.

Dashing into the clearing to take in the stunning structure, Mina gasped loudly.

Her reaction brought a smile to his face. The summer palace had that effect on people.

His ancestors had had a thing for white marble, and it showed nowhere more than here at the summer palace.

Embedded into the landscape, the building incorporated both the forested hill and the natural cliffside, with thick rounded columns, open-air patios, and breathtaking views all the way around. Inside, the palace was completely modernized, boasting every convenience and then some, and was powered entirely by renewable energy.

She was going to love it here—he knew it. It was impossible not to.

Palace staff greeted them at the stairs, and he quickly reassured them of their health and safety, as well as calling for brunch. They had both worked up an appetite after their morning hike.

Like everything at the summer palace, brunch was both elaborate and relaxed. Spread across a long table, the menu included island classics—olives, fresh cheese, bread, and pâté—as well as delicious flavors from farther afield, like coconut pudding, *kheer*, fresh mango, pineapple, and starfruit.

Eyeing the food, Mina sat regally in the chair that had been pulled out for her, though he was sure she didn't realize it. He doubted that she would believe anything she did was regal.

A frown came to his face at the thought. Her self-doubt was, in part, his fault. Which was unfortunate. Freed from her academic disguise, she was truly lovely. Her mind was exacting, and yet she was humble. She had withstood shock, devastation and, if he were being honest, mild humiliation with grace and those squared shoulders of hers. If only she had the ability to hide everything she was feeling, she might have the makings of an excellent queen.

They dined al fresco, on a patio overlooking the island's small bay, falling into what was quickly becoming a pattern of easy conversation.

"That water in the bay looks divine," she said, and sighed, closing her eyes.

He smiled. "It's warm, too."

"I'm definitely swimming. Or not..." Words that had started high ended low.

"Why not?"

"My swimsuit is back at the plane."

Zayn shook his head, laughing. "There's probably a selection for you to choose from in your closet."

It only took her a moment to recover from being taken aback this time. A sign she was adjusting to royal life. That was good.

"It's odd to think of it as being mine."

She still needed to work on that earnest forthrightness, though. Otherwise, sooner or later, she'd be skewered. The thought irritated him.

"Well, I'm sure it will sink in eventually."

The words came out sharper than he'd intended, but she merely glanced at him before turning back to the view, and he was glad. Let her focus on relaxing. She didn't need to know she was tying him up in knots.

CHAPTER NINE

BY THE END of her massage she was a human puddle in all the best ways possible. Each and every muscle in her body had been seen to, and after the dancing, the emergency landing, the hiking, and…other things, each and every muscle in her body had *needed* seeing to.

She was beginning to see a pattern in Zayn's communication with her. He might be presumptuous and autocratic, but he was tender and thoughtful at the same time. Relaxed and pleased, she asked staff to direct her to their rooms.

Not finding him there, she detoured, exploring the closet prepared for her by the summer palace staff. They'd provided a selection of items for her for every possible island activity she could imagine. Spying the tasteful lingerie among the neatly stored clothing, she added emphasis to the word *every*.

For the moment, she thought, she wanted to feel comfortable, but also…*pretty*. Instead of shoving the urge away, she let herself wish for them—for the frivolous things she'd shunned for so long. She wanted to look pretty when Zayn saw her.

And, as if her life had truly turned into a fairy tale, she found what she was looking for in a cashmere lounging set, with an off-the-shoulder top and silk ribbon drawstring pants in a rich, creamy ivory color. The slippers she found were decadently soft, each step a mini foot-rub.

Successfully finding clothing that was both comfortable and pretty, in her own closet, had to be one of the more positive novelties of her new life. And, taking in her reflection in the full-length mirror, she had to admit to herself it definitely had a confidence-boosting effect that was almost magical.

Feeling as soft and decadent outside as she felt inside, she looked for Zayn in his office next, locating it after one wrong turn and a second request for directions, only to find it empty.

She didn't find him in any of the spas, theaters, lounges, libraries, gardens, or patios she checked either. It was only when she stood with her hands on her hips in the foyer, at her wits' end as yet another idea turned up with a gorgeous room but no sign of her husband, that a maid stepped forward quietly and tapped her shoulder.

"If you're looking for His Majesty, Your Majesty, you won't find him here. He's down on the beach."

"Thank you," Mina said to the woman, before heading down to find him.

Beside the front door was an assortment of styles of sandals. She chose a simple thong sandal before making her way to the beach. There she found a small blanket and towel laid out, but no sign of the King.

Scanning a horizon that was growing ever more golden with each passing hour, with her hand held up to shield her eyes from the glare of the sun off the sea, she saw him only when he crested the waves in a powerful butterfly stroke, the sunlight glinting off the bright tan of his broad shoulders, which were balanced with perfect strength and symmetry. His whole body looked weightless for a heartbeat, before he disappeared once more beneath the water.

He was as perfect and natural at sea as he was on land.

She wondered if there was any landscape he wasn't the master of. He certainly never seemed to lose his footing. Perhaps that came with being born a future king.

Taking a seat on his blanket, she was content to watch him as he swam, his body appearing and disappearing in the surf, which crashed with soothing power and rhythm. On the beach, with the waves lulling her heart, perfectly safe here on a private island—as improbable as that was— watching her gorgeous husband swim, she let go of the last of the grief for her broken dreams.

She had achieved everything she'd set out to do. Not many people could say that. And if the triumph hadn't lasted as long as she had imagined it would, she was not so lacking in gratitude that she couldn't be thankful that this was where she had landed after the fall.

There were a lot worse things to be than Queen.

Zayn joined her on the beach not long after, his chiseled body dripping with seawater. As suspected, the reality of it was a thousand times more seductive than the vision her imagination had conjured in the bath the night before.

Staring up at him boldly as he dried fanned the seemingly ever-present flame that existed for him at her core. He watched her just as boldly, noting her every reaction with his amethyst gaze, unhurried by her regard, and when he was satisfied he sat beside her on the blanket, looking out to sea.

"Good swim?" she asked.

"Wonderful. I had forgotten how well the water clears the mind. It's been too long since I've come here."

"When was the last time?"

"Just after graduation. I spent an entire week here with my father and mother. We jet-skied, hiked, spent a night at the cabin, played charades…"

He reminisced quietly as they watched the pink beginnings of the sunset.

She laughed. "It's hard to imagine you playing charades. Or your mother, for that matter."

"But you can picture my father?" he asked, with mock outrage.

Mina nodded. "He had that certain something."

Flat-voiced, Zayn said, "Don't say he was approachable."

"Well, he was…" she hedged.

Zayn growled, and she held up her hands in surrender, giggling.

"He was! But it was more than that. There was something about King Alden that made him seem like he was just like the rest of us. A regular person."

Zayn snorted. "That was just the image he wanted to project. He was a king, through and through."

"You miss him," she said.

He looked away from her then, his eyes going again to the sea. "Every day."

"You were close?"

"Very. We discussed everything—philosophy, economics, justice, rule. He shaped me, even when we didn't agree."

She smiled. "My father was the same. Though he and I were always in agreement. Or at least I always agreed with him," she amended.

"My father sometimes encouraged disagreement, though it was rare."

Intrigued, she asked, "What did you disagree about?"

He looked at her then, considering her before he said, "Love."

"Oh, really? What thoughts did the man who betrothed his son before his birth have on love?" she asked archly.

A lopsided smile tilted Zayn's face. "Believe me, I've asked myself that question a number of times over the past months," he said.

The light chuckle he added took the sting out of the statement. They were no longer adversaries, Mina thought, but in this together. Somewhere in the past two days they'd gone from being two strangers to a team.

"No. Ironically, he insisted that my top priority be falling in love—the very health of the nation depended on it, he said."

Mina frowned. "And you don't agree?" she asked.

He shook his head, not catching her shadowed expression. "I think the nation benefits most from a skilled monarch who brings something of value to the crown."

Keeping her voice light, Mina asked, "And what do I bring to the crown?"

"Initially, I wasn't sure," he said frankly, "but then you took care of me during our hike, so it's obvious you were destined to bring ease to the crown."

He spoke loftily, his nose in the air high enough to ensure she knew he was teasing, and she had another glimpse of the man he'd been before tragedy had replaced his carefree life with rock-steady rule.

Drily, she replied, "I'm so glad I can bring so much value to the crown."

Laughing, he wrapped an arm around her shoulders and pulled her to him. "You keep surprising me with your hidden talents. I'm sure I will never know the limits of your value."

Cheeks now aflame, she didn't know what to say. His smile turning wicked, he leaned closer, and she somehow knew that if he kissed her then—if his lips touched hers while her heart was still stuttering from his words—something terrible would happen…something that would change her forever.

Her mind grasped for the first thing it could, to put space between them before he closed the distance. And because, no matter how her life changed, she couldn't change who she was, what came out was about his work.

"So, tell me about the Ambassadors' Dinner?"

The blurted-out question was enough to halt him for the moment, but rather than look irritated by her evasion, he let his smile turn arrogant.

Leaning back, he said, "This dinner is particularly important for securing a diplomatic relationship with the Farden, a small German-speaking country with excellent mineral resources. This is their first visit to the island and we want them to see that we are sophisticated and modern—that establishing ties with us is not a risk to their reputation. As members of one of the few remaining constitutional monarchies of Europe, you and I represent both our entire nation and an outdated, increasingly unfavored form of rule. As such, it is crucial we convey progressive thought and current awareness."

Mina nodded, finding herself intrigued by the concept of strategizing an event appearance. "That all makes sense."

"My goal is a verbal commitment from the Chancellor that we will formalize a diplomatic relationship between our two countries by the end of dinner. Conversation will be in English throughout the evening, which makes it a great relief to find that you speak it so well."

Mina smiled, warming under his praise. She spoke German like a natural-born citizen as well, having learned in the cradle and spent summers there with her grandparents before her studies began to tether her to her desk, but didn't mention it for fear of looking like she was fishing for praise.

Unaware of her private bashfulness, Zayn continued, "We've secured relationships with England, Sweden, France, Italy, Spain, Australia, New Zealand, Ireland and Greece already, so I have no doubt we can do so with Farden as well."

Mina agreed. "I don't see why you wouldn't. Cyrano shows all the signs of being Europe's next 'undiscovered gem.' It would be in their interest to smooth the way for their citizens to take advantage."

Zayn leaned forward, his eyes lighting, "My thinking exactly. And Cyrano will benefit because the relationship will serve as an example of exactly the kind we need to ensure that it truly becomes just that."

She laughed. "That's a rather calculated game of chicken and egg."

He smiled, his expression wide, open, and genuine. "Not an incorrect description of statecraft."

They continued their conversation on the beach, strategizing on how they would approach the Ambassadors' Dinner, until the beginning chill of the evening and hunger sent them inside.

That night they dined on exquisitely prepared fresh seafood, and then made love in the summer palace's stunning master suite until neither could breathe.

The next three days continued in much the same fashion: hiking, swimming, bird-watching, dining al fresco and, of course, having massages. All too soon, though, it was time to return to the real world—and, more importantly, the Ambassadors' Dinner.

Their plane was due within the hour.

Mina's attire for the dinner would be waiting on her arrival in the Queen's Wing, along with Roz and the entire team, ready to prepare her yet again for the state function. Mina had made it clear following the ball that, while she wanted none of them to feel beholden to her, she would welcome each and every one of them to her permanent team. They had all accepted.

It was good to be Queen.

The King's guards, as well as Moustafa and d'Tierrza, met them at the private airport. Zayn nodded to his guards, who fell into their usual positions around him. Mina greeted her own guards with a smile that was bright and beaming and pulled each one into a hug. Moustafa stiffened, but quickly relaxed into the embrace. D'Tierrza returned it with strong-armed enthusiasm.

Zayn said goodbye to her when they reached the palace. "I need to check in with my assistant before dinner. I'll see you tonight." He bowed slightly to her, kissing her temple before leaving.

Mina, Moustafa, and d'Tierrza met Roz's team in the Queen's Wing.

"What happened to you?" Roz rasped.

Mina laughed. "Too much to recount—and we covered what's important when we spoke on the phone. Tonight it is imperative that I project the correct image—as well as the extra part I mentioned."

Roz nodded, a wicked light brightening her countenance. "Right. Cool, modern, and bringing the King to his knees within the appropriate limits of a state dinner."

"Exactly!" A little thrill trilled through Mina's blood.

The team got to work. Chloe, Roz's assistant, as usual all in black, ran errands for the rest of the team—fetching a brush for Byron, the hairstylist, an eyeshadow for Sabine, the aesthetician with the perfect face, and pins for Catriona, the designer with the asymmetrical haircut.

When they were done, Mina was once again transformed. This time she was all sharp edges and shadows. Her hair had been pulled back into a sleek and elegant French twist, without a wisp out of place, and she wore a custom-fitted black one-piece pantsuit.

Deep V cutouts adorned the chest and back of the suit, with panels of sheer fabric in dark black sewn in for modesty. The design displayed the distinct impression of the curves of her breasts without showcasing any actual cleavage. The sleeves were fitted and full-length, tapering to narrow slightly at the wrists. Everything she wore followed and hugged the lines of her body—no one would dare call this suit boxy.

Roz had chosen diamonds as her only accessory—
enormous teardrops at her earlobes and a monstrous soli-
taire hanging on a long platinum chain in the center of her
breasts.

For shoes, they'd selected simple black leather pumps
with heels high enough to add a few more inches to her
legs. Once again the heels had bright red soles and a foreign name tastefully stamped into the leather.

Sabrina had made her eyes look smoky and large, without being overly dark and dramatic, and used a muted dusky
rose for her lips, ensuring she looked alluring, yet professional.

Dressed in all black, she would be the perfect complement to Zayn, ensuring that they presented an image of
sleek, young and modern monarchs, just as he wanted. She
would be everything he said a queen ought to be: temptation in an untouchable package—at least not until long
after the dinner was over.

His face when she met him in the foyer justified the effort. His gaze heated, igniting an answering flame in her
that she let him see, but she kept tortuously outside of his
arm's reach. He wore a black suit with a black button-up
shirt and tie.

"You look lovely. Excellent choice for the evening."

She smiled at his compliment. Roz had taught her an
important lesson—one she had already subconsciously observed in academia: clothes made the man—or the woman,
the professor, or the Queen. Tonight she had dressed the
part. Together they were a pair of silk-clad ravens, grave
and imposing. And the sporadic flares of electricity between them only emphasized the intense magnetism that
paired them.

Mina inclined her head with a cool, "Thank you."

He led the way to the entrance, where their driver held
open the limo door. Mina thanked the man as she entered

the vehicle, and slid along the smooth leather seats to sit beside the window. Zayn followed her into the car and the driver shut the door.

They arrived at the venue to find a red carpet and flashing cameras. Cyrano was certainly developing a celebrity culture—paparazzi and press included.

Zayn slid an arm around her waist, the heat of the contact branding her through the layers of fabric that separated them, and he smiled, obliging the media covering their arrival and sending a thrill down her spine at the same time.

He was an excellent multitasker.

The dinner was being held in the grand ballroom of the Palace Museum—an aristocratic palace in the capital that had fallen out of the hands of its original owners nearly a century before and had been purchased by a private citizen and art collector. Upon his death, the palace and the collection it housed had been converted into a museum.

Mina had been to private events at the Palace Museum throughout her academic career, but nothing as grand as the occasion before her now. The museum had clearly spared no expense for the evening, and every effort had been made to impress the distinguished guests, which included all of Cyrano's standing ambassadors and their families, in addition to other delegates from the nations Cyrano was courting relationships with, as well as members of Parliament and the bulk of the island's aristocrats.

As they approached the Chancellor Klein, Mina's nerves around the importance of the encounter, coupled with the constant exertion of withstanding her inconveniently relentless attraction to her husband, had her pulled taut as a bowstring. Practiced smile in place, however, she vowed to herself that she would do nothing to jeopardize the relationship Zayn sought.

In fact, filled with an oddly protective determination, Mina reached for Zayn's hand and squeezed it as they walked, unthinkingly mirroring the reassurance her father had used to give her before every big event.

The memory flashed through her without any of the acrid tang that memories of her father had recently taken on, and she was glad, hoping that it meant the process of forgiveness had begun. She might never be able to think of him in quite the same way again, but their love had been real. His peerless rooting for her had been real.

She didn't understand why he'd done it, but she could accept that her father had arranged the betrothal out of love. And somehow, as if acknowledging that had shattered the shield of ignorance that had been protecting her, as her hand clasped his, she realized that she loved Zayn.

Not in the enduring and mellow way she loved her mother, and not in the vague, patriotic way she loved Cyrano. It wasn't the complicated, angry, nostalgic, yearning love for her father either, and it wasn't her captivating love of study.

She loved him the way a woman loved a man.

Passionate, greedy, and demanding. Intense, delicate, and needy. She loved him for trying to make her strong enough for the job at the same time as trying to make up for everything becoming royalty had changed in her life. She loved him with her full self. And so, for the first time, she felt engaged—fully and completely—with everyday life. She was no longer preparing for the future or breaking over the past. She was here, in the present moment, absolutely in love.

And it was time to meet the Chancellor.

The Chancellor, a slender gray-haired woman with impeccable style and wireless glasses, wore a graphite pantsuit and sensible black pumps. Her husband was on a well-televised reconciliation tour of the African continent, so she had brought her college-aged son Werner to attend the dinner with her instead. The two of them stood with a number of other Farden officials who had made the trip alongside the family.

Chancellor Klein's son's interest in politics was well known, and he was expected to make a bid to turn his family into Farden's first political dynasty within the next decade. Already famous in his own right, the striking blond youth also happened to be athletic and highly intelligent, on his way to graduating with honors from Cambridge. Werner was the kind of star pupil Mina had seen pass through her classroom only rarely, as they typically bypassed Cyrano's humble Capital University to travel to more internationally renowned institutions.

Mina smiled warmly as she and Zayn closed the distance between themselves and the foreign visitors, first catching Chancellor Klein's savvy blue eyes before turning her gaze slightly to include her son.

As their eyes connected the young man's expression took on a glint Mina did not immediately recognize, both haughty and hungry at the same time, and she schooled her features so as not to give away her confusion as she allowed him to take her hand. He bent over it with a kiss and a smile while Zayn engaged with his mother.

In English, he said, "I had heard the Queen of Cyrano was a common woman of rare beauty, but the reports do not do you justice."

Rather than feeling flattered, she realized his words had set off an unpleasant sensation, crawling along the outer edges of her skin.

"You're very kind, Mr. Klein. It's lovely to have you and your esteemed mother here in our beloved Cyrano."

"And it is lovely to be here. Cyranese hospitality lives up to its legend."

She had no idea why, but although his words were innocent, Mina felt the urge to use hand sanitizer after he'd said them.

Obviously catching the tail-end of Werner's sentence as he turned from the Chancellor, Zayn said, "I am glad to hear that. We're here to serve. Let our staff know what you would like, and we'll do everything we can to accommodate you."

Having made their introductions and initial contact, Zayn and Mina had turned to make their way to the dining room when Werner Klein leaned toward one of his companions with a chuckle and said, in distinctly audible German, "I'd like to see if his wife could accommodate *me*."

Mina sucked in a quiet breath. At her side, Zayn was suddenly all rapid motion and purpose, closing the short distance they'd walked away from the younger Klein in seconds, to return to his side.

The sudden movement of the King caused a ripple of awareness to go through the crowd, drawing conversations to a halt and bringing all of the attention in the room to him—just in time to witness the precise cocking back of his elbow and the jackhammering of his fist directly into Werner's face.

One. Two. Three. And Werner collapsed on the ground.

Color draining from her face, the Chancellor took a step toward her son but then seemed to hesitate, unwilling to approach the darkly radiating monarch.

Dressed in black, and towering over the unconscious man, Zayn looked every inch the medieval warrior King, despite the modern lines of his suit and his insistence that Cyrano had moved past its history.

Werner's cronies stepped closer, gaining confidence after their friend's embarrassment. In moments, there would be an all-out brawl.

Watching as Zayn's plans crumbled around him, Mina felt something click inside her. Dr. Aldaba might never have been caught dead in her current outfit—too distracting, after all—but the impenetrable professor and scientist was as much a part of her bones as Queen Amina.

She squared her shoulders and crossed the space between her and the two men as if she was strolling across her lecture room rather than a ballroom at a grand event.

She placed cool fingertips on the King's elbow and he stilled, the radiating physicality of his intent toward the younger man dimming. And as she restrained him she also said in soft, smooth, and rapid German, her tone at once censuring and commanding—the same tone her mother had used on her to calm her rare tantrums as a child, "Gentlemen. I don't believe it is considered polite to scuffle indoors. I'm going to have to insist you take this outdoors."

Zayn shot her a glance that she knew had more to do with the fact that she'd held back her language abilities than the censure in her tone. He did step back, however.

The other men, having been accessories to Werner's original comment, were not handling the revelation of the Queen's language skills nearly so well. Two sets of eyes were glued to Mina in abject horror. She recognized the look of individuals staring career failure in the face, but couldn't muster much empathy. She had been a teacher long enough to recognize a group of entitled rich kids a mile away.

As the threat of physical violence dissipated, the Chancellor stepped inside the circle, her hawk eyes taking in the fact that her son was on the floor and that all his cronies had lost their color.

"What's going on here?" she asked quietly, speaking in German as well.

Mina opened her mouth, ready to answer for all of them, using the tone she had used as a professor to report to a parent on a student's progress, but Zayn's hand on her wrist stopped her.

"I would advise that you leave your son at home next time, Chancellor Klein."

Zayn's voice was a whip through the room and Chancellor Klein's mouth dropped open.

Mina grimaced, adding public rebuking to the list of primeval King's rights that Zayn was exercising tonight. But even though she felt for the woman—it wasn't her fault her son's behavior had been inexcusable—Mina couldn't help but observe, as Zayn dragged her out of the ballroom, that he had been right. The open-mouthed expression really did make one look like a fish.

CHAPTER TEN

ZAYN'S REIN ON his temper was hanging by a thin thread, and he had already taken violent action against the son of a head of state.

"You will never speak of my wife again," he had growled in German, just before hitting the man with the cold clarity and precision his instructors had always told him to seek.

As a man, Zayn had encountered Werner Klein's kind many times, and he knew that the best way to deal with that kind of bully was to smash them like an ant and move on. And he'd done exactly that.

That was not, however, how a king dealt with his problems.

Kings treated men like Klein as gnats—unworthy of notice or reaction.

No. He had not acted like a king. He had acted like a man—and not just a man, but a hot-headed youth, the kind of young man he had been when he had gone away to college, wild and unable to carry the responsibility of the crown, rather than the level-headed monarch he'd schooled himself to be.

And it was all because of Mina.

He had acted more like his father than himself, and that was a luxury he could not afford—not when vipers lay in wait to take advantage of his every weakness.

He had put his woman before the needs of the nation.

The thought bounced around inside him like an angry wasp he could neither force out of his consciousness nor bury beneath his growing fury.

"Slow down, Zayn. I'm new to this height of heel."

Mina's breathless voice finally broke through the storm that was his thoughts. Immediately he slowed, turning to take her in.

Her hair was as controlled as it had been the day they had met, but tonight it elegantly highlighted the sweep of her cheekbones, somehow directing the eye to her lush mouth.

Her mouth was, he knew, an erotic playground, barely charted in the handful of times he'd had the privilege to explore it. And her body, contoured and showcased as it was now, in her one-piece pantsuit, was sexy and untouchable at the same time—a frustrating combination that antagonized the hunger that lived inside him even as it stoked it.

He gave his head a small shake. He was thinking about her too much.

Closing his eyes again, he took a deep breath. He would get them to the car, return to his office once they arrived back at the palace, and immediately begin damage control for the evening. Then he would return to his quarters and go to bed.

A desperate and resolute part of him vowed that it would be alone. Not with her. It couldn't be with her. Not until he had regained his control. It was imperative that he master his reactions to her. The night had made it clear that the issue was no longer merely a personal matter.

In the time they'd been married he'd learned that there was nothing he could focus on that was compelling enough to keep images of her at bay. He was helpless against the flow of erotic flashes of her that danced across his mind the moment his guard was down—and he held the fate of a nation in his hands.

Distance was the only thing that would work. And maybe a drink.

"Zayn!" Mina stomped her foot as she said it, standing on the curb, arms crossed in front of her chest.

He turned his attention to her—or rather the real her. His attention had been unable to focus on anything but her since the moment she'd stepped through the chapel door—with effort.

"What?" His voice held all the cutting chill it had held that long-ago day.

"What's going on?"

She asked the question quietly, delicately walking around the words she didn't say. *What the hell were you thinking? You ruined our plan! Where is your self-control?* And he found that irritated him more than if she'd just gone ahead with recriminations. Lord knew he had earned them.

He hadn't done anything so foolishly scandalous since he had been photographed in Amsterdam years ago, as a university student.

"Zayn?" she said again, with a bit more volume but no less grating delicate concern.

"I hit a man in the face, Mina. And as I am the King, I would think it would be clear what's going on now: I'm trying to determine the correct order of operations to begin immediate damage control."

The car pulled up and their driver jumped out to open the door, wisely sensing that conversation would be neither welcome nor appreciated.

Zayn gestured for Mina to enter the car first before following, his every movement brittle and angry. She opened her mouth, but Zayn stopped her with a hand. "If you are about to offer some meaningless condolence, Mina, I would advise against it."

She closed her mouth, and the ever-growing orb of rage inside of him began to take on a more beastly shape.

It was absolutely absurd that he had actually hit the man—defending his lady's honor like some barbarian of old—and all the more ironic for the fact that he, and his father before him, had spent the bulk of his reign working to separate Cyrano's reputation from its tumultuous feudal past. He had just undone all that with a single action.

"Zayn."

Mina's fingertips pressed lightly at his elbow again. She had scooted closer to him at some point, her perfect body just inches away from his now, and he hadn't noticed. He was deteriorating faster than he'd feared possible.

His entire body stilled.

She leaned closer, placing her palms on either side of his face to draw his gaze to her own. Green and gold swam together, warm and accepting, in a loving promise that it was possible to come back from this. That together it was possible to come back from anything.

And then she was pressing her lips softly against his in a kiss that was feather-light and over before it began. Pulling back, she sparkled, an open smile on her face, emanating that same strange sunlight only she seemed to possess.

"It's okay," she said.

She didn't say *I love you*, but she didn't need to. He heard it. And, hearing it, he broke open.

It began as a faint crack in the dam that held back the deep black. His hands thrust out to cup either side of her face, his fingers wrapping around her skull while his thumbs tilted her chin up. His internal structure began to give way as the crack raced across its surface, branching out at rapid speed, freeing the rage of waters held back too long.

Their lips met. Hers were soft and pliant and open, not only willing to absorb the weight and wrongness of his sin, but asking for it, begging him to bury it deep inside her, where she could turn it into something better—something good.

He pulled her into his lap with the force of a wave off the sea. Like so much flotsam, she tumbled into him, ever willing to be swept up in the fierce power of his embrace, open to him whenever he had need. And wasn't that the problem? She was a drug, offered freely, over and over, her only price the abandonment of his honor.

He wanted to push her away.

Instead, he absorbed her.

He demanded her entire focus with his lips, controlled her body, gripping her thighs on either side of him with no intention of allowing her to move, decimating her shields with his will to own and command her entire being.

The car pulled into the palace at some point. He lifted her out, unwilling to break their kiss, and somewhere along his route, carrying her to the Queen's Wing with her legs locked around his waist, the hot core of her scalding even through the fabrics that separated them, he waved off her guards and shooed away the staff.

But he made sure she wasn't aware of any of that. As far as she was concerned, the only thing that existed was him and the sensations he aroused. He would have it no other way. Here, he would be the master and commander. She would experience the feeling of being completely unmoored, completely at the mercy of another human being, her very behavior tethered to whims of another.

He pressed her against the wall in her bedroom, the rigid steel length of him teetering between threat and promise as she leaned into him with force to match his. And then it wasn't enough to press, to be separated by barriers, even those as insubstantial as clothing.

Her carried her to the bed, where he placed her gently on her back before placing his hands on her hips and turning her around until she faced away from him, on her hands and knees. Impatient to have the glorious curves of her at his full disposal, he unzipped her suit and pushed it off her shoulders from behind.

Breathing heavily, she pulled the top half off before he took over, pulling the suit over her hips before lifting her to remove it the rest of the way. Her thong winked at him from between the round globes of her derrière, flimsy and audacious at the same time, like something a French harlot might wear in a bygone era. The image aroused him and gave even greater form to the beast inside him, lending it claws with which to break its way out.

And then he was scraping his teeth along the same trail his caressing palms had taken, tasting her from behind while she cried out his name, the sound an entreaty and a plea at the same time. He happily obliged until she trembled, her body shaking as it dove into bliss.

It wasn't enough to taste her anymore. He needed to possess her. To break her into a thousand pieces and make each and every one of them irrefutably his.

Pulling away from her, he realized he was still fully clothed, but rather than delay to remedy the fact he simply unbuckled his belt and slipped himself free of his trousers. He was straining and hard and ready.

He made quick work of positioning himself behind her before sliding in, thick and heavy meeting wet and tight, against the backdrop of her helpless moans.

He managed to make three long, slow strokes before the beast demanded more. More speed. More pressure. More intensity.

The fire burning inside him was stoked to an explosive level as Mina's cries echoed in the rounded architecture of her bedroom. His hips became pistons, moving in and out of her, helpless to do anything but return over and over again.

Her body was slick with sweat and he sensed her peaking. But he wouldn't allow her release until she felt like him:

weak-willed, insatiable, and selfish. Hammering deep inside her, their bodies in a single rhythm, he refused to take them both over the edge until he knew he wasn't alone and never would be—not in this.

And when she gasped, crying, "Please, Zayn!" and her inner muscles desperately clenched around him, he knew it was true and they detonated.

Hours later, well past midnight, she lay deeply asleep, unhaunted by the ghosts of her father and the wreckage of the evening. He envied her. He was not faring so well on that front, and lying in her bed, listening to the quiet sounds and murmurs of her sleep, wasn't going to make it any better.

What he really needed was a drink. A drink would be the answer to the gnawing craving inside him that seemed to return the instant it was satisfied. He refused to let it be anything else. It was absolutely not the woman who stole his breath, and his attention, and his focus by her simple existence.

Sliding out of her bed, he ignored the tight squeeze the motion brought to his chest. There was no point lying beside her, drawing her into his arms, trusting they would sort everything out in the morning. That was foolish and, worse, neglectful.

He had a job to do.

And he would do it with a drink.

He would call for one as soon as he was out of her rooms. It would be waiting for him on his desk—sharp, no ice, and doubtless strong, just the way he liked it—when he got to his office.

"Where are you going?"

He spun around. She lay on her side, sheets drawn up to cover her breasts. Her head was on the pillow and her stare was wide open.

The image of her like that—relaxed, trusting—clawed at his throat like a choking bramble.

"Go back to sleep." His words were stilted and brittle, tin men in the face of the raw honesty she offered.

"You're leaving."

She didn't say it as a question, and for some reason that rankled him more.

"I have work to do."

"At this hour?"

"At all hours. A king is never off duty," he snapped.

"Typically, it requires a national emergency to force the King into working in the wee hours. Unless I missed an emergency, I can't imagine what is calling you."

This time when he snapped, it wasn't just his voice. "Tonight was an emergency, Mina. An enormous disaster. What's 'calling me' is the need to get my head out of whatever *this* is—" he gestured toward her and the bed "—and back into my work. Unlike you, Mina, people depend on my ability to do my job well."

She winced, her fists tightening on the sheets, but didn't break eye contact with him. "There's no reason to be nasty."

But she was wrong. There was every reason. He had made a fool of himself, and therefore a fool of Cyrano. And all over her.

"There is every reason to be nasty. I swore to myself I would not make the same mistakes my father made—that I would never put my own feelings before the health and safety of my country."

"I don't see how tonight—" she began.

But he cut her off. "Of course you don't see. You may be brilliant, Mina, but don't kid yourself. You're no political mind. Tonight was a travesty, and it was all because I couldn't keep my head together."

"What do you mean?" she asked.

Her obvious desire to soothe him only added fuel to the fire.

"You, Mina. I'm talking about *you*. When you're around I lose control, and that's something a king can't afford. I'm not willing to put the kingdom at risk because I'm in love with you, Mina."

The words shot out—an accusation even more than a confession.

They hung in the air between them, heavy, throbbing, raw.

She searched his face, capturing his gaze with her green and golden stare before asking. "You're in love with me?"

The air whooshed out of him silently, as if he'd been punched in the gut. Still the words hung suspended in air, almost visible, seeming so tangible. She waited for him to answer, and there was grace rooted in her quiet steel. She waited for the truth.

He nodded.

When he did not offer more, she frowned. Then she nodded too, the movement a communication with herself rather than a response to his gesture. It was sinking in—what he was saying to her.

Finally, after the silence had stretched between them and gone past comfortable, she asked, "And you think that's a threat to national security? So you're leaving me, in secret, in the middle of the night?"

Looking deep into the clear sage of her eyes, noting their growing sheen, he pinched off the voice inside him that said he could forge a new path—a stronger path—with the woman he loved at his side, and instead he answered her, "Yes."

He saw his words strike her, saw the gutted agony flash across her gaze and even felt it in himself. He wrenched at it, writhing even as he stood motionless, watching her collapse inside herself. And, unable to bear witness to the havoc he was wreaking, he turned on his heel and walked out.

He walked through the twisting corridors all the way to his office, where he locked himself in on the pretense that he needed to begin developing damage control strategies with Farden.

Six drinks later he'd spent no time thinking about Farden. Alone in his office, and drunker than he typically allowed himself to get, the reins on his mind turned invariably to Mina. Always Mina.

The sharp, raw edges of that hole inside him offered clarity at least. He needed to get away from her. He couldn't go to the summer palace. Not now. Not after the time they'd spent there. Her memory would be everywhere. It would be like surrounding himself with potent traces of the woman he couldn't shake off.

He needed to get away from her—and sooner rather than later. Only time and distance would be sufficient to suffocate the thing that had taken root inside him.

He arrived in Paris through a private airport just before three a.m. A driver took him from there to the apartment his family kept on the Champs-Élysées, and he watched the dark streets of the City of Lights pass by through his window. The cobblestoned streets and sidewalks were deserted this deep into the night, each *arrondissement* at quiet rest in preparation for another day of making up the city of Paris.

Stepping out of the car, he looked up to take in the French apartment. It was the first time he had been here in at least three years, and when he tried to name the sensation drawing his heart down into his gut the word that came to mind was *regret*.

That was absurd, however. Regret was a luxury a king could not afford. He did not regret. He merely wished he had brought Mina along, wondering how she would have received the opulent Parisian apartment, which was classic, traditional, and all things French.

Imagining her wonder brought a smile to lips as he rode the elegant antique elevator to the apartment. But a scowl replaced his smile just as the elevator doors opened, revealing the long hallway that led to the royal apartment. Striding down the hallway, he gave the door guards each a stormy nod before they opened the doors for him.

Inside, he headed straight for the study—and the liquor cabinet. Moving with all the deliberateness and yet none of the care he usually took, he selected a highball glass and rummaged through the assortment of crystal decanters available, all filled with glowing liquids in colors ranging from jewel-toned deep ambers to painfully clear.

He poured his drink rakishly and replaced the decanter with a clatter, uncaring of his lack of grace. There was no audience here. Unlike the kiss at the ball, and the brawl before dinner, there was no one here to bear witness to his absolute lack of decorum.

"Zayn!"

He didn't turn around at once. He simply closed his eyes with a sigh, brought one hand to rub the bridge of his nose and set the glass down with the other. Then he turned around.

A woman stood in the doorway, one hand on her hip, the other pointing toward him, her silhouette backlit by the bright living area behind her.

"Mother."

The light flicked on. His mother no longer stood in the doorway but walked toward him, her silk pajamas flowing with her movements as she put the safety catch on the small pistol she held as she walked.

"This is unexpected," she said.

Though it was four in the morning, she showed no sign of tiredness, no hint apart from her clothing that he'd woken her from sleep. As always, she was perfect. Elegance personified. It wasn't on purpose. In fact, his memories of childhood were full of her eager efforts to disrupt her own natural grace—so at odds with the fire of her personality—to no avail. With her long white-blond hair, delicate bone structure, and wide violet stare, the blue of her blood had shown through even the thickest mud. And all of it had aged well.

"I didn't know you were in residence," he replied—because it was true. He had not thought to check her whereabouts in his eagerness to escape Mina.

"I only just arrived," she said.

Silence stretched between them, two sets of matching eyes meeting each other across the gulf of the room.

Finally, she said, "You married."

And as if the soft, sad words were the spark the dry tinder of his temper had been waiting for, and because tonight was apparently the night he lost all control, the words, "Did you know?" were ripped out of him, raw and acidic because they made him vulnerable.

Startled confusion replaced the look of hurt in her eyes and she demanded, in a stronger voice, "What in the world are you talking about?"

"Did you know about the betrothal?" he barked, willing to make his own demands.

"Young man. You may be the King of Cyrano, but I am your mother and you will speak to me with respect."

"Like you and father respected me? What about my right to choose?"

"Don't be so dramatic, Zayn. There are worse things than finding yourself married to a beautiful, accomplished woman."

"How do you know she's any of those things?" he asked.

The hurt had returned to her voice when she responded. "I've been following the news."

His attempt at censure might not have found their mark, but hers did. "We were married in private by the Archbishop. Not what you would call a wedding."

"A mother still wants to witness such an event."

"There was no event. I told you. Just the two of us and the Archbishop."

His mother frowned. "Surely her parents were there?"

Zayn shook his head, a feeling of defensive shame growing in his gut at his mother's expression. "No," he said.

"Why not?" she asked, and a dangerous and growing note of suspicion entered her voice with each successive question.

"There wasn't time."

"There wasn't time to invite her parents to her wedding?"

Again, Zayn shook his head. "My men had trouble locating her. She does not go by the name used on the betrothal document. I did not want to risk losing track of her once we found her."

"You make her sound like some kind of criminal."

Zayn flinched, thinking back to his use of the national riot team to collect her.

"I had no idea *who* she was."

Finally, he was able to turn some of the censure around. And this time it was his mother who flinched.

Lifting her hands, palms up, she offered, "We always thought you'd get out of it."

For a moment he just stared at her incredulously. "I had the best lawyers in the country look over the contract. It's unbreakable."

She nodded. "Of course. You were the only one who could have broken it. Or her, I suppose…"

A fluttering sensation entered Zayn's chest at his mother's words. He didn't recognize it as panic because he had never experienced it before. He took a seat on the studded leather sofa. Did his mother know some way that Mina might nullify the marriage? If she was free to walk away, would she?

Palms going clammy, Zayn asked cautiously, "Is there some way we could render the marriage void?"

Mistaking the thread of fear that wove through his words for desperation, his mother took a seat beside him, her eyes widened in alarm. "Oh, no, darling. I'm so sorry. It's far too late now. We just never in a million years thought it would take you so long to find love…"

Her voice trailed off, and the slick, oily panic that had coated Zayn's throat at her words began to dissolve.

The marriage stood.

"What do you mean?" he asked.

His mother's alarm warped into guilt before his very eyes, and for the first time in his life he had the experience of seeing his mother ashamed. "We just never thought it would come to this."

He raised an eyebrow "Somehow I find that hard to believe. Father entered into an agreement that would require constitutional amendment."

"That's absolutely absurd. Absolutely." Like a tempest, his mother blew through emotions like mere changes of clothes. Now indignation ruled. "You're the King—you can't marry a cabbage farmer's daughter!" she exclaimed.

The sentiment was the last thing he'd expected from his mother, who had spent her time as Queen championing the rights of the poor, and Zayn found himself bristling in Mina's defense.

"Mina is far more than just a cabbage farmer's daughter, Mother—far more. And, thanks to Dad, we are already married."

The fact that he'd used the cold, commanding tone he reserved for speaking from the throne on his mother startled them both.

She opened her mouth to speak, but closed it again.

Uncomfortable with this discord with his mother, but unwilling to back down in his protection of Mina, he surprised himself by adding, "Besides, you don't even know that her father grew cabbage."

His mother took her seat once more, her eyes growing shrewd. "Of course I know her father grew cabbage. I know everything about the man."

It was Zayn's turn to be confused. "What do you mean?"

"I was pregnant with you—just weeks away from my due date—when I developed anemia. My hemoglobin levels dropped below three and my doctors insisted I needed a blood transfusion. Obviously they looked to Seraphina first, but I have a rare blood type and she wasn't a match. They searched the national donor database, invoked royal privilege to search all private medical records, and even reached out to distant cousins amongst Europe's royal families, but still could not find a match. Then your father had them search an old military database—and would you believe it? A match with a former sergeant. Ajit Aldaba—the one person on the entire island who could save my life."

Zayn's mouth dropped open, hanging wide in the same fish expression he'd accused Mina of having.

Clearly exhausted by the telling, his mother continued, "Your father was out of his mind with worry. My pregnancy had been rocky from the beginning, and we wanted you more than anything in the world. By then we knew I would not likely be able to sustain another pregnancy, so even though there was a risk we approached Sergeant Aldaba."

Zayn's voice rasped out, a dagger in the darkness. "And he said yes, on the condition you gave away your only son in a betrothal?"

His mother's eyes widened, catching enough light in the dim room to shine a clear amethyst. "Oh, no. No. Nothing like that." Her eyes went a bit misty before she continued.

"No. He said yes without hesitation… He was about to have a daughter—she was due just after you—and he said he hoped anyone would do the same for his wife. And, of course, he was a soldier through and through, always ready to answer the call '*for the good of Cyrano.*'" She smiled at the memory.

The echo of the same words he'd heard in Mina's voice pierced Zayn's heart like a poisoned dart. Then his mother shook her head, as if the images were a fog.

"No. It was your father who took it further," she continued.

"What?"

"That man." She crossed her arms in front of her chest, irritated still, even thirty-six years later. "He offered the man anything under the sun—insisted he chose a gift when he initially refused. He even had the gall to remind him to think of his growing family. It was that that did it, really."

"Did what?"

"Gave him the idea to ask for your hand in marriage."

Zayn would have laughed at her turn of phrase if farcical history had not been the stuff of his destiny.

"After your father had all but commanded him to ask for something, and then reminded him of his coming daughter, he threw out the idea of marriage. I think he was joking, really, but once the words were out things snowballed."

"What do you mean, 'things snowballed'?" Zayn's didn't bother to hide his irritation when he spoke.

"I was out of it after the transfusion. Ajit was out of it too. Your father was out of his mind with relief that both you and I had made it through the procedure alive. He needed a grand gesture to show his gratitude. One thing led to another and you were betrothed."

"You make it sound like a one-night stand," he observed drily.

The Queen snorted, continuing, "Your father regretted it before we even left the hospital. So much so that he went back to Ajit—and you know how much pride he had."

As usual, his mother was siding with his father, but her statement, could not go unremarked upon. "I should think so. He was a great proponent for choice and true love, after all."

His mother lifted her eyebrow. "You're emoting rather loudly, dear."

He scoffed. "I'd say I have the right."

"This side of you is all your father."

He ignored that. "You were saying…? He felt bad?"

"He swallowesd his pride and went back to Ajit to amend the agreement. They added a clause. *If neither child should find love before they turn thirty-five, the two shall be joined…* It was a small addition, but we all felt it would do the job."

Zayn didn't try to hide his exasperation. "This is all absolutely absurd, you do realize? You were real monarchs, you know—not fairy tale characters."

She chuckled. "I was on a lot of drugs at the time. And your father… He would have done anything for us."

The look on her face said she was momentarily lost, caught up in the memory of the man she'd loved more than any other soul save the son who stood before her. She came back, though.

"Besides, thirty-five seemed like plenty of time—eons away at the time. Of course, it all flew by faster than we could ever have realized…"

Watching his mother, knowing he was about to lose her to the pull of sorrow, as he had so many times since his father had died, he made his voice bitter when he said, "I should have known."

"Should have known what?" she asked, reluctantly drawn back from the pull of his father's memory.

"I should have known that his unhealthy attachments were at the root of all this."

An edge came to her voice as she lifted her eyebrow to say, "Excuse me?"

"I should have expected this entire fiasco had its roots in Dad's obsessive love."

His mother gasped. "Zayn Darius d'Argonia. How dare you speak of your father like that?"

"My father put love before his duty to the nation time and time again. When he decided to let the prime minister handle public hearings two days a week so the two of you could spend quality time together. When he postponed the national exposition because your due date approached... And this—sacrificing my future, not to mention the fate of the nation, just to say thank you." Disgust dripped from his words.

There was a moment of silence before his mother finally replied, her voice dry as desert sand. "Saving one's wife and child requires something a little stronger than a thank-you, Zayn. But, since you appear inclined toward hyperbolic oversimplification at the moment, I won't be the one to argue with you."

Just as she had always been able to, his mother lanced the boil of his self-righteous anger, revealing his asinine behavior in the process.

He brought his thumb and forefinger up to pinch the bridge of his nose. "I'm sorry."

His mother closed the distance between them and hugged him. "I accept your apology. I am sorry, too. I had no idea you felt that way."

"It doesn't matter."

She shook her head. "No. It's important. Your father would be the first to acknowledge that he put his loved ones before everything, but that's what made him such a great king. He *loved*, Zayn. He loved so fiercely he was willing to sacrifice everything, over and over. But never you."

Zayn reeled. So many pieces of his family puzzle were rearranging themselves in a single instant that the very foundation of his identity shook.

"We never told you before because—well, because it's so complicated. There was so much we didn't tell you. But the betrothal, at least, we thought would never become an issue. We were so sure you would find love long before the terms were up. As the date got closer we decided to tell you when you turned thirty-four. But then the assassination…"

So much had happened in the six months immediately following his father's death—his coronation, the discovery of his uncle's plot, his uncle's death, his mother's departure. His memories of the time were hazy and dark, but one thing was becoming clear.

"Father was right."

Frowning, his mother asked, "About what, dear?"

Instead of explaining how this new information had shed light on the shadows of his narrative, chasing away the monsters he'd feared lived in their depths, he said, "I have to go back to Cyrano," and kissed his mother's cheek.

His mother started. "Right now? But you've only just got here. And it's so late."

But he was already making his way to the door.

CHAPTER ELEVEN

THERE HAD BEEN no word from the King.

The morning after he'd left Mina had waited in her office, sure he would come to make amends for the way they had parted.

He had not.

So she had walked purposefully to the staff office and found the King's major domo and his assistant deep in discussion with the chef when she arrived. Each of them had looked up and straightened when they'd seen who stood before them.

"Get me the King on the phone."

For the first time since toddlerhood, Mina hadn't said *please*. He owed her an explanation and she wasn't going to beg or wait for it.

All three staff members had immediately bowed, working in unison to coordinate locating a phone, dialing, and placing it into her palm.

And as the cold device had touched her skin, it had brought with it the realization that she was the Queen of Cyrano, with all her rights and privileges.

It hadn't been the Archbishop marrying her in the chapel, or wearing a solid gold mask to her debut ball, or visiting the private summer palace, or playing international stratagems that had made it sink in. It had been the fact that she could walk into a room and demand to speak with the King and have it be done.

The line had rung. And rung. And rung. After the fourth ring, his voicemail had picked up, and his voice had been a slick lick of fire in her core, despite all her frustration.

Mina had not left a voicemail. Neither had she let her mouth fall open in outrage, and nor had she made any noise to indicate how infuriated she was. Instead, she had sucked in a breath through flared nostrils, held out the phone to one of the three staff members, who had taken it with a slight tremors in his hand, and then she had turned and left the room.

For dinner that night she had ordered every single one of her favorite foods, called up a priceless bottle of wine, and dined alone while watching period costume dramas, crying only at the appropriate plot points.

And now, this morning, still with no sign of the King, she had returned to carrying out her duties, projecting an image of a warm and doting wife when in reality she was hurt and angry enough that she might have taken her own unannounced vacation.

But, no, that wasn't her. Regardless of how anyone else around her behaved, she would always live up to her own standards.

She had kept her word, enacting every duty required of her as outlined in her schedule, which had included two video calls with heads of state and responding to a number of letters and requests.

This evening, though, there was a shared event on their calendar. On national television.

A public reunion after his abandoning her was perhaps poor planning on his part, but after her failed attempt at reaching out to him she hadn't been willing to try again. She had some pride.

And she had something else, too. It was strange and pow-

MARCELLA BELL 171

erful and new, but she recognized the feeling that coursed through her for what it was: rage.

Shaking her head to clear it of thoughts of him, Mina turned to d'Tierrza. "Roz and her team aren't due for another hour," she said.

D'Tierrza smiled. "So you expect them any minute?"

"Exactly. Though for the life of me I don't know why she seems to delight in catching me off guard so much. You'd think she'd want me cooperative."

"She wants you too confused to say no to her."

"What do you mean by that?" Mina asked—just as Roz and her team burst into the suite.

Mina sighed, but only because she knew she would never get her answer now, rather than over the frenzy that was about to begin. She welcomed that. It was just enough of a distraction—and the only form of armor she had—to keep her mind off the fact that she would be in the same room with Zayn again in a matter of hours.

Tonight, though, she dressed for herself—not for her husband, not for her role as Queen, not for academia, and not for her father. Just for her.

Tonight, she and the King would appear together on the *Jasper Caspian Show*—the most popular late-night show in all of Cyrano—and tonight, and for evermore, she would be herself.

She caught the makeup artist's eye. "Tonight, I want to be as flawless as you."

Sabine laughed, the faintest pink showing on her cheeks as the only sign that she had taken the Queen's words in. "Impossible," she said dismissively—only to ruin the effect with a wink and the words, "But I'll get you damn close."

Mina turned to her wardrobe next. "This will be my biggest audience yet. I want to show the world the everyday Queen Amina, while also looking breathtaking. And I want comfortable shoes. Can you make that happen?"

Catriona snorted and rolled her eyes. "Isn't that exactly what I do every time?"

Mina laughed, shaking her head as she turned to her hairdresser. "Down and free tonight," she said. "I'm tired of tying myself in knots and shrinking myself to fit. Big hair—don't care."

Byron smiled warmly, showing full teeth. "Great minds, Your Majesty." Then he inclined his head toward her, adding a small flourish with a twirl of his comb.

Finally, she came to Roz and her assistant. "How did I do?"

Roz snorted, the sound dry for all that it was nasal. "You managed to get your point across. Passable. An autumnal seventies theme will tie everything together. You're going to charm the nation tonight."

Coming from Roz, that last declaration might as well have been a tearful embrace.

Mina raised an eyebrow. "And here I was, thinking I'd done that with the Queen's Ball."

"Pish. You stunned them then. Absolutely stopped them in their tracks with just an image. Tonight, they'll see you alive, moving, speaking, breathing—your darling, refreshing, self on full display."

Mina winked at Chloe, Roz's assistant, before saying, "Be careful, Roz. All that praise might go to my head."

Roz's voice crackled as it rolled out as casually and slowly as sagebrush. "Keep in mind that 'refreshing' can get old."

D'Tierrza smothered a laugh from wherever it was she had faded into the background and Mina pretended to be offended when, really, she was nearly as content as she had ever been.

In all her years of research, Dr. Amina Aldaba would never have predicted that here she would stand, in a palace, surrounded not by colleagues, but by true, real friends. An unexpected rag-tag bunch they might be, but they were real.

Make-up came first. Once again, Sabine used colorful powders to draw out the gold and green flecks in Mina's eyes, but this time, rather than smoky, the palette the woman chose held tones which could only be described as down-to-earth—rich, deep browns, buttery tans, and shimmering cream.

Wardrobe came next, and Mina pulled on the soft, snug-fitted cashmere sweater they had picked out for her. The sweater was the color of ripe pomegranates and had a simple and elegant wide crew neck. It was paired with a pleated midi-length A-line skirt in the same color, and a thin tan leather belt that cinched her at the waist. The espadrilles that went with it were gorgeously comfortable, as well as flattering, and immediately became Mina's favorite royal footwear.

Her hairstylist left her hair down, using his comb to add mountains of volume and his curling rod to define and touch up individual curls here and there. The highlights he had given her before combined with the artfully tousled curls to make her look simultaneously natural, sexy, and straightforward all at once. She couldn't have asked for better.

When she looked in the mirror, she finally saw herself. Queen Mina. Not boxed-up Dr. Aldaba, and not the bursting star of Queen Amina. Just simple, lovely, honest, and kind Queen Mina. A common woman of the highest quality, showcased as much by the open expression on her face as by the top-tier fabrics she wore.

Her face was, if not flawless, near perfection. Light and breathable, her makeup looked like it was barely there, even as it highlighted and sculpted her features, emphasizing her eyes and lips in a way that made her blush at her reflection.

Her eyes reflected not just her recently revealed beauty—

beauty that even she could appreciate now—but also the intelligence that she had worked so hard for.

She wasn't merely a pretty distraction for her nation. She wasn't merely a brilliant scientist—or even just a gifted linguist and scholar. She was a multifaceted queen, not only fit, but ideally suited to the job.

She had even almost earned the love of her King. She'd known it in the desperate way he'd held her the night before he'd left.

And now, like the straw and smoke they were, her hollow attempts at mental bolstering faltered and dispersed, and she was left standing in front of a mirror, about to join Zayn for an interview, to sit beside him under the public's scrutinizing gaze, knowing that she had offered him everything she had and he had refused it.

But she didn't let any of that show on her face. The people around her had worked too hard to make her look pretty for her to let them down with a frown.

Nothing got past hawk-eyed Roz, though. Catching Mina's eye in the mirror, the woman said, in an overloud voice, "Since it's late-night, we wanted to go with something earthy and sensual while remaining well within the bounds of propriety. With your perfect height and coloring that obviously meant updated nineteen-seventies casual glamour."

Mina's smile finally reached her eyes. "Obviously."

"If anyone asks you who you're wearing, tell them you don't know. It'll be nonchalant and more natural for you, since you'll never remember if I tell you. We sent a press release—they can find the answer there."

"Should I be expecting that kind of question?"

Roz snorted. "Of course. This is television. All they really care about is fashion and sex."

Mina blushed, the heat deepening the brown of her

cheeks and setting off her makeup highlights charmingly. The aesthetician was really a magician.

"Let's hope not." She laughed through it. "I'm better versed in biochemistry."

Roz waved her away. "Yes. Well, one can't help one's shortcomings…"

D'Tierrza's laughter bounced around the room, and the sound of it eased some of the squeeze around Mina's heart.

She squared her shoulders and turned to her two guards. "Shall we go?"

Moustafa nodded, a faint smile softening the seriousness with which she did everything. D'Tierrza grinned like a fox.

Roz draped a sleeveless cape over her shoulders, and handed her a small leather clutch that matched her belt.

Mina turned to her team. "Thank you, as always. Your magic amazes me." To Roz, she said, "You're a queen-maker."

Roz rolled her eyes. "Of course I am. Now, go. And expect miracles."

Mina opened her mouth to ask a follow-up question, but d'Tierrza was already drawing her away.

Stepping into the barrage of flashing lights, microphones and cameras was by far the most challenging thing Mina had done yet as Queen. There had been a red carpet and press at the Queen's Ball, but nothing compared to the walk from her car to what was supposed to be the private entrance for guests on the *Jasper Caspian Show*.

Perhaps it was the combination of royalty and television, but it was all Mina could do to keep a smile plastered on her face and answer the odd question.

When someone shouted, "Who are you wearing?" she turned the plastered-on smile in their direction.

"I have no idea," she said. Just like Roz had told her to.

"What's your favorite sex position?"

She was saved from acknowledging that question by reaching the end of the gauntlet.

Once inside the studio, she closed her eyes, drawing in a long, slow, deep breath before opening them and looking around.

Everything was painted black and, industrial as a result of form and function rather than design. Soundproofed walls separated the set and studio audience from what went on backstage, which mostly appeared to be men walking around with clipboards wearing dark, loose-fitting clothing and headsets.

One such man, slender, pale, and young, with shaggy brown hair and a pair of dusty black cargo pants, met Mina and her guards at the door.

"Right this way, Your Majesty," he said as he ushered her toward a door set apart from most of the backstage traffic.

She grimaced at his form of address, but appreciated the rescue. Inside, the room was a shock of cozy warm-toned beige and tan, with a coffee table set with a lovely bouquet of flowers and refreshments, and an arrangement of plush furniture.

"We've prepared the green room according to your secretary's instructions, but don't hesitate to let us know if there is anything you need."

Unaware that she'd even given instructions in the first place, Mina merely nodded with the words, "Thank you."

The King had not arrived by the time the stage manager came to escort her, ready for her cue, so she walked onstage alone.

The lights on the stage were too bright for her to make out the live audience, for which she was grateful. She didn't need to see the faces of the people she was worried about making a fool of herself in front of, on top of everything else.

Though she couldn't make them out in detail, she could

tell that they, like Jasper Caspian, at his famous desk, came to their feet as she entered the stage. The stage band played the last chords of the national anthem as she took the seat nearest to Jasper's desk, knees together, legs crossed at the ankles, as Roz had instructed.

Angled toward him for their conversation, she got her first view of Jasper Caspian, up close and personal. The first thing that struck her was how large his head was. Not only was it slightly oversized for his frame, it was particularly round. Coupled with his large eyes, it made him look faintly like a cartoon come to life.

Knowing it contributed to his visual interest and appeal, the biologist in her was fascinated.

His hair was white-blond and…*swoopy*. That was the only word for it. Thick, silky, and swoopy. His eyes and eyebrows were deep brown, a startling contrast to the rest of his fair coloring, and the combination was likely what he owed his rise to stardom to.

He studied her in return, his expression cunning as he took in every detail. And as the wild cheering of the audience settled, Jasper's smile grew.

When they'd finally sat down in their seats and quietened, he said, "I'd say let's give the Queen of Cyrano a warm welcome, but any warmer than that and we'd be breaking our fire codes!"

The audience laughed at his joke, but sedately, as he'd clearly wanted. Obviously he was an expert at managing the energy of a large group of people.

Mina was impressed.

"So, Queen Mina—that's what they told me to call her, folks, we're not being fresh—you're finally here. The mysterious, multitalented woman who captured our King's… heart."

The man imbued his pause with the energy of salacious wink and the audience ate it up.

Mina couldn't help the smile that spread across her own face, despite recognizing in him each and every class clown she'd ever had the challenge of teaching. It made her happy to think of any one of them finding their place in the world, as Jasper so clearly had.

"We're all dying to know…well, *everything*. Start with that."

Mina waited for the laughter to die down before saying, "Well, I suppose I should start where it all began."

Jasper leaned in. "Yes. Do."

Mina laughed, unable to fight her growing ease in his presence. She moistened her lips, smiled wide, and said, "It begins with Cyrano, of course. In fact, I was born and raised right here in the capital. A dyed-in-the-wool, tried-and-true, homegrown Cyranese capital rat."

Jasper's eyes flashed his admiration even as he smiled. "That's right…that's right," he said. "They're calling you 'the commoner who caught a king.' You are the very first commoner to marry into the royal family in Cyranese history. Did you know that?"

Mina did not know that—had not, in fact, even ever thought of it. But, rather than miss a beat, she simply admitted it, saying, "No. I had no idea. I must admit for most of my life I've been focused on being appointed to the King's council."

Jasper's smile widened. "Indeed, you are a queen of firsts. But, of course, what we all really want to hear about is how you snared the most eligible bachelor in the kingdom."

Mina opened her mouth to reply, only to be drowned out by the collective gasp of the audience and Jasper at her side.

All the attention in the room was focused on the man walking on stage to join her. And then the audience was on their feet once again.

Without needing to turn, she knew it was Zayn. But when she did turn, he looked different.

First and foremost, he had the beginnings of a beard, the dark stubble lending the hard planes of his face a sense of warmth and wisdom. His hair was styled neatly, but more naturally. And that was not the most dramatic change.

For the first time since his father's death, the King wore a color other than black.

Admittedly, the very deep navy of his trim suit was not a far jump from his usual palette, but in someone as closely scrutinized as the King, the difference might as well have been a shout. Like a monarch of old, he had come out of mourning.

In his lapel pocket was a burst of flowers, their colors a complement to her own attire.

Breathless, she watched him cross the stage, his long legs eating up the short distance quickly.

His scent enveloped her, an erotic caress in the room full of people, as he reached around her to shake Jasper's hand in greeting. It wasn't the King's first appearance on the show.

He sat on the other side of Mina, his body language relaxed and open, for all the world to examine. She wished she could project that kind of ease when she didn't feel it.

"Welcome, Your Majesty. It's lovely to have you back on the show—even if you are late."

Zayn smiled at the mock censure in the other man's tone, and there was a great sense of contentment in his expression. "I apologize for that. Traffic in this city is just out of control. Someone should do something about that…"

The audience laughed, just as Zayn had intended, and Mina enjoyed the thrill of pride that came with recognizing that he was more than a match for Jasper.

And he was hers.

At least on paper.

She was getting used to the stabbing sensation in her chest whenever her mind lingered on him too long.

"Well, before you distracted all of us with your arrival, our lovely Queen Mina here was going to reveal to us all how she captured your heart."

Zayn caught her eyes then. The violet of his gaze was warm and welcoming, with no hint of the resistance she knew he was committed to.

And yet despite that, even in front of an audience, she was still arrested by the locking of their gazes, frozen and lost at the same time.

He would forever be the most beautiful man she had encountered in her life.

His lips curled up at the edges and she felt the movement deep in the wet heat of her core.

"Oh, was she, now?" he said, drawing out the words with a suggestiveness that had her blushing. "I'd love to hear that."

Jasper grinned, sensing the kind of show content that spiked ratings lurking in the heightened awareness thrumming between them, and Mina swallowed.

"Then again," Zayn said, drawing the focus to himself effortlessly, "you could just get the information from the source."

Jasper turned to the audience. "What do you think audience? His or hers?"

Mina's stomach dropped, and in that instant she realized she didn't know which would be worse: hearing his answer, or having to fabricate her own.

The audience, it seemed, was most concerned with accuracy, choosing to go with testimony from the primary source, and Mina braced her heart—as much as it was possible to brace the kind of organ that attached itself to another person regardless of whether or not he reciprocated that attachment or not.

Zayn turned a wide smile toward the audience, ready to tell some canned lie, no doubt. "Now. You were asking how to win a king's heart?"

Jasper pointed to the King and said, "This guy!" before shrugging and adding the words, "Close enough."

The audience laughed, but quietened quickly. They wanted to hear what he said.

Mina's stomach turned.

He slipped his hand around hers and squeezed, before beginning. "It helps to be the most brilliant scientist in the country. That's a strong first step to getting caught by a king."

Rather than cringe, Mina found herself fighting the urge to snort. Getting "caught by a king" was certainly one way to say *getting arrested*. The tight knot in her chest eased just a fraction.

Jasper pretended to take notes on his desk. "Step one: be a rocket scientist."

Zayn laughed along with the audience, the sound unfettered and genuine and, for Mina, completely disorienting.

"Next," he said, "one must naturally be stunningly beautiful."

Jasper nodded mock seriously, "Naturally."

"But I don't mean just ordinary beauty. I mean a beauty that collects everything there is to love about our island nation and puts it into the form of a woman."

An instant of silence greeted Zayn's statement, wherein not even Jasper Caspian could think of something clever to say.

The words sank into all of Mina's soft tissues, anchoring themselves in a way that she knew would make every other compliment pale in comparison for the rest of her life.

The audience recovered first, responding with a loud sigh of longing.

Looking at Mina, Zayn began to speak again. "But that is the mere surface. The kind of sparkling tinsel that catches the eye of every foolish man. In order to truly capture a king, you must first make a habit of squaring your shoulders and facing every challenge head-on."

The tenor of his voice had changed, and despite the fact that he spoke for the all the world to know, in truth it was as if he spoke to his Queen alone.

"You must be cool-headed and controlled when your dreams are crushed. You must be earnest. You must meet every curve ball thrown at you."

Mina's mind was filled with their hasty chapel wedding with the Archbishop, its details becoming even more surreal in memory.

"You must be willing to walk miles when you have just fallen from the sky, finding beauty along the way. You must know how to cook a mean tagine."

Here Jasper broke in with, "A queen that cooks? Now, there's a keeper, folks!"

The audience took the break as an opportunity to let out the collective breath they were holding on a laugh, before leaning closer for more.

Zayn continued, his attention still focused on Mina. "It takes more than a surprising talent to steal a king's heart, of course. You must offer true partnership, a safe haven, and a place to be an ordinary man."

Mina's eyes pricked with the tears, but she would be caught dead before she'd let herself shed them during her first television appearance.

"You must also be willing to stand up against the opinion of a king. You must be indomitable. You must accept what you cannot change, but demand change when you know you can. Most of all, you must never accept less than you deserve."

Mina swallowed again, the knot in her throat bearing

a suspicious similarity in thickness to barely restrained emotion.

Letting Zayn's words rest in the air for a moment, Jasper was less irreverent when he next spoke. "Well, my dears. There you have it. What it took to woo the King. Sounds easy enough—am I right?"

The audience chuckled appreciatively.

Eyes still on Mina, Zayn said, "She certainly makes it look so."

More of that internal knot loosened, even as a part of her grabbed at its strands, trying to keep it together, a tight ball of resentment to block him from digging in any deeper.

Jasper fanned himself. "Folks, it is just as hot sitting here by these two lovebirds as it seems. I admit I didn't expect the change in you, Your Majesty. It seems like it was only a few months ago you were here on this show, a completely different man."

"That's the impact of a good woman."

"I can see why you were so quick to scoop her up into matrimony. Though you denied us all the pomp and fun of a royal wedding!" Jasper's pout was a consummate expert's.

A mischievous glint lit in Zayn's eyes. "You know, Jasper. You're right. I acted quickly when the opportunity presented itself. But you, and certainly my lovely bride, deserve something better than that."

And then he got down on one knee in front of her. Jasper and the audience gasped, and a sheen of tears came to Jasper's eyes that Mina knew had nothing to do with romance and everything to do with ratings.

The audience erupted into applause.

Zayn smiled. "I would marry you every day, Mina. Over and over again."

She wanted to believe him. She did. But they were in front of a live studio audience and he had a scandal he wanted people to forget about. Even though he was asking, he wasn't really.

She had a clear line in this drama and she did her part, nodding, and the cheering went up another few notches before it began to calm down to a reasonable level.

When the moment came, Jasper said, "Well, you saw and heard it on the *Jasper Caspian Show*, folks. We're going to get a royal wedding after all!"

The audience came to their feet in raucous applause and Mina let Zayn clasp her hand, lifting her arm high as they came to their feet before he led her off the stage.

As soon as they entered the green room, however, Mina shook her hand free.

"No," she said.

"What do you mean, 'no?'" he asked.

"I'm not going to marry you again in a big public display in order to distract your people from your recent behavior. Our relationship will not be a tool in your arsenal, and what's more I will not be Queen on your terms. I'm tired of being swept up in the plans and requirements of the men in my life, never being asked what I want. If we're to do this like colleagues, then we keep to business hours and business topics. If we're to be more—" she took a breath before meeting his eyes "—then you owe me an apology."

He stared at her, left her words hanging between them.

She frowned as his silence grew, her eyebrows drawing slowly together and the corners of her mouth tilting down just slightly, her always too revealing eyes wounded. He just watched her as she gave up hope and then squared her shoulders.

She took a breath and said, "I've lived my entire life on other people's terms, Zayn. My father's, academia's, yours..." She used a finger to quickly dash away a falling tear. "I'm done with that now. I will be Queen on my terms.

You can contact my secretary to coordinate our activities, but I will not put my heart on the line for a farce."

And she turned her back on him and started toward the door.

"Stop."

The word wasn't a command, but a plea.

She stopped, blowing out a frustrated breath, her heart in her throat.

"You're right. I apologize, Mina."

She turned around, her attention caught.

"I should never have left you like that. I was scared—of what I feel, of how I lose control when it comes to you." He laughed, and the sound was self-recriminatory. "It's not comfortable to know I have it in me to cause a diplomatic incident where you're concerned."

"About that—"

She opened her mouth, ready to tell him that she had secured the relationship with Farden. It had taken a long video-call, in which she had explained what had happened to the Chancellor and bonded with her over their shared love for the same chocolate bar. The call had ended not only with the establishment of a diplomatic relationship, but also a sincere apology from Farden over Werner's conduct.

"It's not important, Mina. Nothing is more important to me than you. Not Cyrano, not being King—not a thing."

Mina's heart thundered but she kept her eyes shuttered. "What changed?"

Facing her, he smiled. "The difference between a boy and man is that a man can admit when he's wrong," he said. "You have made me a better king at every instance, Mina. My loving you is not only no threat to the nation, it will be its savior."

"How do I know you won't disappear again?"

He smiled, likely sensing the weakening of her defenses. "You will have to trust me. But to help…no more separate wings. And we're going to have a real wedding, with both of our mothers in attendance. And this."

He dropped to one knee again, pulling out a small black box.

Opening it to reveal the astounding diamond ring within, he said, "Dr. Amina Elin Aldaba. You alone have shown me what it means to truly love. I can think of no woman better suited to sit at my side as my Queen. Will you marry me?"

Mina nodded through happy tears and a wide grin stretched across her face, her wild curls bouncing with the movement. He slipped the ring on her finger before coming to his feet. Weaving his fingers through the soft springs to cup the back of her head, he pulled her close, and as their lips met she realized that, although she hadn't always known their shape, her dreams had finally come true.

* * * * *

MILLS & BOON

Coming next month

THE COST OF CLAIMING HIS HEIR
Michelle Smart

'How was the party?'

Becky had to untie her tongue to speak. 'Okay. Everyone looked like they were having fun.'

'But not you?'

'No.' She sank down onto the wooden step to take the weight off her weary legs and rested her back against a pillar.

'Why not?'

'Because I'm a day late.'

She heard him suck an intake of breath. 'Is that normal for you?'

'No.' Panic and excitement swelled sharply in equal measure as they did every time she allowed herself to read the signs that were all there. Tender breasts. Fatigue. The ripple of nausea she'd experienced that morning when she'd passed Paula's husband outside and caught a whiff of his cigarette smoke. Excitement that she could have a child growing inside her. Panic at what this meant.

Scared she was going to cry, she scrambled back to her feet. 'Let's give it another couple of days. If I haven't come on by then, I'll take a test.'

She would have gone inside if Emiliano hadn't leaned forward and gently taken hold of her wrist. 'Sit with me.'

Opening her mouth to tell him she needed sleep, she stared into his eyes and found herself temporarily mute.

For the first time since they'd conceived—and in her heart she was now certain they *had* conceived—there was no antipathy in his stare, just a steadfastness that lightened the weight on her shoulders.

Gingerly, she sat beside him but there was no hope of keeping a distance for Emiliano put his beer bottle down and hooked an arm around her waist to draw her to him.

Much as she wanted to resist, she leaned into him and rested her cheek on his chest.

'Don't be afraid, *bomboncita*,' he murmured into the top of her head. 'We will get through this together.'

Nothing more was said for the longest time and for that she was grateful. Closing her eyes, she was able to take comfort from the strength of his heartbeat against her ear and his hands stroking her back and hair so tenderly. There was something so very solid and real about him, an energy always zipping beneath his skin even in moments of stillness.

He dragged a thumb over her cheek and then rested it under her chin to tilt her face to his. Then, slowly, his face lowered and his lips caught her in a kiss so tender the little of her not already melting to be held in his arms turned to fondue.

Feeling as if she'd slipped into a dream, Becky's mouth moved in time with his, a deepening caress that sang to her senses as she inhaled the scent of his breath and the muskiness of his skin. Her fingers tiptoed up his chest, then flattened against his neck. The pulse at the base thumped against the palm of her hand.

But, even as every crevice in her body thrilled, a part of her brain refused to switch off and it was with huge reluctance that she broke the kiss and gently pulled away from him.

'Not a good idea,' she said shakily as her body howled in protest.

Emiliano gave a look of such sensuality her pelvis pulsed. 'Why?'

Fearing he would reach for her again, she shifted to the other side of the swing chair and patted the space beside her for the dogs to jump up and act as a barrier between them. They failed to oblige. 'Aren't we in a big enough mess?'

Eyes not leaving her face, he picked up his beer and took a long drink. 'That depends on how you look at it. To me, the likelihood that you're pregnant makes things simple. I want you. You want me. Why fight it any more when we're going to be bound together?'

Continue reading
THE COST OF CLAIMING HIS HEIR
Michelle Smart

Available next month
www.millsandboon.co.uk

COMING SOON!

We really hope you enjoyed reading this book.
If you're looking for more romance, be sure to
head to the shops when new books are
available on

Thursday 10th December

To see which titles are coming soon, please visit

millsandboon.co.uk/nextmonth

MILLS & BOON

LET'S TALK

Romance

For exclusive extracts, competitions
and special offers, find us online:

f facebook.com/millsandboon

🐦 @MillsandBoon

📷 @MillsandBoonUK

Get in touch on 01413 063232

MILLS & BOON

THE HEART OF ROMANCE

A ROMANCE FOR EVERY KIND OF READER

MODERN

Prepare to be swept off your feet by sophisticated, sexy and seductive heroes, in some of the world's most glamourous and romantic locations, where power and passion collide.
8 stories per month.

HISTORICAL

Escape with historical heroes from time gone by. Whether your passion is for wicked Regency Rakes, muscled Vikings or rugged Highlanders, awaken the romance of the past.
6 stories per month.

MEDICAL

Set your pulse racing with dedicated, delectable doctors in the high-pressure world of medicine, where emotions run high and passion, comfort and love are the best medicine.
6 stories per month.

True Love

Celebrate true love with tender stories of heartfelt romance, from the rush of falling in love to the joy a new baby can bring, and a focus on the emotional heart of a relationship.
8 stories per month.

Desire

Indulge in secrets and scandal, intense drama and plenty of sizzling hot action with powerful and passionate heroes who have it all: wealth, status, good looks…everything but the right woman.
6 stories per month.

HEROES

Experience all the excitement of a gripping thriller, with an intense romance at its heart. Resourceful, true-to-life women and strong, fearless men face danger and desire - a killer combination!
8 stories per month.

DARE

Sensual love stories featuring smart, sassy heroines you'd want as a best friend, and compelling intense heroes who are worthy of them.
4 stories per month.

To see which titles are coming soon, please visit

millsandboon.co.uk/nextmonth

JOIN US ON SOCIAL MEDIA!

Stay up to date with our latest releases, author
news and gossip, special offers and discounts, and
all the behind-the-scenes action
from Mills & Boon...

 millsandboon

 millsandboonuk

 millsandboon

It might just be true love...